Heart Journey

Robin D. Owens

B

BERKLEY SENSATION, NEW YORK

THE BERKLEY PUBLISHING GROUP
Published by the Penguin Group
Penguin Group (USA) Inc.
375 Hudson Street, New York, New York 10014, USA
Penguin Group (Canada), 90 Eglinton Avenue East, Suite 700, Toronto, Ontario M4P 2Y3, Canada
(a division of Pearson Penguin Canada Inc.)
Penguin Books Ltd., 80 Strand, London WC2R 0RL, England
Penguin Group Ireland, 25 St. Stephen's Green, Dublin 2, Ireland (a division of Penguin Books Ltd.)
Penguin Group (Australia), 250 Camberwell Road, Camberwell, Victoria 3124, Australia
(a division of Pearson Australia Group Pty. Ltd.)
Penguin Books India Pvt. Ltd., 11 Community Centre, Panchsheel Park, New Delhi—110 017, India
Penguin Group (NZ), 67 Apollo Drive, Rosedale, North Shore 0632, New Zealand
(a division of Pearson New Zealand Ltd.)
Penguin Books (South Africa) (Pty.) Ltd., 24 Sturdee Avenue, Rosebank, Johannesburg 2196,
South Africa

Penguin Books Ltd., Registered Offices: 80 Strand, London WC2R 0RL, England

This book is an original publication of The Berkley Publishing Group.

This is a work of fiction. Names, characters, places, and incidents either are the product of the author's imagination or are used fictitiously, and any resemblance to actual persons, living or dead, business establishments, events, or locales is entirely coincidental. The publisher does not have any control over and does not assume any responsibility for author or third-party websites or their content.

PRINTING HISTORY
Berkley Sensation trade paperback edition / August 2010

Library of Congress Cataloging-in-Publication Data

Owens, Robin D.
    Heart journey / Robin D. Owens.—Berkley Sensation trade paperback ed.
        p.   cm.
    ISBN 978-0-425-23454-9
    1. Life on other planets—Fiction.   2. Space and time—Fiction.   I. Title.
    PS3615.W478H45 2010
    813'.6—dc22

                                                                    2010014279

PRINTED IN THE UNITED STATES OF AMERICA

10   9   8   7   6   5   4   3   2   1

"If you've been waiting for someone to do futuristic romance right, you're in luck; Robin D. Owens is the

Rob... ...ens

Heart Fate

"A superb romantic fantasy filled with heart."
—*Midwest Book Review*

"A touching tale of learning to trust again . . . Even for readers unfamiliar with the Heart world, Owens makes it easily accessible and full of delightful conceits."
—*Publishers Weekly*

"A true delight to read, and it should garner new fans for this unique and enjoyable series."
—*Booklist*

"[This] emotionally rich tale blends paranormal abilities, family dynamics, and politics; adds a serious dash of violence; and dusts it all with humor and whimsy . . . Intriguing."
—*Library Journal*

Heart Dance

"The latest Heart fantasy is one of the best of this superior series . . . retaining the freshness of its heartfelt predecessors."
—*The Best Reviews*

"I look forward to my yearly holiday in Celta, always a dangerous and fascinating trip."
—*Fresh Fiction*

"The world of Celta is amazingly detailed, and readers will enjoy the bits of humor that the Fams provide. Sensual, riveting, and filled with the wonderful cast of characters from previous books, as well as some new ones, *Heart Dance* is exquisite in its presentation."
—*Romance Reviews Today*

Heart Choice

"The romance is passionate, the characters engaging, and the society and setting exquisitely crafted."
—*Booklist*

continued . . .

Titles by Robin D. Owens

Anthologies

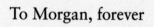
To Morgan, forever

Acknowledgments

Thanks for the company and motivation go to: the Live Journal Toono/ Word Warriors community, the Fairplay Hand Hotel weekend retreat writers, and the Low Country Romance Writers November retreat writers. You are all very special.

Characters

The Cherrys:

Cerasus Cherry (Raz): The son of GrandLord T'Cherry. Formerly the heir to Cherry Shipping and Transport, a rising actor. Secondary character in *Heart Fate* and *Heart Change*. He provided the voice for the Turquoise House.

T'Cherry: Raz's father and titular head of Cherry Shipping and Transport. He is a HeartMate.

D'Cherry: Raz's mother, formerly a scholar of ancient Earthan language and early colonist language. She is a HeartMate.

Seratina Cherry: Raz's younger sister, in charge of Cherry Shipping and Transport and heir to that business. She is a HeartMate and has a kitten Fam.

The Elecampanes:

Helena D'Elecampane (Del): She is a master cartographer and has charted the western part of the two continents. Del is often on the road and in the field.

Shunuk: Del's FoxFam. He met and became Del's Fam on the trail.

Helendula D'Elecampane (Doolee): Del's young cousin. She is the daughter of Elfwort and the granddaughter of Inula.

The Blackthorns:

Straif T'Blackthorn: FirstFamily (highest noble title) GrandLord: Hero of *Heart Choice*, the best tracker of Celta. Ex-lover to Del. His Family has a fatal genetic trait that makes them very susceptible to disease. He is a HeartMate. His Fam is Drina (Queen of the Universe).

Mitchella Clover D'Blackthorn: HeartMate and wife to Straif, heroine of *Heart Choice*. She is from a large commoner Family who is moving up in rank. She is an interior designer and is sterile.

Antenn Moss Blackthorn: Their older adopted son, he is studying to become an architect. His natural brother was a notorious murderer.

Cordif Blackthorn: Their younger adopted son.

The Actors and Theater Folk:

Trillia Juniper: An actress from an acting Family, she's been in the business all of her life, another rising star. Ex-lover to Raz.

Klay St. Johnswort: Friendly competitor to Raz.

Lily Fescue: Leading lady in the mystery Raz is starring in.

Reing Galangal: An actor somewhat older than Raz who plays the villain in the mystery Raz is starring in.

T'Spindle: FirstFamily GrandLord who owns the theater the Evening Primrose.

Other Characters:

GreatLord Rand T'Ash: Jeweler/blacksmith, T'Ash sells his creations in T'Ash's Phoenix. (*HeartMate*)

GreatLady Danith Mallow D'Ash: HeartMate of T'Ash, Danith is an animal Healer and the person who usually matches intelligent animal companions (Fams) with people.

FirstLevel Healer Lark Holly: One of the three FirstLevel Healers of Celta. She is a HeartMate. (*Heart Duel*)

Captain Ruis Elder and Nuada's Sword: Ruis is Captain of Nuada's Sword, the last starship. (*Heart Thief*)

Guardsman Ilex Winterberry: Druidan Guardsman who is assigned to the FirstFamilies. (*Heart Quest*)

GreatLord Muin (Vinni) T'Vine: The young prophet of Celta.

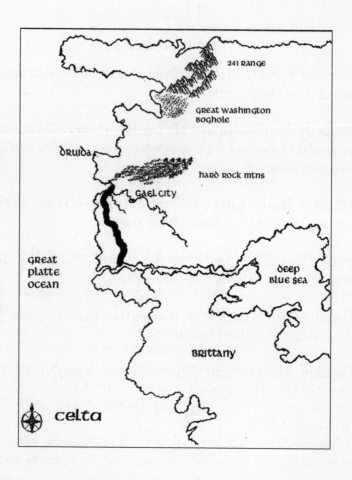

241 RANGE

GREAT WASHINGTON
BOGHOLE

DRUIDA

HARD ROCK MTNS

GAEL CITY

GREAT
PLATTE
OCEAN

DEEP
BLUE
SEA

BRITTANY

celta

One

*R*az, *Cerasus Cherry, shuffled the oracle cards for his breakfast table* mates, a half smile on his face. Of them all, the cards looked best in his long-fingered hands—good tools for an actor, as was his face and his smile.

He had breakfast at the Thespian Club every morning—late mornings for those who were working, earlier for those who were between jobs. The full complement of the group was six, three men and three women, none of them couples. Three of their group had eaten earlier and were gone by the time the rest of them had arrived at their reserved table.

A daily reserved table at the Thespian Club! His smile bloomed. They were all in their late twenties, rising fast in their careers, all talented, all ready to leap into stardom and excellent gilt. Not to mention the fame. Fame brought better, more challenging parts.

"You gonna shuffle all day to look at your pretty hands?" asked

Klay St. Johnswort, Johns, with his patented sneer. If you wanted a rough-hewn pure alpha male hero type, Johns was your man.

Raz considered himself elegant . . . and with an edge. More versatile.

"Lay out the cards, me first!" Trillia wiggled in her seat, her voice higher than usual, anxious. She'd gotten bored with the secondary lead in her play and had resigned the night before and was worried that she'd jumped when she should have stuck.

Raz handed her the cards—they belonged to the club—so they'd absorb her energy. Praying under her breath, she shuffled, cut the deck thrice, and laid out a six-card pattern. Her breath whooshed out, then her praying went to muttering as she studied her divination. "Crimson Nuts of Knowledge . . . the six of blazers, Goddess of the Rising Star, the six of wands."

"Looks good," Raz said. "New opportunities, gilt, success. But you might have to travel."

Johns said, "Could go to Gael City."

Trillia made a moue at the mention of the smaller town. "Gael City."

Raz tapped the six of wands. "Success."

"Oh, very well. I'll go straight to the guild from here."

"Might want to wipe the egg off your chin first," Raz said.

She rubbed at her face with her softleaf then flung it at him. "Oh, you."

"I heard The Rep in Gael City was reviving *Heart and Sword* in an updated production," Raz said.

Trillia sat up straight. "Fern Bountry, the *Nuada's Sword*'s Captain's wife! I could play Fern, kidnapped from the cryonic tube by evil mutineers . . . Wait, wait, she was dark." Trillia grabbed a handful of her hair and brought it in front of her face. It was fading from a blond rinse back to brown; she grinned in relief. "I can do this."

"Of course you can." Raz collected the cards.

Johns grunted. "Gonna show us all your fine fortune cards again, Raz?"

Raz quirked a corner of his mouth. The cards had foretold an excellent future for him lately. "What, past, present, and future? I was just going to draw an 'energy of the day' card."

"And he hasn't had all good luck," Trillia said. "There was that break-in at his apartment. Have the guardsmen found the thieves?"

"No. I didn't lose much." Raz frowned. Putting his space back in order had taken time, and he'd arranged for a decorator. He blew on his hands and the cards to dispel the negativity of the mention of the theft and the images that had trailed through his mind.

Drawing in a breath to center and bring in more positive energy, he shuffled on the exhale, inhaled, and pulled three cards from the deck and laid them out.

"Past." He flicked it over, the same Goddess of the Rising Star that Trillia had pulled. Trillia sighed. Raz liked it when women sighed, especially if they were in the audience.

Grunting again, Johns said sourly, "Prob'ly gonna be all major named cards, from the GreatSuite, all from the Ogham." Since their culture was based on the ancient Ogham alphabet, it wasn't surprising the major suite of divination cards were, too.

"One hopes." Raz grinned. Fully expecting to flip over The Oak King, solid success for years, as he had every time in the last few weeks, he turned it over.

The Summer Queen. The HeartMate card if drawn by a man.

Surprise flooded him. He'd always focused on his career, no time or inclination for a serious, permanent woman in his life.

Trillia whooped.

"Personal success and the fullness of creative expression." Johns snorted a chuckle. "Changes are coming for you, man. A Heart-Mate. A love life distracts from a single-minded career climb."

Raz couldn't tell if he was envious or not. Johns *was* taking some delight in the upset of plans a HeartMate could cause. Raz wasn't pleased. He liked his love life just as it was, full of casual sex and no expectations.

"Future?" Johns jutted his square chin at the cards.

His own jaw flexing, Raz revealed the last card. The Birch Wand. "New beginnings!" caroled Trillia.

He didn't want a new beginning or a HeartMate. He was doing just fine.

Johns stood, drew a card from the deck, The Oak King, tossed it down, then clapped Raz on the shoulder, grinning. "HeartMate, huh? Couldn't happen to a nicer guy."

STEEP SPRINGS, CELTA
That Afternoon

*H*elena *D'Elecampane, Del,* rode into the mountain town, hot and dusty from the frontier. It had taken all day by stridebeast to wind up the rough road from the plains to the town and was now late afternoon. After two months in the wilderness, she was longing for a soak in a private hot spring, a good meal, and a bedsponge. And her HeartMate.

Not necessarily in that order, though it would be another couple of weeks before she arrived in the capital, Druida City, to meet and claim him.

She'd felt him during his final dreamquest to free his psi power a while back. That made him younger than her, by how much she wasn't sure, but it didn't matter. She'd liked his mind touch and would no doubt like his physical touch . . .

"Hey, turn down that music!" a man shouted from the street, and she reluctantly thumbed off her saddle music player. From his scowl, the guy didn't appreciate the sophisticated sound. Del loved jazz. It was a music that only a few enjoyed.

Stup has no taste, said her fox Fam, Shunuk, raising his nose. He was riding on a pad behind her saddle. *Smells bad, too. Eats mostly vegetables.*

Del snorted. "There are a couple of jazz clubs in Druida. I heard places are admitting Fams. A good reason to visit the big city. We can stock up on new holobooks and vizes." They'd watched all she had dozens of times. Maybe she could see a play or two. "Druida will be fine."

Many busy people, Shunuk said, watching a man hurry down a street.

"Yes, and a lot more there," Del said. "Too many people for us."

Foxes are doing well in Druida. Shunuk grinned.

Del wondered how he would be accepted there, though he was as able to take care of himself as she was . . . and she'd be walking into a structured society, too. As a GrandLady from a House that had been founded three centuries ago, she could attend any society parties she wanted. If she wanted to be a social butterfly like her parents had been. Which she didn't.

All she'd ever wanted was to satisfy the itch to *explore*, to discover or see other places on Celta that no Druida noble even knew about. Most nobles only traveled back and forth from Druida to their country estates if they left the city at all. Oh, she supposed some visited Gael City, which was much smaller and more provincial than Druida, but that was it.

"We don't have to stay there very long." Only the time it took her to claim her HeartMate and meld him into her life. "We'll be back on the road soon." She'd wanted to see everything, and she'd done a good job of traversing the western parts of the north and south continents. She'd *made* maps of the continents and refined details.

As a girl she'd apprenticed herself to a cartographer and left on her first trip as soon as she finished her Second Passage—a dreamquest to free her psi power, her Flair—at seventeen. By that time her parents had been glad to see her leave. They didn't understand her and she was too young to want to understand them. Everyone was relieved the awful arguments were over.

She touched the long, cylindrical security pouch containing her maps that hung from the stridebeast's withers.

Maps are good. Shunuk gave a little yip. *Pretty.*

Del smiled. "Yeah, they are." Her Flair had changed and the maps were now fully three-dimensional. She thought the HeartMate connection during his Passage had sparked that change.

You will take me with you when you deliver the maps to the Guildhall?

Ever since she'd told Shunuk about the great Guildhall in Druida, he'd wanted to visit.

"I said so." She grimaced. "Sometimes city people move slowly, like in the government. The Councils always take a while to assign a value to the maps." She rolled her shoulders. "There's a great amount of paperwork."

They will like new maps.

"Yes, I've fulfilled my annual NobleGilt and more with these."

Her stridebeast whiffled, then whined. He didn't like the paving stones under his hooves. Steep Springs was growing slowly, in small increments, as all Celtan towns grew.

More gliders on the streets, Shunuk said. *Will we get a glider?*

"No." Del smoothed a tangle of the stridebeast's long hair, patted him. "Gliders aren't good if there isn't smooth, solid earth. They're too big and take too much energy to power. Spells I don't need to spend gilt on." Del shook her head. "More buildings here, too." More two-story brick and stone buildings rather than wooden, and there were *streets*, not just one circled drive around the park in the center of town. Two narrow spokes ran along the valley, and houses climbed up the hills. Pretty houses tinted in pretty colors with fancy carved trim. Del scowled. Fancy enough to appeal to some city folk as "quaint." Steep Springs was definitely growing.

"We'll stay at our usual place." The inn with the best private hot springs. She guided her mount to an alley behind the inn. "Unpack first." She wanted to put her precious maps and the new landscape globes she'd made with her creative Flair into the room's security no-time. "Then we'll eat."

As she swung off her mount, she stared into Shunuk's yellow eyes. "I'll bring you a roasted clucker. I don't want to hear about any missing town cluckers this time."

He spoiled his innocent look by licking his muzzle. *Crackly skin?*

"Yes. Better than a mouthful of feathers."

He shifted his eyes. *Maybe.* Then he hopped down and grinned. *Will be juicy rats in stables. More stables here, too.*

"Yes."

Shunuk stretched. *See you later.*

"Later." Since she traveled light, the unpacking went fast, though she'd frowned at the new person behind the counter when told the room and spa she liked best was booked.

The stable prices had gone up, as had those in the eatery, which was now called a restaurant. She ordered pasta with spinach in a cream sauce. Vegetarian. She chuckled as she thought of Shunuk, but she was tired of killing and eating animals. The meal was good and the place was playing new, excellent music.

She left a good tip with coin she didn't often use. Then she strolled back out to the summer day, lingered in the sun, and watched the world go by. How pleasant just to do *nothing*. That mood wouldn't last long, she was a restless person, but for now it was good.

There was a jangle of bells on the door of a nearby shop and Del realized it was near closing on Midweekend and most places wouldn't be open the next day of Ioho.

Which meant if she wished to head out tomorrow or early the next day and wanted good caff to drink and more medicinal herbs, she'd better get moving.

She crossed the street to the Herb and Caff Emporium, which also carried her landscape globes. There she settled at a tiny table and ordered some caff with cinnamon and white mousse.

Her gaze went immediately to the dim corner where she could see the faint gleam of her creative work—glass globes, each on a rock base. Except for a small coating of dust, they appeared to be exactly as she'd left them. No one had held them, felt the energy within tune to them individually. No one had breathed a little Flair upon them or simply shook them to see the bits of plant and soil and other items in the fluid of the globes. Not one had attracted a buyer.

She suppressed a sigh. They were less refined than the ones she had now, but they *should* have drawn someone who'd look beyond the little bits of wood and stone and plant settled in the bottom of the liquid-filled sphere.

She *knew* they worked. Her creative Flair was just as strong as her cartographic Flair. A globe should draw a person, someone strong in creative Flair—and wasn't everyone?—to come and hold it, look inside, shake it.

Then the Flair in the globe would react with the person's Flair to show them their perfect home.

Del finished her caff, hardly tasting the cinnamon, a rarity. Years ago her survey of a valley that grew cinnamon for T'Hawthorn had been her best-paying job.

Ever since she'd connected with her HeartMate, she'd been impatient with her travels, had an urge to find him. She was pretty sure that he hadn't sensed her during his Passage, not enough to track her if he'd wanted.

Most people wanted HeartMates, a true soul-binding love. Del was a little uncertain about the whole thing herself, but still there was this pull to him . . . and had been since her own last Passage seven years ago. Now it was stronger, a true link.

She went to the counter and addressed the proprietress. "Hey, Hysa, I'll have a half a pound of light roast caff and a pound of hibiscus tea." She always yearned for the ultracivilized drink after time on the trail, a throwback to her childhood. "I got tired of trail caff and chicory a while back."

The plump, matronly woman smiled. "Some FemCycle Leaf tea as usual?"

"No." Del leaned companionably on the counter. "I'm going up to Druida City to claim my HeartMate." She winked. "Or let him claim me."

Hysa's mouth fell open. "You? *You* have a HeartMate?"

Del straightened. She'd known Hysa for years, had thought the woman had known her.

Guess not. Hysa had never paid any attention to more than Del's frontier woman appearance. What did the store owner consider her, a mule? Some sterile animal? A person without needs or passions? Hadn't her passion for exploration gotten her to this point? And she wasn't that old, only thirty-six.

"No," Del repeated in a clipped tone. "No FemCycle Leaf tea. If I want to get pregnant, I will." Good boast on underpopulated Celta.

They stared at each other with irritation.

"Hey, that you, Del?" A man walked through the door and let it slam behind him.

She turned to see the town's communications chief. "Yes, do you have something for me?"

"I'd say so. An official notice from the FirstFamilies Council itself, a big actual papyrus envelope." He grimaced. "And a holosphere from FirstFamily GrandLord T'Blackthorn."

Probably jobs. Del shook her head. "That Straif, he tracked me all over Celta once. The second payment of my yearly NobleGilt come?"

The man grinned, hooked his thumbs into his belt. "Got a confirmation from your bank right on your Nameday, a month ago, *GrandLady* D'Elecampane," he teased.

The title got Hysa moving, which was all to the good. Yes, she'd only bothered with Del's outer appearance, not considered their talks, Del's creative Flair, her background. The noble background that Del didn't much consider, either.

Del said, "Just give me a stock of the standard med herbs, the caff, and tea. I'll pick anything else up in Druida." She turned to the comm chief. "I'll be right with you." Expression smooth, she gestured to her six landscape orbs. "I'll take those with me, too."

Now a hint of a blush stained Hysa's cheeks. "Of course, of course." She bustled over to them, set them out two by two on the counter for Del. "They just didn't sell."

Del shrugged, pretending she wasn't sensitive about her work, that the woman's comments didn't hurt. Tried not to feel pity for her creations. This one had a glitter of silver snowflakes, that one an interesting, gnarled twig. She *knew* they could build a person's dream home—city or country, cottage or castle.

From her bag she took out softleaves and padded pouches she'd made on the trail to fit her hand-sized globes.

"They just didn't sell," Hysa repeated with a touch of accusation as Del wiped them clean, wrapped them, and placed them in the pouches.

"That's all right." A little spurt of glee ignited inside her. "I got word from a merchant who will handle them."

"Oh? Who?"

Del met her gaze and smiled. "T'Ash, in his shop in Druida. T'Ash's Phoenix." *The* most prestigious jewelry store on the planet.

"Good one." The comm chief winked and Del's mind went back to the letters. She frowned as a tingle slithered down her spine. An official notice from the FirstFamilies Council was serious business.

Two

A septhour later Del was leaning against fluffy pillows, her legs stretched out on the bedsponge, a meter of softness under her butt. Luxury. A fire was nicely tamed behind glass and pretty to look at. She never got tired of watching campfires.

She'd had her soak in peace. As she'd sunk into the heated and mineralized water, she'd let her mind drift until she was in a meditative trance, setting all concerns, even the papyrus envelope from the FirstFamilies Council and the holosphere from T'Blackthorn, aside. It had been a long time since she didn't have to keep her wits keen for predators in the night around her.

Something to be said for cities, though they had their own predators. Still, other humans were sometimes easier to face than beasts that would rip you apart with a slice of their claws.

She was dressed in a civilized silkeen nightshirt that slid across her skin. No sleeping in her clothes tonight, either, another luxury.

Now it was time to open the envelope or look at the sphere, and a prickle of dread went through her, vanquishing the last bit of peaceful contemplation from her mind. Which to open first? Straif T'Blackthorn's probably had a job offer in it, maybe a long journey that he didn't want to take now that he was settled down with wife and babies. He had a HeartMate, too. She smiled. If he could make a marriage work, then maybe she could. He'd been on the road as long as she had, longer, and running from problems, unlike her.

Yeah, if Straif T'Blackthorn, her occasional lover a while back, could take a partner and be happy, she could, too.

Though she didn't want to settle down like Straif, especially not in Druida City, nor did she want babies. She just wanted her Heart-Mate and her maps and the trail curving around the next mountain or through the next stand of trees.

She took the small sphere, remembering Straif T'Blackthorn. They'd had good, fast sex and longer, interesting conversations. He was a FirstFamily lord now, not journeying much. Could hardly get more restricted than the duties of a FirstFamily lord.

Flicking the gray sphere with her thumb, she smiled as his tall, broad-shouldered form solidified in the holo. He was wearing expensive clothes, looking more like a lord than the rough tracker she'd known. His expression was stern, his sandy brows down, his muscles tense as if facing a threat.

Another frisson passed through her.

"Greetyou, Del. There's no easy way to tell you this news." He paused and her gut clenched. She wanted to put the holosphere down, now. Sweat sprang to her palms and caused the thing to roll a little. The image stayed vertical. Straif's nostrils widened as he took a big breath.

Del braced.

"I'm sorry to have to tell you that your Heir, your G'Aunt Inula, and her Family have died in a fire . . ." His lips compressed, then he went on. Cold crackled into ice inside Del. *No!*

"They didn't burn, most perished of smoke inhalation, suffocation," he said as if trying to comfort her. He glanced away as if he could see her shock and grief.

Even more horrible, their name-plant, Elecampane, was known for freeing congestion in the lungs. Did Straif recall that? Probably not. Del's own chest tightened. Tears welled in her eyes, trickled down her cheeks, and the rushing in her ears had her missing the rest of the message. Straif's image was lost as the holosphere rolled from her hand onto the bedsponge.

She brought her knees up, curling, put her head on them, and let grief tears follow shock tears as she tried to make sense of things. Celta was hard enough with sicknesses and low birthrate keeping humans scarce. Why did other things like this have to happen?

Her mind grappled with the news, even as a small portion of her knew this information was hitting her harder than she might expect.

She wasn't close to her Family, never had been. In their social striving, her parents had distanced themselves from the middle-class branch. Del herself hadn't met them very often. But she'd always known they were there, carrying on the Family name if something had happened to her.

Now she was the last of her Family. How much would that affect her plans and her life? Never much wanted the title, but she'd gotten it. Resentment and anger flared inside her. She didn't want to be the last of her Family! Didn't want to have other people's, city people's, expectations dragging her down.

There was a slight *whoosh* and the scent of the night air. Shunuk landed next to her and she raised her head. He stared up at her with dark, concerned eyes. *Something is wrong.*

Del moved cold lips. "All the rest of my Family has died."

Shunuk's tail plumped in distress and he swished it. *That is not good.*

"No." How "not good" she still didn't know. But she grieved for the people who had also carried the Elecampane name. Her Heir, G'Aunt Inula, and her husband; their two children, older than Del; then the third generation, young Elfwort and his wife and child . . . Del swallowed. The baby had been named Helendula, very close to her own name, Helena. She shuddered. She'd only seen the newest Elecampane once.

Lying down next to her hip, Shunuk was added warmth, but he must have touched the sphere, because Straif's voice rumbled into the silence.

"All but one died, but one *did* survive." As Straif paused, Del lunged toward the sphere. Shunuk yelped and leapt away.

One had survived! Lady and Lord's blessing! Who? They'd be cursing her at not being there to help, though they should have had enough funds to do whatever was needful. Had they been hurt much? Were there medical bills to pay?

". . . Little Helendula's room was at the end of the wing. Her door was closed and she was sleeping on a floor bedsponge. The fire mages got to her in time. She was taken to the Maidens of Saille House for Orphans until you returned."

When? *When* had this happened? Del had been out of touch for nearly a *year* and Straif sure wasn't telling this properly. Letting her think she was the last.

But she was the last adult.

"As soon as I heard I arranged to take over your affairs here in Druida . . ." Good! She'd owe him. Her fingers curled over the sphere, she sat up with a grunt and stared at Straif. Shunuk sat next to her and did the same.

Straif looked grim and raked his hands through his hair. A touch of red lined his cheekbones. He cleared his throat. "The Noble-Council took my word we'd been lovers and I'd know what you'd want." Well, he was a FirstFamily lord, they would take his word. But with him wed to his HeartMate, that must have been interesting. Del definitely owed him. "You've probably got a formal notice from the FirstFamilies Council that you are the last adult of your line."

Again he looked aside. His shoulders set and he stared directly back at her. "When my wife and I heard of little Helendula's circumstances we went to the Maidens of Saille House for Orphans and removed her into our care."

Del's hand went limp again and the sphere rolled away, onto the bedsponge and down to the floor, where it bounced on a rag rug. Del watched it go, as did Shunuk. His tail flicked. He turned to meet her eyes.

You have a kit, he said.

She had a child.

She ripped open the envelope. In stilted, formal, legal terms, it told her what Straif had. She let it, too, flutter to the floor, stunned.

The last of her Family, herself and a child a little over a year old.

Shunuk put a paw on her knee, looked her in the eye. *Kits must be cared for until they are old enough to fend for themselves.*

Yeah, that made her gut feel worse. He rubbed his paw along her leg in comfort. *We can do that.*

"We'll ride at dawn. Then we can make it to Gael City before the last express airship leaves for Druida." She flipped up the covers, slid between soft linens, and said a Word that made the room go dark. Shunuk settled near her feet on the bedsponge. *We can take care of the kit,* he repeated.

Could she? She set her teeth. She'd have to.

The night deepened, darker, darker and she was sad and alone. She reached for him instinctively, and he was there, sharing her dream. "Lover," she said, her voice breaking. She needed the contact now that she knew there'd be no more hugs or kisses or even conversation with her lost Family. "Lover." She touched him "physically" and her hands felt the smoothness of a muscular back. She didn't know who he was, couldn't see him with blurred eyes in the dark . . . though she thought she heard city sounds.

He was larger than she—taller, and she was a tall woman. Broader, but she was tough whipcord, every muscle honed, and he lean male strength.

He rolled to the side and gathered her close, front to front, skin to skin—he was as naked as she, and aroused. She was hurting and needed him emotionally and the small link between them had widened and he had come to her in her dream . . . It would turn erotic, she knew that, welcomed that, but for now he held her. He kissed tears from her cheek.

Ssshhh, he said mentally, and she felt the comfort of it, the tenderness that was more than sex, the HeartMate connection that had already formed between them.

He stroked her back, over the curve of her butt, back up. Then his lips trailed from her cheek to her jawline and down her throat, where he licked and her sadness melted away with his gentle touch . . . that became more insistent. His hand went to her breast, cupped it, stroked her nipple, and she arched into him. Sweet desire flickered into greedy passion. She needed him.

He'd given her tenderness, but now she wanted more, wanted like he did. His erection was strong and hard, nudging her stomach, and she shuddered at the sleek length of him, remembering the feel of him inside her during their previous dreams.

She hooked a leg over him, opening her physical self, and felt his slow penetration that made her dampen even more, made her yearn to strive for release . . . and the joy of orgasm and simple forgetfulness. He rolled atop her and she locked her heels behind his back and moved with him.

Passion throbbed through her, faster than his thrusts, flashing hot, faster than her pulse beating in her head. He was taking her away from herself, her life, and that was what she wanted. For now.

HeartMate, she chanted it mentally, though she knew he didn't hear, kept it a tasty secret in her mind, naming him what he was for her, cherishing the fact of him, the reality of him.

He panted and his back dampened and she was with him for every step that wound hunger and yearning and pleasure tight until bright stars exploded in the night around her and she fell apart and was remade.

Her HeartMate. The heavy knowledge that she had lost her Family had returned, but she also understood that she still lived. Life went on.

Distantly, she thought she felt him wake, swear. Then the link between them snapped shut and he was gone and her bed was empty.

DRUIDA CITY

*M*idmorning the next day, pounding came at *Raz's* dressing room door. He jolted awake and rose from the sofa where he'd been sleeping after a very late night—and a disturbingly sexual dream that he didn't want to think had involved his HeartMate. Not now, not so soon.

Cursing accompanied the rapping. He glanced at the wall timer. Yes, he should be getting ready for the afternoon matinee.

"Raz Cherry, you speak to me *now!*" Lily, his leading woman, shouted with more knocks.

He opened the door and Lily stormed in. "Dammit, why have you been messing with my stuff?"

His character adored Lily in the play, and she was a fine actress, but Raz found her difficult off stage. She carried a negativity around her.

"I haven't touched your things," he said.

"It had to be you. You were the only one here in the theater this morning."

"What are you talking about?" Irritation suffusing him, he followed her to the hall where he heard weeping and raised voices from the cast who shared a common dressing room. Their possessions had been rifled through and things were missing. Everyone converged outside Lily's room, which was slightly closer to the stage than his own. She flung her door open.

"See!"

It looked no messier than usual to Raz. He shrugged his shoulders. "What?"

Her mouth pinched, then she said, "I lost some jewelry."

"So did I," chorused two more women and a man.

Raz raised his brows, rocked back on his heels. "And why do you think I'd take jewelry?" He waved a hand so the ruby signet ring on his hand flashed, the only jewelry he wore.

Lily glanced aside and Raz got the impression she was hiding something from them.

"It wasn't only jewels," one of the men who hadn't spoken before grumbled. "My script has been ripped, pages scattered everywhere."

"An old *real* book of mine has been pilfered," the villain of the play said, eyes narrowed.

"I prefer vizes and holos myself," Raz reminded them all coolly.

The manager showed up, frown lines creasing his long face, his shock of wiry white hair standing straight up. "The actors' and guest book in the green room has been stolen. The small paintings of Booth and Alyssa Primrose are gone, too."

Silence fell. Everyone liked the paintings of the famous actors who'd founded the theater, considered them mascots.

An actress sniffled. "Someone found my stash of gilt."

"Stup," her partner said and put an arm around her.

Raz stared at Lily. "And you accuse me of all this?"

"No one's accusing you, Raz," the manager said.

"My things were all right last night when we left." Lily tossed her head. "You were here this morning."

"Because my apartment's being retinted."

"Being retinted because you had a theft there, too," said the villain of the play. "Quite bad luck for us all."

The manager asked, "Raz, you were here this morning, did you hear anything?"

"No, I was sleeping."

"I'll call the guardsmen. Everyone make a list of your missing or destroyed property. Meanwhile I will remind you that we are giving a show in a septhour." The manager loped away and the others, still loudly upset, drifted back to their room.

Raz propped his shoulder on the doorjamb of Lily's room. "What was taken that you aren't telling about?"

"Nothing." She tried to close the door on him but he stopped it with a foot, gave her a fierce smile.

"Lily?"

"I need to make that list and get ready. Go away."

"Like to give me orders today?" Then his eye caught a piece of crumpled papyrus with a distinctive golden flower mark in the corner. He straightened away from the door frame. "Is that a script by Amberose? Is she writing again?" He swung his gaze back to Lily. "*You* got a script from Amberose?"

Scowling, Lily set manicured red-tinted nails against his chest and pushed. "None of your business. *Go away.*" She added the Flair of a woman who'd been pursued too much by men and knew how to handle them. Her Flair sent him back through the door and into the hallway.

Raz frowned and decided to scry his agent and ask about a new play by Amberose. Then he heard the back doorman's raised voice, the clump of heavy feet. His nose twitched as he scented a slight, unfamiliar odor. The guardsmen had arrived. He hurried back into his room and began to don his first costume, gathering his Flair to accentuate his features for the audience.

*T*he day was Ioho, the last of the three weekend days, yet Del managed to do a great deal. Her first stop was her home, where she sent the windows up and the doors open and initiated all the housekeeping spells. Her house wasn't an intelligent Residence yet, though she felt the faint stirrings of sentience deep in the bowels where the HouseHeart ritual room lay.

Another thing to tie her to Druida City, along with the child, if she let it. The longer a house was occupied, and by the more people, the sooner it would become self-aware. She shoved the thought aside. There was plenty of time to think of options when she didn't have so much to do. One step at a time.

She contacted Straif T'Blackthorn's Residence—a true and mighty being—and was not put through to Straif or his HeartMate,

Mitchella. So Del left a message that she wanted to speak to them about her cuz Helendula and meet the child, then went on to her next task.

The City Guildhall was open but practically empty. Shunuk trotted around, exploring the building, yipping, and listening to echoes off the marble walls. Del heard him in the Guildhall clerk's office while she filed her maps with the clerk on duty. That lady had unrolled the maps to log them in and had made many admiring compliments that fed Del's ego. Her maps *were* superb.

After that she pleased her fox Fam even more by walking to the southern edge of town where G'Aunt Inula's house had been. There was nothing but seared land. The Councils had cleared the hazardous ruins. Del swallowed hard, tears stinging the backs of her eyes as she recalled the sprawling red-brick building that had been the home of several generations of Elecampanes. The house and the people in it and the laughter and busyness that had resounded throughout the halls—it had never been a quiet place—were all gone.

She stood alone, the remaining adult member of the Family, and though she wanted to mutter curses at fate, she breathed the soft summer air with the hint of flowers and began a blessing chant for the area and the souls of her lost Family. Her feet tingled as she felt the formal blessings of a priestess and priest from the ground. It had been cleansed after the fire.

The closest houses were many meters away. Del looked at the grass that had begun encroaching on the burnt area. She strode over uneven ground to see a plant or two had been spared, though the rest of the gardens were gone, as were the sheds that had held the Family research workshops. The Family Flair was for scrying—communication—developing ever-better spells to be coated on bowls and panels for houses and vehicles.

A year and a half ago Elfwort had developed new glassy pebbles encasing a droplet of water for individual mobile scrying. Del herself had very little of the Family Flair.

Brows knit, Del tried to recall what she'd heard about what the oracle had said at Helendula's birth. The baby had good Flair, and the Family sort, hadn't she? There should be copies of the Family papyrus at the NobleCouncil Clerk's Office and maybe even a set at Del's house. She wasn't accustomed to thinking of Family matters, hadn't looked for such papyrus at home. Her inefficiency bothered her.

More was the underlying feeling of helplessness and her life spinning out of control.

Children's shouts from neighboring grounds twisted the sorrow inside her until it cut like a knife instead of being a raw ache. Who knew she'd miss her Family like this? Cherish the idea of them now that they were gone? If she let herself, she could feel deep guilt. But she had followed her heart as they had followed theirs, and the two paths had not often met.

She shrugged the feeling off. Too much feeling, not enough thinking. Scuffing her boots into the dirt, she settled into her balance and again let the atmosphere of the city surround her, press hard on her with the different smells and the faster pace . . . and mentally followed the link to her HeartMate.

To the entertainment district where eateries and social clubs and night clubs were. She'd already scouted out the two jazz places and they were both in that direction.

He was there, and she sensed he was *working*. She let a smile curve her lips. Could he possibly be a jazz musician? That would be perfect. Maybe fortune's wheel was turning better for her.

With a whistle, she called Shunuk, though he was reluctant to come since he'd smelled fox-spoor and was tracking it to the closest dens.

After a half-septhour PublicCarrier ride, she and Shunuk stood in the large flagstone rectangle that was ringed by the city's theaters. They walked to the Evening Primrose Theater. Del stared at a short animated holo projected from a poster that showed a brief scene from the performance inside. Raz Cherry and Lily Fescue starred in a sophisticated mystery. Del's gaze was riveted on Raz as she watched the holo time and again. Looked like she'd go to a play tonight.

Shunuk pointed his narrow muzzle to the poster. *We know that man.*

Her HeartMate was Raz Cherry. She'd had a viz of one of his performances, had watched it time and again, and hadn't understood that the actor was special to her. But the man in this poster was older and smoother and more accomplished than the young man who'd played second lead in the viz she'd watched.

He's my HeartMate, she said.

He is a pretty human?

Yes. Her heart beat faster, her gut clenched with wanting, but she managed a casual shrug. Then she thought of her strong shoulders, her strong muscles, her less than smooth skin. Not much like Lily Fescue, for sure, or the man himself.

What kind of partner could Raz Cherry be?

Three

Raz didn't sink into the character he was playing completely, was oddly distracted. He told himself that his failure to stay in the present was the thought of a new play by Amberose.

That famous and reclusive playwright hadn't issued a work for more than a decade. What a triumph it would be to star in it. He could only hope the male lead didn't call for a big bruiser like Johns.

Lily slapped him on stage and it was more than they'd practiced. Fire was in her gaze, her sharp words, the way she flounced away. Raz set his jaw. She'd been right to bring him back to the here-and-now and he didn't like that he'd slipped. So he concentrated and became the hero, followed Lily across stage to grab her arm and swing her back—with the exact force they'd done for one hundred and eighteen performances.

By the time the traditional curtains closed, he was pleased with his work and grinned at the loud "bravos," some of which were for him alone. He and the cast took several bows and he soaked in the applause. There was nothing in the world like it.

He returned to his dressing room imbued with satisfaction.

Until he opened the door and found his room ransacked, objects scattered, possessions broken.

His shout gathered them all, brought the two guardsmen who had lingered to see the play for free. The sweet pleasure of triumph transformed into fury. He plunged forward to the broken models of the three starships that his father and he had made when he was a child. *Arianrhod's Wheel* and *Lugh's Spear* were twisted metal as if they'd been stomped on, *Nuada's Sword* was unrecognizable. A groan tore from Raz as he picked up *Lugh's Spear*, the ship of his ancestors. One of the models had always stayed in the theater while he was on a job.

"Sir, you shouldn't—" started a guardsman.

Raz whirled on him. "This happened during the show. Where were you?"

The man winced. "In the front." He widened his stance. "We talked to all'a you, all'a the stagehands and crew. Got lists of missing items. No one saw anyone, anything." He glanced at the gathering in the hallway. People shook their heads. The guard turned back to examine the room. "Can you tell if anything has been stolen?"

Curling his lip, Raz scanned the mess, nodded to the shelves dangling from the wall. "Holospheres, old scripts." His favorites.

The other guard had a sensorball, recording the chamber with sweeps of his hand. "Papyrus, holos taken. You keep a journal?"

"No."

A throat cleared. The manager stood in the door, folded hands over his small paunch. "Sorry, Raz, but you should leave this room as much like you found it as possible. You and the two guardsmen were the only ones in the room since this morning?"

"Yes. Had to happen since my last costume change. 'Course I was on stage for the last half septhour." Raz found he was stroking the cool metal of the *Lugh's Spear* model with his forefinger. He followed the guards from the chamber, stepping over debris, avoiding looking at the fat cushioned couch that showed puffs of stuffing leaking from slices; the crumpled, ripped, and ruined world map tapestry that had hung on the wall. Sparing a last glance over his shoulder at the other models, he let loss fill him, then let it go, searched for a positive spin in all this.

Perhaps when he told his father, they'd repair *Lugh's Spear*, make new miniatures of *Arianrhod's Wheel* and *Nuada's Sword*. Maybe reclaim some closeness they'd lost when Raz had turned his back on the Family business to train as an actor.

As he stepped into the hall he bumped into someone, then squinted at the usual dark aura of a crewman that let him move around on stage unnoticed. "Who the hell are you?"

"Sorry." The shield was dropped and Raz stared at a short, familiar woman.

Sighing inwardly—he liked to be charming to all women, especially the ones he worked with—he bowed and said, "My fault. I ran into you."

Her face was puffy and eyes red, probably why she'd shielded. With a grimace, she looked in his room, then away, her lips trembled. "They broke the stuff in my locker. Earlier." She glanced around, shifted from foot to foot. "Bad luck."

The manager clapped. "People, the guardsmen will have my office. They have requested that none of us leave until after the performance later tonight. I've ordered catering in. While the guards are investigating, we will be using the Noble Lounge. Raz, let wardrobe know what you need for the show tonight."

Raz's mouth twisted. "Everything except what I'm wearing now."

"A priestess and priest will be coming to cleanse the area after the guardsmen are done. If any of you want counseling, they will provide it. Performance in three septhours." The manager's lip curled. "Let's show everyone that we are the best troupe in the business."

*   *   *

*A*fter *Raz's dressing room had been cleaned, repaired, and blessed,* he'd spent a few minutes lying on the new couch, testing it and meditating before his performance.

A lingering scent of serenity herbs combined with an atmosphere of soothing calm brought by the priestess and priest. Lily's area felt less negative than it had since the run had started.

He'd contacted his father about making new starship models and had seen pleased gratification flash in the older man's eyes. They'd settled on dinner and work at T'Cherry Residence Midweek when he had only an afternoon show. That had felt good.

The rest of the cast and crew seemed equally relieved at having a cleansing and a blessing in the theater. Those who'd lost gilt and jewels had already been reimbursed by the theater owner. A few of the women were looking forward to shopping the next day.

Once Raz took the stage, he knew it would be a good night. There was something about the audience, a certain Flair, that ignited his own. An energizing buzz slid along his skin and sank deeply into him. He sensed the energy of the audience more clearly. They were in a mood to be more entertained with the wit of the play than the mystery so he modified his part. Lily and the rest of the cast picked up on his slight change of character and adjusted their own.

At the end of the last act he was revved as the audience gasped at the final twist, shouted as the curtain came down.

The villain rose from the stage and plucked the dummy knife from his chest. He linked hands with Lily as Raz did, and when the curtain rose, the three of them took their bows.

"Few times in a lifetime do we get energy like this," the villain muttered from the side of his mouth. "Damned if the place doesn't feel better than last night, despite everything."

Lily smiled and bowed with them, angling toward stage left, center, right, talking softly through curved lips. "It will be back to normal tomorrow night."

The villain lifted her hand and kissed her fingers. "That's what I adore about you, your unwavering optimism."

One last bow with all the cast and Raz left the stage with the others, retired to his dressing room. Unlike in the morning, he locked it. The day had been long and weariness hovered on the edge of his mind, ready to crash on him.

He hadn't had enough time before the show to prowl his refurbished room, arrange his remaining possessions, and in two days he wanted to walk into a space that felt right. Tomorrow the theater was dark. He had the day off, but there was a party that night to celebrate this one hundred and twentieth performance.

A good number, and maybe that factored into why the night had been so successful. Appeared he'd be employed for another one hundred and twenty and that was good.

He arranged his belongings, packed the remnants of *Nuada's Sword* and *Arianrhod's Wheel* in a shielded box, placed the battered *Lugh's Spear* in the center of a very empty shelf. He left, spellshielding the door. As he stepped into the hall, he realized everyone was gone and it was later than he thought.

He looked at the wall timer—a septhour before midnight. He'd be returning to another place that wouldn't feel good. The decorator would have left her energy in his rooms. Muttering under his breath, he strode to the stage door, stopped when he saw a female guardsman. Raz cleared his throat, smiled, enjoyed the little flush that came to her face. "Good night. Take care."

She nodded. "You, too, GrandSir Cherry."

He caught an echoing sound. "Are there more of you?"

"Three. One for the main entrance and one to patrol."

Now he felt her strong Flair, which reassured him. She was tall and the guard uniform couldn't hide her breasts and hips. She wasn't a member of the stage or the crew . . .

The HeartMate card came to his mind's eye and he gave her another smile and a wave and hurried out the door. He couldn't be too careful with new women coming into his life.

How was he to know who'd be safe for a nice, brief, sexy affair and who wouldn't? Cave of the Dark Goddess.

He knew HeartMates usually connected during Passages—dammit, he'd had his last Passage at twenty-seven, a year ago!—and that they could have erotic dreams about each other, especially during Passage. He'd enjoyed those dreams, the slide of his hands along her skin, the slide of his body on hers, the slide into her . . . and damned if he wasn't getting aroused.

As he left the building he thought he could almost recall her scent . . . an exotic mix of spices, the slight taste of salt on her skin. He tucked the memory into the back of his mind where it would be for comparison to women who came into his life.

Three steps into the street and wariness feathered up his spine as if someone watched him. He tightened his grip on the box containing his destroyed treasures. He was angry and *wanted* to smash anyone who attacked him, so he decided to walk the half kilometer to his rooms instead of taking the PublicCarrier home. He'd like to catch this vandal and thief.

Yes, he was actor enough to know when eyes watched him, a glance slid over his body. Adrenaline rushed through him and he loosened his muscles, kept his stride easy. His expression showed a man thinking of other things than his surroundings.

His footsteps tapped lonely on the street, though he thought someone followed close. He watched for shadows and saw nothing, listened for the slightest hint of another footfall, a brush of a shoe against a curb. Nothing.

Soon he was at the roundpark in the center of his neighborhood that catered to artists with unique shops and small restaurants and apartments. There were no footsteps, though he thought the watcher was still there. He stepped into the deep alcove of his doorway that led to the staircase to the four apartments above. With a murmured Word he was through the new, stronger spellshield and the sturdy door closed behind him. All the tenants had been burgled.

He'd spoken to the guardsmen at the theater about both thefts. They'd taken notes but had only mumbled at him that they didn't think the break-ins were connected. He didn't think the guards would pay any attention to a report that someone was watching him since he had no proof.

When he opened his door, a dim glowing ball of spell-light came on, illuminating the newly tinted walls of his rectangular room. Sucking in a breath that brought him the fragrance of vanilla, he relaxed. There was no lingering or clashing vibration of energy left by the decorator. Three of his walls were a light terra cotta hue, the fourth with the two windows onto the street a bold red.

The broken light-colored wood shelves were gone. Instead there were six deep reddwood shelves in a pyramidical pattern, long lower shelf to small upper shelf. He grimaced at their emptiness. Nothing was on the bottom two, a few sculptures were on the middle, but the top meter-length shelf had been made to fit the three starship models.

His arm tightened around the box that held the fragments of *Arianrhod's Wheel* and *Nuada's Sword*. Flaired craftspeople could repair them, but the damage was so great that the models would resonate more of the repairer than of himself and his father. It wouldn't be the same. He was a little surprised to realize how much he'd liked the reminder of his Family, the vibration of them and his childhood in his rooms.

He took the box to an ornate cabinet, the one piece of Family furniture that he'd wanted, placed between the windows. As he put the container on the large empty bottom shelf, he saw the colorfully patterned divination cards, also antique.

Family legend said that the pack had been created by their colonist ancestress, Mona Tabacin, who had trekked with others from the crashed *Lugh's Spear* to Druida City. Since none of the cards were exactly the same size, he could believe the story. The cards were based on an ancient Earthan divination system and images, not the Celtan Ogham one, but he had taken pride in learning their meanings.

As soon as the psi power of his Family became strong Flair, each card and the deck itself had been shielded, a blessing since they'd been scattered around his rooms during the theft. He'd have been in a great deal of trouble from his Family if the cards had been damaged or lost. They were his sole inheritance of the Family treasures—his younger sister, the child with the Family Flair, was Heir to the shipping empire.

On impulse he took the deck from the cabinet, fanned them out. Family energy caused more of the day's tension to drain. He particularly loved these cards because each of the backs was different: bold and cheerful patterns of colored bands from deep purple through the spectrum to light yellow.

Closing his eyes he drew in a deep breath and plucked a card from the deck.

The card showed lovers holding hands. He dropped it. This card meant *choices*. Behind the man there was a landscape with a tiny tower that resembled Druida City Guildhall. Behind the woman was an equally minuscule shape, a crunched starship, *Lugh's Spear*.

Choices.

Raz had been set determinedly on one path for a long time: his career. He *liked* that path. But inside him a seed of a thought sprouted, of loving and being loved by a HeartMate.

How would a HeartMate change his life if he chose her? Choices. He must make the right one.

The next morning Del walked several kilometers from her Family estate to T'Blackthorn Residence in Noble Country. She had an appointment at MidMorningBell.

The sky was a lighter blue in the city, though it was more north than she'd been for a while. The roads were smooth for foot and glider and PublicCarrier traffic.

She breathed deep of the city air, with city scents. Smells of Earthan and hybrid flowers that didn't grow well in the wild, cut and trimmed hedges that had a subtly different fragrance than when they tangled outside the city.

Shunuk caught up with her as she turned down the road bordering

Straif T'Blackthorn's estate. She hadn't seen her Fam this morning. Now he trotted beside her, mouth open as if laughing.

"I hope you had a good evening," she said.

I did, he said. His tongue lolled. *Many excellent, intelligent fox in the city. Good to hunt with, good to share food, good to talk with.*

"I'm glad."

You're not. He gave a short bark. *But I love you best.*

"Glad someone does." She'd been having doubts about Raz Cherry as a travel companion. He'd gloried in the applause of the show she'd seen last night. And he'd done extremely well, was a superb actor.

It annoyed her that she was having doubts about anything.

Doubts about Helendula, too. When Straif Blackthorn had returned Del's scry this morning, he'd told her that he and *his* HeartMate, Mitchella, had come to love Helendula and wanted to adopt her.

That statement had closed Del's throat even as she studied the landscape globe she'd made for the child during her long and restless night. She'd stood, stunned, options crashing through her mind, unable to puzzle out what she felt. She'd been getting accustomed to the thought of having a child, working on how she'd fit little Helendula into her life. How she could compromise to give them both what they needed.

Then Straif had pressed for her to come and see them, meet Helendula. Gestured to the background of the scry where his wife held a toddler. The baby Del had hardly known was gone, had become a child with a tragedy in her past.

Would it be selfish or selfless if Del left Helendula with the Blackthorns?

Four

Shunuk wove a pattern in front of Del, drawing her mind back to the present. He angled his narrow muzzle at her. *I heard that your kit has found a home with folk who take abandoned kits.*

Del winced. If she'd been in town, she'd have cared for Helendula. She hadn't meant to abandon the baby. The thought hurt. At least there had been gilt enough to give the child the best. She owed Straif a big debt, but she didn't owe him Helendula.

Shunuk coughed and Del understood that he wanted more than a grunt as an answer. "That's right," she said. "You remember Straif T'Blackthorn? He joined us a few times when we were on the road. Made me set up a permanent message cache at the Steep Springs communications center."

The man who smelled like celtaroon leather and wood shavings and grief. You played with him.

Del chuckled. "Yes, I did." Drawing her brows together, she

looked down at Shunuk. "He's mated for life now, so be careful when we meet them."

Another short bark. *I am not going into T'Blackthorn Residence.*

Del stopped. "Don't you want to meet Helendula?" She'd been counting on Shunuk for support.

Young child will smell like all other young children. His nose wrinkled.

After a deep breath, Del said, "We may be taking that young child with us on some trips."

A ripple went down the fox's back from neck to tail. *Maybe. May stay here in Druida—*

"No!"

Kit may stay with Blackthorns. I will meet her when she becomes our kit.

Before she could say any more he raced to the greeniron gates set between high brick walls and slid through a gap between the bars that appeared too narrow for him.

Del stopped at the gate, touched a scrystone in a pillar, cleared her throat, and said, "Helena D'Elecampane to see Straif and Mitchella Blackthorn and my cuz, Helendula Elecampane."

"You are expected," the Residence said in a voice deeper than Straif's.

She bowed reflexively as she would to anyone who'd helped her in this polite city. "Thank you."

The gate swung open and she walked up the well-kept gliderway to the elegant house with rows of Palladian windows. All was neat and tidy and gorgeous, unlike the last time she'd been here, several years before.

Straif had abandoned it. Left no one to tend to the Residence or the estate.

At least she'd never done that, and well to remember it. Before she'd left last time, she'd funded her house with spells to keep it clean and safe for two years.

People were people, everyone had faults. She would not let gratitude or guilt sway her in what was best for Helendula.

Straif opened the door himself, still lean and fit. She looked into his eyes and clasped his hand and felt nothing but friendship.

Nothing like the trembles when Raz Cherry had walked onto the stage last night. She'd gone a little dizzy at the sight of him and the rush of feelings for him, deeper than the lust of the erotic dreams they'd shared.

"Welcome to T'Blackthorn Residence." That was Straif's Heart-Mate, Mitchella. She was as tall as Del, with voluptuous curves and long red hair. Lovely woman. She held out her hands, too, though there was weighing in her green gaze and strain around her mouth. Was that because the woman knew Del and Straif had been lovers? A HeartMate thing? Del hoped not. She didn't want to think of all the times this could happen with her and Raz. A HeartMate shouldn't feel jealousy, should she? Not when she knew that the man was bound to her until both their deaths.

But she confronted this particular problem like everything else, straight on. Gripped Mitchella's hand and liked her firm shake, met the woman's eyes. "Yeah, Straif and I rolled around with each other when we met up on the trail. Five, maybe six times."

A strangled sound came from Straif.

"Glad Straif has a HeartMate, good to meet you," Del said.

Mitchella threw her head back and laughed. She squeezed Del's hand and Del felt a warmth, realized the woman had natural charisma. Despite them both, a friendly feeling flowed between them. Then Mitchella dropped Del's fingers and stepped back. "You're very direct."

Del entered the grand entrance hall and looked at the couple. They'd already drawn together. A tiny knot squeezed inside her. She wanted that. "You wish to keep my cuz, Helendula."

A small breath whooshed from Mitchella. She glanced up at Straif. "You were right." Then, chin set, she met Del's eyes. "Yes. We have come to love her and have adopted other children and they love her, too. Our *family* loves her." She made a sweeping, graceful gesture. "The Residence can house many children. We hope to adopt more, take six or seven."

Del nodded, inhaled, released her deep breath slowly. "I will do what's best for Helendula." She touched the small landscape globe she'd made for the girl that was in her leather trous pocket. The couple before her were dressed in the height of fashion—Mitchella because she seemed to be that sort of woman, Straif because he was a FirstFamily lord and knew the value of appearances.

These people could give Helendula every material thing. Did they really love her? Were they good parents?

"Helendula is in the playroom, watched by the Residence while we came to answer the door." Mitchella took off toward the end of the entrance hall, turned right at the corridor. "She's only a year and a month old; we don't like to leave her alone."

Del had to lengthen her stride to keep up. Straif passed her and caught Mitchella's fingers in his, linked them.

"How many children do you have?"

Straif threw her a serious look over his shoulder. "Three, including Helendula."

He and Mitchella had been married only three years. They must have had no doubts about adopting children.

Unlike Del. "Where are your other children?"

"My youngest son is with his nanny in the nursery. My oldest is studying architecture with a master," Straif said.

When they reached the playroom, Del spared it a glance. It was easy to see this was the family center. There was a wealth of toys scattered around cat perches. It smelled like children's food and drink and was just right for a growing family, with sturdy furniture a girl could knock over with no reprimand.

Then her gaze was riveted to the little girl walking, running, staggering toward them: Helendula. "Gaaaaa. Mmmm. Dddd."

She looked like the Elecampanes. Bright blond hair that would shade into nearly yellow, tightly curled. Pale green eyes.

She looked like Del.

But Helendula's lashes were long and her smile triangular and sweet, like her dead father's, Elfwort's.

Del's knees collapsed and she plunked onto the couch.

Mitchella scooped up the child, squeezed her, and put her back on her feet, pointed her in Del's direction saying, "This is your cuz, Helena. She has a name like yours." Mitchella caressed the little shoulder as she urged the girl forward. Helendula walked to Del and stared up at her with huge peridot eyes, barely taller than Del's knees.

Del cleared her throat. "You can call me Del. I mean, when you begin to talk, you can call me Del." She drew in a long breath. "I have something for you." She pulled out the small landscape globe she'd made the night before after *feeling* the link between herself and the child. It had pieces of wood and gray stone; some minuscule flower petals and greenery; a hair from Del's head, short and fine and blond; and a tiny beige feather.

The young child looked at it and gurgled. She smiled widely, showing a few tiny teeth and drooling. She shook the globe, watched the bits inside settle, then shook it again, holding it in both hands. She wobbled then plopped down on her rump to roll it, tilt it side to side, raise it to her eyes . . .

"She likes it." Mitchella's lips curved, her hands clenched.

Del raised her eyebrows. "I made it especially for her. My creative Flair." She wasn't about to tell the woman that the globe would help Del make up her mind. If the child considered T'Blackthorn Residence "home," it would show.

Straif frowned. "She's already played with it longer than most toys." At that moment their oldest child, a teenaged boy, hustled in. He stopped and gave Del a hard stare, then changed his stride to a casual stroll. "Greetyou, parents, greetyou, D'Elecampane."

"Our son, Antenn," Straif said.

"Greetyou," Del responded.

The boy folded himself onto the sturdy carpeting next to Helendula, watched as her little fingers shook the globe once more. "Whatcha got there, Doolee?" He reached for it.

She shouted, pulled the globe close to her chest. "Mmmaam!"

"Yours." He nodded. "Sorry. Would you show it to me?"

Sniffing, her face scrunched up and she offered him the glass globe, now grubby with finger smudges.

"Thank you." He peered inside the curved interior, shook it, looked at it from all sides, shook it some more. Shrugged and gave it back to her. She grinned, rubbed it on her soft top, and looked inside again.

The teen glanced up at Del, hunched a shoulder. "Don't know what she sees in it."

"A gift from her true Family." Mitchella's voice shook.

He scowled, sat straight, puffing out his chest, met Del's eyes. "We're her true Family. *We* love her."

Del nodded, gestured to the globe that continued to occupy Helendula's attention. "I may be a cartographer, but our Family Flair is for scrying. Her father was brilliant; she could be, too. Try her with water in a reflective bowl."

Antenn went to the end of the room where there was a sink. He opened a cupboard over it and took down a smooth, thick granite bowl with rounded edges. The inside was coated with glisten, a shiny silver-with-rainbows metal. A real scrybowl for communication.

"We had to move all the scrybowls that were anywhere within climbing range of Doolee . . . Helendula," Mitchella said, shifting from foot to foot. "Now I know why; she was trying to scry."

"I should have recalled, but I didn't." Straif was stiff.

"Not like you had anything else on your mind," Del said.

Antenn came back with the bowl half full of water and set it in front of the child. She stared at it, looked at Mitchella and Straif.

"Go on," Mitchella said.

Dropping the landscape globe to the rug, Helendula looked into the bowl and cooed, made faces. With another scrunched face, she ran her baby hand around the bowl's rim, hummed.

"She's initiating the spell to make the bowl scry again!" Mitchella said, staring. "We didn't know she had such Flair. Who's she calling?"

Helendula looked into the bowl, grumbled. She let out a baby sigh, then ran her hand around the rim again. An image formed in Del's head. A baby's view of her old nursery, her mother. Nothing happened, no answer.

"She's thinking of her old home," Antenn said. His mouth set and he looked aside, but his hand went to the girl's head and sifted through her blond curls. Del shared a glance with the older Blackthorns. She realized they were all connected enough with Helendula to have seen the image.

The toddler smacked the water with her hand. She whined, then circled her hands around the rim once more, visualizing a different place—a bowl in Del's den. This time Del's scrybowl cache answered. "I'm not here, leave a message." The child looked from the bowl to Del, face crumpling. She stood on wavering legs, marched over to Mitchella, and held out her arms. Mitchella lifted her, cuddled the girl. Straif came to hold them both. Del's heart twinged. The child *was* loved here.

A noise caught Del's attention and she turned to see Antenn carefully carrying the bowl to an area with a semitransparent privacy shield of a rosy color. "This is Doolee's personal section of the playroom," he said. He put the bowl on a miniature red table.

Helendula took her thumb from her mouth and smiled at him, babbling baby words.

Straif and Mitchella stood together. "There are other Families here in Druida who have scry Flair. We can apprentice Helendula to the best, give her the best. Let us keep her." Straif's voice was thick.

Del rose and strode forward, picked up the landscape globe and gave it to Helendula.

"Mm-ah-na-mmm-ma!" The girl clutched the dome and smiled at Del, though Del knew the child felt safe in the woman's arms, embraced by the man.

Del met Straif's eyes. "I know you can give Helendula every advantage, the same as the rest of your children." She glanced at a glowering Antenn, who wore expensive clothes, had a costly haircut. Everyone knew he'd been a lost and wayward orphan.

She lifted her chin, set her stance, looked at Mitchella, then Straif again. "But I can remember the Family spells and traditions that she had already begun to learn." Del was recalling more all the time and knew, at least, she'd have to record them for the child, no matter what.

Inclining her head, Del crossed to the door. In Mitchella's arms, Helendula was playing with the landscape globe. "I am her closest relative, she is my Heir. Nobles won't overturn that, I'd win a legal fight, but I don't want that. We'll all think hard about this."

"We love her," Straif, Mitchella, and Antenn said at the same time. Antenn continued, "Do you?"

"Antenn!" Mitchella scolded, blinking tears. She was holding tight to Straif and Helendula. "I apologize. He's nervous; we all are."

Del stared at Antenn, her jaw flexed. "I can love her." She left, walking through the halls of the lovely, Family-filled T'Blackthorn Residence. She thought of Helendula with the scrybowl and the globe. Del wondered if her plan would work. What would Helendula's landscape globe show? What if it showed a home that was lost to her forever?

*R*az was confronted by a fox when he stepped from his apartment building that morning. Tongue lolling, the animal lay circled in the middle of the sidewalk, making passersby smile as they walked around it. Obviously the fox had supreme confidence that no one would step on it.

From the intelligence in its eyes, Raz concluded that the fox was a Fam animal. Someone had gotten lucky. Fams were still scarce, most of the matches of Fam and human conducted by Danith D'Ash. And most Fams were cats or dogs, though a rage for fox jewels, faux fox fur, and images had occurred a while back.

When the fox saw him, it sat up and yipped. *Greetyou, storyman.* Raz halted. "What did you call me?"

Storyman. The man in the viz stories that my person and I watch.

That sounded reasonable. A couple of his plays had been recorded. "Storyman." Raz allowed himself to be charmed. He inclined his torso in a half bow. "Greetyou, FamFox."

I am Shunuk.

"Greetyou, Shunuk." They were taking up the whole sidewalk. Raz gestured in the direction he was going—to the Thespian Club for breakfast.

You rise late, the fox commented. *I have cleaned out all the mice in the alley this morning while waiting for you. Cached a few for snacks later.*

"Ah." Raz cleared his throat. "I was in a story last night, it runs very late."

Shunuk bobbed his head. *Do you go for morning food now?*

"Yes."

You do not make your food?

"I go to congregate with other story people in the morning. We work together and talk."

Ah, clans and circles and dens.

"Somewhat." Raz stopped at the PublicCarrier plinth. The Thespian Club was a long walk and he had errands to run. He had a glider, but he wanted to save the energy needed to power it for that night. This evening's party would be work and he had to be fresh. He was already running behind, but if the fox proved amusing, he could delay his chores for a while.

The carrier glided up and Raz stepped through the weather-shielded door to the interior, took a cushy seat. To Raz's surprise, the fox hopped onto his lap. He held it as the carrier accelerated, looked down to see big yellow eyes with a black-slit pupil staring up at him. Glinting with laughter? Raz frowned. "Why are you here?"

I like eggs for breakfast.

Raz was sure that wasn't the only reason. The fox was being cagy. "I suppose I could order you some eggs. Didn't you say you have a Fam person?"

I am new to Druida City. I wanted to see the storyman. Smell if he is a good human or not. Many things to do and see in the city. The fox sniffed lustily.

"And . . . ?"

I like your scent. It is good.

Raz was sure that the fox didn't mean the slight scent of cleanser that lingered on his skin. He supposed he should have been grateful that the fox didn't bury his nose in Raz's groin.

I am not so rude. Shunuk narrowed his eyes.

A little shaken that the Fam had answered his thoughts, Raz replied telepathically, *You heard me?*

I saw an image of myself and you in your head. You visualize well, storyman.

It is part of my craft.

We speak well together. It is good. Shunuk sat up straight in Raz's lap, pointed his muzzle at the opposite window. *Tell me of the city. Especially if you know where other foxes' den.*

I don't. But I know of Danith D'Ash, she who matches Fam and human. Raz could be indirect and cagy, too. Who was Shunuk's person?

The fox flicked a dismissive ear. *She is only for city Fams, those who cannot find their humans themselves.*

Oh? Where do you come from?

I have been many places. Last was Steep Springs and Gael City. The fox slanted him a sly gaze. *Came to Druida on a shuttle with cherries tinted on the side. Smelled a little like you.*

My Family's business, Raz said shortly. *Why are you here?*

To smell you. Shunuk's tongue flicked out and across Raz's chin. *You taste good, too.*

Staring into those eyes, Raz knew he'd get no more from the Fam, and he had the feeling he was missing something important.

Five

That evening Del barely ate due to unusual nerves. Tonight she'd make contact with her HeartMate. She wanted to be perfect.

After a hefty donation to the Flair for the Arts of Druida City organization, her scry cache had clogged up with invitations, including the one she'd wanted. The Spindles, owners of the Evening Primrose Theater, were giving a party to celebrate the one hundred and twentieth performance of the mystery Raz Cherry starred in. Del got the idea that it was just an excuse for a summer party like all the rest.

The donation had been a good investment, and Lady and Lord knew she had more than enough gilt from all the inheritances she'd received—the Family had been wealthy since they'd sold the scry-bowl spells and business a couple of generations back.

Elfwort had also sold his spell for personal scry pebbles the year before. That had made him, and his side of the Family, and now Del, very rich.

When she'd studied the accounts, she'd felt guilty about how much she'd received from Inula and the others, and the insurance, and how little outlay she had for her own tiny household of two.

One of whom she hadn't seen all day and wasn't at dinner, and she wanted his company.

Even as she thought of him, Shunuk trotted through the Fam door and into the kitchen where she ate at the cook's table.

"Done anything interesting?" Del asked Shunuk.

He yipped at the pet no-time and a tray extruded with crispy clucker strips. Laughing up at her, he said, *Yes. Your HeartMate is a nice-smelling man.*

Del's fork fell from her fingers. "You went to see him." She wanted to know everything. "How is he?" As if Fam judging would be like human. She couldn't even think well, let alone talk.

Shunuk buried his nose in the food and ripped at it, bushy tail waving. Without looking at her, he said, *Our lives are changing. Your kit lives here in the City. Your HeartMate lives here in the City. Good fox community here in the City. We may stay.*

Del's throat constricted. "I will not live in this city. I don't like it and things will be expected of me from other folk that I won't do."

Now Shunuk slid her a glance. *Like wearing shiny clothes, going to gatherings with many strangers.*

"That's right, and attending rituals to keep the City and the planet and our culture going." A good idea, but she didn't want to be part of it. "Lots of rules in the City." She gave her Fam a thin smile. "People care if cluckers go missing, people want to know who prefers clucker meat. Fams of noble houses have rules and duties and responsibilities, too."

He chewed, gulped. *I could have mate, kits. Nice den.*

"You are welcome to stay and do so." He wouldn't leave her, he loved the wild, of course he wouldn't leave her.

You will not stay.

"I can't imagine anything that would make me stay here." Del thought of taking and raising little Helendula while she continued her exploring. She'd find a way.

A calendarsphere materialized with a chiming that made her flinch in surprise. "Time to leave for the Spindles' party."

Del set her teeth, rose, put the dishes in the cleanser, washed her hands in the sink. She strode barefoot down the long corridor to the modest entry hall. A section of wall was a mirror and she stared at herself, winced.

The first time she'd dressed formally in over a decade. But she wanted her HeartMate to look at her and see an attractive woman, not a dusty frontier gal who could take on a slashtip.

She could hardly believe the reflected image was her. Long, firm limbs, yeah, those she recognized. Her hair was shorter than ever in tight blond curls due to the closeness of the ocean.

Her pale green eyes had tinted color on the lids, and her eyelashes were dark and long. She'd reluctantly practiced enhancing spells several times. Her long gown was thin silkeen, the bodice was square cut and showed the tops of her breasts. The whole thing was a flaming red. There were no trous that went with the gown and having her legs bare felt odd. Instead, she had a long damask jacket of the same color, with reinforced long square sleeve pockets so she didn't have to carry a pursenal.

She looked down at the sandals next to her feet dubiously. It seemed indecent to be wearing just a sole with a bunch of straps, and with her toenails tinted the same red as her gown. When she was a girl, children wore such shoes in the summer, but not adults. Her feet hadn't been exposed in public since then. Good, sturdy boots always protected them.

A snake or an animal could bite her! She grimaced, shook the thought aside. The shoes had cost a lot, but the tailor had insisted. She put them on, frowned at the fit. Shouldn't they feel better?

Shunuk trotted up, angled his head back and forth, studying her feet. He gave a foxy grin. *Nice.* Then he sniffed at her, even swiped a tongue across her toes. Del hopped back, forgot the short heels on the shoes, fell into the wall. Shunuk laughed.

"Ha. Ha. Ha," she said to her Fam. She'd be clumsy.

You smell and taste good, he said.

She'd rather Raz Cherry had told her that.

A knock came on the front door and she crossed and opened it to find a man in uniform there. "GrandLady D'Elecampane? I'm your driver for the evening."

She started to grunt acknowledgment, then recalled she was in the city being a noble and would need words. So she nodded and stretched her mouth in a smile. "Thank you." She'd paid an outrageous fee to a glider service to be available for a month. She prayed she'd be done in Druida by then.

Shunuk barked. The man glanced down. "Greetyou, FamFox. Do you attend the Spindles' party, too? They have Fams in their Residence."

Shunuk snorted and bolted out the door. The driver offered his arm and Del laid her fingers on it as if she'd need his assistance to walk the couple of meters to the glider. As she slid into the vehicle, she saw Shunuk sitting in shadows, ready for the adventure of the night. She wished she were anywhere but on the way to a party. He turned his head, lifted his lip, and his teeth gleamed. *You smell and taste good,* he said. *Complementary to your mate.*

Her heart gave a fast, hard thump. She hoped HeartMate mutual attraction would be good enough, because she felt gauche and wordless.

*R*az made his entrance into the Spindle ballroom on a wave of applause that warmed him. He smiled, bowed, and began to mingle. Everyone here liked the play, appreciated theater.

Most of the faces in the packed room were familiar. Some were wealthy producers who fanned hope that his success was being noted for the future. He wondered if any of them had a copy of Amberose's new play.

As he sipped springreen wine, he scanned the crowd. His gaze stopped on a woman in red who he'd never seen. She was across the width of the ballroom, hovering near an arbor twined with honeysuckle, wearing a simple red gown and long jacket. Her hair was short, soft blond curls. Her skin held a golden tan, and he thought her eyes were pale green. Striking.

She appeared slightly awkward in the setting . . . her body quiet and stiff, not open and pliable. Observing, not part of the party, and not observing like an actor . . . or a writer or an artist. Like someone who didn't entirely like people or being around them.

Interesting. Why was she here?

Not someone he knew, not someone who should have attracted him, since she also radiated impatience. But there was a certain something about her . . .

A look of contempt, hastily masked, crossed her face when two married-to-someone-else lovers discreetly slid into the arbor next to her for conversation. More and more interesting. Not a city woman, then, who was accustomed to marriages of convenience . . . but the way she held herself was noble . . . or so completely confident in herself that she knew she was a master of her craft. What could possibly *be* the craft of such an individual?

The unique puzzle of her pricked his curiosity.

"Wonderful play, I like this role much better than the last. You were fabulous," a woman gushed and he turned with a practiced smile that became sincere when he took Signet D'Marigold's offered hand. She belonged to a Family who had supported the arts for generations and she still glowed with love for her HeartMate whom she'd wed in the spring.

"Thank you," Raz said. He kissed her cheek, not having to bend much. She was tall and willowy, about the same height as the unknown woman in red. He glanced that way. She remained by herself.

Signet turned to follow his gaze. "Who are you . . . oh, very interesting person. Do I know her?" Signet's eyes unfocused and Raz watched fascinated, knowing she drew on her Flair to *see* the psi power of the woman in red.

Signet's husband, Cratag T'Marigold, slipped an arm around her waist and Raz smiled at the big man. It amused Raz that the warrior eyed him with suspicion. As if Raz had pursued Signet instead of just acting god to her goddess in a couple of nonintimate rituals.

After reflexively scanning the room once more, the man met Raz's eyes and said, "Saw your play last night. Good job."

"Thank you."

"But I could teach you a better punch—showier—to take the villain down. Better theater."

"Really?" Raz was hooked and they discussed it.

Signet smiled at them, then took a glass of something pink and frothy from a passing waiter. Raz watched as she crossed to the woman, tilted her head, and spoke.

The woman narrowed her eyes, then a smile bloomed on her face, showing dimples in each cheek that softened her. She responded to Signet, her stiffness relaxing, becoming as animated as Signet.

"Huh," Cratag T'Marigold said. "I think I know her, too. And not from here in Druida."

That both satisfied Raz's ego that he'd guessed correctly about the woman and increased his curiosity. "Who—" But Cratag was moving off. If Raz didn't want to appear like he'd been deserted by his friends, he needed to catch up with the man, which he did, amused.

"It's so good to see you again and know you're doing well," Signet said. She turned to them as Raz and Cratag stopped. Cratag slipped his arm around Signet once more. "Let me introduce you to—" Signet started.

"Del Elecampane." Cratag stuck out his hand. "Long time since we met on the trail. Don't know that I ever thanked you for helping me get to a Healer after that slashtip incident."

The woman took Cratag's hand, squeezed, then dropped it and shrugged attractively toned shoulders. "No thanks necessary. You'd've made it on your own. I just helped."

Cratag ran a finger along a white scar on his cheek. "Signet, Del tended my wounds. My scars would have been worse without her."

The man's scars were bad enough.

"Scars aren't important," Signet said.

Scars like that would ruin Raz's career.

"No, scars aren't important," Del agreed.

Signet beamed at her.

"Appearances count less than most folk think," Cratag said.

Well, Raz was certainly in the minority in this foursome.

Signet met his eyes, lifted her brows. "Raz, a good actor can have many appearances, yes? One of your skills is to change characters or nuances of character by a slight change in appearance?"

That he could agree with. "Of course."

Del smiled at him, flashing those dimples again. She offered her hand. "Helena D'Elecampane—Del."

"Cerasus Cherry—Raz." He took her hand and a sweet surge of lust went through his fingers directly to his groin. With a deep breath he caught her scent, wild lavender. Her hand was not a soft, city hand. She had calluses and her grip was firm. He swallowed.

"I admire your work," she said. "You were wonderful in the play last night."

She meant it, was completely sincere. This was not a woman who would be indirect or lie. The compliment meant more to him than many others he'd heard that night. "Thank you." He let go of her hand and felt a pang at the loss of contact with a unique woman and turned to Cratag and Signet. "So you, Cratag, knew Del from . . ."

"Brittany."

Raz stared. "The southern continent?"

"That's right," Cratag said.

"I know her because our parents were friendly," Signet said, "and she was in a grovestudy group that met in Celandine Park, like mine did."

"An older group," Del said with a smile.

"Circles and circles," Signet said. She leaned against her husband, looked at Raz. "Odd how that happens, isn't it? Del is a cartographer."

"Cartographer," he said. "Mapmaker?"

"Yes," Del said. "I scout and measure the terrain of Celta. I'm on the trail most of the time."

Why did that seem like a challenge?

On the dais, musicians struck up a Grand March. Signet linked her arm in Cratag's and pulled him away to take a place in the dance line.

Del flinched. She hoped Raz wouldn't ask her to dance; she'd forgotten the intricate steps of the pattern. More and more her thin layer of civilization was eroding. Raz obviously was more comfortable with Signet—that type of arty woman—than with her.

She was warm, heated from the inside out since he'd grasped her hand, her blood hot and racing. Her tanned skin would keep her from showing a deep flush. A little pinkness might hit her cheeks, but Raz would be used to women flushing in his presence, probably liked it. Preferred pale or pinkened skin to golden.

He turned with courtesy. "Would you care to dance?"

She shook her head. "I don't recall the steps, thank you very much."

His smile showed in his eyes as well as his lips. She felt her breath actually catch. Lady and Lord!

Their gazes locked; she could almost feel a link between them unrolling like a string that led through a dangerous maze.

"Raz, shall we?" The question came from their hostess. She smiled benignly on Del. "My HeartMate will be opening the dancing with Lily Fescue, the lead actress of the play."

"Of course," Del said. She should have figured that out, shouldn't she? She was so rusty at social events. "Thank you for the invitation, I'm enjoying myself."

The older woman beamed at Del, then whisked Raz away.

That Del *was* enjoying the event surprised her. But she liked Cratag and Signet Marigold, though Signet had stretched the truth when she'd said their parents had been friendly. Within the ranks of GrandHouse and GraceHouse nobles, status was mostly based on how early the house had been founded. Sometimes that could be overcome by wealth. Del's parents had certainly believed so and had done their best to raise the Family a few notches in the social scale. They might even have done it, Del didn't know. It must have been bitter to them that all they'd "worked" so hard for would be left to a daughter who didn't care a silver sliver about Druidan noble society.

She'd stopped talking to her parents years ago and had only a twinge when she recalled their deaths a decade before from a sickness that had swept Druida. Another reason she disliked the city; too many people close together to spread disease.

She watched the dancers, all lined up according to status. Status meant nothing in the wilds, and she preferred that. The atmosphere that had smothered her when she'd walked in began to descend again and she rolled her shoulders and went for another glass of springreen wine.

The party had been uncomfortable and tiresome before Signet D'Marigold had come up to Del. Talk had been boring and the people shallow. Her gown—with no trous!—had been restricting; she had to watch how she held her arms so the long pocket sleeves didn't sweep around ridiculously. Her shoes hurt. That was what she got for being on time. She should have known that Raz Cherry, an actor, would make an entrance.

All the actors made entrances. It got so she watched to compare their styles. The rushing-I-am-late-but-so-cute of one young actress; the hauteur of the man who played the villain in Raz's mystery; the intense virility that preceded a large man with rough features whom she recognized as Klay St. Johnswort, a leading man about the same age as her HeartMate.

The food was good and so was the wine. She nibbled and sipped and observed. There was social jockeying and deals being done off the dance floor.

On the dance floor her HeartMate moved with a grace that stirred her. Straif T'Blackthorn, tracker and noble, didn't move that well. Cratag T'Marigold, a warrior, didn't move as well.

Del wasn't quite sure she could define what set Raz apart, but it was there. Charisma? The man had that and she'd never valued the trait. He wouldn't be at a loss speaking to anyone and that baffled her.

She retreated again to near the arbor; the light wasn't as bright here and she liked the natural scent of the flowers more than any of the perfumes people wore.

She watched Raz in one of the least intimate dances of their culture and ached with desire. Taking another swallow of wine, she wondered if she could bring him to her in another erotic dream that night. Heat flooded her.

Six

Raz danced in between conversations with those who could advance his career. He enjoyed the party and interacting socially, but that wasn't as important as work.

He still wasn't sure why Del Elecampane had come and that continued to pique his curiosity. He kept an eye on her and was amused to see that some people gravitated to her simply because she was different. Occasionally she became animated, her hands expressive, her dimples winking as she spoke of . . . maps.

A satisfying septhour passed before he gave himself another break from business.

Trillia walked up to him with a sloppy grin and a drink he knew was over her limit, another one of those pink foamy things most of the women were guzzling. She wobbled and he steadied her. She came from an acting Family and had worked most of her life, knew the inside of the business and all the gossip for two decades past.

She'd been the first to welcome him on the stage of his first show and a very sweet lover. They'd remained friends after their affair had ended. Both of them had a policy of staying friends with their lovers.

Standing on tiptoe, she kissed him with a damp smooch on his cheek, looked up at him with wide blurred blue eyes, and gave a little hiccup. "Got the part of Fern Bountry in Gael City. I am hoping it will make my name, separate me from the rest of my Family." A loud sigh escaped her. "Gael City." She shrugged soft, round, white shoulders. "Well, we've never played there for long; it's time." Trillia tried to straighten but leaned against Raz instead. "I'll miss the Thespian Club and you." Her smile held deep humor. "Would *love* to see you with your HeartMate."

"That's me," Morifa Daisy purred. She was a socialite Raz had broken up with the week before. She slipped her arm between his biceps and his side, giving his muscle a squeeze.

His stomach sank. He had hoped to avoid a scene, especially here. He made sure from the outset that his casual partners knew he was uninterested in just one woman for the long term. Hell, everyone in Druida knew that from the newssheets' social columns.

Trillia hauled herself up, and this time she stood, not even swaying, her gaze sharp on Morifa. Trillia shook her newly long and dark curls. "No, you aren't his HeartMate. You don't have the stamina to keep up with him, not to mention the heart." As the woman gasped, her nails digging into Raz's arm, Trillia walked away and was scooped up by her current partner and left the party on a laugh.

"That bitch," Morifa said.

"Trillia is one of my oldest and dearest friends."

"Were you making love to her at the same time you were me?"

"No. I don't believe in more than one lover at a time," Raz said.

Morifa was spoiling for a scene and he didn't want adverse gossip tonight. He tried an easy smile and played along with her first statement. "You're my HeartMate?" He sincerely doubted that. "Isn't it illegal to tell me so? Takes away my choice or something?"

Morifa's lips pursed into a sulky pout. She lifted her chin, glanced around as if she hoped to gather a crowd. Worse and worse. With a simple turn and some pressure on her arm, he led her to the vacant arbor, though Del Elecampane stood close. His eyes met hers and he gave her a rueful smile.

She would be a minor audience but a critical one and his pride stung that such an intriguing woman would see him in a poor light. She glanced aside, took a few steps to the closest group, and introduced herself. From the tautness of her back, Raz thought she was still aware of what was going on with him.

Raz allowed a charming smile to curve his lips as he looked down into Morifa's petulant brown eyes. "HeartMates?"

"I wouldn't have had to tell you if you hadn't broken it off with me last week."

Ah, that was the problem. He had done the ending, not her. Nothing to do but to play this scene she'd set up to the finish.

He let out a soft breath, drew one of her hands to rest on his chest. "HeartMate, you know we've connected during those wonderful dreams." He lowered his lashes and looked at her from under them, saw she was becoming nervous. "When will you give me the HeartGift you made for me?" His smile widened. "I could feel you working on it years ago." Morifa was older than he, four years, five? Now that he thought on it, so was his HeartMate, but by so much? He didn't think so.

She stilled, and he sensed that she regretted staging the scene, too.

"You know I would give you anything you wanted." She pressed her lush breasts against him. They both knew she wasn't wealthy enough to give him much if he'd wanted to go the gigolo route, which he didn't. Gilt wasn't as important as his craft and his career.

He ran his hands down her arms, then back to her shoulders, gripped her, and set her a pace away but kept his glance intense. "Isn't the best way to claim a HeartMate to give me a HeartGift?" He dropped his hands and stepped back. "You present the gift you made for me during your last Passage. I accept it. You let me know it is a HeartGift and claim me as your HeartMate." He looked at her expectantly, lips still curved.

Morifa frowned, but it was the most graceful way Raz had thought of for letting her save face.

She stared out of the arbor. "Tomorrow," she said.

They both understood she wouldn't be seeing him again. Not tomorrow, not in the future. She turned sharply on her heels and her gown swung around her. Her narrowed, predatory glance swept over the crowd, landed, and she swished away. Raz thought he'd already vanished from her mind.

He let out a long, quiet breath and found Del Elecampane watching him with interested eyes. She held out a glass of pale green wine to him, sipped one of her own.

"Excellent job, MasterLevel Actor."

He didn't pretend not to know what she was talking about. Here was a woman who didn't play games. Whom he wouldn't have to play games with, wear masks with. Take her or leave her as she was. For the moment, she was a very nice change.

His smile went wry. "The best I could do."

Del turned and looked at his ex-lover. Morifa had latched on to Guy Balsam. Thank the Lady and Lord that friend of Raz's preferred men. Del studied the woman and said, "Yes, you handled that well. I think she could have turned nasty. And I think she's going to be disappointed again." Del shook her head, met Raz's eyes once more. "You would have been in a bind if she called your bluff, made a firm date to come by tomorrow with a HeartGift."

Raz hesitated, then answered openly. "She's too old to be my HeartMate. Must be thirty-three at least. I think I felt the HeartGift thing when I was going through my own second Passage at seventeen. My HeartMate's probably no more than three years older than I."

"Ah? You did say that you connected during dreams. Did you make a HeartGift, too?"

He had, a tiny model of the lost starship, *Lugh's Spear*, no more than ten centimeters long. Heat edged his cheekbones as he held her eyes. He lifted his glass, shifted his gaze from her eyes to his wine.

"Your eyes are the same color as this wine and the coloring as rare. Lovely."

"Ah, springreen wine. A nice compliment, thank you." She smiled and downed a mouthful. He sensed she did most things in her life lustily. "You know that the grapes for springreen wine prefer higher valleys and cool, steep slopes with plenty of sun, more mountainous locale than regular white or red wines. The grapes prefer a sweeter soil." She smiled, showing white, even teeth, raised her brows. "I'm not that sweet."

She looked luscious to him. His pulse kicked up.

"*Your* eyes are the blue of the Deep Blue Sea, gorgeous."

Again he felt heat in his cheeks.

"But you've heard that all your life, I'm sure."

He inclined his torso, lifted his glass. "Always good to be complimented by a fascinating woman."

Her brows lifted. "Always good to be complimented by a handsome and smooth man. Very accomplished actor." She sipped, kept her gaze on his.

"I'm not acting." He took her free hand, looked into her eyes with true sincerity, let a smile hover. "You are the most bewitching woman in the room."

She gave a short laugh. "Only because you don't know me."

"Not only. Though you're right, I know everyone else here and I do know why they are here—to party, to mingle, to be seen . . ."

"I wanted to meet some of the people I watched on my holos the last few years."

He sensed that was true and untrue, which was even more intriguing. A woman returned to the city who watched holos, a deduction clicked in his head. "You have a fox Fam."

She laughed with more amusement. "Yes, Shunuk. He told me he met you."

"He wheedled breakfast out of me, and that Fam can *eat*."

Her body relaxed completely, the mask over her face dissolving, and Raz congratulated himself on a good job of putting her so at ease. To have her focused on him was another boost.

She narrowed her eyes. "I don't think I like that smile of yours."

He took her free hand and lifted her fingers to his lips. Her palm was warm, her fingers strong. He brushed a kiss on the back of her hand, liked the zing of attraction between them, let his smile broaden. "My very satisfied smile that I have exclusively claimed the attention of the most riveting woman in the room?"

"That's the one," she said, and though her fingers tensed a bit, she didn't pull them from his grasp. "So, I'm the new face and thus the new toy and object of conquest?"

"No one, lady, would ever think you a toy, and it is a rare pleasure to be in your company." That was the truth, too. The air seemed to sizzle around them. He enjoyed the sensation of blood rushing through his veins. He took a sip of wine again and the vintage was less dizzying than the woman. "You are more dazzling than anyone here, more pleasurable than drinking this fine wine."

A flush had come to her cheeks, showing peach under her golden skin, accenting the green of her eyes, her bright curls. He breathed in her scent of wild lavender, more . . .

"You are a man who works with words. You have a very smooth tongue."

"I could show you better things to do with my tongue than to speak," he said.

Her breasts lifted in a deep breath and he wanted to put his hands there, his tongue in her mouth. He was becoming aroused, feeling the flush of desire. Not the place, not the time. Maybe later, if he was lucky, he could taste that mouth, smell the change in her fragrance as he kissed her and her passion rose.

She pulled her fingers away. "Use that facile mouth of yours to drink your wine."

"It's not what I want to taste."

Del stepped from the shelter of the arbor and gave a passing waiter her wineglass.

Raz followed her. As she'd left the shadows for the lit room, he'd seen her face go immobile just for an instant—as if she was putting on the thin veneer of a social mask. She didn't hide much of herself, certainly not as much as most people. Again he wondered why she'd come to the party. He drank the last of his wine a little too quickly to savor, then gave the waiter his glass.

The musicians struck up a waltz and couples left the dance floor or went onto it. The first to match their steps were Cratag and Signet Marigold. Raz smiled. He turned to Del, offered his hand. "Do you waltz?"

"Yes." She put her fingers in his, pivoted, and placed her hand on his shoulder. The touch of her, the closeness, went to his head faster than the wine, was tastier, more delightful. He was taller and broader than she. He hadn't quite realized that until she was in his arms, she had such an indomitable spirit—presence. Once again words escaped him without thought. "How old are you?"

She threw back her head and laughed and he saw the enticing golden column of her throat. "I'm thirty-six, pretty boy." The way she said it, laughing at herself, had him sweeping her around and around in a whirl. Her body was strong and supple and he thought he might be able to do anything with it. Her pale green gaze glinted with humor. "Eight years older than you."

He pulled her closer. "You can't be," he murmured into her ear, once again catching her fragrance—the scent of lavender that wasn't the same in the city. He was a city man through and through, but attraction wove between them as she matched his gaze with that sparking green of her own. Her body pressed along his, warm, exciting. She was completely unlike any woman he'd ever known.

And she'd be leaving Druida soon.

Maybe she was safe to make love with. He looked down into her eyes and slid his hand down her back just above the curve of her bottom, feeling the flex of her muscles. Even if she wasn't safe, he'd make love to her.

As soon as they finished their dance, Del was asked by another man and accepted. She danced a few more times with men other than Raz, then excused herself. She made her way to the Marigolds to say good-bye, then to the Spindles to pay her respects and thank them again for the invitation.

If she danced one more dance with Raz she might spontaneously combust. Best to leave him curious . . . she was woman enough to know that, and to know that passion was smoldering in him as well as herself.

So she left with a wave to the room, blessing the cool outside air as it wrapped around her. Her driver was there, the glider waiting.

She slid into the vehicle and the springreen wine made her head a little muzzy—enough to speak to the man about the state of the City, the rehabilitation of what had once been known as Downwind, and whether new maps would be a boon.

The night had been good, nicer than she'd expected, and she'd make sure her dreams were better still.

The party had turned out to be one of the best of Raz's life, mostly because of the woman in red who had become a potential lover, Del Elecampane. True, Del had left after a conversation and a dance, but when she was with him, his blood pumped faster. He hadn't managed to seduce a kiss from her; her eyes were too knowing. She'd gone without any promises to meet, though he was sure that she felt the same sweet zings of passion that he did.

A very unusual woman, she had made no overtures, had not flirted. Had left him aching with arousal after she'd gone . . . and had challenged the hunter in him to pursue.

He wasn't the only one she'd danced with. She'd waltzed with Johns and they had looked good together, like a study in athletic grace. Damn Johns. He'd nipped Del away from Raz just because they were competitors, but two minutes later was laughing with her. Yes, the hunt was on.

Before the dullness of her absence from the party could set in, he'd received a couple of compliments on his work from people he'd admired, then an agent had hinted to him about a part in a new play by Amberose. Raz hadn't been quite able to show simple casual interest, he'd pressed the man, who had smiled enigmatically, changed the subject, then slid away. Raz had seen him talking to Johns, who had gone as impassive as a rock face—a sign he was suppressing excitement. Another thing to compete for.

Raz didn't know which he wanted more, the woman or the part. He'd had another glass or two of springreen wine. Almost enough to affect his timing so that he remained too long. He liked to exit an event at the right time—leaving people behind charmed and wanting more of his company.

But now he breathed the soft summer night air as he stood on the terrace above the side grassyard where about twenty gliders were parked in three rows.

He inhaled the scent of full-blown roses trained over the terrace wall, and the heavy air made him yearn for one more whiff of Del's scent. He glanced toward the gliders, grinned. He had his own, just like the wealthiest nobles, a gift from his Family, and he'd named her Cherry. She was parked at the far end of a row, a few feet before a tangle of forest.

With three tuneful notes, he summoned her. Saw blurs of men tumble from his glider as she moved—someone had been on or in her! "Hey!" Raz shouted.

"I told you these damn shields would take too long to breach. Should have just smashed it, searched, and run," a low voice said, beginning to swear. The man should have known better than to talk in that pitch.

"We had to disable the stun!" a smaller man said. He muttered something and the vehicle stopped, stands clicked down.

Raz jumped over the low terrace wall, grunted as he hit the ground three meters below. The thieves weren't running away. Noise of shattering glass came. Raz didn't waste breath shouting.

His glider was shrieking: "My virtue is threatened!" The old-time melodramatic phrase had seemed funny when he'd programmed the alarm, but now it fed his ire.

The night of black and white was hazed with the red of his anger. Not this time. His home had been violated, his work area defiled, his property smashed. Putting some Flair into his leaps, he bounded down the rows of parked gliders to his vehicle.

There were two people burglarizing Cherry. The smaller one was inside, rifling through her. He heard rips.

Raz yelled as he hopped up on a large, old, Family glider parked close to his, jumped toward the large man with a flying kick to his head. The big guy got an arm up, threw Raz off balance. He landed, rolled, came up swinging.

His knuckles connected with the man's jaw and he grinned, hardly noticing the sting. The large guy swung back; Raz slid aside but caught a fist on his left shoulder that numbed his arm. He led with his right and got the man again. As the vandal stumbled back, Raz hooked a foot around his ankle and brought him down.

More slashing noises behind him—the smaller guy! Raz whirled. "Open!" he yelled, realized the frame was bent too much for the door to rise. Reaching through the broken window, he grabbed at the other thief, caught fabric, and did some ripping of his own.

He was yanked back and spun around by the big one. Raz jerked his head aside and the large man's hand skimmed his temple, then he hit Raz in the stomach. He oofed out a breath, gasped, ignored the pain.

"My virtue is threatened!" screamed Raz's glider.

"Hey!" someone yelled from the terrace—Johns. The sounds of footsteps running toward them and shouts from more people were mixed with other car alarms. "Back away, I have stun," came from the Family glider Raz had hopped on.

He kicked at the big guy, connected. The man fell back. Raz followed and pounded short jabs on the thief's stomach.

"Gotta go!" squeaked the man in the glider. He kicked Raz through the broken window, sent him into the big man's fist. Pain shot from Raz's cheek to rattle his brain.

"No!" the first man said. "Get him and hold him. Play actor too damn much trouble. Who'da thought?"

"Have a problem with actors?" Johns asked, grabbing the big guy from the back and throwing him aside.

"I'm getting out of here," the smaller one yelled.

"Won't get your gilt," the big man snapped, panting. He slugged Raz on the left shoulder again. Raz punched with his right to the guy's jaw.

Yelling, the smaller man flung himself on them. They all went down. Raz's head cracked against metal. He landed badly on Johns, whose breath escaped in a grunting *whoof*.

"Gotcha!" The smaller man yanked at the larger, dragged him free, and they teleported away.

"Uhhhn." Raz sat up slowly, put a hand to his head. His lip was cut and bleeding and he thought his cheek was fractured.

Johns lay flat and spit out words in short pants. "Sorry. Too late." He groaned and it seemed to take all his breath.

"You did fine." Raz wiggled his jaw; it hurt, too. A dull throbbing came from his temple. "Many thanks, I'm grateful."

Sudden quiet descended, except for Raz's glider. "My virtue has been violated," Cherry said mournfully.

Seven

*D*el took a long waterfall, letting the hot water roll over her. She liked real waterfalls, too, but they were invariably cold. So she hummed and did a slick wiggle to shake off the energy of others. There was something to be said for civilization, since it provided hot water-falls and steaming bathing pools laced with lovely fragrances upon demand.

After stretching to loosen muscles she hadn't used lately but that had been put to the test when dancing, she hit the bedsponge and leaned against fat pillows propped against the headboard. Sighing in contentment she drifted into a meditative trance.

First she thought of Helendula and her chest tightened. How could she love the child so quickly? Except to her, the little girl seemed to embody all the best traits of Del's Family. Curiosity, happiness with what she was given, generosity, love.

Just how generous and loving was Del herself?

Loving and generous enough to walk away and leave Helendula with the Blackthorns?

No. Not totally.

Helendula was an Elecampane and should learn Elecampane traditions. In fact, Helendula was now Del's Heir. This house and everything else would belong to Helendula if something happened to Del—and much of the Elecampane knowledge could be lost. Including the way to the HouseHeart and the small flame of sentience being born in that sacred space.

Del hadn't thought much about Elecampane traditions. Because G'Aunt Inula knew everything, more than Del. How much of her own heritage was lost now?

Probably not a lot. Inula would have kept meticulous records and a Family journal off-site of her own home. She'd come to check this house once a week and would have updated a journal here.

Del faced the question of selfishness. Did she really want to take care of Helendula, change her life for the child? A part of her echoed *yes* and she was pleased at the answer. She wasn't totally selfish and self-absorbed then. She could change her life to fit Helendula into it, take shorter jobs or city jobs until Helendula could come with her . . .

Despite herself, her life was changing. She'd have fought against it harder if she hadn't had a child to think about. She hadn't thought about having a child so soon.

Part of her wanted Helendula, maybe even a stable base camp instead of complete freedom to wander the roads. Perhaps a nesting instinct was activated when HeartMates connected.

Most of her wanted to continue as she had been, rising with the sun, searching out new places, making them known on papyrus for others. The whole world used her maps, and that was a real achievement. She wasn't ready to stop her travels yet.

Lately she'd yearned to go east, beyond the far edge of the Deep Blue Sea, the huge inner ocean of Celta to the Bluegrass Plains. There had been tiny communities from Druida City to the western half of the continent since the disastrous landing of the starship *Lugh's Spear*. In the last few decades people had been moving east instead of north or south. The Bluegrass Plains were verdant and Celtans had more knowledge and Flair than ever. That was where the new cities would rise, Del felt it in her bones.

Even as her thoughts spiraled out to that idea, she yanked them back to Helendula. Should she take the child away from Straif and Mitchella Blackthorn, uproot her once again?

If Del wanted the Elecampane Family to go on, she should claim Helendula. Somewhere along the way through all this mess, Del had decided that she would grieve if she knew she was the last of her Family. Grieve for the future more than the past. Each person and Family had unique gifts to contribute. Helendula would be no different.

But the child was loved by the Blackthorns. Was claiming the girl just because she was the last of Del's Family selfish, too? Del winced. She thought so, yet she couldn't let the Family vanish; that was beyond her. No solution now, the matter of Helendula would have to wait another day.

Now she could consider the matter of her HeartMate, Raz Cherry. Her lips curved and sweet delightful desire sifted through her.

He was gorgeous. She loved his coloring, the auburn hair and coppery skin, his blue eyes. More, she liked watching him move. His voice was mellow, with a nice range, didn't offend her ears.

She had it bad.

She wanted him bad.

And she wanted him to need her bad.

She unfolded her legs, thumped the pillows, and lay down. One last thing before she *reached* for Raz—and surely he'd be done with the party, now? He wouldn't be with anyone else, would he? Jealousy stabbed. She was sure he'd felt the same attraction that she had. But men did stupid things.

Hell, women did stupid things, too.

All these *feelings* involving Raz, since she'd strengthened the bond between them. How he felt about the woman, his friends— that Trillia and St. Johnswort and Balsam—*she* felt that now. She hadn't anticipated that, didn't like it much.

She didn't think she projected much emotion, so maybe he

wouldn't feel hers through their bond. Maybe he wouldn't guess she was his HeartMate. He'd run—no, he'd shut her out—if he learned that. Keep her away longer than she wanted to stay in Druida.

He wasn't ready for a HeartMate. She'd gotten used to the idea. He just needed a little more time to see what they could share.

She called mentally for her Fam, *Shunuk.*

I am here, he said.

Where?

I am hunting in Landing Park. I have learned that the primary fox den is near here.

Why do you want to see that? Do you want to join them?

Want to see how the best den lives in the city.

We won't be living in the city.

Maybe not, but I want to see all, anyway. Get ideas for my own den.

You want to start a den?

Maybe, maybe not. I am not getting younger. A rush of joy at the scent of rat came from him and Del narrowed their link.

She had no idea how old Shunuk was or how old foxes were when they mated and made dens or how long they stayed with mates. He'd been with her for three years.

She was fine with mating for life, having a partner. She wasn't so fine with staying in one place. She'd think of that later. Right now she planned on seducing her HeartMate.

Del had given the setting some thought, had wanted it to be special. She was used to having sex outdoors, though sometimes it wasn't very romantic and she figured Raz would go for the romantic stuff, at least until sexual frenzy kicked in. She grinned. Nothing wrong with a little sexual frenzy.

But she didn't want to give him anything to deduce who she might be—no tropical forest setting with lush blossoms never seen in Druida city. No high mountain glen in the summer. She was uncommonly nervous. Relax and breathe and think of *him.*

That was easy. His coloring, his grace, his long, lean body.

The way humor lit his eyes, how he was courteous to everyone, how he bowed over women's hands, pleasing them.

Pleasing her.

How his hands had felt on her during their dance, the warmth of his touch through her clothes right above her butt that had sent sizzles through her . . . and lower. How their bodies had brushed until hers had heated, readied for him. How she had actually leaned against him, wanting more touch.

She opened her mind, found their connection bright and golden, and let a bit of consciousness flow toward him.

He was sleeping.

That surprised her, he'd be used to late nights.

All the easier for her to craft a dream.

She opened herself wide, sensing what he did . . . the glide of fine linens on his naked body, soft stuffing over harder bedsponge. The quiet steadiness of his breathing, and the absence of any sound in his apartment, though city noises came from outside.

There. She was ready.

So she slipped them mentally into a dream, and to the center of the Great Labyrinth north of Druida, a sacred space more than one pair of lovers chose for sex.

He lay on the thick grass with wildflowers surrounding them, cool summer night air laden with a medley of scents—roses, trees, ripe fruit, flowers. He was nude, and she was dressed in a gossamer white robe, open in the front, kneeling beside him. The whispering leaves of the great ash tree near them cast ever-moving shadows. Dark enough that he wouldn't see her well.

She didn't need to see him to know him.

With a light touch, she ran the tips of her fingers along the wide sweep of his brow. His hair formed a slight widow's peak, dramatic. His cheekbones were wonderful. Her fingers brushed them, then she touched the fullness of his lips. A face easy to fall in love with. Many must have. But she was his HeartMate and they would have more.

She shaped his face with her palms. Following desire, she bent over and kissed him, swept her tongue along his mouth, tasted him. Cherry with a hint of cinnamon and sweet. A gurgle of laughter rose from her, escaped her to join the night birdsong. Why had she thought he'd taste differently?

He opened his eyes, blinked. His hands went to her head.

With a thought, she made her hair long, and it became full and curly.

"Soft," he mumbled.

It was probably the only soft part of her, but she didn't care, not now, not here, not in this perfect dream.

She kissed him again and his eyes fluttered closed. His hands went unerringly to her breasts, holding them, thumbs playing with her nipples, and she moaned. She let the passion spin between them, let the dream take her as well. Shared with him.

She traced the line of his fine collarbone, trailed her hand down his chest. Strong, defined muscles. He wore clothes well, but they didn't do his body justice. Lean, but with a subtle muscularity. He would consider it a part of his art to have a beautiful body.

She'd never seen him naked in reality and she yearned for that.

The scent of his skin rose to her nostrils and she had to taste him again. She leaned down and licked the small line of hair from his chest down his abdomen, smiling when his sex rose thick and hard. His hips were lean, his thighs toned. She dipped her tongue in his navel, had his hands clamp around her upper arms.

She knew he'd roll them so he was on top. "No," she whispered, "let me lie on you." She wanted him beneath her. Wanted her body caressed by moonlight and not pressed into the earth. She'd want him over her later. Right now she needed the freedom of the skies, not any ties to the ground.

He let her move as she'd wanted, to lay atop him, her heated skin to his, her head angled to nibble at the underside of his sculpted jaw.

A low moan came from him, his hips moved, and he thickened more against her stomach. Enjoying the sensual deliciousness, she rubbed herself against him. The light hair on his chest caressed her nipples and they tightened and caused her core to melt. She matched his groans. Her hands went to his, to twine in his fingers, to meet palm to palm.

Energy, Flair, sparked between them. He thrust up and she slid down and let him pierce her with his body, let their emotions, their desire, whirl into passion and rise and rise. She bent to kiss him, taking his tongue into her mouth as their sexes joined. Joined all together.

Eight

*R*az woke and stumbled from the bed into the waterfall room, panting.
By the Lady and Lord, what a woman that one had been in his
dream. The thought made him shiver. He'd never had such a climax,
never been so drained. He shook his head and felt the dampness of
perspiration on his face. Incredible.

He let the water cool him. He didn't recall being so hot from sex,
either. Again he shook his head, just to make sure it hadn't exploded.
For a while all his thoughts had vanished in a puff of smoke. Even
sensations had blurred until all he felt was a striving for release.

For completion.

Every thought about that bout of dream sex was a superla-
tive: best, most, greatest . . . He groaned and leaned against the cool
stone-veneered wall of the stall.

He hadn't experienced an erotic fantasy. This had been well and
truly sex with another person.

She hadn't said anything, but it didn't take the dregs of his mind to understand she was his HeartMate. The mental—and physical—sex was hotter, sexier than when he'd had his last Passage a year back, and Passages were supposed to be the most intense feelings of your life.

This was more.

The water was cooling . . . even in the middle of the night the building didn't have a large supply of hot water, and he didn't want to use energy to heat it. But he'd chosen the building for the charmingly unique rooms—an excellent frame for himself when he entertained. He closed the waterfall spell and murmured a dry spell. Enjoyed the soft whirling heat a little too much since he became aroused again. Somehow the spell seemed more like her hands than a mere whisk of air.

Must be his HeartMate.

He didn't want her now . . . well, not the intimate connection of the HeartBond. His career was more important to him and he wanted to concentrate on that. Though her body and the sex, the lovemaking, would be something he could become addicted to. But maybe not every night, his mind, senses, *feelings* had been blasted so.

His legs still weren't altogether steady as he walked back into his bedroom. Clearing his throat, he said, "New sheets." The bed that was a gift from his mother flipped and tossed. Linens were stripped and new ones appeared.

He still enjoyed watching the magic, still didn't understand how it happened. He'd had to "load" four sets of linens under the soft mattress top and the cover always was crumpled at the foot of the bed.

New technological Flair. He loved it. He'd been one of the first to buy the tiny gilded stone droplets that were miniature personal scrys.

His system was leveling after the fantastic sex and he slipped between the clean sheets. They caressed his body and he shuddered then willed his arousal away. He suspected he wouldn't fall asleep soon, though more often than not he had to fight rude sleep after sex.

A thought niggled at his brain. He *had* satisfied her, hadn't he? He struggled to recall, but much of the dream was fading into a haze. Not to mention he'd stopped thinking very soon after her hands had explored his body. He recalled how he'd gotten overflowing palms full of breast, cupped her ass in his hands, plunged in.

Sucking in a deep breath, he relaxed muscle by muscle, even said a little spell to move his blood from his groin to throughout his body. A good spell for adolescent boys—and one he had rarely used since then.

He could only hope he satisfied her, because he didn't know, and that was a new experience.

Breathing deeply, he calmed his mind again, relaxing and enjoying the sounds of the summer night in the city. There was the steady whoosh of the PublicCarrier—little more than a large glider at this time of night—and night birds warbling.

Had she deliberately drawn him into a dream or had it been unknowing on both their parts? He considered that, then decided it must have been instinctive. She'd felt, smelled, familiar in the sense that he'd known her loving from the dreams before, but also unfamiliar . . . the soft cloudy hair that he'd speared his fingers through close to her skull.

Closing his eyes, he sank into serenity, weaving in birdsong and the steps of a passerby. He felt loose but a little achy.

The memory of the fight painted the inside of his eyelids red and bold and jolted him. He'd forgotten that.

Amazing. He tested his limbs. The Spindles' Healer was good; he'd barely had a bruise after she'd worked on him and any lingering aches had been wiped away by the fabulous sex.

But he suspected that now all his troubles would hit the newssheets. His host, T'Spindle, had been stiff with pride, insisting on taking care of the damage to Raz's glider.

He'd spent two septhours with the guards going over every detail of the burglary here, at the theater, his sense of being watched, and the glider incident. No one had any explanations.

Restlessly, he got up and walked to the windows covered in gauzy cream curtains. He glanced out, frowned. One of the shadows was different. He'd had enough sleepless nights, come home at all hours of the night, to know the shadows. Anyone who teleported observed the fall and shift of light.

As he watched, a man-shaped dark patch vanished. Raz blinked, trying to grasp the form. It might have been the big man from tonight. It hadn't moved like it had been hurt in a fight. But neither did he.

With a sigh Raz went to the no-time food and beverage storage and took out a potion that sent thin tendrils of gray steam into the dark. He swallowed the mild sleep-aid in a gulp that made him recall Del Elecampane—who'd also faded to the back of his mind with all the events.

An intriguing lady. She held a GrandLady's title, though he hadn't remembered that until someone had referred to her after she'd left. She'd left him wanting.

Uneasily he went back to bed. Could she be his HeartMate? He worked on the calculations, when he'd first felt the touch of his HeartMate . . . Second Passage at seventeen, as was becoming usual. If his mate had been four years older than he and had *her* Third Passage at twenty-one, the connection would be strong. Stronger than what he'd felt?

He grunted. Del was eight years older than he, and his dream woman had had long hair and had been romantic and . . . gentle?

The next morning he called the guards again to report the shadow of the big man who could have been the one who'd assaulted him at the party. He was told that his neighborhood would be patrolled at night. The residents and shops would be cautioned to watch for any unusual incidents. Raz figured he'd have to turn up his charm to remain popular.

A guardsman also firmly but gently told Raz that he was an actor in a mystery, not a sleuth himself, and to leave any investigation to professionals. Raz had cheerfully replied that with ten performances an eightday, he didn't have the time for sleuthing.

No other disturbing events occurred over the next two busy days and the feeling of being watched faded, as did the details of the erotic interlude. He didn't know whether to yearn for more dream sex or be glad he wasn't being pulled into an irresistible web of temptation that would complicate his career.

The dream woman was replaced by Del Elecampane. Not that they met, but he seemed to notice her often.

That night she'd come to the show again. He'd been pleased to see her in the house and the energy continued to be good. The cast and crew were cheerful, especially when new portraits of the Primroses by the great artist T'Apple were set into place and a priestess and priest came and blessed the theater again.

The next day he'd seen Del with T'Ash, the jeweler and blacksmith, walking in a local park and having a lively discussion. About what? What could she have in common with the tough and brooding T'Ash . . . unless it had something to do with the rehabilitation of the area that used to be the old Downwind slums. He'd overheard T'Ash say "landscape." Then the man had become aware of him and scowled. Del had laughed and winked at Raz but had diverted T'Ash's attention. Even more intriguing.

Midweek matinee went well, though not as well as the previous evening performances, and he looked forward to dining with his parents and working on the new model spaceships with his father.

He actually smiled at the thought of seeing his Family. Progress. On all their parts. They'd moved beyond disapproving of each other this last year and he hadn't realized it. He wondered if anyone had except his crafty mother. She'd gently made the change happen. The rest of them—he, his father, and his younger sister, the Heir—had been too stubborn to make the first move.

His mother had asked for tickets to the play he was in at the time to entertain business associates. Apparently the associates were impressed with Raz's acting. Their Family reconciled.

An easy action, but beyond his father or sister to take.

His Family ate early, so Raz picked up flower bouquets from a local shop for his mother and sister, then put the box with his broken models under his arm and stepped into the small square area in his mainspace marked off as a teleportation area. His glider wasn't back from being repaired. Raz was grateful that his Cherry was getting the best treatment and being paid for by the Spindles, but if he'd had it taken to the Family shop, it would have been done by now. He had dreaded breaking the news of Cherry's harm to his Family, but they had learned it from the newssheets the morning after the attack.

So dinner might be a little touchy, but nothing they hadn't negotiated through before, and he had the virtuous feeling of being the one to call his father last week.

He thought of home, simply home, and was there on the private teleportation pad of the Residence playroom. The scent was the same—brandied cherries—and the atmosphere wrapped around him like an old and familiar childhood blanket he'd outgrown.

His mother was there, smiling, arms open. He bent down and kissed her cheek. She and his sister were small. He'd gotten his height from his father, who was built on heavier lines.

"Mother, I love you. Here." He offered her the bouquet of cottage-garden flowers. She refused to cut any of her own, preferring to see the pretty blooms outside her windows.

She squeezed him, stepped back, buried her face in the delicate blooms and lacy greens. "Gorgeous. Thank you."

His sister strode into the room, dressed in business clothes, moving rapidly as usual. Raz wasn't the only one who'd gotten a dash of charisma Flair. Seratina exuded Presence.

She was frowning. "Your glider still not fixed?"

She'd refused to call his glider Cherry. He smiled and offered her flowers. "What can I say? The Elders are slower than your shop. But I didn't pull folk away from work on your transports to repair my vehicle."

"True," she said. Taking the mixed colored roses, she went straight to a vase and put the blooms in it, said a Word to keep them fresh until she'd get the proper nutrient-laden water for them. His sister liked things done right and in a proper order.

There came a tiny sniff, followed by a tiny mental voice. *Is this the male littermate?*

Raz stared down, openmouthed, as a small white kitten tumbled into the room.

"Yes!" Seratina said and swept up the young cat to cuddle next to her cheek, suddenly looking six years old.

He kissed her cheek again. "Lovely woman, my sis."

She blinked at him. "Thank you."

I am pretty, too, said the kitten and Raz knew it was female.

He studied her. "Very pretty." He gave her a lopsided smile. "A superior cat for a superior woman."

A loud purr revved. *I am a Fam. My sire is Zanth. My Dam is Drina, the Blackthorn Fam.* She lifted a pink nose and gave him a little pointy-toothed smile, then curled her tongue in the way cats had of using their additional sense, as if tasting his exhalations, the atmosphere around him.

Raz wanted a Fam. Now. Wanted the companionship. Wanted the caring, the love. No one in the theater had a Fam, not one of his friends. Actors were not high on the list of people to be matched with sentient animals.

The door off the hallway opened and his father's voice boomed out from his ResidenceDen. "Good doing business with you." He was respectful and sounded as if he was bowing.

"Here." Seratina thrust the kitten at him and he took her, settled her along one arm and petted her with his fingers. Yes, he'd love a Fam. He thought of the fox. A fox wasn't for him, nor was a puppy. A Fam who would amuse with its poses, its pride—a cat.

He lifted the little one to his eye level, saw that her own eyes were a pale yellow shading into a pale green. Her little round stomach was cute. "Beautiful," he crooned. She shut her eyes, her tiny tongue came out and swiped her whiskers, then she cracked her eyelids and said, *I could have a treat. Just for being Me and beautiful.*

He laughed.

"You want a kitten desperately, don't you?" asked his sister, plucking the thought from his head as she could often do.

He raised his brows, but before he could say anything, his father strode into the room.

Followed by Del Elecampane.

Nine

*L*ike you to meet my wife," Raz's father said.

His mother swept up to him, smiled at him, then Del.

"GrandLady Helena D'Elecampane, my wife, Emilia D'Cherry."

Del shook his mother's hand and Raz could tell his mother had given the woman a limp hand. Both appeared a little surprised.

"Del has skinned us on some maps of an additional pass through the Hard Rock Mountains." Since he was rubbing his hands, Raz didn't think his father was too upset at Del's prices.

She chuckled. "I think that I got the worst of that deal, T'Cherry."

Seratina hurried to the pair, a gleam in her eyes. "We got the maps."

"Yes," his father said.

His sister beamed, turned to Del, tried and failed to look solemn. "You really think the pass can be widened for regular airship traffic?"

Del nodded. "With current and upcoming technology, yes."

"We need to get the right-of-way, better yet, the land," his sister said.

His father's hand came down on his sister's shoulder. "Already did, sweetheart, bought it when you left to greet your brother." He gestured to Raz. "My son, Cerasus Cherry, the master actor."

Del smiled at him. "We've met. I admire his work."

Since Raz had wondered whether he'd imagined how strong the spark between them was, he gave his sister her kitten then held out both hands to Del.

She looked surprised but put hers in them. When he closed his fingers over hers, the warmth, the desire was there, zipping between them. He was pleased to see a slight glaze come to her eyes, pink edge her cheeks under the golden tan of her skin.

His mother made a small humming noise. Raz smiled and Del drew her hands away.

His father's bushy auburn brows lowered. He stared at Raz, at Del, a corner of his mouth quirked. "Stay for dinner."

Shaking her head, Del said, "No. It's obviously a Family get-together and I won't intrude."

"You're not—" his father said, but his mother had made a soft exclamation.

"I'm so sorry for your loss, D'Elecampane."

Del swallowed. "Thank you." After an exhalation, her expression relaxed and she spoke to his father again. "Excellent doing business with you."

He nodded. "Anytime."

Del slipped her hands into a bulging pocket of her trous. "A little something extra." She handed a round glass ball full of clear fluid with a standing-ring on the bottom to Seratina.

"Wonderful," Seratina said.

Her kitten opened her eyes, sniffed at the globe. *I know these. These are fun toys.*

"Yes," his sister said.

"What is it?" asked his mother.

"The result of my creative gift," Del said, looking much more comfortable now that they weren't talking about whatever loss she'd suffered, something Raz would ask his mother.

Del rocked back on her heels, a half smile on her face. "I call them landscape globes." She brought another one out and gave it to his mother. Del frowned at the bits and pieces floating around in the liquid. "Though I don't know that either of you ladies would need them." She turned her springreen gaze on Raz. "The items inside will arrange and build to show an image of one's ideal home." She shared a smile with all of them. "I'm sure it will reveal this lovely Residence." She met his father's gaze. "Certainly if I gave one to you, it would."

His father dipped his head, though his gaze was on the globe in his mother's hand. "Surely."

"I've heard of these. Each one is different." Seratina compared her globe to their mother's. Neither had any of the same contents.

"Of course," Del said, her fingers twitched as if she wanted to shove her hands in her trous pockets. She wasn't wearing a gown with sleeve pockets, not the sort of woman who would customarily wear tunics with oversized sleeves.

Raz stared at the globe. He'd heard of these just this week. One of the women in his breakfast club had bought a going-away gift for Trillia, one of these landscape globes, and Raz had contributed to the purchase. He'd heard she'd loved it.

"T'Ash sells them," his mother said, shaking the thing and watching a tiny fern swirl around.

So that's what Raz had heard earlier.

Del was smiling; her stance had shifted to easy hip-shot. "Lucky on my part. They're selling well."

Raz met his father's gaze, and he became aware again of the box tucked under his arm. He moved to grasp it with both hands. His chest hurt from the contrast between the broken bits of metal inside that had been perfectly crafted models and the whole, pristine landscape globes his mother and sister held.

His father's mouth went grim as he met Raz's eyes, neither of them happy that their work had been violently destroyed.

"Are you sure you won't stay for dinner?" Raz's mother said and Del shook her head, started moving.

"No, Family only." Her eyes were a little sad. "Blessings and be thankful for what you have." She walked back to the ResidenceDen and left quiet behind her.

"What happened to her?" asked Raz's father.

"All the Elecampanes except a babe died nine months ago in a fire at Yule," his mother whispered.

Raz's stomach tightened.

His father stepped up and put an arm around his shoulders and drew his wife and daughter close. "Family Blessing," he said, and for the first time other than holidays they prayed together to the Lady and Lord.

The kitten sniffed. *You can all be thankful for Me.*

Raz was.

Dinner passed in cheerful conversation and Raz was relieved. Finally, finally he could talk to his Family about the theater and his friends and his craft.

After the meal, Raz walked with his father into his workshop. "Maps from D'Elecampane?"

His father's grin was wide. "She contacted us first this time, not the Eryngos." The Eryngos were rivals for the southern transport trade.

With a puffed-out chest and a lifted chin, his father said, "But we've edged them out in business over the last year. They're a little shaky. The Heir didn't want the job, so old Eryngo is looking for a good husband for his Daughter'sDaughter that might want to take over."

Heat flushed through Raz. Sounded like his own circumstances. His father had wanted him as the Heir, but his sister was so much better suited. He wondered if another argument was shooting his way.

His father continued to his workbench, turned with an outstretched hand for the box, then his eyes widened as he saw Raz hadn't kept pace.

"M'apologies," the older man rumbled, glanced away. "You're a fine actor, Raz." He cleared his throat. "And that's what you should

be doing. Your sister is an excellent Heir to my business." He shook
his head that only had a few strands of gray. "Sometimes ancient
instincts rise up and bite you on the ass. You being male made me
want you as my Heir, when I knew all the time your sister could
handle the job, would like the job better." His lips compressed, he
shrugged hefty shoulders, then met Raz's eyes. "You gonna show me
what's in that box, son?"

Raz lowered his chin in a slow nod. "It's pretty pitiful." He took
the few steps that had him meeting his father and offered the box.

His father nodded, too, opened the box and winced, sucked a
breath in through his teeth. "Nasty."

Swallowing, Raz said, "Yes."

The older man lifted the twisted metal of the ships from the box,
a few clinks came when more broken bits fell off. He'd taken out
Arianrhod's Wheel. He pursed his lips, glanced back at Raz. "*Lugh's
Spear* is good?"

This time Raz winced. "It's not as bad as these. I thought we
might do the worst first."

His father looked into the box and shook his head. "*Nuada's
Sword* is flattened beyond fixing."

"I thought so, but you're the expert."

Stroking a finger along a battered piece of thin metal, his father
said, "You're as good at this as I am." Again he cleared his throat.
"Still have the little *Lugh's Spear* you made as a HeartGift?"

Raz kept himself from stiffening, but tension tightened every
nerve in his body. Someone at the Thespian Club had been talking.
"You've heard something?" He kept his voice bland.

"That Trillia, real nice girl, is still friends with your sister. She
called to say good-bye. Heard the scry myself." Like most people, his
father smiled at the thought of Trillia. "She was giggling that you'd
be getting your HeartMate soon?"

With a sigh, Raz moved to the table, took the squashed *Nuada's
Sword* from the box, and set it aside. He had no doubt that his
father would keep it somewhere, since it meant so much to the both
of them, the hours they'd spent building the ship.

His father had a wide streak of sentimentality. Probably why he talked the way his transport workers did instead of the proper noble Celtan that he'd been brought up with. He identified with his job and the men and women who made and repaired and flew the airships. A very good thing. Raz was uncomfortably sure that his younger sister could swear the ears off him, too. The men and women in Cherry Shipping and Transport were tough.

To his surprise, he thought of D'Elecampane. She was tough, too. Had that innate self-sufficiency and confidence that she knew her craft well. Of course she also had that frontier aspect going, too. He had no doubt that she could take care of herself in the wilds.

Raz himself had polished away all innate mannerisms. He was an actor and could don many, but he reflected his mother's smooth manner more than his father's bluff and burly one.

The older man had already straightened out a panel with a stroke of his finger, had arranged the pieces of *Arianrhod's Wheel* meticulously. Raz got his creativity from both parents.

As well as his sensitivity, his depth of emotion. "Thank you."

His father glanced up. "Huh? For what?"

Raz smiled, came up, and threw an arm around his father's shoulder, squeezed. "For teaching me so much."

The man turned red and narrowed his eyes. "You didn't answer my question."

Raz thought back and his smile tightened. "Yes, I still have my HeartGift, safely shielded and put away. Yes, our little daily divinations at the Thespian Club indicated that my HeartMate would be coming into my life. No, I haven't met her yet." His face hardened. "And yes, right now, I will be putting my career first."

His father shook his head, sighed, and said, "Let's get to work."

*T*he next morning Del sat in the courtyard grove of AllClass Healing-Hall and waited for the Healer who had done her physical examination. She shouldn't be waiting for easily discovered results. The fact that she hadn't had an immediate response set her nerves—and teeth—on edge. It was all she could do to pretend to sit serenely on the carved stone bench where plenty of other butts had rested—enough so there was a slight rounded depression. She stared at the shade of the trees and the colorful flowerbeds and saw little.

A year ago it wouldn't have mattered if she'd picked up some sickness or injury that had made her sterile. Now it did—and her small time with Helendula made her want children, the miracle of loving and being loved, of seeing the delight as a child discovered the world.

Del cared for Helendula, but cared for her Family line, too, both new feelings. She'd usually been more interested in the act to procreate than the actual procreating itself.

The small swish of a door alerted her that she wasn't alone, and she turned on her seat to see Lark Holly, one of the FirstLevel Healers of all of Celta, walk toward her with a smile Del didn't trust. This was not the Healer who had examined her.

Lark, a small, dark-haired woman with a heart-shaped face, very pregnant, sank down next to Del, offered her hand. "Greetyou, GrandLady D'Elecampane."

"Del." Her voice came out raspier than she liked. Reluctantly, she put her fingers in the Healer's warm, strong, and smaller hand.

Lark nodded, rubbed her thumb over the top of Del's hand. Del didn't mistake the gesture or energy for anything but what it was, another examination. She searched for words that wouldn't be rude and betray her anxiety.

The Healer smiled sympathetically and made Del grit her teeth more before she consciously relaxed her jaw. Lark said, "We don't often see nobles here. Most go to Noble HealingHall or Primary HealingHall."

Del rolled a shoulder. "Healers are good everywhere, a simple exam shouldn't need a FirstLevel Healer."

Another smile and a squeeze of her hand. "Maybe not, but I asked my associate if I could relay her conclusions."

They wouldn't have sent a greatly pregnant woman to give her bad news, would they have? That would have been the height of insensitivity.

Swallowing hard, Del nodded, rubbed her free hand on her thigh, felt smooth linen for the city summer instead of leather for the high mountains. "And your conclusions are?"

"You wanted specifically to know whether you are sterile."

For once Del wished someone had been a little less direct. "That's right."

Lark bent a sympathetic gaze. "You aren't sterile; you should be able to conceive as well as any other woman on Celta."

Del narrowed her eyes. "Celta's harsh on all Earthan creatures. I have problems?" She felt great, how could her body betray her like this?

"You're as fertile as we all are." Lark patted her stomach. Surely she didn't have too much longer before she delivered.

"But?" Del asked.

"You're a successful woman who spends much of her time away from Druida. My husband is concerned about his cuz, Straif Blackthorn, who wants a child of your Family."

Huge relief slid off Del like an avalanche down a mountain. "This shouldn't be any of your business."

"I love my husband and he loves his cuz. That's why you want to know if you're fertile, because it will help you understand whether little Helendula could be the last of the Elecampanes." Lark flashed a smile. "We've all met her, the Blackthorn-Holly-Heather clan. Even my father, T'Hawthorn."

That man had been the Captain of All Councils, the most powerful man on their world. Del narrowed her eyes. "Don't try to intimidate me into doing something that isn't the best thing for me or Helendula."

Lark's expression turned cool. "As long as you *do* the right thing for Helendula."

"Being a child of the highest noble Families—like the Blackthorns—doesn't always mean that the child has the best. A baby needs love." Del looked aside.

"I think you know already that Helendula is loved by the Blackthorns, integrated into their Family."

"Not totally," Del said. "She remembers her old Family." She wanted to add that she thought Helendula remembered her, too, but that could be wishful thinking. "I care for her, too."

Lark gave a little cough and all Del's fears came pounding back in the rush of her pulse. She turned her head slowly to meet Lark's violet eyes. "What else?"

Sighing, Lark laid her hand on her stomach. "The energy of your womb is sometimes associated with women who have problems carrying a child full term."

It was a blow so sharp, Del didn't know when she'd feel the pain. She stared at Lark's belly. The woman flushed, lifted her chin. "But you are a woman in the best physical shape that my associate and I have ever seen. I mean that, Del. You should—"

"What are the chances that I can have a baby?"

Lark puffed out a breath. "With diet and rest and under a Healer's care, I would say sixty-five percent."

Not great odds, but better than zero. Hopeful, even.

"More than one child?" Del grated.

With a purse of her lips, Lark said cautiously, "You are fertile; you *may* just need to be careful after you conceive. We'll take it one child at a time, shall we?"

She smiled and shifted and Del stood and helped the Healer up. This was Lark's first child and she'd been bonded with her Heart-Mate for four years. Typical for Celta.

"Thank you," Del said. "Glad to know so I can make good decisions about the future of my Family."

"I'm sure you'll make the right ones."

"Helendula displays our Family Flair for scry work. Elecampanes *do* have Family traditions, and she's my Heir."

The Healer gazed at her steadily. "I'm sure no one expects you to stay out of her life. But you have your career." Lark looked at the HealingHall with an expression that showed she'd never retire. She seemed to understand both sides of the conundrum facing Del. "And the Blackthorns will be dealing with providing tutors for the different Flairs of all their children."

"Thanks again," Del said. "I've transferred your fees to the HealingHall."

"And I've had documentation sent to your home cache," Lark said.

Del nodded and walked from the grove. She already loved Helendula, and Del had a duty to her Family line . . . and Helendula. The child must not be deprived of her heritage . . . but she must have a loving Family and that could be the Blackthorns. What was best for the girl? And why was this hurting so much?

That evening Del rode through the gates of T'Blackthorn estate again. Both Straif and Mitchella welcomed her though Del realized she'd interrupted their dinner, and they invited her to join them. Happening a lot lately. Hell, she didn't know the rules for casual Family dinners. Her own parents and she had always eaten fashionably late.

So she ate with them and watched the freewheeling Family dynamics and tried not to be envious.

After dinner she went with Straif and Mitchella to the den to speak privately. Even this room smelled like children, and she could sense the vibrations of their voices outside the room. Antenn and the Residence were keeping an eye on the younger ones.

Straif and Mitchella sat in a twoseat and Del in a leather chair angled toward them.

"You two look good together. You match," Del said. They did. The tough guy, the voluptuous woman. Made for each other. Heart-Mates. Would Del *ever* have that kind of look with Raz? She swallowed the doubt.

"Are you going to take our child away from us, Del?" Mitchella asked.

Ten

Mitchella stared at Del with eyes that were greener and bigger from tears.

Fligger.

Del looked at Straif. His face was impassive but his muscles had tensed. "You love Helendula, Straif?"

"Yes."

Del rubbed the back of her neck but kept her gaze straight. "She's my Family, too. The last of it."

Mitchella frowned. "Like so many on Celta."

Oops. Del had forgotten Straif had that bad-gene thing and Mitchella was sterile.

"I don't believe you'd take a child on the road with you, Del," Straif said.

She could. It would be difficult, but she could. Make sure the young one was well protected. Not go into dangerous areas. Limit her jobs. Limit her life.

"It's a hard life," Mitchella said, leaning against Straif. His arm came around her.

Sudden envy burst inside Del. She wanted that. Sex and more, loving. Had she been lying to herself all this time? Or was this a new thing? Who cared? "One of the reasons I came to Druida was to find my HeartMate."

Mitchella sucked in a breath.

Del tensed.

Then the woman smiled with sincerity. "That's wonderful." Her lips trembled. "If you're going to make a Family and want Helendula . . ."

"You've already found him, know who he is," Straif said.

"Yeah."

Curiosity shone in both the Blackthorns' eyes.

"No, I'm not going to tell you."

"HeartMate love doesn't always go quickly or smoothly," Mitchella murmured.

Straif winced, moved even closer.

"You will have children of your own," Mitchella said, but Del caught the echo of an old pain, that Mitchella was sterile.

"Maybe," Del said.

Straif quirked an eyebrow. "Staying here in Druida?"

Del let out a breath. "No." Her shoulders felt tight so she shifted them. She glanced around the room again. A FirstFamilies couple could give Helendula more. A HeartMated, honorable, *solid* couple . . . Family . . . could give Helendula everything. Almost.

"We won't change her name," Straif said.

"Names don't mean as much as . . ." As love. Helendula should have more than Del had; a childhood with people who loved her.

Helendula was her last Family. Del had a duty, too. But duty wasn't the same as love. She knew that all the way down to her bones, figured Straif and Mitchella did, too. Del couldn't sit still; she stood and paced the room. Everywhere she looked spoke of people who took care of what was theirs.

She didn't usually hesitate over decisions, made them quickly and got on with her life, but she'd been thinking about this one for days. Even the ride to the Great Labyrinth and treading along the path until she got to her Family shrine and tidying up the area hadn't helped.

She stopped in front of Straif and Mitchella. "All Families have traditions, pasts, histories. If you have Helendula, then she has your traditions and not mine, ours. I'm not willing to let that happen. Not willing to lose the last of my Family." She sucked in a deep breath. Mitchella was trembling.

"But Helendula is loved here. Don't change her name. I want equal legal custody, but her primary home will be with you. I will be Auntie Del." Just as she had always been. It didn't feel like enough anymore, but it was the best for Helendula. Del didn't need to wait to see the home in the child's landscape globe to know what was right.

Del was changing. It hurt and she didn't like it, couldn't see the road of her future stretched out before her like she'd always done before. Huge boulders in her path. She couldn't see the shape of the vista beyond, either.

"Done," Straif said. "I'll have my attorney draw up the papers."

Del grimaced. "All right. I'll have mine look at 'em."

Both he and Mitchella sprang from the sofa and embraced her and she was surprised at being hugged by two people. Couldn't even remember the last time that had happened. She swallowed hard, blinked fast.

"Let's go tell Antenn and the others," Mitchella said.

A good mother, thinking of her children first. Del was swept along to the playroom. The children were all there—Antenn, the teen, a boy under two running around yelling, with Helendula staggering after him, making noises.

Mitchella swooped down on Helendula, picked her up, and swung her around. Straif picked up the boy and set him to ride his shoulders. Both children squealed in high pitches that made Del's ears ring.

Antenn was in a section of cool blue—his own personal area—where he'd been building a structure with wooden shapes that looked a lot like the very Residence they were in. A small pinkish cream cat had been supervising. The teen stood and picked up the cat and moved out into the center of the playroom.

"Antenn," Mitchella raised her voice. "Del's made a decision. We'll share custody and she will always be in our lives, but Doolee will remain with us."

His tense, thin shoulders relaxed and he yelled, too, adding to the noise. The cat made a sympathetic sound, then projected mentally. *I am glad My girl is not going away.* His purr was loud from such a small body.

Of course she must stay, she is a member of My daily adoration hour, said a different Fam.

Del looked around for the source, saw a small beige and white cat sitting atop a tall, carpeted pillar in the corner of the room, looking down on them all with a queenly regard.

"My Fam, Drina. I don't think you've ever met," Straif said.

Del stared at him. The FamCat appeared more demanding than Mitchella. "*Your* Fam?" That cat wouldn't have lasted half a septhour on the road, would have been a tidbit for a slashtip or grychomp.

"My Fam," he returned with a straight face.

"Dwina, Dwina, Dwina!" yelled the little boy, pulling on Straif's sandy hair. He didn't even wince.

Del eyed the pillar Drina was sitting on, the top was still out of reach of those chubby hands. Straif didn't move toward it. He continued, "And this is my son, Cordif. Say hi to Auntie Del, Cordif."

Mitchella snorted. "Introducing your Fam before your son." She laughed and bounced Helendula—Doolee—nuzzled the little girl's curls.

"'Nother Auntie?" Cordif said, a gleam coming to his sky-crystal blue eyes. Obviously he found women a soft touch. He held out his arms to her.

Del's mouth dropped open.

Shifting grips, Straif lifted his son and handed him to Del, who took him automatically. The boy grinned up at her, showing dimples. "Auntie Del," he cooed. He leaned his head against her breasts, stuck a thumb in his mouth.

"That's my charmer." Straif beamed with pride, winked at the boy.

Warmth swept through Del, from the ease of the child with her . . . not even a child of her blood . . . the approval shining in Mitchella's eyes, Straif's wink—at her this time. Her throat closed.

Doolee's face scrunched as she stared at Del. "Ddd, ddd, ddd . . ." She reached in the center pocket of her tunic and pulled out her globe.

"Yes, Auntie Del gave you that toy," Mitchella said.

There wasn't as much floating free, the contents had begun to settle into a form. Del was sure whatever Doolee's Flair built in the globe would reflect the Blackthorns.

"Wah! Want!" Cordif's thumb was out of his mouth, his brows were down. "Want, want, want!"

"You have to ask Auntie Del. Nicely," Mitchella said.

The boy tugged at Del's tunic. When she looked down at him, she saw widened, rounded eyes. He grinned again. "Pwesent?"

"Yes, I'll make you a present," Del said, before she thought, then considered the amount of globes she'd already promised to T'Ash, others she'd want to give away to folks she'd be meeting . . . like the Cherrys. But she couldn't resist the boy's gurgle of happiness.

She met Mitchella's eyes and said, "I won't be giving you or Straif a globe. They only show a person's ideal and true home, and you both have one here."

"Waste of time and gilt," Straif agreed.

Del angled toward Antenn. "I can—"

"I don't want one," the teenager said. A flash of something— fear? dread?—showed in his eyes. Shock rolled from Mitchella.

Antenn flushed. "Beg pardon, but I don't need one."

"All right," Del said mildly. She understood that it wasn't her he was rejecting, but the globe for some reason.

A soft snore came from the child in her arms. Cordif had gone boneless in sleep.

"I'll take him," Straif said.

Del reluctantly gave him up. She drew in a deep breath, knowing her next words would break the mood and hurt them all. "I have to ask one more thing," Del said.

The Blackthorns stiffened.

Antenn scowled and cradled his cat closer, stared at Del.

She jerked her head toward the sitting area.

"Let's put the children down," Straif said. He laid the still snoozing Cordif on a wide soft section. Mitchella hugged Doolee, then set her on the rug where the little girl shook her landscape globe.

There had been a beige feather in that globe. Now it was the color of Mitchella's hair.

None of them sat.

Del gritted her teeth, her jaw flexed. All her teachings, everything inside her told her she was doing something wrong, but it had to be done. The secret had to be shared, and she couldn't give it to Raz yet.

"Who of your Family is the best at scry talent?"

Antenn pointed to Doolee.

Del grimaced. "I was afraid of that." She studied Straif and Mitchella. She had trusted Straif with her life, with her body, but that was when he was a Flaired tracker running away from his problems. Now he was a FirstFamilies GrandLord. She didn't trust him enough.

So she studied Mitchella. The woman was beautiful, talented though not greatly Flaired. But she came from a very large Family, a commoner Family moving up rapidly due to their numbers and talents and skills. Del couldn't bring herself to tell Mitchella, either.

Her lips compressed. Perhaps she'd keep this secret after all. She shrugged and began to turn away.

"Let me guess." Straif's voice was low; Del could barely hear him. "You want someone to know how to get into the Elecampane HouseHeart for Helendula."

"Doolee's too small to remember stuff like that," Antenn said.

Straif put a hand on Antenn's thin shoulder. He would never catch up with the stature that should have been his if he hadn't been born in the slums Downwind and scavenged on the streets.

"Antenn can be trusted. He is training to be an architect." Straif smiled. "He could consider this his first professional secret."

"He could be spelled to not remember the way or the Words that could open the door," Mitchella said.

Del raised her eyebrows. "You sound as if you've—"

Mitchella's smile was cool. "I've been asked to design and decorate a HouseHeart."

Del's eyes widened. She would never have considered a Family would have asked that of an interior designer in a million years. Once again she looked at Mitchella, but Del just couldn't bring herself to trust a woman she'd known so shortly, one whose loyalty would be to her husband and her Family.

Streaking fingers through her hair—it was getting too long, especially in the city summer heat—she lifted it away from the dampness of her neck. "I don't want him to forget the way. Doolee, Helendula, must know the HouseHeart, be taken there often." Del huffed out a breath. "It's her right." She met Straif's eyes. "Her responsibility."

Straif nodded.

Del examined the boy-turning-into-a-man. "How old are you, again?"

He straightened to his inconsiderable height. "Fifteen."

"He could be spelled so that he could never reveal the information," Straif said.

"An architect?" Del asked.

The boy met her gaze with a steady hazel one of his own. He jerked his head in a nod.

"Gone in any HouseHearts?"

Antenn hunched a shoulder. "Maybe." He jutted his chin. "Maybe with the master architect I'm studying under. Maybe I can't say."

Del was both insulted and amused.

She looked at Straif. "Does he go into the T'Blackthorn HouseHeart?"

"Yes, and alone. He's my son."

Narrowing her eyes, she examined the boy. He had been a Downwind orphan, part of a gang. That didn't matter. It was the past and she knew what it meant to be an outcast—even if it was only from your Family and not the city. Straif trusted him with FirstFamily secrets and wealth, so he must be trustworthy in that way. Wouldn't steal from her, vandalize her house.

On a long exhalation, Del locked her gaze with Antenn's. "The Elecampane house is not a Residence yet, but there are ... stirrings ... in the HeartStones. They need to be, uh, encouraged."

Interest leapt into his eyes, then his attitude turned more hostile. "You're going to abandon them?"

Straif winced.

"My Flair is cartography. It requires me to travel." Del bit off each word.

"Antenn," Mitchella said.

"Sorry." But he didn't look it.

"I want someone reliable to take Helendula to the Elecampane HouseHeart, to promote sentience in the HeartStones when I am out of the city." Now Del shrugged and turned away.

"Which will be most of the time," Straif said behind her.

She nodded. "Which will be most of the time. I don't like Druida City. I'll go consult with the priestess of the GreatCircle Temple; perhaps she can give me a name."

"Del would be *trusting* you, Antenn," Straif said.

It was then Del recalled that the boy was brother to a murderer who'd killed several FirstFamilies lords and ladies, a madman. Not many would really trust him, especially of the older generation, and they ruled long since lives were long.

"Wait," Antenn called.

Del turned her head.

He gulped. "HeartStones beginning to think. A HouseHeart I could visit whenever ..."

"At least once a month with Doolee. Not more than once an eightday by yourself. T'Blackthorn is your Family and your Residence, not Elecampane."

Antenn hunkered into his balance. A less well-trained boy in fighting would have shifted from foot to foot. Yes, this youth had been given advantages, though the strain of living with his previous life showed in his eyes. Not many would forget his circumstances like Del had.

She plucked Doolee off the floor, swung her around like the

toddler loved, stuck the girl on her hip as she'd seen Mitchella do.
Oh, how good the child felt! Del never would have expected this
rush of feeling for her—or for Cordif—but there it was.

She enjoyed the sweetness of having a child in her arms for a
minute then held out the child to Antenn, the boy the girl considered
her brother. Doolee went willingly and grinned up at him, shaking
her landscape globe and drooling. He cuddled her close but kept his
gaze on Del.

They stared at each other.

Could she really trust him with her Family's deepest secret?

This time as she looked at the boy, she probed as deeply as she
could with her Flair. She saw a boy who prized his place in this Family. She sensed, through their mutual link with Doolee, the respect
and love he had for structures, for Residences. As much as she
yearned for the open road, this teen wanted to understand houses
and Residences.

She nodded acceptance. If this was to be done, it should be done
quickly. "You and Doolee be at D'Elecampane Residence tomorrow afternoon after your studies end. You will not speak of this to
anyone."

Frowning, Antenn cleared his throat, looked at his father. "I was
supposed to go away for an eightday with a study group. Examine
the architecture of Gael City."

Del could have told him that the unimpressive Gael City architecture could be seen in an afternoon. She stopped a sigh. "It can
wait, then. Scry when you return." Her smile was nothing but a
slight turn up of the corners of her mouth. "I'll be careful here in
the city." Del wanted to reach out and hold Doolee again, feel the
weight and softness of the youngster in her arms.

But the girl was happy in her Family.

Del turned and walked away.

"This has been as hard on you as it has been on us," Mitchella
murmured.

Del glanced back and saw that Straif held his younger son again, stood with the child next to Mitchella and behind Antenn who still held Doolee.

The picture of a Family unit. Mother, father, three children. There would be more children for them, she knew.

She didn't know if there would be more children for her. It was an ache deep in her chest.

"Celta is a hard planet," Mitchella said.

"Celta can be hard on Earthans. But it is a wonderful and glorious place," Del said and left. She had a lot to do. Too many people to see. None of them Family.

After he left the theater that night, Raz spotted Del Elecampane sitting on a white marble bench in the park nearest to the entertainment district. She was dressed as if she'd been to a play, elegant tunic and trous, sparkling sandals. Pain pinched him. She hadn't been in *his* house again, he'd have noticed her. Especially since the energy of the audience had been a little flat tonight and the whole company had struggled to keep the story fresh.

As he watched, Del tilted back her head so her face was touched by the twinmoonslight. It occurred to him that the trimmed and pretty park would be a far cry from the wild.

Something about her drew him . . . something different than attraction tonight. He stood for a moment and let the sensations emanating from her wash through him.

Sadness.

Her body language didn't show grief, but he felt that. He hesitated a moment and went to her, joined her in silence on the bench.

Her breathing was slow and steady, her body was relaxed, but her inner self throbbed with hurt.

Grief.

He couldn't imagine losing his Family. Didn't know what to say. He usually had a lot of facile words, but this woman was already more than an acquaintance but less than a friend or lover.

"I wasn't close to them," Del said, and he understood that a thread had spun between them to let each other sense feelings. "My Family." She grimaced. "Definitely not my parents. But it was a shock to hear I was the last adult." She shrugged, still not looking at him. "I hadn't planned on having a child so soon."

City and nature sounds mixed. Muted conversations. Crickets chirping.

Raz waited.

Del cleared her voice. "I was gone when the others perished."

He only heard a small note of guilt in her voice and guessed that was good.

She shook her head. "Straif stepped in and took the baby, Helendula, from the Maidens of Saille House for Orphans."

"Straif?"

Del glanced at him. "Straif T'Blackthorn. We knew each other from meetings on the road."

Raz understood the allusion. She and Straif T'Blackthorn—a FirstFamily lord!—had been lovers. Close enough that she called him by his given name, that the man had taken in a babe belonging to her. A sizzle went through him. Heat. Jealousy? Possessiveness? Stupid.

"Straif and his HeartMate are adopting children." Layers of shared history was in her mind. "They love my Helendula already, so I let her go to them today." Her tones were quiet, her voice steady, but the hurt intensified.

She was a strong woman, even now. But she looked at him with her tumbled blond curls, silver in the twinmoonslight, her eyes wide and vulnerable.

Nothing like a vulnerable, strong woman for pure attractiveness. He kissed her.

Eleven

❤️

*S*he tasted of tears and springreen wine and opened her mouth to him. When he tangled his tongue with hers, she gave a soft growl and her breath sighed into his mouth, dizzying him. This was more than just a condolence kiss. The nibbling and rubbing and tasting. Quick actions, great results. He was lost in her.

Her strong fingers clamped over his shoulders as she moved closer; he put his arms around her back and held her to him. The ripe softness of her breasts against his chest fired him and he closed his hands over her slim hips. His palm pressed against her lower back, before the tight rise of her bottom, pulling her lower body against his heavy arousal. They tilted downward, he wanted on top of her.

With a smooth twist, she was out of his arms and standing before him. At the loss of the warmth of her body the night air encompassed him, chill on his heated skin.

Her eyelids were full and lowered. When she spoke, her voice was husky, coming through lips swollen from his kiss . . . and her own passion? "Thank you," she said. "You're a nice man."

For some reason, Raz heard an unspoken "young." He checked the thread of connection between them and couldn't even feel it. Didn't know whether it was there and completely closed down by her or gone altogether.

He shook his head, hoping sense would come back into it. Del was eight years older than he. He knew that in his mind, but his body certainly didn't care. She'd been lithe and her muscles tight . . .

"I know you just ended an affair." Her lips lifted in a faint smile. "That scene about HeartMates at the party. You can't be too interested in a casual relationship."

His mind had begun to clear, then the word *HeartMate* clouded it again.

She moved to the park teleportation area. "Raz, thank you for taking my mind off other matters."

Before he could say a word, she 'ported away. Raz was left churned up, lust mixing with wariness, and physically aroused. It would be best to walk home tonight, even though he certainly had the energy to teleport.

It would be a long night.

Unless his dream lover visited him. His heart rejected that notion. He didn't want her.

He wanted Del.

Wanted to explore her. Everywhere. And he didn't intend to let anyone stop him.

*W*hat was she thinking to teleport home? Energy, flaming desire, zoomed through her. Better to have taken a good, long walk home.

Not that her shoes could have handled it. Even specially bespelled to feel good, the shoes weren't sturdy enough to be walking kilometers. Del undressed, putting her new clothes carefully in her closet, though as far as she was concerned, she'd never wear them after this business was over.

City life wore on her.

She couldn't sleep—how she had loved touching Raz in person, actually *feeling* the flex of his muscles under her palms, the surge of his body against her. Having his tongue in her mouth for real.

She moaned and picked up a pillow from the bedsponge and threw it across the room. *Looked* at this room. She didn't like it. What was she doing sleeping in a room she didn't like? This was not some hotel where she'd spend a few days; this was her home. The Elecampane Family home, and it would always be hers.

No.

She didn't like it. Didn't like Druida. She could not stay here. The city suffocated her. *This* home would be Doolee's. Del would make sure of that. The girl could have it with her blessing.

When Raz's landscape globe HeartGift showed his ideal home, they would move there. Pray the Lady and Lord that it wouldn't be in Druida City. Surely that wouldn't be demanded of her? Surely someone who was her HeartMate, bonded soul to soul, would not insist on being in Druida.

She didn't know. Things were not progressing as she'd planned. She'd reluctantly admitted to herself that she'd have to compromise if she wanted a life with him. He wouldn't be scooped up to be a partner to her in her work; he had work he loved of his own. She hadn't anticipated that.

Or hadn't figured that his work might be incompatible with her own.

An actor. She didn't want to manipulate Raz, but she *did* want him to fall a little in love with her before she gave him her Heart-Gift. Because she was falling fast for him.

He'd been nice. Kind. He had a good heart. He'd come to her when she'd been brooding in the park about Doolee. The child she had rarely thought of . . . before the loss of everyone else. The loss of her whole Family was no stinking fair.

But life—and Celta—wasn't fair.

She'd been lucky to make it on her own in the wilds as long as she had. Maybe continuing to go out alone wasn't so smart. Even Cratag Maytree, one of the toughest trained warriors Del had ever known, had nearly died alone in the wilderness.

Del had thought to have a partner. Had thought her partner might be her HeartMate. Now she doubted.

She walked through the house to see how it could be modified for Doolee. Del funded the housekeeping spells with her own energy and cleaned the MasterSuite that she took for her own. With a designer for a mother, Doolee would have plenty of ideas on how she wanted this house to look, so Del authorized a decorating account. She found G'Aunt Inula's journal on Family history and secrets and put it aside to read later but spent time recording her own experiences into memory spheres.

She arranged her affairs so they would be easy for the girl—or Straif—to take over if need be. Kick in the butt that Del was now— and forever—connected with a FirstFamily lord. The Elecampanes would always be linked with the Blackthorns . . . and by extension the Hollys . . . and maybe other FirstFamilies who married into those clans.

How her parents had yearned for something like this to happen, and it came about because of the loss of all the rest of the Family and Del's connection with an old lover.

Life was unfair and damned odd.

Finally, as the night septhours slipped into early morning, and she was at the nadir of her energy, Del unpacked her HeartGift. She looked deep within the landscape globe she'd made for her Heart-Mate during one of the Passages that freed her psi power.

She saw nothing but the floating bits: a flake of pure gold, leaves of plants she couldn't recall, small white twigs. Raz's ideal home did not appear. She set the thing—still shielded so it wouldn't trigger sex dreams between them—on one of her workroom shelves with others.

She'd dealt with her problems the best she could. More would come.

*   *   *

The next morning the pressure began. The scrybowl shrilled in her bedroom when she was creating her landscape globes in the workroom converted from a sitting room. Above the bowl wavered graytinted light, no one she knew. She wouldn't answer.

A smooth, plummy voice issued from the bowl as a message was sent to the cache. "Greetyou, GrandLady Helena D'Elecampane. I am GrandLord Pym T'Anise of the Bloom Noble Circle of Druida."

He said that as if she was supposed to know what it meant.

"Your dear parents had risen to the level of our circle and we would like to invite you to our social activities—and to assist us in our rituals to improve the city." He gave a little cough. "I am pleased to say that we have been complimented by the lords and ladies of the FirstFamilies themselves." Pride radiated through the air. "Please join our next ritual in three days for Full Twinmoons. A light repast will be provided at my antique shop at EveningBell, then we will congregate in my own ancient grove. Welcome again, we are happy to have you as a part of our group."

Del found her teeth grinding. Happy to have her Flair and her gilt, she figured. She could ignore the man and his circle for a while.

Raz was irritated and intrigued as Del Elecampane eluded him over the next week . . . as if she was avoiding him. He couldn't understand why she would duck him. Was she embarrassed at being so vulnerable?

He'd sent her wildflowers after the kiss in the park and had received a polite note of thanks.

He only caught glimpses of her . . . but observed that she seemed to be making the rounds of the shows. He wasn't surprised to see her fox with her. Shunuk would grin at Raz, flip his tail, and head off after Del as she strode away up the avenue farther into the clubbing district to some place she favored for late-night entertainment.

She wore masculine dress of elegantly cut but narrow-legged trous that showed off an excellent derriere and a shirt with slightly bloused sleeves. From the looks she got, Raz thought the woman might bring such clothes into fashion.

He'd dropped a few conversational starters about her and listened to very thin information. The newssheets had run an article on her maps and the city museum would be hanging holographic copies. Apparently all the good recent maps they had of Celta had come from her hands and brain and Flair. Fascinating.

Raz resorted to bribing the fox. Shunuk had shown up that morning for breakfast at the Thespian's Club and been pampered by the actors and the staff. Raz had discovered the Fam had a fondness for clucker and rabbit and had had a dish made up especially for him.

Muzzle deep in the bowl, tail waving, the Fam had assured Raz that he would keep Del in the long cobblestoned rectangle between the theaters until Raz got there after his performance.

The play went better that night, since Raz had an extra spark of excitement. He kept mental contact with Shunuk to ensure Del was staying put until he could reach her. Raz dressed well, but casually, in a blue that picked up the color of his eyes.

She sat on a bench near a tinkling fountain floating with colorful and fragrant water lilies. He'd noted if there was some sort of natural setting around, Del would gravitate to it.

The minute he saw her, his lower body tightened, his pulse sped up, and he felt an underlying flush of anticipation. Yes, this was the woman he wanted, for now.

He bowed and offered his arm and a sincere smile.

She raised her brows. "GrandSir Cherry?"

Shaking his head, he said, "You know it's Raz . . . Del."

"Raz. Thanks again for the flowers." Her dimples showed, the first time he'd seen them since the party. He was charmed.

She linked arms with him and his nerves quivered. He concentrated on keeping his blood in his head and not pooling lower. Maybe he'd get another searing kiss tonight, but he didn't think he'd get more, no matter how much he seduced. But it would be fun to try.

"Where are we going? Am I walking you home?" she asked.

An image came of them together on his bedsponge, him plunging into her slick heat. He swallowed, discreetly, he hoped. "Wherever you go in the evenings after the theater."

"Been watching me, huh?"

"Oh, yes." He slid his hand down her forearm and took her fingers. Skin to skin. Very, very nice.

The thready link wove stronger between them.

Shunuk yipped. *I will meet you later. I have a couple of food caches to check and nibble.* The fox melted into the dark shadows before Raz could comment.

"You've discovered his weakness."

"We all have them," Raz said. "You knew Shunuk visited me?"

"He told me of you. Over the last few years, we've watched two of your holospheres many times."

Raz smiled.

"Among others," she ended.

He started walking in the direction that she always went. At the end of the flagstone rectangle where several streets branched off, he made a half bow and waved his hand. She glanced sidelong at him, gave him a mysterious smile. "Trust me?"

"Yes." The answer came out of his mouth with the force of utmost truthfulness. That surprised him, but Del walked on as if it meant little to her.

She was used to being trusted. She was honest and would limit contact with dishonest people. So if you didn't trust her, you got out of her way. Admirable, if a little daunting. Much of the theater world included masks and manipulation. Even if actors didn't intend to slip into characters, their nature sometimes had them doing just that.

With Del, you saw the real person and accepted her or not.

And she might not care if you didn't accept her.

Raz found that he cared very much that she accepted him.

Twelve

Soon they were out of the theater district and walking toward the less popular clubs. Del had a long, easy gait that told him she spent a lot of time walking. He smiled at the thought of her hiking all over Druida. It looked good on her.

They turned down a street that opened onto a strip of shabby park. A loud mixture of eye-crossing music blasted from the open doors of several clubs. Raz walked to a beat of dance music. Couples were dancing in the park, and some were fading into the shadows of large trees. He'd like to do either with Del.

She passed most of the doors, strode to one that was shut. There was no name above it. She rapped briskly and it opened. The greeter bowed. "GrandLady D'Elecampane." He turned to Raz. "And guest . . . ah, Raz. It's been a long time."

"I didn't know where you'd moved to," Raz said, though he could have found out.

Del's lips quirked. "You like jazz, Raz?"

"Yes." He kept his voice down. Musicians were on the stage and the club took jazz seriously. Slipping an arm around her waist, he nodded to the doorman and spotted Shunuk at a table in one of the best areas.

Two full glasses of wine were on the table. Shunuk didn't turn his head, kept it focused on the small stage. *The music is good tonight. Mellow with no instrument screeches.*

"Ah," Del said.

Shunuk likes jazz, too. Her telepathy was a lovely brush against Raz's mind, clear, almost familiar. As straightforward as her words.

What's not to like? Raz asked as he seated her and pulled his own chair close.

She smiled at him, wide enough he saw both her dimples. Then she turned toward the musicians, head tilted, sipping her wine. He moved their linked fingers to his thigh, enjoyed the sweet bite of desire . . . anticipation. Yes, he would definitely have this woman.

He watched Del for a while, saw her eyelids lower, felt her move into a state of absorbed listening. Since he admired the music and respected the musicians, he gave up his plan of seduction.

The music might be seduction in itself. It was low, throbbing, wove an atmosphere of sound pulsing with Flair around them, different beats, different instruments, all pleasure. The best pleasure was Del's relaxed fingers on his leg. He let himself sink into a semi-trance state, too.

This was good. He drank a few swallows of his wine, unsurprised to find it the best the place carried, and he lost himself in the present. Each improvised note was unique, the tune never to be the same again. Sharing such a fragile and fraught moment with Del was perfect.

He didn't know how long the time out of time lasted, but he was on his feet clapping when the last low wail of the saxophone stopped. It felt nearly as good to give applause as well as receive it. Nearly.

Del stood beside him, clapping, then she reached into the pocket of her trous and took out some folded bills with golden edges. Shunuk set his teeth carefully around them, hopped from his chair to weave through the crowd and drop the gilt into a stone urn on the stage.

A ripple of laughter and applause followed Shunuk, but the musicians nodded to him and squinted out from the brightly lit stage into the dimness of the club. Impossible to make out people from that vantage point, but the whole quartet bowed.

Shunuk barked and headed for the door. Though the crowd settled, Del remained standing. She smiled at him, then sighed.

He'd have liked to think the sigh was for him but figured it was for the delight at the music. Her body seemed looser. "I must go now," she said with regret in her tones. "I have an early-morning appointment."

"Can I take you home? My glider is behind the theater. I wish more of your company."

After a pause, she replied, "I'd like that. Thank you."

When she preceded him, he set his fingertips on the small of her back, enjoyed the surge of desire when they touched.

On the way out, Raz stopped to hand additional coins to the doorman for the service and the musicians. It was obvious that Del was a member of the club and ran a tab.

People yet danced in the park as they passed. Once again Raz had taken Del's hand. Walking hand in hand with her was a simple pleasure he couldn't forego. If he was with Del, he'd be touching her, linked with her through more than just the emotional bond forming between them.

When they reached the street across from the theater rectangle, Raz was within spell-calling distance of Cherry. She'd been returned in perfect condition.

He stopped Del by slipping his arm around her waist, pulling her close. She didn't object and Raz's blood pulsed at the thought of a good night kiss. She wouldn't invite him inside her home, but at least they'd savor another hungry kiss.

Cherry zoomed up and Del exclaimed. Even the tough wilderness woman wasn't immune to a bright and gleaming red sports glider. He lifted the door for her, and the scent of new furrabeast leather wafted out.

She sniffed and slid into the single passenger seat. He walked around the glider with a grin. He was impressing the woman, and he liked that. Once inside, he gave Del's address and Cherry slid into the night. He touched a button and the speed slowed.

"Very pretty car," Del said.

"Thank you, a gift from my parents. Cherry, please play jazz."

More jazz floated on the air.

Del chuckled. "Your glider has a name."

"Wouldn't you name yours?" He leaned closer, wishing for the first time the vehicle had a bench seat.

"My stridebeasts have names, of course . . . but a glider? I don't know." She shook her head.

He took her hands, brought one, then the other to his lips. Had he felt a throb of desire from her through their bond? He hoped so. Turning one of her hands over, he kissed her wrist, swore he could feel the rapid beat of her heart. He let the tip of his tongue touch her, taste her. Sweet saltiness, herbs, Del.

She flinched, and he knew it couldn't be from fear. Overwhelming desire? Good, because his body was heating enough to simmer the thoughts from his brain. He kissed her other wrist and her pulse picked up, or maybe that was his own. "We have a mutual attraction."

"Yes."

"Is that why you avoided me?"

She withdrew her hands. "I don't know what you want from me."

He wasn't stupid enough to say "sex."

"I don't want to be a few-week fling easily forgotten by a sophisticated man," she said. "You play by different rules here in Druida. I'm not accustomed to playing at all. When I want sex and a man is available, I have sex. Then we go our separate ways . . ." Her voice turned harsher. "I don't want you using me . . . for any reason."

Raz sat up straight, met her gaze. "I wouldn't. Only use you as you used me. Equally. Passionately. To discover the pleasure we *will* have together." He ran his forefinger along her jaw. "We have a bond, don't we? An attraction and a bond." An image of his Heart-Mate dreams flickered through his mind, vanished. Imagination. This was reality.

"I want to have sex with you," she said.

He shuddered. "Yes. But I want more. I want to spend time with you. You are different from anyone I've known."

She turned so she was looking forward, not angled toward him. "I've spent much of my time on the road, in the wilderness. Alone. I don't play games."

"Oh, Del, don't you understand that I know that?" He took one of her hands from her lap, linked his fingers with hers. "We have an attraction, a desire, a bond. Isn't that enough?"

"Is it too much for you, Raz? Too intense?"

He let a breath out on a laugh. "You see? You know. *We* know that it's intense, not simple and not unimportant between us. Already."

Again he reached for her other hand, took it, twined his fingers with hers. Flair, feelings, cycled between them.

He could sense the liquid heat in the core of her body. How she liked looking at him. His aspect and form pleased her. That triggered his arousal and he knew she'd sense the thickening of his shaft, his yearning for her. "Only you," he said.

She laugh-coughed. "Never enough sexual encounters in the wild. Either no sex, or lots for a few nights. Still, I like to know who I'm rolling around with."

He wasn't too pleased that she'd reduced his romanticism to a basic urge. He pressed their palms together, and they fit. As closely as their bodies would fit. "I know that you love jazz and have watched my holos and attended my show. You said you admired my work. I admire *you*. I'm certain that when I see your work, I will admire it, too." He straightened their hands until he could nibble her fingertips. "I want to learn you, Del." He left it at that, let the link reinforce the fact that his body ached for sex with her, that his emotions were as confused about her as ever but his predominant feeling was sheer fascination.

He felt her need, deeper than he'd anticipated, as if it were a great whirlpool that could drag him down. If she let it. Which she wouldn't. She was a woman in control.

But it would be interesting to be involved in an intense relationship, one that was emotionally dangerous.

Or that could be a rationalization.

He was already hooked.

"The D'Elecampane gates are ahead," said Cherry, beginning to slow. They reached tall cobblestone stacked pillars and Del lowered her window and murmured a lilting spell. The gates opened. A few minutes later—too soon—they were in front of her house. It was three stories of red brick, a pleasant but uninspiring home, though he didn't think Del felt about the place the way a person should feel about their home.

"Did you make a landscape globe for yourself?" Raz asked. Now that he knew that was her talent, he noticed more of the orbs around.

Del opened her door and hopped from the glider. "No."

He wasn't about to let her go into the house without a kiss. "Too bad," he said, using a long stride to catch up with her before she set her hand on the door latch.

"Yes," she said.

He slipped one arm around her waist, his other hand curved around the back of her head, his fingers weaving through her silky curls. He brought his body to hers, bent his head, and took her mouth.

Del had known he would kiss her, of course. Had let Raz make the moves. If she went after him the way she wanted, she'd scare him away.

Then her length was against his and he was taller and wider and the passion coming from him engulfed her, torched her as if she were a twist of paper in flames. Even as she stroked the length of his back, snugged her lower body into his, feeling the thick length of his shaft, she fought for control. She could not touch him, woo him, respond to him the way she did in their erotic dreams. If she did, he'd withdraw and she might as well ride out of town.

So she gave herself up to fine sensation and rubbed against him, teasing them both, knowing that she wouldn't allow herself to touch him in person or in dreams tonight. She sucked at his tongue until he groaned, felt the connection between them double and redouble. Knew she was an instant away from lifting her legs and wrapping them around his waist, teleporting them both to her bedroom.

She nipped his lip, and when he hauled her even closer instead of releasing her, she pushed against him, wrenched from his clasp. Jumped away from the heated desire that raked them both with needy claws. Now was not the time. Too soon, too soon.

She gasped and panted for breath, aware only of his taste, dark sweet man, and leaned against the door. "Had a good time with you," she said, grabbed the latch of the door, yanked it open, then teleported immediately to her waterfall and ordered it cold.

As she stood dripping in her clothing, she felt his anger—at his own lack of finesse. When she checked the connection between them, it was stronger than before. She ignored the fact that it yet showed red with arousal . . . for them both.

Thirteen

The next morning *Antenn and Doolee arrived to be shown the Elecampane HouseHeart.* To Del's surprise—and she thought Antenn's, too—Doolee recalled the HouseHeart door was hidden behind a false no-time panel in the pantry. The child knew the pattern to open both the door to the slide to the corridor below, and the knocking rhythm for the HouseHeart door. Though she wasn't old enough to say the Words correctly to enter the obsidian bubble itself.

Antenn was fascinated by the spherical room, particularly the hot spring in the bottom that was covered with vented thick glass that Doolee crawled along, patting as if she wanted it open. Though Del didn't reveal the spell to slide away the glass, she didn't discount the children's cleverness and made Antenn promise to get antidrown spells on both himself and Doolee—and have them learn to swim.

A tapping came, then Raz's voice. He was up early. "This is

Raz Cherry, requesting permission for the gates to the estate to be
opened. Del . . ." His voice rolled the word like a caress that had
been lingering on his tongue. "How about an outing with me?
Brunch?"

Del felt her skin heat under Antenn's gaze. She walked stiffly
over to a scrybowl set on a tall pillar. With a touch on the rim, she
connected to the scrystone at the front gate.

Raz's visage rippled in the water, more handsome than ever. He
was smiling cheerfully, a weathershield nimbus around him. The
rain pattered behind him, soft but steady.

Del blocked any sight of the HouseHeart or Antenn. "I'm sorry,
Raz, I'm busy at the moment." She hesitated. "There's a gazebo in
the gardens if you want to wait. It's down a raked gravel path and
shielded from the rain. I won't be too much longer." She waved a
hand over the bowl and the gates opened.

"Is he your HeartMate?" Antenn was frowning, hands on hips.

"Not all of my business is your business, too."

The boy's mouth tightened but he said nothing more. Del had no
doubt that he'd spill everything about Raz to his parents. She just
hoped they all kept their mouths shut.

Antenn picked up Doolee, who struggled and whined as he
walked to the door. "Glassheart," he said the opening Word. Nothing happened.

"The exit phrase is 'through a glass darkly,' " Del said.

The door slid open and they walked to the steep upward tunnel.
His mouth opened, closed. "How do we get up?"

Doolee had already wriggled from his grasp, turned around, and
set her bottom near the slide.

"Ooo, ooo, ooo!" ordered Doolee. She put her arms around
Shunuk, who'd sat down near her.

Del moved toward Doolee. Antenn stepped aside. Del sat down,
put her legs around Doolee and Shunuk, and held on, grinning at
Antenn. "Up, up, *up!*"

They were whooshed up backward, Doolee chortling, to the
floor of the pantry.

Dizzy, Shunuk said and staggered away—faster than Del thought he should, then out of the kitchen Fam door toward the gardens.

Entertain Raz, she sent to him mentally. He yipped assent.

Del stood with the child—Doolee wanted to slide back down—and moved into the kitchen until she heard Antenn's shout and he was in the pantry. She let Doolee down as soon as he'd locked the door, then she removed a beverage from a no-time and handed it to him. "This drink holds the best silence spell made."

His grin faded and he matched her serious expression.

"On your honor, as a nobleman, do you promise not to divulge any Elecampane secrets you know now or learn in the future to anyone else unless I am dead and you are in peril of your life or dying?"

He paled, set his lips, nodded, and repeated the conditions, then drank the mixture down. Surprise came to his eyes as he licked foam from his lips. "It was good."

Del smiled. "I tried." She jerked her head toward the kitchen entrance. "I'll show you the journals—"

But Doolee was screaming, tugging on Antenn's full-legged trous, reaching up for the cup.

"No, baby, you can't have any," he said.

She stuck her bottom lip out, narrowed her eyes, and said, "No, no, *no!*"

Del scooped her up and got images from the little girl's mind: Elfwort playing with her in the kitchen. Her mother and father and Doolee sliding down into the HouseHeart, and Inula.

"Shhh, shhh." Del turned the child into her shoulder and hurried through the door onto the terrace where the rain added a comforting swish. Del glanced over her shoulder to see Antenn following them.

"She's overtired," he said.

"Yes, and thinking of her lost Family." As Del was. Useless regrets; she wouldn't have changed her life unless she'd been told of the future tragedy. She loved her life. Too bad she hadn't realized she'd loved the people in her Family a lot, too. "We'll look at the journals later." They returned to the house through the sitting room doors and went to a teleportation pad. Doolee fussed, tears trickling down her cheeks, sobbing.

Antenn took her and she buried her face in his thin shoulder, not looking at Del. Hiding from the past?

Del couldn't blame her. She pulled a landscape globe from her pocket, shook it and handed it to Doolee. "Here's my gift to Cordif that you can give him." Dooley peeped out at her and took the globe.

"D'Elecampane?" Antenn said, his brows down.

"Yes?"

"In the HouseHeart . . . I couldn't sense the HeartStones."

Del smiled. "I could. They responded to both Doolee's and your energies. They'll be fine."

His breath expelled with a little spit. "Raz Cherry is your Heart-Mate." He grinned. "That's not an Elecampane secret I'm forbidden to tell."

Boys. How long had it been since she'd been around boys? Since she'd been a girl. "I'm sure that your parents will teach you the discretion that a FirstFamily son needs," she said. "Merry meet," she began the traditional good-bye.

He stood straighter, rubbed his hand down Doolee's back. "And merry part."

"And merry meet again."

He was gone before the sound of her voice was absorbed by the silence of the empty house.

The image of Antenn and Doolee lingered. Children of the next generation. Both orphans given a good home and now sister and brother. But Doolee would vaguely recall her Family, even as she grew to look more like a female version of Elfwort.

The past was sad, the present had to be lived and guided well for the future to prosper.

And Raz waited for Del in the gazebo. She hoped he would be part of her future, soon.

Del glanced down at her clothing and shrugged. She'd dressed in good leathers for her time with Antenn and Doolee. What she was most comfortable in, what reminded her who she had become once she'd left this place and her parents.

Raz hadn't seen her in her usual garb. May as well find out how he would react. She hid only that she was his HeartMate, conforming to the laws of their society.

She walked into the light rain, let it dampen her hair that would curl tightly, dew on her face . . . though the city air felt different than that of the wild. The city had more crafted Flair, more psi power from people. A benefit of city life for a change.

Her leathers were treated both physically and magically to repel wet, so she wasn't uncomfortable as she strode through the gardens. They'd been excruciatingly formal when her parents had been in charge, then Inula had shaped them to be more practical and useful, augmenting those of her own household. Some of the cuzes had loved to garden. She'd have to hire a trustworthy landscaping company when she left.

Was she sure she would leave?

Yes.

When she reached the pretty octagonal gazebo, Raz was staring out into the distance at the starship, *Nuada's Sword*, his back to her. Even that view gave her a jolt . . . to her sexuality and to her heart. Lean and proud of his body, that was Raz. Next to him, on the wide sill, was Shunuk.

Raz turned and his smile melted her further, even though she knew he was using it for just that effect. His eyebrows winged up and he scanned her up and down. She was suddenly aware that though these were her better leathers, they had white scars where the butterscotch color had been ripped away by a branch, a slide down a rocky hill.

"Did you take another job? Will you be leaving?" He frowned.

She stopped on the lowest stair of the gazebo, sheltered from the rain, hooked her thumbs in her belt. "Do you care if I'm leaving soon?"

"Yes."

He walked to her and boards creaked. He lifted both her hands, kissed them. "I want you, Helena, in my life and my bed."

"Nice leading-man line."

His expression darkened and his grip tightened on her hands. "It's the truth. I'm not acting."

"But you could, Raz, and we both know it. I want honesty from you. You actors hide under masks so easily."

"I am and will be honest." He gestured to the fancy greeniron table. A dark blue tablecloth draped it and pretty china and silver was set for two. He held out a chair.

Before he could take the other, Shunuk, who'd been watching them and keeping his thoughts to himself, hopped onto it.

Raz laughed, hauled a third chair to the table and moved the setting. He poured springreen wine for them, clinked his glass against hers, and said, "To your fascinating eyes, part of your fascinating self."

His gaze met hers and he sipped, not breaking the contact. She found herself dropping her eyes, thinking she might reveal too much. The link between them thickened and shone inside her mind. He touched her shoulder where a patch of white showed rough in the leather, his lips curved. "My wildcat." His hand curved around her cheek and his thumb brushed her lips.

Del couldn't look away from him. He could move her so easily, this man, her HeartMate.

There are no such things as real wildcats, Shunuk said. *Only in story holos. There are feral cats, but they are not the same. What are we eating?*

Raz laughed. "I have thick porcine sandwiches. Fruit tarts."

Shunuk rotated an ear. *I like porcine. I might eat a berry tart.*

"I'm glad to provide you with a good meal." Raz set out a soft-leaf, unearthed a sandwich from a large picnic basket, and stripped thick bread from it, leaving a large slice of porcine.

We are Fams, Del and me, Shunuk said. *We go together.* He didn't stay to see how this pronouncement was received by Raz, but abandoned his manners and nipped the porcine from the table, hauled it over to a corner to feast.

Raz filled plates, then sat and drank more of his wine. Del watched him move like a dancer, graceful—the fantasy of them making love had spun heatedly in her mind. Raz bit into his sandwich. "Mmm, excellent."

Food from Thespian Club is always good, Shunuk said.

Del's sandwich had tart mustard and a thin herbal spread, the porcine was crispy on both sides. Good food indeed. She ate and the quiet between them was friendly.

"I would like to see you exclusively," Raz said.

A bite got stuck in her throat. She washed it down with wine that lay like a blessing on her tongue, complementing the meal. "Exclusivity works on both sides."

"Of course," he said. He popped a strawberry into his mouth, grinned when he noticed her focus had gone to his lips. She was beginning to forget why she had to keep control of this situation, why she couldn't give in to their urges to have sex right here and now.

Shunuk gave a little cough. *I would like another piece of porcine to cache for a snack later.*

Del frowned. "The pet no-times are fully stocked. Plural, no-times."

He looked up at her with big eyes. *The taste of meals from the no-times and meals from the ground are not the same.*

She stared at him.

Shaking his head, Raz went to the basket and handed another slice of meat to the fox. Shunuk took it carefully in his teeth, but a string of drool fell from his muzzle. *Thank you!* With a swish of his fat tail, he leapt through the weathershielded window and out to the raindrop-glistening grass and wildflowers.

The sun shone and a brilliant rainbow graced the sky, seeming to curve around the starship in the distance . . . starting in the ocean to one side of the ship and ending in Landing Park in the city.

"Gorgeous," Raz said as he looked at it.

"Yes."

He turned and she realized she'd stood and been drawn closer to him than she'd known. Their bodies brushed.

Once again he took her hands in his, linking their fingers, and Del knew she'd forever associate that gesture with him.

He bent his head. She leaned forward.

The roar of applause filled the air.

Del jerked back, stepped aside.

Raz flushed, dipped his hand into his trous pocket, and brought out a tiny glass sphere encasing a droplet of water. The object nestled in the center of his palm and he brought it eye level.

One of the new personal scry pebbles Elfwort had invented.

"Here," Raz said.

"Raz, you're not at the Cherry Transport yard. Thank the Lady and Lord!" The words exploded from his father.

"What? What's wrong?"

"Fire," the older man said, his face set in grim lines.

Fourteen

T'Cherry wiped his arm across his forehead. "You told me you might drop by, thought you mighta been caught—"

"Seratina? Others?"

"No one's hurt, but there's plenty of property damage, Cave of the Dark Goddess!"

"I'll be right there."

His father squinted. "Is that Del Elecampane?"

Del stepped close, marveled at the tiny portrait of Raz's father in the glass and water droplet.

"Yes," she said.

The flesh of T'Cherry's face went heavier, his dark red brows angled down. "Sorry to say that the map you gave me earlier of Fairplay Canyon was lost. They torched our old den, been there for a century!"

"I'll be right there," Raz repeated. His fingers started to curl over the drop, ending the call, but Del touched them.

"I have copies," Del said.

"Copies?"

"Yes. Even if I didn't, I know that canyon well enough to reconstruct them."

T'Cherry puffed a breath. "I'm grateful."

Raz grabbed her hand. "We're teleporting—"

"No!" yelled T'Cherry. "The yard's a mess. The light is odd, you might not visualize right. Come by glider. Helluva thing."

Someone shouted at him and the older man nodded at Raz. "See you soon." The droplet in the glass turned cherry red, then clear.

"Fire," Del murmured. Her heart clutched, but she hadn't been in Druida when her Family had perished. Fire didn't bother her. The little personal scry, perscry, that Raz carried touched her more. "Let me get my maps. I'll meet you at the front door. Did you come by glider?"

"Yes."

She nodded and teleported to her den, strode to the cubbyholes that held her maps, and pulled out those showing the terrain of Fairplay Canyon. Setting them on her draft table that was stacked with papyrus, she put her hand on the top one, said a couplet, and the maps were copied. She took the new sheets, rolled them up, put them in a leather holder, and was down at the front door in minutes.

Raz's face was tense, his glider already humming with power.

She flung up the door and slipped inside the vehicle and they were off before the door slid closed. Raz didn't set the glider on automatic, but drove himself. He was a good driver. Whether he wanted to admit it or not, he had plenty of Cherry Transport blood in his veins. He probably had driven gliders since grovestudy. She wouldn't be surprised if he could pilot a cargo transport or even an airship. Working Families were like that. Everyone on Inula's side of the Elecampane's had worked with scrys.

"I've given it some thought," Raz said abruptly. He moved

smoothly around a clunky PublicCarrier. "Dad must have meant the old, historic den, not the new building. It is—was—wood. Just a couple of rooms with some old stuff in them, on the outskirts of the old yard, not near the new buildings or the hangers. Dammit."

When they reached the large port, Raz was waved through the gates and they entered an area of organized chaos.

Buildings of all sizes held gliders and cargo transports and even a few airships. The acrid smell of smoke hung in the air. Raz wove through the buildings to the far edge of the place, where the most activity was happening.

He parked Cherry and they stepped onto paved concrete. There wasn't much dampness around and Del figured the southern part of the city hadn't gotten as much rain as the northern.

T'Cherry was in the center of a group, barking out orders. A few nearby buildings showed singes on their brick or metallic skins. Behind him was a large seared area of collapsed beams burnt completely black, smoking in spots. The building was gone, nothing but wood and rubble.

Del's heart squeezed. She didn't want to think that this is what her cuzes' home had looked like. No, not quite. That home had been brick. She found herself panting, slid her glance away to focus on Raz's sister, Seratina, who was speaking with fire mages . . . the people who smothered fires. Two small groups of them looked around the busy yard interestedly.

As soon as she saw them, Seratina sighed and nudged her father toward them. Del held up the map case.

His eyes brightened and he stopped talking, hurried over to them. He nodded to Raz but his gaze was fixed on Del's tube. His ruddy complexion went deeper. "I, ah, was comparing your map to one of the early ones we had, left it there last night." He glanced at the destroyed building, scrubbed his face.

Del avoided looking but couldn't get away from the smoke-filled air. "The fifth survey was when gliders and airships were developed enough to make the long trip to Gael City." Her lips showed in a brief smile. "Or I should say that was when our human Flair became strong enough to power good gliders and airships. I have fifth survey maps at home." She hesitated, glanced at both Cherry men, then Seratina, who was gesturing to her to move her father along. So Del issued the invitation, "If you want to come by, we can compare them in my study. Like I said, Fairplay Canyon has been too narrow to handle traffic, but not only are our vehicles sleeker, I think you'll find that it will be cost effective to smooth the floor for a gliderway and widen the walls for low-flying airships."

T'Cherry turned and stared at the destruction. "I'm needed here."

"Everything's under control, Dad," Seratina soothed. "I can handle it, just cleanup—"

"Meaning you don't want me around," T'Cherry said.

Seratina puffed out a breath. "Meaning that I think things would go more smoothly if you left it to me. Go. Look at the maps. You know you want to."

Brows lowered, T'Cherry grunted, shook his head, pivoted back. "I'd like to see your maps." He eyed Raz's glider. "I haven't driven that baby since I bought her for Raz." He went over and opened the side of the glider, gestured to Raz and Del to sit in the passenger seat. His eyes twinkled. "It'll be tight, but I don't think you two'll mind that."

Before she got in, Del stroked the glossy tinting on the hood, thinking as she had when she'd first ridden in the vehicle that this beauty couldn't be taken into the wild . . . nowhere off the sometimes problematic roads of Celta. It was a city glider. Raz was just as glossy.

She sat on Raz's lap. He was grinning like his father and the resemblance was strong. He put his arm around Del so his hand lay just under her breast. There was no use fighting the enforced closeness, so Del relaxed into him. He smelled wonderful. His grin became a satisfied smile and his eyelids lowered. She noticed he didn't wear much of a mask when he was with his Family. There was still the hint of Raz the son and Raz the older brother, the roles he'd grown up with.

T'Cherry winked at Raz, closed the side, freed the driver's bar from the console, and flexed his fingers. As soon as his door lowered, they were off.

Raz was an excellent driver. T'Cherry was exceptional, a master. She'd never been in a glider with such a good steersman.

She'd never been in a glider that went so fast. She hung on to Raz. He tightened his grip on her and chuckled. They arrived at her house in half the time it had taken to get to the Cherry yard. Del was breathless, her legs a little trembly. She hadn't known a glider could corner so well without tipping over.

T'Cherry handed her out, his arm strong when her stance was unsteady. "This baby sure goes, doesn't it?"

"I think I'll stick to stridebeasts," Del said. She strengthened her knees. "Or walk."

T'Cherry laughed. Raz climbed from the glider and set an arm around her. His hand curved around her hip.

As they walked up the front steps, it occurred to Del that it was time for midday meal. She and Raz had just eaten, but she'd bet that T'Cherry had risen near dawn and had a hearty breakfast septhours past.

"Let's go into the dining room. Plenty of space to spread out the maps on the table," she said. "And I can get you some lunch, T'Cherry."

She led the way, wondering what the no-times held that he liked.

Raz met his father's eyes as they walked through Del's house. It was furnished in the most elaborate fashion of a decade past. The atmosphere was one of a rarely tenanted place, one of quiet occasionally broken with small human sounds.

Del hesitated at the dining room door, opened it, and a little sigh escaped her. Raz sensed that she hadn't been in this room since she'd returned, that it didn't hold happy memories.

With brisk movements, she spread out her wide map on the long, polished table that could seat twenty. "I'll go get the Fifth Survey Map, Area Between Druid City and Gael City. Be right back." She left through a white-paneled door.

Raz's father stuck his hands in his work trous pockets and glanced around the white dining room with fancy gold medallions on the wall. "Doesn't look much like Del, does it?"

"No." Raz hesitated. "Did you know her parents?"

T'Cherry lifted and dropped his thick shoulders. "Not much. Started out below us in status, ended up equal or so, with a lotta socializing and being free with gilt. Knew the other line of the Family a little better. Inula Elecampane and her get. Good people. Terrible tragedy, their deaths."

Del entered again, with a rolled map that appeared as pristine as those in the Guildhall. She took care of her tools. She spread the map out, flicked her fingers until the maps lay correctly to compare the landscape of Fairplay Canyon.

She and Raz's father leaned over the table. "You can see that there's been erosion in the last three centuries, and no offense to the surveyors, but they got the dimensions wrong by tens of meters." With a tap of her finger, areas on the map enlarged and became three dimensional. She looked at T'Cherry. "You must know the measurements of your transport gliders and airships. Too bad we don't have the technology to fly over the mountains instead of through them."

T'Cherry grunted. "Don't like the idea of being high in the atmosphere where you can freeze and can't breathe on your own. Above the mountains would be faster, though," T'Cherry said. "Stridebeast takes a week, an eightday, to Gael City. Even a glider runs a couple of days by Ambroz Pass. My best express airship time now is six septhours." He eyed the narrow canyon. "Ambroz is wide enough for two ships. This one is only good for one, with a fast glider road in the middle and a slow lane for stridebeasts on the eastern side."

T'Cherry opened a belt pouch and took out a small pad of papyrus, handed a sheet to Raz. "You make the CH-90 airship."

Raz set his fingers on the papyrus to ensure the proper folds. He visualized the sleekest low-flying airship Cherry Transport and Shipping had, gathered and sent his Flair to the papyrus. The sheet twitched and folded, tore and bent until it became a miniature papyrus model of the CH-90. With another stroke of his finger, he tinted it silver and red, with the flowing name of *Del's Delight* across it. Humming, he sent it rocketing through Fairplay Canyon, wasn't too careful and it scraped along one side. "Hmm. Tight fit, but it can be done." He smiled at Del. "A challenge for our pilots; they're going to love you."

Meanwhile his father had made the fastest glider they had for the transport of perishable luxury goods, tinted it a red with orange flames, and zoomed it along the twists and turns of the bottom of the canyon, his brows knit. The words *Elecampane Express* on the model blurred with the speed. He grunted a laugh as the model sped from the canyon right off the table, caught it with his Flair, and sent it to hover before Del. With a little bow, he presented it to her. His face had lit with glee. "That cuts the time we currently take for this model by a third. Even with the canyon being east of the direct route." He rubbed his hands. "Thank you."

Del smiled and stroked the little model with her forefinger. "It occurs to me that we might have done this when I first presented the maps to you."

His father shrugged again. "I trusted you and your rep and the eyeball we did. Had to move fast to get the land."

"Yes," Del said.

Raz bumped his airship against her nose and she laughed, took it, and examined it, looked at his father's. "These are wonderful."

"Our creative Flair," T'Cherry said, "making models."

"Something to be truly proud of," Del said. She waved and the holographic canyons collapsed. The maps rolled up and lifted to a side table.

She turned to his father and said, "Would you like lunch? Lots of stuff in the no-time. I think there's furrabeast steak and vegetables."

"Mmmm, my thanks. I like it rare."

Del went through another door. "Be right back. Thought I'd have some soup. We have all kinds, but I'm going with potato cheese with herbs, Raz?"

"You have beef broth with vegetables?" His father and Del stared at him, both very active people. The play had occasional physical demands but nothing like the professions of the other two. "Sure," Del said. "I'll get it all."

There was a small pop and Shunuk sat in the corner. *I could eat again,* he said. He pointed his muzzle at Raz, *Greetyou, story-man.* The fox slid his gaze to T'Cherry; he raised his mental voice. *Greetyou, sire of storyman.* Sniffing, Shunuk added, *Greetyou, pilot. I am Shunuk, Del's Fam.* His bushy tail wagged.

"Greetyou, Shunuk," T'Cherry said gravely. He stared at the fox. "You don't eat kittens, do you?"

Shunuk sniffed. *No, not even non-Fam kittens or cats. Humans get angry if you eat pets.*

"That's right," Del said, bringing in a tray full of food. The mingling of smells made Raz's mouth water. He saw she'd given him some herbed flatbread that steamed with warmth. Both he and his father rose to relieve her of the weight of the tray.

T'Cherry was closer. "I've got it," he said, then, "I think I might like a fox Fam. You got any brothers, Shunuk?"

"He comes from the south," Del said. "I don't think so, but he's made friends with most the fox dens here."

Shunuk said, *Since we are Fams and not lowly fox and we are prized now, all our kits survive, even the runts. I will ask if any want to be with a pilot.*

His father had winced at the mention of a runt, but inclined his head to Shunuk and rumbled, "My thanks."

A kitten would feel superior to a runt fox. I have noticed that it is best to let cats feel superior.

They all laughed. "Wise fox," his father said.

Del said, "Raz, there are spelled placemats in the sideboard. I don't much like this table, but no use ruining it."

The mats were golden. Raz quickly set them out, and he took his soup and bread and flatware, gave Shunuk his plate of furrabeast bites in the tiled corner.

Del served his father first, then sat down at the table, looked to T'Cherry. "Blessing?"

His father rumbled. "We thank the Lady and Lord for the skills of those past and present who have provided us with this food. Blessed be."

"Blessed be," Raz and Del echoed.

Shunuk slurped his meal.

There was silence as they all ate, then Raz sent his father a straight look and said, "Shunuk called you a pilot."

"I am," his father said comfortably, forking a nice chunk of steak into his mouth.

"Yes, you are. But I don't think any of us want you taking runs through Fairplay Canyon Pass when it's done."

T'Cherry's brows dipped. He chewed. "Think I can't handle it, boy?"

"I love my father," Raz said.

"No use giving Celta an extra life through . . . misadventure," Del said. "Life's tough enough here. Sicknesses. Low birth count. Sterility. Fires."

Raz met his father's eyes. "I am definitely talking to Mother and Seratina about the pass runs." He smiled. "Maybe we can go down several times to look at the place when the gliderway is being built— good Family outings that will give our women good visuals."

"And the rock walls should be sheered some," Del said. "Yeah, could be plenty dangerous at high speed." She frowned. "I didn't much consider that."

"You travel by *stridebeast,* girl," his father said with the superiority of a man who used technology and Flair to travel. He stared down his nose at Raz. "I wasn't the one who scraped the side of my model going through Del's canyon."

"You are an excellent driver. But I wish you wouldn't take many chances," Del said, smiled. "I like my friend."

His father's face tinted a little red. "Thank you, but, you, Del Elecampane, you've lived a chancy life. How many chances are you gonna be taking in the future?"

Fifteen

Del stared at her bowl, her expression sobering. "Not as many as in the past now that most of my Family is gone." She drew in her breath. "There's plenty of work around here and Gael City." Her lip curled. "I've been asked to map the new streets of what used to be Downwind. Came from Steep Springs, pretty sure their maps are out of date, too." She sighed. "City maps."

Quiet gathered again and Del spooned a few bites of potato soup into her mouth, but Raz didn't think she tasted them. Her stare was fixed out the window that looked onto a formal garden. He didn't think she saw that view, either. "I've been wanting to travel again to the Bluegrass Plains," she said. She grimaced. "I'm not really a city woman."

His belly coated with a chill that Raz didn't like. He was most definitely a city man.

"Thank you for an excellent lunch, Del." T'Cherry burped

discreetly in his softleaf. Pushing back from the table, he lifted his plate and silverware to clear. Del rose hastily and took them, arranged them tidily with her own on the tray.

Raz reluctantly chewed the last of his tasty flatbread and put his things on the tray, too, then lifted it. "I'll take these to the kitchen."

He followed Del and helped her put the plates and flatware in the cleanser. "Thank you for lunch, Del, and for the companionship."

Her dimples showed. "Always a good time with the Cherry men."

"I'm glad you think so." He took her hands, just stared at her, her pretty springreen wine eyes, her curly hair of many shades of blond. Fascinating.

He kissed her hands, leaned forward to brush his lips against hers.

His father coughed loudly in the dining room.

Del chuckled, squeezed his hands, and drew away to go back into the dining room. His father had taken the new copy of her map and waved toward the roll. "I want to take this back home for safe-keeping, then return to the yard." His lips flattened. "The fire mages informed us that we were lucky that it was raining. The fire started in the old den, then the smoke alerted us to the problem, but the rain confined the flames to that building until the fire mages were called. It's a total loss."

"Sorry to hear that," Del said.

Raz went and threw an arm around his father's shoulders, hugged. "None of our original stuff in there, right?"

Grimacing, his father said, "No, but a lot of centuries-old copies of our oldest documents. They had value, too, scribed by different ancestors. That stings."

"Better things than people," Del said.

His father flushed, said gruffly. "Sorry, didn't mean—"

She patted his shoulder. "'Course you didn't." She took the map and ran her fingers along the roll and it was encased in a protective covering—both physically and with a Flair shield. "I'll show you to the teleportation room in the entryway."

"Thanks." His father glanced at Raz and sighed. "Guess you won't let me take your glider, Cherry."

"No, and it's really too bad that you promised Mother that you wouldn't get a sports vehicle." Raz shook his head in false commiseration.

They trouped out of the dining room that none of them liked and to the entry hall, which was even more gilded. His father kept his face expressionless, Raz thought that the previous Elecampanes had taste that wasn't quite top-notch, and he didn't think that Del even noticed her surroundings.

His father stepped into the teleportation area, initiated the spell, saluted Del with his rolled map, and disappeared.

Raz stepped close and put his arm around her waist. "It's been an eventful day."

"Yes, it has," she said. She looked up at him and blinked. "You have a performance tonight, don't you?"

"Yes, the fifth time I take the villain down this week. I want to continue to see you, Del."

"You will."

He bent and pressed his lips against hers in a gentle kiss, swept his tongue along the sweetness of her mouth. "A lot. Exclusively."

Her eyes were serious as she replied, but he noted her breasts rose and fell with her quick breath. "I agree."

"For as long as you're in Druida."

She stiffened a little, lifted her chin. "All right." She tilted her head and Raz realized she was listening to the rain that had started up again. For an instant the charred, blackened, and smoking timbers of the old den at the yard came to his mind, then he shuttled it away.

"Come on upstairs to the green parlor. It's cozier. We can talk and listen to music strips."

He lifted her hand to his lips. "Learn to know each other."

She cast a narrowed gaze at him. "That's definitely one of your actor voices, Raz."

He laughed, clasped his hand with hers, and walked to the base of the stairs with her. They had no sooner gotten to the top and turned down the corridor before a chiming sound reverberated through the house, announcing visitors.

A few steps later, they turned into the green parlor and Raz saw Straif Blackthorn, *FirstFamily GrandLord Straif T'Blackthorn*, holding a little girl in his arms that was the image of Del.

Raz's spine stiffened; he tightened his clasp on Del's fingers. This man had been her lover, close enough to her to manage her affairs when her Family died while she was away. He was father to this child . . . the remaining child of her Family. *Her* child, also. Too many strings between the two of them. Strings that seemed to vibrate.

"Greetyou, Del." T'Blackthorn moved forward with the same easy stride Del had, one that spoke of many miles walked and ridden.

"Greetyou, Straif," Del said. Her gaze seemed fixed on the little girl, as if she was unaware or unconcerned with the tension between Straif and him. Raz rubbed the back of her hand with his thumb. Straif did not miss that action.

"Straif, Doolee, this is Cerasus Cherry. Raz, this is an old friend, Straif T'Blackthorn, and my cuz, Helendula Elecampane-Blackthorn." She untwined her fingers from Raz's, walked toward them, and held out her arms to the child. "Greetyou, Doolee, good to see you back again so soon."

"Dd . . . dd . . . dd." The little girl took her thumb from her mouth and flashed a dimpled smile at Del, held out her arms. Del took the child and kissed her cheek, settled her on a hip.

Raz's insides pitched.

Straif said easily, "Quite a picture. Del, since you're in town for a while, I'd like to arrange for you to sit for T'Apple, so he can craft a holo painting of you and Doolee."

Del shifted with the child, they looked at each other. "Sit. Like sitting still, right?"

"Right," Straif said.

To Raz, both females appeared nearly incapable of being quiet for more than a few minutes.

"For a long time, and not just once?" Del questioned.

"I'd like this holo of you," Straif said, in the tone of a FirstFamily GrandLord.

The man was dressed in the finest of bespelled clothes, tailored for him, in the latest fashion. Raz could only hope to make enough gilt from his career to someday wear such clothes. The Cherrys were an old house, but the highest in nobility, riches, and status were the FirstFamilies.

"Why can't you just take a recording and T'Apple can work from that?" Del grumbled.

"Because he's an artist?" Straif raised his brows.

Raz's jaw tensed. He couldn't prevent how his body straightened, angled toward Del as he stepped to block her from Straif's vision. It didn't matter that the man was happily wed to his HeartMate. He was a past lover of Del's, a man who mattered to her, who she'd cared for and who had cared for her. A man who would be tied to Del for the rest of her life through the child she held.

A man dangerous to all Raz's possessive instincts.

Scowling, Del moved beside Raz and said, "All right, set up the appointment. We'll do our best, won't we, Doolee?" She jiggled Doolee on her hip, smiled at the little girl with such tenderness that Raz's heart gave a hard thump in his chest.

"Ya, ya, ya!" Doolee said. She leaned against Del and turned her head to look at Raz, fluttered her eyelids.

A flirt in the making. He had a flash of the baby as a young woman, pretty and aware of her own appeal. Not like Del, who was still frowning as she looked at Straif. "You could have scried to tell me that."

"So I could have," Straif said. He was staring at Raz. "But I wanted to take a look around the house again. It's been a long time since I was here and you said something to my son about a journal? My HeartMate and I wondered if you might have children's books of Family tales." He smiled and didn't sell the sincerity. "We like to read to our children at night."

Del grunted. "Yeah, children's tales somewhere. Holos in my old room or the nursery. I'll get them later." She ran a hand over Doolee's curls, handed the child back to Straif. "I'll send them all to your cache."

"You asked Antenn to make sure Doolee was taught to swim and had an antidrowning spell . . . my son was vague . . ."

"That's right. You'll have to trust me on that. I'll see you *later*, Straif."

Raz gave Straif a smile of his own, slow and triumphant, as he wrapped an arm around her waist. The woman wanted to spend time with him, not her old lover. "Pleasure meeting you."

T'Blackthorn narrowed his eyes. "Right." He was all tough guy; Raz didn't think the tracker had gotten soft since he'd taken up his title. But Raz wouldn't back down. This was *his* time with Del. Her time with T'Blackthorn and whatever romantic involvement they'd had was past.

"Bye, bye!" Doolee made kissing noises, and Straif held her out to kiss Del's cheek.

"Tomorrow, Del," Straif said. He took a couple of paces back and vanished.

With her free hand, Del rubbed her face, shook her head. "Lady and Lord, I love Doolee and respect Straif, even though he's gone all nobleman on me, but all these complications . . . and being tangled up forever with a FirstFamily . . ." She shrugged.

It was the most natural thing in the world for Raz to pull her into his arms.

She came willingly, the tenseness in her muscles as she'd faced T'Blackthorn easing, turning her supple against Raz, and that was a very unique pleasure. She tilted her head back and wrapped her arms around his neck and opened her mouth to his, let his tongue invade her.

Passion exploded inside him, shot straight to his sex. He grabbed her tight, one arm around her shoulders, one curving around her derriere, pulling her against him, her belly against his hard and throbbing shaft. Then he bent her back, so they would be close, close, as close as they could get, clothed.

Fire raged in him, running through his blood. Hunger. He *needed*.

Then they weren't in the wide, white and gold corridor, but in the dimness of a room that smelled of her, just like the taste of her that tantalized him until he was mad with longing to kiss her and learn all the flavors of her—mouth and neck and shoulder and breast and sex.

"Clothes off!" Her voice was guttural, her short-nailed hands ripping open the front tab of his shirt . . . but he was used to quick changes and was naked and wanting before she was. Leathers! He yanked on them; they didn't part.

"Clothes *off*," he ordered, swore as his fingers fumbled. No damn tabs. He broke away, gasping, jerked off her belt, pulled her tunic up over her head . . . finally found a front tab for her trous, ripped it open, shoved her leather trous and pretty pantlettes down. Her boots would have to stay on.

His hands went to her breasts and fondled as she fell onto the bedsponge. He followed, panting, then he tested her, found her ready, and he plunged.

She was hot and wet and tight and he lost himself in her, could only feel her body as her hips pumped, shooting them to the top of ecstasy and explosive release.

Then all he knew was that she was naked under him and her breasts were soft and full and her skin smooth and he struggled to stay awake, give her words. "Wonderful, lovely woman. Beautiful Del." He sucked in a breath, but sleep loomed in the back of his mind. He couldn't rest now, here, or he'd succumb.

He rolled to his side and struggled up on an elbow, forced his eyes open. Del looked shocked and humor rippled through him. Her curls stuck out, her eyes were wide and a touch wild. He liked that. He put a hand over her breast, feeling the small nub caress the center of his palm, sending a last frisson of delight through him.

She blinked and blinked again, reached up to run her thumb along his jaw. Her heart pounded under his hand, her chest rising and falling; there was a gleam of perspiration that added a glow to her skin.

He breathed her in and the spicy lavender was less than a hint of sage and some other scent he didn't quite know.

"Pinyon pine," she said, answering his thought. Then she smiled and her lashes lowered to half cover her eyes and her lips curved. "I think that's what you smell." She drew in a deep breath. "I like the fragrance of cherry myself."

"Surely you jest."

"Surely, I don't. That's what you smell of, pretty boy, hasn't anyone told you so?"

He was affronted. A leading man smelling of cherries? "No, and it's not true."

"I smell cherries, and it's not true that I am beautiful, either."

"Wrong." He shaped her breast with his fingers, the womanly softness of her, stared into her eyes that had turned a deeper green, her wide pupils. "There is so much more of beauty than the surface." He let his hands skim over her torso, rest just above her sex. "Though your surface is attractive enough . . . such a fine body. Such a pretty face, especially the dimples. I love when your dimples peek out at me."

Her eyes narrowed. "I don't have dimples."

He laughed. "Oh, yes, you do. You obviously don't spend much time in front of a mirror."

She jutted her chin, no dimples in sight. "I don't carry one with me."

He believed that. He shook his head. In his profession a mirror was always around the corner to check that his body was right, that he was looking like the character, or just to practice facial expressions, gestures, postures, whatever.

Bending down to kiss her nose, he said, "If you want to see your dimples, just look at Doolee; she's the image of you."

"She is *not*. She has Elfwort's pointy chin. I don't have that chin." Hers angled even more, so he stroked her neck.

"You might see other Family members in her face, but the Family resemblance between you is startling." Raz followed the curve of her collarbone to her shoulder, let his smile linger. "You'd admit she's a very pretty child."

With wariness, Del said, "Yes."

His smile broadened. "So you must know you're a very attractive woman."

She shrugged and he felt the firm muscles move.

He cupped her chin. "Believe me in this, Del."

She stared into his eyes and he became aware of himself, sensed how she saw him, his good features, his hair falling around his face, his own blue eyes. Sensed more than how he looked. He did *not* smell of cherries.

Del grinned. "Yes, you do. Cherry liqueur." She sat up, appeared startled at her garments caught on her boots. A laugh rolled from her as she shook her head. "We were in a hurry."

Raz took the opportunity to trace the fine dip in her spine, admire her toned back, stare at her very nice ass. "Yes, we were." He let out a satisfied sigh. "Though I didn't show my best."

"Nah, I *felt* your best." Del looked over her shoulder, eyes merry. She bent over to take care of her boots and clothing and stopped Raz's breath with the view. His mind went dizzy, but his hands reached for her. She whisked away. "Waterfall for us. Then you might as well stay here for a nap. When do you need to be at the theater?"

His brain wasn't working. "Calendarsphere," he said.

"Of course you have one. It'll get you up? How many septhours ahead of time do you go into the theater before the show?"

"One. Maybe. Meditate." All he wanted to do was see her bent over like that again, so he could take her again, ease this need again. His sex stirred.

Del had turned around. She took his hand and pulled him to his feet, glanced down, and laughed again. "Something to be said for younger lovers."

"I'm not that much younger than you."

She shrugged again.

He caught up with her, put his arm around her waist as they walked to the open door of the waterfall room. "Our age difference doesn't matter. Get that in your beautiful curly head."

She glanced up at him. "You like my hair, too?"

With a shift and a slide, she was in his arms. "I find all of you extremely attractive. Body and spirit."

Her expression was one of surprise. "You have some muscle there."

"Let me show you my favorite one again."

"Oh, yeah."

Sixteen

$\mathcal{D}$el watched Raz nap, nude. She wanted activity. She'd like more sex with Raz, but he needed to sleep for his performance later. If she couldn't have sex, she'd like a ride out of the city . . . but she wouldn't leave Raz alone to believe he was abandoned when he awoke and she was gone. Fligger.

If she couldn't get physical activity, she'd settle for mental. She went into her landscape globe workroom.

Sex—no, *making love* with Raz had been more wonderful than she'd ever imagined. Better than the erotic dreams they shared. She wanted more, and more often.

HeartMate sex. The thought shivered her nerves. She let out a long breath and set two completed globes on her "done" shelf with ten others, including her HeartGift.

HeartMate and HeartGift, realities of her life.

* * *

R*az woke, mind sharp, as always. He knew where he was . . . in* Del's bedchamber. It was dim, with closed curtains, though a shaft of sunlight came from the open sitting room door, showing that it was late in the afternoon, nearly time for him to eat if he wanted a bite before he went on stage.

He considered food or sex and figured if he was lucky he could have both. As he rose and stretched, he scanned the room. The walls were bare, though he thought they might have murals bespelled for a touch.

Experimenting, he went over to a press-point and found himself in a noisy party filled with nobles all dressed formally and elegantly— a hologram projected from all four walls. He was naked and it felt more like a nightmare to him, especially since no one paid any attention to him. Then the late, unlamented FirstFamily lord T'Yew, a stickler for manners, turned to him and said, "I respect your opinion on that, T'Elecampane." The moment was just too strange—a dead man talking to a dead man. Raz shuddered.

"I see you're up," Del said from the doorway, wiping her hands on a softleaf. She watched the mural cycle, shook her head. "My parents valued social connections." Making a face, she continued, "I've got a guy named T'Anise calling to include me in all the rituals of something called the Bloom Noble Circle." Her shoulders moved as if trying to shift a burden.

Then she glanced at him and stared. His body had reacted to her husky voice.

"Turn off the mural 'compliment,'" she said. The party winked out.

He smiled his lopsided smile, made light of the eerie disturbance that had crawled down his spine. "I don't usually attend gatherings nude."

"Or in that condition, I hope." She smiled and flung the softleaf aside. Stepping from the sitting room—that wasn't a sitting room from what he could see of a workbench—she began undressing and his mouth went dry.

She stripped with efficient movements. Light summer work tunic side tabs opened with one slip of the fingers, drawstring trous shuffled off. She was barefoot, and to his surprise her toes were tinted the rich red he'd recalled from the first night they'd met. He'd rarely seen her in sandals since, felt through their link that she didn't like open shoes, and the fact he was seeing her feet now was an additional boost to his lust.

Straif T'Blackthorn might never have seen her feet.

The stray thought was all too male, and from Del's expression, she'd caught it telepathically. She laughed, shook her head. "No, Straif never saw my feet." She paused and Raz got the impression of dark, rolling around in a tent, and regretted his stupid digression since she was thinking of another man. He strode to her and picked her up, tossed her on the bed. She spread her arms wide and laughed again, flashing those dimples.

He was beside her the next instant. She'd be open and ready for him, but he denied his lust. He wanted to explore her. So he swallowed hard and ordered the curtains open.

She reacted to that, her nipples tightening. She wouldn't have often made love in the day, would she have? And that was the last damn time he was thinking about her previous lovers. Now she was here and his.

$\mathcal{D}$el should have felt vulnerable, her body so open for Raz—for his pleasure and her own. She didn't. She felt powerful, with a buzz under her skin that sensitized it, ready for his touch.

When his fingers feathered on her, the sensation was so wonderful that she arched into his hand, her body demanding more. He touched her everywhere, his blue eyes intent, noting when she reacted, remembering it . . . telling her with fingers and mouth alone that he would please her now and every time they made love by keeping what she liked in his thoughts until his body knew her completely. Then instinct would take over.

She let her mind blur, until she heard their ragged breathing, was only conscious of his hands skimming her, shaping her breasts, sliding between her legs to pleasure her until she moaned with greedy hunger and finally reached out for him.

He grasped her wrists, held them with one hand, and only then did she realize how much larger his hands were. How much smaller her bones were. Her breath hitched with the delight of being overwhelmed, out of control in this loving.

His mouth took hers and he covered her and lay atop her and she felt the heat radiating from him, sinking into her bones until she simmered in passion. All his muscles were hard against her, and a fine tension imbued them. He was building the yearning desire until they both would be frantic for mating.

It wound tight, the heat, the longing, the need. Until she twisted under him, until she could only groan demands, until her teeth found his shoulder and she nipped and he moaned and slid into her and they stormed the heights of ecstasy together and she tumbled off the cliff of passion.

This time she was limp and Raz was revving . . . thinking of food and the performance before him. She smiled at the change in their energy. He scooped her up and took her to the waterfall and they played again. She thought it odd that he wanted to carry her around—she wasn't a small woman—but found it unexpectedly delightful.

He left the waterfall before she did, and when she walked back into her bedroom, he was nowhere to be seen. Her heart jumped in her chest at the thought of abandonment before she heard a rustling from the workroom.

When she turned, he was at the threshold, wearing only a towel around his waist. Looking great. "I couldn't resist your work, Del. Fabulous."

She joined him at the door. "Not much to see."

"The creative process, which is fascinating, like you." He kissed her.

"Would you like one?" Her pulse thumped hard throughout her body. Her HeartGift was arranged with the others. She'd put it there for contrast, since she'd made it, as usual, when she was seventeen during her second Passage to free her psi power, Flair.

Raz knew about HeartGifts, hadn't she overheard him speak of them with his previous lover? Would he recognize it?

The globe was shielded with spells—if it wasn't it would be emitting such sexuality that she would feel nothing else—and when she and Raz were in the vicinity, they'd do nothing but make love.

She'd also put a security spell on it that only she and he—her HeartMate—would see it clearly.

"I'd love a landscape globe!" His smile went brilliant, lighting his eyes.

Her chest tightened. Were there formal words involved in giving a HeartGift? If there were, she didn't know them. She waved her hand. "Take your pick." After a long steadying breath in, she said deliberately, "A gift from me to you."

Seventeen

He strolled in to study the shelves. *"You do exquisite work."* He glanced back at her. "Like most of the people who buy them, I don't *know* my perfect home. My ideal setting." He shook his head. "Not my parents' estate, T'Cherry Residence, no matter that they want all their Family close. Not my current apartment." He slanted her a look. "Have you heard of the Turquoise House, the house becoming a Residence?"

"I think so."

Pride filled his tones. "I did the *voice* for that house, even considered someday moving there." He laughed. "But I'm not so egotistical that I would enjoy living with my own voice every day." Again he shook his head. "I don't know where I really belong . . . except on stage, but that isn't truly a home. A theater is always shared, with cast and crew and audience. Even with the shades and vibrations of those who worked there in the past, and a slight anticipatory sense of those who will follow in the future." He sighed. "A home of sorts, but not *the* home."

"Um-hmm," Del said. She tried to keep her face pleasant as he stopped in front of her HeartGift.

It was larger than most of the ones she made now and set on a pretty, polished reddwood ring. Rounder, easier to see. Good stuff inside. She could barely breathe, barely hear over the rushing of blood in her head as he reached for it.

She was giving Raz her HeartGift. If he accepted it, held on to it long enough to allow his ideal home to form, she could claim him as hers. Legally. In the eyes of the entire world. She dragged in a breath.

He cradled the glass globe, stared at the bits swirling around. "Wonderful."

Glancing sideways at her, he shook it.

"It won't break." Her voice was tight. The HeartGift reflected her essence, was imbued with it. That globe would be the sturdiest she'd ever make.

He shifted his fingers until one hand was under the base and the other trailed over the glass. Then he shook his head, his expression dreamy. "A lot of very interesting items you have in here. I can't imagine how they will become a model of my perfect home."

"Flair," she forced out. A model. She blinked. She'd never thought of her globes that way. She thought of them as base and glass and tiny found objects and various liquids imbued with her creative Flair. She cleared her throat. "My Flair interacting with yours. Unique."

"Oh, yes." He raised his brows and his eyes were wickedly intent. "We are definitely unique when we interact."

Her turn to flush. "Yes. We are."

"I'll take this one." He shook his head and scanned the others. "If I were less greedy, I'd choose a smaller one. But this one calls to me."

Whew. He'd seen it, he'd picked it out, the HeartGift was his! "That's how it's supposed to happen," she said, then made a depre-cating gesture and smile. "I'd given a few to a store in Steep Springs on commission and none of them sold." She hadn't meant to ever tell that to anyone. Hadn't realized how much the idea still hurt.

"Obviously the people of Steep Springs have no taste," he said with a noble hauteur.

"Thank you."

He shook his head again and smiled down at the globe, tilted it right and left. "This is the most amazing thing."

"I'm glad you like it." She turned back into the bedroom and headed for the closet.

They dressed—Del in her most comfortable and casually elegant masculine-cut clothes—and ate a light dinner. She sensed that he expected her to come with him to the theater and watch his show again. She was amenable. When she was on the trail, she watched the same holos over time and again. Since she knew the story so well, maybe she'd examine how the actors played it. Always interesting to see masters at work.

When she'd first seen the show, she'd noticed how Lily and Raz had interacted but hadn't quite been able to separate what was real and what was show between them. Through her link with Raz, she'd sensed he had respect for Lily but wasn't attracted to her . . . or wasn't attracted now. She didn't think they'd ever been lovers. She chuckled.

"What?" asked Raz, spooning up another bite of clucker in cream sauce.

"Just that it seems my jealousy has kicked in for you . . . I don't think you and Lily Fescue were ever lovers?"

"Jealousy is a terrible emotion, but a little . . . desire for exclusivity . . . is good. I didn't like meeting T'Blackthorn in this house."

"Hmmm." She drank a sip of wine.

"I didn't like it at all, but I liked that he went home and I stayed here." He smiled. "Made me feel like I was a victor. As for Lily, no, we were never lovers." His exhalation was quiet. "I don't like to speak ill of my colleagues . . ."

". . . But I am your lover."

He nodded. "But you are my lover, and Lily is . . . not always of a positive disposition."

Del wondered what he meant by that, but just shrugged. "What do you think of the villain of your play, Rieng Galangal?"

"I think it's good for my career that he likes playing villains."

They put the tableware in the cleanser. "You're more handsome than he and have more charisma," Del said.

Raz's glance was considering. "Thank you. He has great craft and presence. I think he should broaden his range." He smiled and it was more sincere. "But I'm glad he hasn't." He glanced around. "Where's Shunuk?"

"He is scouting around fox dens for a kit for your father."

"Ah. What will we owe him?"

"FoxFams aren't like cats. Sometimes they are generous for their own satisfaction."

Raz laughed and his fingers sifted through her hair. "I thank you for the gift again, and we were very generous for our shared satisfaction today." He bent down and kissed her until her mouth warmed and her body went liquid. "You're an excellent lover, Del. Now come watch me work."

"A pleasure," she murmured.

The performance was the best Raz remembered. His Family was there, parents and his sister and her HeartMate. They were enjoying the play, though they'd seen it before. He got the idea through their Family link that they were taking their minds off the fire at the yard.

Del was there—and now he had cautiously deduced the show was so good because of the energy cycling between them. Why hadn't he heard of this phenomena before? Lovers in the house could boost you. It should have been common knowledge, but apparently it wasn't.

Anyway, he had charisma going on, the other actors responded, and the whole theater shook with the standing ovation. Raz was particularly pleased because a holo spell had been recording the show for a viz. It should sell well.

When he and the villain and Lily linked hands, the other two stared at him.

"Lady and Lord, what did you *do*, Raz?" Lily asked, keeping her brows up though he thought she wanted to frown.

"Took a new lover," he said smugly, basking in the applause, bowing left, right.

As soon as he entered his dressing room after his last—record—bow, he was informed that a guardsman wanted to see him as soon as he changed and that the secondary lounge was reserved for him and Del, and his family.

T'Spindle and Winterberry, the guardsman assigned to the First-Families, were there. The guard made it plain that all the incidents of vandalism were connected to Raz and the Cherrys and now the investigation was very official. T'Cherry—and Raz—were asked to leave any investigation in the hands of experts.

His Family went home to the securely shielded Residence and Raz wrapped an arm around Del's waist, looked down into her eyes. "Will you spend the night with me?"

Her quiet breath out was less than a sigh. "I would love to." She smiled and he had to kiss her, a tender kiss, one that only had the seed of passion. "I'd love to see your apartment."

He smiled. She wouldn't care about how he'd decorated, whether it was a good setting for him. She'd be interested in what he had there—the things he kept around him that showed her who he was. Fine with him.

"What of your house?"

She shrugged. "It will be fine."

She was obviously not attached to her home, and Raz wondered how that might feel. He'd taken care with his living space, so it would be comfortable, as well as where he could entertain—friends . . . his agent . . . he wouldn't be ashamed to invite T'Spindle there. Raz took his settings seriously. He got the impression that Del took her settings seriously when she was measuring them . . . or it was an exterior instead of an interior.

He wanted to show her his apartment and share himself with her more than he expected. More than he'd wanted to share with other lovers in a long time. "I need my keys from my dressing room."

This time she took his hand and linked fingers, and he knew that was progress. As they walked down the dim hallways shrouded with shadows, she said, "Guardsman Winterberry didn't question you as closely as I thought he would. Did you get the idea that he wasn't telling everything he knew?"

Raz's mind was jerked from romance and the image of Del on his cream-colored sheets back to mystery and the enigmatic guard. "Yes," he said. He wasn't sure whether his Family had picked up on that. "But I don't tell everything I know to T'Spindle, either. Do you tell everything you should to the FirstFamilies?"

"I only know Straif, and though I told him a lot . . . it was before he took up the title. Since then . . ." She hunched a shoulder.

"I think it's a rule: Never Tell Everything You Know To A First-Family Lord or Lady. Which is probably why they are so curious and controlling. As for Winterberry, he's an interesting character study. Such the epitome of a guard."

"He struck me that way, too," Del said. "He is a man who *is* his work."

"Like you are a cartographer," Raz said softly.

"And you are an actor."

"It's not just a job for us."

"No."

He lifted her hand to his mouth, brushed her fingers with a kiss. They descended the stairs to the backstage area in silence.

Del glanced at him. "You don't seem too concerned about being a target of thieves."

He shook his head, squeezed her hand. "That's one way to break a romantic moment."

She blinked up at him. "I didn't know we were having a romantic moment."

"Here." He picked her up and carried her down the hallway, feeling utterly masculine.

Laughing, she put her arms around his neck. "Nice." A small sigh escaped her. "Nice." Her eyelids fluttered shut. "Can relax, not handle everything. Sometimes that gets tiresome."

He kissed her brow. With amusement lacing his voice, he said,

"Dear heart, you *will* be handling something later on tonight . . . otherwise, I'll take charge."

Del lifted her lashes just enough to see Raz's strong jaw, his handsome features. Another sigh got trapped in her chest. She wouldn't think about the future, would think only about the now. The matter with Helendula was handled. Caretaking for the Elecampane HouseHeart was handled, her commitment to T'Ash for new landscape globes was being met, no problem there . . . Ah, she had misspoken about the number of FirstFamily lords and ladies she knew. She knew T'Ash, but he hadn't struck her as a FirstFamily lord. Like Straif when she'd met him, T'Ash had a tough, commoner-type manner.

Raz was the elegant noble, even when he was completely himself. He'd been raised in privileged circumstances, like she, but he hadn't rubbed those manners off; instead, he'd polished them. A contrast between them.

She had nearly sunk into a doze by the time he murmured a Word and the spellshielded door of his dressing room opened. He lowered her to a couch that smelled of new furrabeast leather. She sat up, opened her eyes to see his tender smile. "Sleepyhead," he said.

Raising her brows, she said, "I didn't get too much sleep last night . . . too aroused."

Fire lit behind his eyes. The bones of his face seemed to sharpen and his lips curved in desire. He stepped toward her, eyeing the couch. "I haven't broken this in . . ."

"Good. We won't. Get your things." She stood and wandered around his dressing room. It was larger than she'd thought, plenty of space to pace—a screen in the corner if he wanted to change when others were with him, though nudity didn't concern most Celtans. The only time it bothered her was when she was outdoors where there might be predators.

She looked around while he tidied up the dressing table that held tools of his trade and gathered a few things into a satchel. The leading lady, Lily Fescue, had kicked up a fuss with Del staying backstage before the show, so she'd spent a few minutes in the green room, reading the guest and performers book and studying the holograms of the founders. The *new* holograms done by T'Apple. Since she and Doolee would be sitting for that artist, she'd paid attention to his technique and approved. The holos had matched the old-fashioned atmosphere of the room . . . It had the feeling of being classic for the theater.

Here in Raz's dressing room, there were bare shelves and a square of pale-colored wall where something had hung. The place was emptier than she'd imagined and she was reminded once again of the burglaries.

Raz gripped the handle of the bag and joined her. He glanced at the wall. "That had a tapestry of the world."

"Really? You put it up?"

"Yes." His smile flashed, showing his even, white teeth. "Cherry Transport has always valued maps."

"Nice," she repeated and took his fingers again; she liked being physically linked to him. "What era of the world did the tapestry show?"

"Second century of colonization." His smile was self-deprecating. "Those tapestries were all the rage a decade ago, easily and, ah, inexpensively obtained. Good value for a small budget." He opened the door, closed, and spellshielded it behind them.

"Mmm. I think I might have one or two myself. You want a replacement?"

"Sure. But you don't need to give me gifts."

His words struck them at the same time and they stopped, looked at each other. His face showed more color than usual. "I didn't mean that the way . . . I'm not a gigolo. I don't take money from women."

His explanation hurt more than his first careless words. "I think you're having a problem with my age."

"No, I'm not. No, I don't." He closed his eyes, opened them, smiled a deliberately charming smile that was reflected in his eyes. Turning fully to her, he took her other hand, kept his gaze on hers.

"I am deeply attracted to you, Helena D'Elecampane. I value you as a friend. I would treasure any gift you would give me." He nibbled at her knuckles and she felt heat rising between them. His voice thickened. "As I hope you would treasure any gift I give you."

"Yes." She wanted to believe him . . . could feel he was sincere through their bond. But this was an issue she couldn't let slide. Not with her HeartMate. If he'd been a regular lover she could have ignored it or walked away. They had to thrash this out, and now.

Eighteen

The theater was full of patches of light, shades of dark deepening into black shadows. Dim. Odd, unfamiliar noises came to her ears. His world, not hers.

"I'm sorry, Raz, but—"

His grip tightened on her hands. "No. I won't let you go because of one stupidity I said aloud." His expression was stark in the silver light. "I am an *actor*."

"We agreed that you took your profession seriously, Raz," Del said mildly. "You are an excellent actor."

His muscles eased and he shifted his stance slightly, but he didn't loosen his grasp on her hands. He wanted her, and that was good. "Women have tried to buy me."

"I'm sure they have, but I wouldn't. I want your respect, Raz. I am not a woman who would buy a man."

"No, you aren't." He grimaced. "I know you aren't."

"But still you insulted me."

His jaw flexed. "A foolish moment. A defense. I apologize. Don't go away, Del."

She let the silence hang and seethe for a moment, learning the trick from him, and was that good or bad? How much would being with him change her? A question for another time. She let out a sigh. "I won't go away." She could have made light and cynical, said he was too good a lover, but that would hurt them both. Looking deep into his eyes, letting the link between them widen so she felt his self-anger, let him feel her hurt—he flinched, brought her hands to frame his face, leaned down, and kissed her on the mouth. It was a kiss of promise.

She didn't sink against him, kept herself separate. But she let her lips soften under his, let his tongue into her mouth, tasted him and let him taste her. Then she stepped back. "I won't go away." Not soon. She was beginning to think she was in trouble, her options in life narrowing. Another consideration for another time. She stroked those wonderful cheekbones. Didn't say she was falling in love with him. How easy it was to forgive him . . . because their link gave her what he was feeling.

She'd had flashes of the past from him when he'd been young and struggling and poor and a woman had wanted to buy him. A beautiful, accomplished woman and he'd been tempted . . . until he'd seen her selfishness . . . and that he'd be another accessory.

Del wound her arms around him, sent her desire for him, the caring for him that welled inside her to him through their link, kissed him. She broke it when they began to pant, and stepped back completely from his embrace, angled her head to meet his eyes, and smiled. "I'm not going away soon. But I think we need to know each other more."

His answering smile was wicked. "I agree. We should go to my apartment and work on that."

"Out of bed, too."

"Of course." He took her hand again and swung it as they walked toward the stage door. They signed out with the guard and stepped into the summer's night. They'd driven to the theater in his glider, which had been parked a couple of blocks away, but now waited, gleaming red, under the new security light.

Del did a rapid calculation as she let Raz open the door and hand her into the vehicle with the courtliness he did so well. When they'd accelerated, she said, "I anticipate giving you two more gifts."

"Cherry, on auto," Raz said and turned to Del with an anticipatory gleam in his eyes. "Two gifts."

Del nodded. "A world tapestry to replace the one you lost."

"Yes. And?"

"A surprise," she said.

"A surprise," he breathed, his voice infused with delight. Again he took her hand, kissed it. "My favorite." Then he winked. "But I will remind you that earlier we agreed I would be in charge of our entertainment for the rest of this evening . . . to let you relax and enjoy . . ." he added virtuously. "You are only expected to handle one easy thing."

Del shook her head. "Raz, you're too good."

"I know."

"But you are deluded if you think you are easy."

*His apartment was as handsome as he. There was a nice-sized main-*space that she felt he used for entertaining with light brown walls and one red wall where the windows were. All was streamlined and tidy, with less stuff than she'd imagined. A battered model of *Lugh's Spear* sat solitary on one shelf. His HeartGift wasn't here; he kept it in his dressing room at the theater.

Through an open door she saw that the bedroom was equally large and a shade darker than the mainspace, almost like a cozy cave. There was a puffy quilt and more pillows on the big bed than she had.

Then Raz distracted her as he ordered some music on and led her into a dance. She wondered why until he brought her close to his aroused body and she realized he wanted to romance and seduce her. She was in a mood to be romanced and seduced.

She let all thought siphon from her mind and reveled in physicality. Their bodies moved together and she liked the pressure of hers against his. She became aware of the underlying fragrance of his space . . . a hint of cherries, cocoa, all those sweets that didn't last long in her pack on the trail. His hands guided her in a turn and she knew he was a much better dancer than she, but it didn't matter.

With her hand around the nape of his neck, she played with the silky hairs there and his breathing went ragged, as fast and choppy as her own.

He was ready.

So was she.

He guided her to the bed and the music throbbed with the beat of her heart. Definitely making-love music. The man knew what he was doing. That didn't bother her, either; they'd both had other lovers, but he was her HeartMate—and she kept that last smug thought to herself.

Instead, she opened the link wide between them, so he *knew* what she was feeling. Her yearning for him—his body with hers—atop or under, but bare skin rubbing against bare skin. Her passion and desire for him.

She grabbed his head and pulled it down and kissed his mouth, hard, opening his lips with her tongue, and he let her in and she stroked him—with her tongue and with her hand. She knew when his mind hazed dark and red and he thought of nothing, letting lust claim him as she fed his and hers.

He muttered thickly, but the spell to undress them both didn't take and he ripped at her clothing. With a flick of her fingers, she freed him from his trous. This she understood, half-dressed, frantic coupling, the surge of sex against sex, letting desire run free and high and wide. Falling to the ground—bedsponge—rolling and panting. Hands on her breasts, stroking, sending shocks into her core, until she *must have* this man.

Then they were plunging together, rocking, clawing, zooming

up the mountainside of ecstasy, and jumping and falling and falling and shouting their release and collapsing in pure pleasure against each other. Sprawled on the bedsponge, legs tangled together, side by side.

As unsteady breath matched unsteady breath, pulse beat kept pace with pulse beat; Del opened her eyes and struggled to focus on her HeartMate. When she saw his eyes were wide and glazed, she found the energy to smile.

"Lover," she said, her voice a husky rasp.

His mouth opened but nothing came out, not one wisp of word from a master of words. A bubble of laughter rose through Del, bringing energy. They were still linked, physically and emotionally, and she kept the bond wide, pushed him back, and rolled with him until she straddled his hips, atop him, looking down. His white shirt was open in a wide V to the waistband of his black trous, and at the reddish bite on his chest, her eyebrows rose and she rubbed it. "I don't recall doing this."

He groaned, closed his eyes, whispered, "Do it again."

She wiggled her butt, got a satisfactory response from Raz. Taking his hands, she meshed fingers with him.

She bent down and licked, sucked, the skin over his collarbone and he arched under her, spearing her with pleasure. Everything inside her heated and tightened, ready for another climb to the peak again, this one long and slow. She rose and fell, testing them both, and his eyes sharpened, his stare latching on to her own. Then he deliberately rolled his eyes back in his head. "Older women are known to be able to wipe a man out."

She liked that he could laugh at himself, at the dregs of their argument, gurgled with laughter again, kissed his swollen lips with her own. "Pretty boys."

A fierceness came to his gaze. "I am not a boy." He rotated his hips precisely and orgasm roared through her, taking her breath. She gasped.

But he didn't stop, tightened his grip on her fingers. "Look at me."

Trembling, she met his eyes. Blue and wild and thrilling. He thrust again and she rode him for a minute, then her lax muscles revived and she took the rhythm from him. Their gazes locked and she saw his rising passion, knew her own pupils dilated as they moved together faster, faster.

His eyes went blurry again and she saw him fall, pushed herself a little and fell with him again, loosed his hands as her arms wrapped around him, and he held her tight, and they fell all the way into sleep together.

D*el awoke in the morning naked and tucked into Raz's bed, feeling* incredible, loose and relaxed and able to concentrate on her Heart-Mate and only her HeartMate. He was gone from the bed, and the scent of caff pervaded the apartment.

The scrybowl jangled, some ancient, bouncy Earth tune that was associated with the theater, but that she didn't know the name of. She was beginning to realize that the theater world had more ties to the past than she'd ever thought. She was usually focused on the now and the future—what was around the next bend that she could put on the next map.

Raz walked into the bedroom and handed her a mug of caff, then strolled over to the scrybowl with a grace that was a pleasure to watch. He ran his finger around the rim of the bowl. "Here, Johns."

Del recognized the name as the actor, St. Johnswort. She pulled a sheet over her breasts, but Raz didn't activate the spell that would send the image of Johns from the water in the scrybowl to hover above it as a two-way viz. Good.

Johns grunted. "Got lucky last night, eh? Meet me at the Thespian Club in a half septhour for breakfast. Got news of an . . . upcoming project."

Through their bond, Del felt Raz's excitement. "I'll be there," he said.

Del drank her caff. It burned her tongue. After she set the mug on a coaster on the wooden nightstand, she rolled from the bed-sponge and headed into the waterfall room, washing briskly and keeping her mind blank and her emotions tamped down. Raz had his life, and he'd shared a lot of it with her. She shouldn't expect to be included in everything he did. She hadn't included *him* in much, so she had no cause for complaint.

Raz joined her in the waterfall, grinning as he resoaped her body. "Good idea. We don't have much time to spare."

"We?"

His expression stilled, eyes cooled. "You don't want to see the Thespian Club, breakfast there?"

She hated feeling stupid and female, but it had to be said. "I thought you didn't want me to come."

He caught her fingers, slipped soap into them, and brought her hand to his chest. Del rubbed, he felt good. His hands feathered through her hair, he tipped her head up and kissed her on the lips, then broke away. "Del, we're going to spend time with each other, right? That means coming with me to the Thespian Club, where I often eat breakfast and stay around to talk and be with others of my ilk." He turned around. "Now scrub my back." As she did, he glanced over his shoulder at her, his eyes serious. "And that means *you* invite me to participate in activities with you. You've been the evasive one."

Happiness flooded her, but she didn't show how delighted she was. She nodded. "Fine, but I don't belong to a social club."

He shrugged. "Plenty of things to do in Druida."

They took the glider to the Thespian Club. The humidity was high today and Del could feel her hair curling tighter and shrugged. She'd look like a fuzzy dandelion. It had taken both Raz and her to mend her clothes—they both had mending spells but hers worked on lea-ther better—and both trous and shirt had tinting spells on them so now she wore an ice blue shirt and dark blue slacks. And boots with ventilation spells. Her feet wouldn't get hot, they'd be protected, and they wouldn't stink if she and Raz got naked again. All worth the price.

The Thespian Club was on a tree-lined street that would have shade all day, the building was old, well-maintained red brick. As soon as she passed through the double smoky-glass doors, the atmosphere of *theater* wrapped around her. Not quite the same as a real theater, with the addition of outsiders—audience—but all the drama and unique emanations of actors.

Hand in hand they walked through a comfortably shabby lounge to a back room. There was an unexpectedly elegant dining room, complete with white tablecloths and softleaves and fancy silverware settings . . . for actors to practice with, she understood from an idle thought of Raz's. Both for actors who came from less privileged backgrounds as well as for certain obscure plays.

The carpet was a faded red with a muted design in other colors that had once been bright.

Johns scowled when he saw her; he'd obviously expected Raz to come alone. But he rose when they approached the round table and held a chair for her. "Pleased to meet you again, GrandLady D'Elecampane."

"Thanks." Del sat. "Call me Del."

"I'm famished," Raz said, smiling at both of them as he sat. He looked up at the waiter. "I'll have the scrambled eggs with porcine strips and a flat muffin." He took Del's hand, twined fingers with hers, and set their hands on the table for all to see, including Johns. "Order something you can't get on the trail." He grinned. "Something lavish, since it's Johns' treat."

It only took a glance at the menu. "I'll have the poached eggs in sauce on a flat muffin with spinach and porcine slices."

"Raz—" Johns began, glanced at the waiter, and said, "My usual."

After the waiter strode away, without even glancing at Johns, Raz said, "One look at Del shows anyone that she can be trusted implicitly. She won't say a word about any secrets."

There was a note in his voice that snagged her. She frowned at him. "What secrets do you think I'm keeping that you're not happy about?"

"And she's very direct, doesn't play games." Raz spoke to Johns, but stared at her. "Secrets with T'Blackthorn."

Del blinked. "I don't have any secrets with Straif."

"It seemed to me that you do. I pick up nuances, Del."

She straightened her spine, sat stiffly. "Straif's son has been shown my HouseHeart since my Heir is too young to access it. I only have a house, not a Residence, but the HeartStones need tending."

Johns' eyes widened; he leaned back in his chair, as if not wanting any part of a lovers' disagreement.

Raz's turn to flush. He inclined his head, then raised her fingers to his lips and kissed them. A stream of understanding and comfort came from him, an apology, and she relaxed. He turned to Johns. "And Del is one of the most trustworthy people I know." His brows rose. "In fact, I trust her more than I do you." He flashed a grin. "Because she and I won't ever be competing for a part."

Del sniffed, shuddered. "You couldn't get me on stage." She nodded to Johns. "You're an excellent actor, too."

Johns' expression was torn between pride and wariness. He shook his head, lifted his hands. "All right, all right."

They were served their food and ate a few minutes before Johns leaned over and said, "Amberose definitely has written a new play and was circulating it, looking for interest. Lily Fescue was approached, but when she lost some pages in that theft you had at your theater, Amberose's agent was none too pleased and revoked Lily's offer."

He caught Raz's gaze and the two men stared at each other. Johns chewed and swallowed before saying, "There are two male leads. Wide-ranging emotion, good character arcs."

Raz's pulse spiked under Del's fingers.

Johns forked a couple of mouthfuls of eggs into his mouth before saying, "I've seen the script, Raz. The parts could've been written for us." He grinned. "Maybe they were, got the feeling Amberose is up to date on what's happening in the theater. A part for your villain,

Rieng Galangal, too, one where he starts out evil and is redeemed. He'll love that. This could really make us, *shoot us to the top.* We'd be good with the material."

"Yes. We'd play off each other well. Which is what I will tell Amberose's agent if he approaches me."

Sighing, Johns said, "Me, too. But if there'd been only one part . . ."

"Understood," Raz said. He glanced around the room. Johns narrowed his eyes and slid them to both sides, checking out the other diners.

Del shrugged. "No one's paying attention to our conversation."

Raz sipped his caff and said, "Did Lily say which actresses Amberose sent the script to?"

"Nah," Johns said. He poured another cup of caff and stirred sweet into it. "And I asked." He raised an eyebrow. "Lily likes me better than you. I've been smoother with her."

"She got a script before you or I did," Raz said. "Amberose must want her more." He stabbed at a porcine strip and crunched.

Johns shook his head. "Lily's a good actor but . . ."

"Yes, negative. I feel that, too. I'd much rather have Trillia and she'd jump at the chance," Raz said. "Did you wring any more information from Lily? Like who might produce? What Family? What theater?"

"No. But I think more than one is interested. Amberose's plays always sell very well. She's made actors' careers before."

"Good job, Johns."

A corner of Johns' mouth quirked. "Thanks."

"What of the story?" Del asked.

Raz chuckled and squeezed her hand, then turned back to his food. "Story's not as important as the character for us."

Del thought of Amberose and frowned. "Is it dark and grim? Amberose likes dark and grim, and that's not what I like to watch, whether she sells out or not." Especially when she was on the road, but she'd decided to minimize references to that for a while.

Johns was shaking his head. "Not dark and grim. The story has it all: mystery, twists, humor, romance." He gestured with a large hand. "I'm not good with words, but Amberose is. I was dazzled." He winked at Del. "The roughly handsome big and tough guy gets the girl." He turned to Raz. "But there is hope for the slender, elegant, smooth guy."

"I'm not slender," Raz said.

"Relatively slender," Johns said.

"Leanly muscular," Del said, and Raz grinned wickedly at her, dipped his head. "Thank you."

Pushing away his plate, Johns sighed. "Problem is, I saw Lily's copy before she gave it back, and the whole deal seems to have gone under since then." Again he waved a hand. "Various rumors about that."

"It's the artistic control thing," Raz murmured. "People might be having second thoughts."

Johns nodded. "Understand that. T'Spindle wouldn't front the gilt for it if the whole thing wasn't in his hands; nobody else I can think of, either. Wouldn't let Amberose pick the actors, even if we are perfect for it."

Raz grimaced. "Stalemate."

Nineteen

Johns shook his head. "I wouldn't let a playwright have full control if I were a producer. Not that I want to direct, like Raz here."

Del glanced at Raz. "You want to direct?"

He laughed and shook his head. "Maybe someday, but right now I want the acting and the applause."

Del thought of the trail. Clapping echoed lonely in her mind.

She remained silent and neither man seemed to notice, both talking about their craft. It was interesting to hear them dissect things in plays that she'd never noticed and she guiltily liked the occasional gossip about other actors that she knew.

For a moment she thought how it might be if she spoke with other cartographers, but her old master, the one who'd trained her, was irascible and wouldn't appreciate her dropping in on him when he could no longer be in the field. She'd learned that lesson a decade past.

There weren't that many cartographers around that she knew of, not that she professionally respected, and the ... two ... she thought of as near her equal were in the field.

"Del and I should go see more of the plays together, don't you think so, Del?" Raz said.

She yanked her attention back to the conversation. "I've seen all of them already, but it would be interesting to go with you," she said politely.

Johns roared with laughter, stood, and threw his softleaf on the table. "You come see mine again, I'll play to you."

Warmth crept up Del's neck to her cheeks. She raised her brows. "That would be interesting, too. Something new."

Circling the table, Johns bowed to her. "I'm sorry if our craft-talk made your eyes glaze over." He shrugged. "Nature of the profession, talk, talk, talk."

Del smiled and stood. "I just got lost in my own thoughts, and if I didn't want to listen to actor-speak, I shouldn't have come to the Thespian Club for breakfast, should I?"

"A wise woman," Johns said. As he straightened, he scowled. "There's that damn fox again. You should never have brought him here, Raz. I swear the staff and the others think of him as a mascot ... but he's—"

"He's Del's Fam," Raz said, at the same time Del said, "He's a moocher."

"Ah." Johns snapped his mouth closed.

"He *is* clean," Del said. "I know he looks scruffy, but he won't be bringing in any vermin. Though I suppose I should pay for any meals he's gobbled."

Shunuk yipped to those who turned to watch his progress, fluffed his tail, and trotted toward Del and the men, angling his head to check out any food left on their plates. With the unerring knowledge of all animals of those who disliked them, he came and brushed Johns' legs, leaving a nice lot of hair on his trous. Tongue lolling, he managed to attach a small string of drool, too.

Raz's laugh was cut short when Del, wincing, then frowning at her Fam, stepped up to place both hands on Johns' wide shoulders. She met the big actor's blue gray eyes. "Hold still a minute and I'll clean you up."

She glanced at Shunuk. "You were rude, apologize."

He smells very good, Shunuk said with a sulky sniff. *Irresistible. But I won't approach him again.*

"Just get it over with, will you?" asked Raz as Johns stepped closer to Del, looking down at her with a charmingly crooked smile.

I will have clucker for breakfast. Shunuk pointed his nose at Johns, and said, *You were going to insult me.* Shunuk lifted his muzzle. *But I have killed all the mice and rats around here, so I get to eat whatever I want free.*

Shunuk was making up for the past. They rarely stayed in an area for a long time, and he'd had to abandon most of his caches.

Johns shuddered under her hands and she caught a loathing for rats, a wariness of all animals, including Fams. Too bad; he was such a nice guy otherwise.

She drew in her breath and focused on the new spell Danith D'Ash had given her when she'd asked the woman to keep an eye out for a kitten for Raz. Naturally, Del hadn't cared whether she'd had hair or spit on her leathers in the wild, but it was totally different here. She concentrated on the flow of her Flair from the soles of her feet up her body, said a Word, and Johns' clothes fluttered with the cleansing. Johns made an exclamation of pleasure and Raz was there, pulling her away, putting his arm around her waist. "Good job, Del. I wonder if my sister has that spell. I've noticed cat hair on her."

"My thanks." Johns bowed again.

Shunuk had hopped up to an empty chair, and though he examined the remnants of Del's and Raz's breakfasts, he didn't move over to finish up the food.

A short fox bark came from Del's trous pocket. Since she'd seen how useful Raz's perscry was, she'd activated the experimental one

Elfwort had made for her a few years ago and put it in her pocket. "Hey, Del, you have a call," said a voice—the voice of her deceased cuz, Elfwort. She'd never update the greeting he'd inserted into it.

Reaching into her trous pocket, she took out the small scry. It was tinier and different than the one that was being sold, more like a stone disc with a little half-spherical drop of encased water atop it. Unlike Raz's iridescent turquoise one, this one shimmered a golden bronze color.

Both men's gazes fixed on it.

"What's that?" Johns breathed.

"Perscry," Del said.

Johns pulled out his. It was the regular sphere, purple with the shimmery droplet of water trapped inside.

"Was experimental," Del said, even as her perscry announced again in Elfwort's voice, "Del, incoming scry."

She answered, "Here."

The stone projected a viz that went from ceiling to floor. The location was the Guildhall clerk's office.

The men blinked. "Some perscry," Johns said and slipped his back into his belt pouch. "I've never seen one that shows life-sized."

Del shrugged. The assistant clerk of All Councils stared out at them, a gleam coming to her eyes as she saw Raz and Johns. Del didn't know whether it was from the newssheet story on her and Raz the day before or something else, but that clerk had usually been bored whenever they'd had to interact.

"We have had a request for your presence, D'Elecampane."

"Yeah? From who?"

The clerk's voice lowered. "Captain Ruis Elder on behalf of the starship *Nuada's Sword*."

"Ah." The waiter appeared with Shunuk's clucker and Del went over to cut it into respectable bites he could eat without gulping. She set the perscry on the table.

". . . As soon as possible," the clerk emphasized.

Del met Raz's eyes. "I have other plans," she said. "Maybe tomorrow."

Johns goggled at her.

"And you might give the Ship the coordinates to scry my house or me."

"It is my understanding that the Ship can only connect with true Residences." The clerk lifted her pert nose.

Now Del grimaced. "All right. But the Ship always wants me as soon as possible. Did you send it my maps?"

"Of course," the clerk huffed. "It says there are some discrepancies."

"From the last time it mapped Celta, four hundred and seven years ago? I should think so." Del began to think that she wouldn't be able to put this off. "Was Ruis civil?"

The clerk sniffed. "*Captain Elder* was very courteous."

Then Del should go see him. The Ship was probably nagging him about the maps. She sighed, turned to Raz, and smiled. "The day has clouded over, looks like it might rain. Nice time to visit the starship?"

He glanced out the large bay windows, nodded. "Perfect. But we should go soon; I have a matinee today."

She nodded. "As long as Ship doesn't rile me about my maps, it's fun . . . Ruis and his children, their Fams, the Ship itself."

Raz was smoothing his shirt. She'd bet he hadn't been on the starship since he was a child during a grovestudy trip. When it was still cursed. "When was the last time—"

"Before Ruis Elder became Captain."

She'd been right. It would be good to see Raz in such surroundings— with people she knew and was comfortable with, a great being she generally liked. Someplace she could take *him*. "Tell Ruis, Captain Elder, I'll be there within the septhour. We'll take a glider." Since Ruis Elder negated all Flair, there were only a few areas available on the Ship where a person could teleport. Most people 'ported to Landing Park then walked to the Ship.

Raz should like the place since he and his father had made models of the starships. She and Raz had plenty of differences, but this might not be one.

She didn't know whether they could overcome their differences now or if it would take years. Stupid thought, stupid doubt. Forget the negativity. She'd have to craft options for compromise. Her brows knit.

"I will inform Captain Elder." The scrystone went dark.

Heh. Shouldn't have scowled at the clerk. That woman could make trouble. Maybe Del would drop by with a landscape globe, her creative Flair was going strong. Lots of material to pick up she didn't often see . . . scraps of papyrus, city flower petals, strange little items dropped from someone's pursenal or pocket. Discarded broken bits.

She would go mad if all she did was make landscape globes for T'Ash. Creative Flair was supposed to be fun, a hobby. She'd tire of it as a profession fast.

She turned to Johns and smiled, holding out her hand. He'd made her feel comfortable, too, hadn't worn any false mask that she'd noticed. "Good meeting you again."

"My pleasure." He took her hand and bowed over it with a flourish, brushing his lips on the back. Not a hint of a tingle of attraction.

Raz grumbled beside her anyway.

"I meant it," Johns said. "I'd play to you."

"Thank you." She didn't know if that would be good for the story or not but figured he was an actor who could make it work. A man good at his profession.

He nodded and let her fingers go, glanced toward the windows in the direction of the starship, but though the Ship itself was two kilometers long, it couldn't be seen. "*Nuada's Sword*, eh?" He rocked back on his heels with a considering expression. "I haven't been there since I was a student, either. Might be good to see it again." He gestured with a broad hand. "New experience."

"Actors are curious," Del said.

"Always," Raz said.

Me, too! Shunuk snorted down a last gulp of food, leapt from his chair. *I have only been to the great starship once.*

Del grunted. "You'll have to be nice to the cats and the dog."

I can do that.

Raz nodded to Johns. "Good conversation. I'll keep you updated if I hear anything about that script."

"Me, too," Johns said. He'd retreated a little from Shunuk.

Winking at the fox, Raz tugged Del's hand. "Cherry's outside."

The temperature was cooler than when they'd entered, the air so humid Del felt dampness against her skin.

She got into the glider and Shunuk hopped onto her lap, pressed a paw so the window thinned to nothing, and stuck his nose out.

Then Raz was in the driver's seat. He pushed the bar into the console, set navigation on auto. "To *Nuada's Sword*," he ordered the glider. "What entrance, Del?"

"The north, closest to Captain Elder's office," she said.

The trip was short and pleasant and silent, broken only by the patter of occasional drizzle. Del let herself relax and snuggle with Raz until they were in Landing Park, then at the entry ramp of the great Ship itself.

"Nice glider," Captain Ruis Elder said from the wide opening of a docking bay. He was a tall man, taller than she, with chestnut colored hair and brown eyes. She'd thought him the most handsome man she knew . . . before she'd met Raz. Her HeartMate.

Captain Elder didn't come close to examine the vehicle. He was a Null, a man who suppressed Flair—both of objects and people. Del didn't mind the uncomfortable feeling of losing one of her senses much when she was with him, he was such an interesting man, but that had been when she was alone.

With her Fam and her HeartMate, the effect on her was greater and lived like an unscratchable prickling under her skin. She ignored it, saw Raz cover his own discomfort and offer his hand to Captain Elder, saying, "Raz Cherry," before she could introduce them. She shrugged. She cared little about formality, even though Elder was now in the ranks of the FirstFamilies Council.

Raz had taken his cue from her—and Shunuk who had given one courteous bark and disappeared into the Ship. Ruis had been an outcast and didn't insist on noble manners.

"Pleased to meet you, GrandSir Cherry," Ruis said. "We watch and enjoy your holograms."

Raz's brow wrinkled.

"The Ship has become adept in translating magical energy and spells into nanotech videos that I can use," Captain Elder said.

"Ah. Thank you."

Del grasped both forearms with Ruis. "Good to see you again."

Elder shook his head. "Ever since we've seen those fabulous maps, Ship has been nagging me to get you here for a consult to reconcile its own charts."

He stepped back and patted her on the shoulder, turned, and led the way to the interior. The iris door wheeled shut after them. Raz laced fingers with her.

"Greetyou, Helena D'Elecampane," the Ship said. Its voice didn't sound like just one person to Del.

"Ah, you have a composite voice," Raz said.

She should have known he'd pick up on that.

"You have a companion, D'Elecampane?" Ship asked.

As if it didn't have video and audio and already knew who Raz was.

Raz turned to a point and bowed. Following his gaze, Del noticed the camera.

Bands of rainbow light flashed through the curving metallic corridor, running up and down the tube.

"Stop that," Ruis Elder snapped. "It's rude to body scan visitors, especially since you know who the man is. You have his work transcribed in your archives." Elder sighed. "Cerasus Cherry, please meet the Ship, *Nuada's Sword*."

Raz bowed again. "A pleasure indeed." He used one of his mellow actor's voices.

"Greetyou," the Ship said, with a grudging note in its tones, then continued. "You are not of the genetic heritage of one of *my* colonists."

"No," Raz agreed easily. Del noted that he was holding his body in that casual way that meant he wasn't casual at all. "My Family is descended from colonists of *Lugh's Spear*."

A loud whispering hiss whirled through the corridors like dry and crackling autumn leaves caught in a wind scraping against buildings. "I am the last starship, the only one who survived."

"Everyone knows that, Ship," Captain Elder said, tromping with fast paces down the hallway to the area Del was most familiar with, one of the chambers where the Ship kept its maps.

"My Captain was more skillful than poor *Lugh's* was, set me down right here near the coast and river just as planned. A fine place for colonists. My sentience remained entire and grew."

"*Lugh's Spear* was less intact, more fragmented after the generations of travel at the time of landing," Raz said. "Her Captain was extremely skillful in getting her down to the planet with only one breach of the hull. And the land he chose was good, fertile, between Fish Story Lake and the Deep Blue Sea."

"The land may have been fertile, but it was weak and collapsed beneath *Lugh's Spear*, burying it within weeks of the landing. Then the location of *Lugh's Spear* was lost," Elder said.

"People have looked for it but never found it," Del murmured.

Raz sighed. "My ancestress kept a journal of her life and the landing and the trek to Druida after the cave-in of the land under *Lugh's Spear*. But the diary, too, was misplaced. That can happen over four hundred years." Now Raz was stiff.

"The Tabacin Diary!" the Ship said.

"Yes, that was her name before she adopted 'Cherry.'"

"I knew that," the Ship said.

"Of course you did," Captain Elder soothed.

"I am recalling your Family legends," Ship said.

"What?" Raz said.

"One or two were entered into my database a couple of centuries ago."

Raz swallowed. His eyebrows rose. "Really?"

"Yes. I believe I was consulted for information on your Family and *Lugh's Spear* because the journal went missing."

Raz made a noncommittal sound.

The Ship continued, "It was said the diary described the exact location of *Lugh's Spear*."

"So we were told," Raz said. His face was stiff as if he covered anger or shame on behalf of his Family. He glanced back over his shoulder the way they had come, and Del knew he was considering leaving, even though he was still curious, and the Ship had tempted him with information.

"I thought you were interested in speaking with Del about her new maps," Elder said.

"Maps, yes." The Ship was distracted by the Captain's change of topic. "My maps *must* be updated. That is of primary importance."

"As opposed to old Cherry legends," Raz murmured in Del's ear. If the Ship heard him, it ignored them. Captain Elder threw them a humorous glance over his shoulder as he rounded a bend in the corridor.

"We'll get back to that," Raz said, his brows lowering in determination.

One more thing that weighed heavy on Del, that she hadn't considered when she first went searching for her HeartMate. Raz was close to his Family.

"Maproom Two, Del," Captain Elder, now out of sight, called.

She and Raz were lagging. She because her head was throbbing with problems, Raz because he was craning to see everything.

"Maproom Two," she muttered herself, knowing that it would soon be her turn to argue with the Ship.

Twenty

Captain Elder showed them to a chamber with metallic walls. Del blinked to see all her new maps hung, the individual ones and the two huge ones that compiled the work of her last five years.

"Fabulous," Raz breathed.

"They are the best charts since the colonists have landed," Captain Elder said.

"There is a discrepancy in this map"—the Ship pulsed a green glow around it—"and one of the maps you did fifteen years ago." The one next to it was backed by a blue glow. Del strode up to the older chart and nearly winced. Her early work. A little crude.

"You're right." She traced the outline of a lake that had become larger on her newer map, touched a point. "There has been an increased flow in the river. There's an underground spring and a fault opened more." She stopped and cast her mind back to the first time she'd seen and mapped the area.

Since it was just off the road to Gael City, in a location where there were noble estates, current charts were always wanted. "I did the first map in the spring, and the second last year." Before she'd met her HeartMate and had fully mastered the 3-D holos that now projected out from her later maps like they were miniature terra-forming projects. From the corner of her eye she saw Raz studying one that she'd done lately.

"Thank you," said the Ship. "And the elevations on this chart"— the glows had faded from behind the maps she was standing before and the backlight came from one across the room—"are not congruent with the maps I have."

"Of over four centuries ago. Let's see yours." She waited until the wall turned into a screen and a map was projected on it. The thing was fuzzy and colored oddly. "From space?"

"Yes," the Ship answered.

She waved a finger. "Move it fifty degrees west." The ship did and Del saw the blue green curve of the planet. A little more green than she recalled seeing from charts made by the Ship. The wrong color. "Ship, is this a viz *you* made?"

The Ship hummed. "Accessing data." There was a short silence, and it said in a slightly higher mass voice, "My memory of the origin of the chart is not available."

"Very agitating time," Captain Elder soothed. "Entering a planetary atmosphere after centuries, with physical deterioration of all Ships, and the unfamiliarity and excitement of the crew."

"Discovery Day," Raz murmured. "Such an eventful day would tax any being to keep track of every little detail."

The Captain smiled at him. "Exactly."

Del nodded, rocked a little, heel to toe. "Ship, show me the entry path and planetary circling of *Arianrhod's Wheel*. That data should be recorded as a greater priority to you and may still be in your memory."

The chart shrunk until it was a full planet, rotating, a streak of bright yellow appeared.

"Now show your trajectory and *Lugh's Spear's*."

Bright blue showed as the well-known path of *Nuada's Sword* circling the planet, landing where it was now, on the edge of the continent, the western boundary of Druida City. Then a bright green streak appeared, circled, and landed between Fish Story Lake and the Deep Blue Sea.

"*Lugh's Spear*." Raz's breath sighed out. "Could we find exactly where it landed and was lost from this?" He'd gone tense with excitement beside Del.

"The data has deteriorated over the centuries," the Ship admitted.

Del said, "The landing streak is wide, too wide to figure out an exact location, I think. And the margin of error—"

"Is too great," the Ship said. "I never knew the accuracy of these trajectories. Nor the accuracy of *Lugh's Spear* and *Arianrhod's Wheel*'s measuring instruments. Also their comm systems may have distorted the data."

"All the ships were relaying information to each other," Captain Elder said. He laid a hand on the wall. "Massively busy time."

"Yeah," Del said.

Raz came behind her until his body brushed hers and took her mind off charts and maps and planets and the exciting and significant event of Discovery Day. Her body pulsed with longing. She was becoming used to him, to sex—loving.

He set his left hand on her waist and reached out with his right to trace the touchdown of *Lugh's Spear*, the ship in which his forebears had arrived. "Captain Hoku of *Lugh's Spear* fought to make a good landing in a good area. Panic among much of the great crew. Calmness on the bridge. The set down rougher than he'd thought. The ship breaks. Atmosphere pours in. So does glorious sunlight." His finger stroked the end smear of *Lugh's Spear*'s trajectory.

Del turned in his arms. "That's from your Family stories?"

He blinked, shook his head, lips curving. "Yes."

"Good stories," Captain Elder said.

"We don't have that one in our databanks," Ship fretted. "It must be from the lost diary. We would like to hear everything you recall of such stories. No one ever tells me everything. Humans keep secrets. Then they die with them."

"A cheerful thought," Captain Ruis said.

"Both *Lugh's Spear* and *Arianrhod's Wheel* had casualties. I had none." The walls around them rang with the pride in Ship's voice.

Captain Elder winced, then touched the end point of the green path. "*Arianrhod's Wheel* broke in more than one place when it landed in what became Chinju, was cannibalized later." Again he touched the wall of his sentient home.

"It had not developed intelligence," the Ship said, and all three humans sighed again.

"We don't have many here in Druida City that arrived on *Arianrhod's Wheel*," Captain Elder said.

Nuada's Sword continued, "They were more skilled craftspeople, only a couple were of the FirstFamilies who financed the colonization. That ship was the least well built. *I* was and am the one who developed intelligence during the voyage. I carried most of the First-Families, and the DNA of Earthan animal and plant life. *Arianrhod's Wheel* had the best libraries of Earthan crafts and technology."

"And *Lugh's Spear*?" asked Captain Elder.

"*Lugh's Spear* carried the most information regarding the type of psi powers of the original colonists, both those in the cryogenics tubes and that which the crew developed during our long flight."

"What treasures we would find on *Lugh's Spear*!" Raz said.

"It would make the discoverer wealthy beyond all imagination," Captain Elder said.

He'd know. He and *Nuada's Sword* had become incredibly rich since he'd become the Captain.

"We were talking about my maps and discrepancies." Del reeled them back on topic. She tapped the first yellow path. "See, it's *Arianrhod's Wheel* that had the trajectory to feed you the information about that first map we discussed."

"Very well," the Ship said.

"That all the discrepancies you have?" she asked the Ship.

"Yes," the Ship answered, but she got the feeling that *this* sentient starship was brooding on the blanks in its memory.

Raz cleared his throat. "Ah, *Nuada's Sword*?"

"Yes, Cerasus Cherry?"

Raz shifted even closer and Del knew it was because he was nervous . . . and she gave him comfort. Nice. "My father and I share a hobby of making miniature models of yourself, *Lugh's Spear*, and *Arianrhod's Wheel*. It's occurred to me that the plans and specifications we have may not be correct. Is it possible—"

"You *do?*" the Ship said.

"Yes."

"Models. Plans. Another thing we could market . . ." Captain Elder said.

"I will give you our plans as you wish. In what proportions?"

"Ah, I will have my father, T'Cherry, contact you," Raz said.

"Done," *Nuada's Sword* said.

Raz said, "And you might want to check the specs at the Guildhall to make sure there aren't any discrepancies there. And, ah, I'd like to take a tour with my father . . ."

"Visitors are always welcome. I authorize Captain Elder to show you all my restricted places."

"Thank you," Raz said and bowed to the camera. Once again he'd noticed it sooner than Del. She was more interested in the feel of Raz against her than history, no matter how exciting Discovery Day had been.

"In return for your Cherry stories," Ship added.

Raz laughed. "We'll do that. I'll tell him to think about the stories."

"You might ask your sister, too," Del said.

"She's younger than I am."

"You, an actor, should know that different people remember different things, can learn differently"—she gestured around them—"express themselves differently."

This time Captain Elder gave a little cough and looked at her.

"Yes?"

"You make those landscape globes, right?" he said.

"Yes." And once again she became aware of the lack of Flair around her. She'd been able to ignore it.

"Could I buy one for my wife's Nameday? She can keep it at her offices in JudgementGrove."

"I'll be glad to give you one"—she made a half bow—"for all your help here."

He snorted. "My duty, to interface between Ship and the rest of Celta."

"Ah, Ship and Captain Elder?" Raz said. "It occurs to me that you might want to know there is a revival of the play *Heart and Sword* in Gael City. Do you have contacts there?"

"I want a viz of it!" the Ship said.

"The Ship is very noble in that play," Captain Elder said.

"As are Captain Bountry and Fern Bountry."

The present Captain shrugged. "The Ship's technological connections with Flair don't work as far as Gael City."

"My friend is playing Fern Bountry—" Raz said.

"We could travel down and viz it for you," Del said. She'd been wanting to get away with Raz, and more than once. "The Cherrys' express airship takes only a few hours."

But Raz stepped away from her, his face impassive. Dammit! She'd moved too fast—had been moving slower than she'd liked and now had pressed too far too fast. It had been easier when her mind and emotions had been more focused on Helendula.

She took her own pace or two away from Raz. No use letting him think that she would pursue him if he ran. Not only did she have her pride, but she was trying to be subtle.

So she shrugged through her hurt, put a calm expression on her face. They'd been together a lot over the last couple of days and she wanted more, especially time alone with him. Yearned for that. Too bad.

She smiled at Captain Elder, dipped her head. "I'll work on that landscape globe for you."

When she turned to Raz—who had his hands in his pockets—she

said, "I know you have a matinee performance. You need to get home and change, or to the theater." He liked to meditate before a performance on that couch of his. She'd already ordered a world tapestry delivered to the theater that morning, so it would be there when he walked into his dressing room. That would remind him of her. She didn't know if that was good or bad right now, whether it would push him away or not. "Shunuk and I will run home," she said.

"It's raining," Captain Elder said. "But there's a public teleportation pad in a gazebo in Landing Park."

Del shrugged again, shifted. "A little rain won't hurt us. We're used to it on the trail." May as well not watch her tongue around Raz since he'd withdrawn for her. She'd remind herself who she was and what her future plans—to map the world—were. But she stepped up to her HeartMate and kissed him on the mouth, only feathering her tongue along his lips.

She stepped back. *Shunuk,* she called mentally, then recalled where she was. No Flair worked here; she shifted mindsets. "Ship, can you ask my Fam, Shunuk, to meet me at the south entrance?"

"I could," Ship said, "but he is here."

There was a bark and the door slid open. Shunuk trotted in, his muzzle stretched in a grin. She knew that smile. He'd been fed well. Again. "Let's go home," she said and winced inwardly. The estate wasn't her home. She'd always considered the trail her home, had been fine with that.

"I'll see you soon." She smiled at Raz, let it become a real, sexy smile, as if she still didn't have a pang in her heart. Just a hot-affair–type of smile between lovers.

Then she turned to Captain Elder again, nodded. "I'll see you soon, too."

"We'll do dinner sometime this week?"

"Sure. Have your wife send a message to my cache. Later, Ship."

"Thank you for coming," Ship said. "I will notify you if I find any more discrepancies."

"I'm sure you will." She strode from the room without another look at Raz.

Shunuk followed, but his eyes narrowed. Del figured he was trying to tell her something mentally but couldn't. Finally he huffed and kept up with her pace down the long straight metal corridor. He stopped at a branching corridor that would lead to the eastern entrance and wagged his tail.

"South entrance, running home."

The fox sat and yipped. Decidedly.

"You're getting too citified," she said. "Maybe even plump."

That didn't move him. He just pointed his nose in the direction of the eastern entrance and Landing Park and the teleportation pad that would be there.

"It's not more than five or six kilometers to home," she said, and again the word *home* nearly stopped her, seemed to echo in the metal hall.

Shunuk barked, deeper, then headed down the hallway, turning his head back to see if she followed.

With a puff of breath, Del went after him, though she needed good exercise, some thinking time, and not at "home," a place that didn't appeal to her.

When the round iris-opening door expanded, she saw the rain beating down. Her half-formed plan of a ride vanished. No use taking a stridebeast out in this, let alone a horse, making them as miserable as—no, she wasn't miserable. She just needed to think on things.

Shunuk shot away, angling through the rain to a small gazebo that held a teleportation pad. No one was there. No one was in the entire park, not even in the other structures. City people. A little rain put them off all sorts of pleasures.

Del's imagination flashed a scene of her and Raz rolling around in bed while listening to the patter of raindrops. She put it aside and inhaled deeply. Less conglomeration of Flair here . . . but still very lush and green. A pretty park she could appreciate, even during the gray day and as the steady rain became sheets.

The fox stood on the top step of the shelter and shook himself, flicked his tail at her. *Fam Woman?* he said mentally.

Yes?

We are not riding in the pretty red glider?

No.

Her Fam was wise enough to say nothing more about the glider or Raz.

"I think I'd like some hot clucker and noodle soup when we get home," Del said.

Me, too.

She walked to the gazebo, stepped on the teleportation pad, picked Shunuk up, and visualized the empty house that was not a home.

A bad time to realize she already loved Raz.

*R*az *watched as Del walked from the room, a little shock shimmering* in his nerves.

She'd mentioned going away and he'd balked. His feet had removed him from her even as his hands ached to keep touching her.

He was torn. He wanted her, but everything was moving fast and more intensely than he'd anticipated.

"When would you and your father want to tour the Ship?" asked Ruis loudly.

Raz turned smoothly to face the man. "How about Midweek, MidEveningBell. That's when we work on the models."

"Ship, did you make the appointment?" Captain Elder asked.

"Yes. We will see you then," Ship said.

Raz and the Captain bowed farewell at the same time. Raz noticed the man's manner was cooler toward him now that Del wasn't present.

"Merry meet," Raz said.

The Captain's eyes warmed a little. "And merry part," he gave the traditional response.

"And merry meet again," Raz said. He kept his spine and shoulders straight. He was the lower one in status here, but he wouldn't fawn, even though the Ship and the Captain impressed him. The Captain nodded and turned in the opposite direction, toward what Raz deduced was his own rooms, and Raz could only wonder what they looked like. A curiosity that might not be satisfied without Del's—or his father's—presence.

Raz walked through the Ship to the bay door through which he and Del and her Fam had entered. He missed Del's hand in his. To Raz's surprise, his glider had been brought into the Ship.

Absently, he told Cherry to return home, then shifted in his seat. He was uncomfortable with himself and his reaction to Del.

She'd put on a little mask. Had dropped one over her features after he'd instinctively stepped away.

He didn't like that.

He'd hurt her, and he liked that even less.

But *he* had been completely honest and open . . . even as he was hurting her. A grumble escaped him and he tunneled his fingers through his hair. They'd been open and honest, then he'd hurt her and she'd had to cover her feelings.

Yes, their affair was getting intense. Far more intense than anticipated.

Then she'd mentioned the trail, and his stomach had clenched. She hadn't spoken of leaving Druida City for a while, and though he didn't want her to go, it was also a reason why he could be so honest with her. Because the time of the affair was limited.

He was torn about that, too.

She'd said she couldn't live in Druida City and he knew that to be true. The restrictions on her, the expectations for the single head of a noble household, would stifle her, erode what he loved—liked—best about her.

His career was in the city. That was the only way he could become what he wanted—a famous actor whom people would pay to see, whom they'd talk about. Who would continue to work at what he did best, at what fulfilled him most.

As being on the trail fulfilled Del.

He snarled at the thought. Too damn conflicted.

*S*ince it didn't seem like she'd be exercising outside, Del took herself down to the HouseHeart to soak in the hot spring and brood.

Walking or running or riding kept the broods away and she rarely gave in to them, but now she would actually have to think and plan. Maybe even strategize.

The HouseHeart soothed her, as it was meant to. There was little of her parents here, more of Aunt Inula and even Doolee. Del sighed as she sat on the underwater bench, let the spring bubble around her.

A year ago Del would have assessed the situation and left Raz alone to build his career, gone off to continue her own. Wouldn't have stayed in the city for an eightday.

She was the last Elecampane. That had knocked one of the stable supports out from under her. She had always known that the other side of the Family was solid and procreating and would continue the name and traditions.

Doolee had presented another problem, making Del change her life to accommodate someone else. Now Doolee was a beloved part of Del's life that she couldn't walk away from.

She was a different person than a few short weeks ago. Looking back, she didn't think it was wise to crawl back into that brittle cocoon of self-sufficiency. Much as she hated to admit it, she *had* been on her way to becoming a frontier woman uncaring of much other than her own passions.

She had wanted Raz as a partner but hadn't been interested in compromising. If he'd been another cartographer, or a tracker like Straif, or someone who had a solitary path of an outdoor career— even a landscaper or gardener, they might have made do. But Raz was Raz, charming, gregarious, outgoing, opposite her.

Honest, caring, determinedly striving in his career, like her.

If she hadn't stayed and gotten to know him, she might have

been satisfied with occasional HeartMate sex dreams. Since she had, she wanted the man. The question was what she'd have to do to keep him and whether she could compromise enough to do that.

He'd have to compromise, too. She *couldn't* stay in Druida. The city would drive her mad in a couple of months. That was the main crux of their problem, would be the breaking point. But Raz's compromising wasn't something she could control, so she dismissed it. Worry about that later.

T'Anise had continued to call and pressure her to meet with the Bloom Noble group, especially since she hadn't attended Full Twin-moons last week. He'd chided her and mentioned her parents again. There seemed to be a social event every other day, usually at his antique shop, which she figured was old and musty. She shuddered; she wouldn't be caught in that web.

Thinking of her parents and their determination to raise the status of the Elecampane Family had her remembering their advice as they plotted the next step up in the social ladder. "Give him what he wants and he will give me what I want," was a favorite saying of theirs.

She only hoped she could give Raz enough.

Twenty-one

*W*hat *did* R*az want? She'd discovered a few things. He wanted a* kitten Fam, and Del was pretty sure that a mongrel would be more loved by him than a purebred—and what did that say about his feelings for her? That he preferred the unique? Something else they had in common.

She'd already arranged that the next time a commoner litter of Fam kittens was brought to Danith D'Ash, Del would get one. She'd taken a cut in her commission with T'Ash for the landscape globes, but gilt would never be a problem. She'd finally totaled up everything, including the massive amount of income from each individual scrystone sold due to Elfwort's genius, and she had enough wealth to fund the Family forever.

What else did Raz want?

He wanted to star in Amberose's new play. That was evident from this morning's discussion with Johns at the Thespian Club.

Johns wanted that, too, and so would Trillia. If Del produced the play and hired the actors that Raz respected and liked to work with, he might be more amenable to moving from Druida.

Bring them out of Druida, to some other place. But where? Even Gael City felt too big to Del. Maybe she could manage the outskirts of the town. She didn't know. But not Druida.

This Amberose thing was key to pleasing him. The playwright wanted to choose the actors and director. Raz and Johns thought they and Trillia were right for the play, but they didn't like Lily Fescue.

Despite being in the heated water, Del's neck muscles had tensed, a headache tightened like a band around her temples. Too much maneuvering. There were too many pieces of this particular puzzle to fit into a good map right now. Needed more exploration and knowledge. Let it lie and take it step-by-step.

All she wanted was to be a partner with her HeartMate.

But she had no idea if Raz wanted more than a hot, brief affair. In Druida.

She gritted her teeth then deliberately relaxed and let her mind drift, directed the bubbles to loosen her knotted muscles. As she settled, she instinctively *reached* for her HeartMate, found the connection between them had widened from yarn width to strong, thick rope.

He was meditating, too. In a semi-trance before he went to work, stepping out on stage to practice the profession he loved.

She would take that away from him.

No.

Compromise. She would ask him to leave the audiences of Druida. Find a base where she could practice her craft and he would be satisfied with his. Though the thought of leaving him for long treks in the wilderness didn't appeal.

She'd tensed up again, so let out a steady breath. She had changed. He could, too. Naturally.

Being HeartMates would do that, she hoped. He would want to be with her more than . . . Her mouth twisted. More than be on stage in Druida?

He was concentrating on his part and dissipating the negativity that Lily Fescue had smudged on him with some sort of argument. Some actor thing that mattered to him but would never affect Del except as it impacted him.

She probed his emotions lightly, hoping to find out how he'd felt when he'd walked into his dressing room and had seen her gift. Her world tapestry was more colorful than his beige and gold and green one had been. He liked it. In fact, now that she'd pushed his thoughts in that direction, he smiled and she felt affectionate warmth from him.

Then his calendarsphere chimed, announcing that it was time for him to don his costume.

So Del withdrew and hauled her wrinkled self from the pool, waved a hand to circulate the water and rid it of any city dust. With another Word she closed the glass cover, walked on it to make sure it was safe for the children.

The scrybowl in the HouseHeart tinkled. Even though Del *knew* it couldn't be Raz, she glanced over—to see Straif T'Blackthorn's colors. They had a bond between them, too, a present bond of Family due to the child they loved.

Darkening the background and draping a bath sheet around her, Del answered. "Here. What?"

"Charming," Straif said. He was grinning.

Del huffed.

He said, "I've set up an appointment with T'Apple to meet with you and Doolee for your holo painting. Here at—"

"No, not at T'Blackthorn Residence."

Straif scowled. "T'Blackthorn Residence is one of the most beautiful places on the planet."

"Sure, but it isn't Elecampane land. I want it here."

"Have you really looked around your house? All white and gold . . . not flattering to your or Doolee's coloring, I might add."

Del's jaw flexed. He was right. "Here or not at all." She perked up. "Maybe we should cancel—"

"No. We are not canceling the professional, artistic holo painting of you and Doolee. I insist," Straif said.

"Then it will be here. In my map room or workroom or—"

"You really want a young child in a place where you work?"

Maybe not. She couldn't hold Doolee all the time. That would be rough on both of them. "I'll find someplace. Outside, the gardens maybe."

"It's raining now, could rain again."

"I have a gazebo. More than one. A pool house. Something. When did you say the appointment was?"

"He can fit you in today, MidAfternoonBell."

"All right."

"I'll be there with Doolee and T'Apple."

"Fine."

Straif stared at her a minute, then finally said, "I hope everything resolves well for you, Del."

She did, too, but she only inclined her head. "Merry meet."

"And merry part," Straif replied.

"And merry meet again," Del ended.

As she dried, she thought of the invitations that had been coming her way, sighed again, and lowered the energy to the candle in the room. Time for her to haul her sorry butt out of the HouseHeart and put on party clothes. Having a great amount of gilt was like bait on a fish hook and would bring people to her, such as Amberose's agent. But she had to drop the line.

*D*el wasn't in the audience. During one of his short breaks off stage, Raz searched for her mentally. They had a nice, strong bond between them and that worried him. But it irritated less than the fact she wasn't here, that he'd taken a step away and she'd taken three.

Then he caught a swatch of her thoughts and knew she was at some noble garden tea party. After a rapid review of social events, he recalled there was a charity fund-raiser for additional beautification of the old Downwind section of town.

He smiled. Del had agreed to map Downwind, and she did

believe in nature. She hadn't told him that she had planned on attending. Or had she decided to go after their mutual withdrawal? He couldn't see it; Del was more of a loner than anyone he'd ever met. It must have been a big step for her to ask him to go on a trip with her.

A simple overnight getaway out of Druida. The city got on her nerves, and it was hot and muggy at this time of year.

The stage manager poked him in the back and he started, knew he was a second late for his cue. Lily glared at him from on stage and he cursed under his breath. He'd made two errors in the last week. Nearly unacceptable, no matter that he'd performed the best ever in the last couple of eightdays.

The rest of the performance went well enough. After the standard number of curtain calls, they trailed backstage, Lily scolding him all the way. He winced and tried to ignore her by escaping to his dressing room across the hall, shutting the door.

Only to find that his sister was sitting on his couch with tears running down her face.

Raz's gut jolted. He went to her and took her hands, sank into the couch next to her. "Seratina, what's wrong?"

She gulped and hiccupped. "Our Gael City house." Her lips quivered. "It was robbed, too. Torn apart. We just heard."

She hugged him hard.

The door opened and his parents and Seratina's husband entered. His mother carried a loudly purring Fam kitten.

Raz's dressing room was now crowded. He stroked Seratina's back and met his father's serious eyes.

"One of us needs to get down to the house in Gael City," T'Cherry, Raz's father, said.

A burn of irritation started in Raz's head, flowed under his skin. He knew what was coming.

His sister's hands clamped around his shoulders as she sobbed. "I . . . I don't think I could . . ." She shuddered, took a breath. "I don't think I could face it."

She wasn't lying or acting. She'd always liked that house best.

Had lived there until their mother had asked her and her husband to move in, Seratina to take over more of the business.

T'Cherry's jaw clenched as he stared at Raz. "I'm in the middle of delicate negotiations with old Eryngo for one of his runs." He glanced at the women, squared his shoulders. "I can—"

Angry at this whole mess, Raz disentangled himself from Seratina and stood, letting her husband take his place. Raz squared off against his parents. "Just because I am an actor doesn't mean that my work ethic is less flexible. I do ten performances a week, including weekends. It *is* the weekend and I just came off stage, am expected to be back on tonight."

"We know that, Raz," his mother soothed. She thrust the kitten into his hands, and he began to stroke the little feline.

"My career and *business* is no less important to me than Cherry Transport."

His father jerked his head in a nod, pivoted to leave the room. "I'll contact Eryngo." He bit off the words.

"No," Raz said. "I hate being put in this position, but I can do it." He let his jaw flex, sent the negative energy—from Lily's sniping and this whole mess—through his body to dissipate in the floor. He felt the loss of the energy, his soles grew hot, the down payment on this trip that could be expensive. "I have an understudy," he said, resigned.

The kitten licked his thumb. *Thank you. FamWoman sad. Doesn't want to go.*

That was the truth. He looked at his sister, who was sniffling into a softleaf, leaning against her husband—her HeartMate. Her eyes were red and swollen with tears.

It occurred to him that Del would never fuss like Lily had over a minor glitch in her work, would never ask anyone to take care of a problem for her, like his sister.

But Del had had a harder life.

He looked at his mother. Her arm tucked in his father's, she watched him with a smile on her lips but concern in her gaze. She could, of course, go and take care of everything, but she preferred to stay with his father and work as his partner. She'd be entertaining Eryngo; the negotiations were probably taking place at T'Cherry Residence, and that was her province.

Now Raz could see Del in his mother, standing with her partner through everything, able to ask anyone else to solve a problem if it meant he was spared worry.

"A Family matter." His exhale became a sigh, but his throat tightened with love as he looked at them all. His sister and her HeartMate linked, his parents a unit, the kitten snuggled in his hands. He was a part of them.

Del was alone, almost defiantly alone, with no one to solve any problems she might not wish to shoulder.

Then his father moved forward, hugged him. "Thank you, Raz. I know what you're giving up for us."

Of course he didn't. His father knew very little about how the theater worked.

"I shouldn't suffer," Raz said.

He thought of the Ship, who wanted a viz of *Heart and Sword*, thought of seeing Trillia again. Thought of taking Del with him. She'd like that, she'd already said so.

"Thank you, Raz." His sister blinked and stood, hand in hand with her husband, who nodded with relief. He was estranged from his Family in Gael City but fit in well with the Cherrys.

There were all sorts of Family permutations in the world. Raz *did* cherish his, especially with his father's thick arm lying across his shoulders in easy pride.

His mother came and slipped her arms around his waist, leaned against him, and she was the softness and the scent that meant "love" for all of his life.

Family. They could be maddening, but they were worth it.

A knock came on his door. "Come," Raz said, and the stage manager walked in, frowning. Behind him was the guard, Winterberry, who was handling the investigation into the thefts and the fire at the yard.

Twenty-two

Everyone in the room stiffened. Raz's father transformed into T'Cherry, equal in status to Winterberry.

"We received notification of the theft and vandalism of your Gael City estate," Winterberry said.

"What do you need to know?" Raz's father asked. He glanced at the stage manager. "Sorry to tell you that right now, Raz is the only one who can be spared of the Family to take care of this matter. With the express—"

"I don't anticipate being gone long," Raz informed the man, handing the kitten back to his mother who joined his father. "Overnight."

The stage manager's brow creased. "Might be good if you took a couple of days. If you're going soon . . ."

"Today, I'm afraid," Raz said.

"Take the entire weekend. The day after that we're dark, that should give you plenty of time."

"Yes, I'll also be arranging for the show *Heart and Sword* to be vized for the starship, *Nuada's Sword*," Raz said.

The manager rubbed his hands. "That play hasn't been staged here for nearly a decade. T'Spindle might consider a revival. Might be a good amount of interest." He stared at Raz. "If it's doing well in Gael City."

"I can check that out for you."

The manager looked around the room full of people. "I'll inform your understudy, then. He and Lily might need work."

Raz's frown matched the manager's. Lily wouldn't like that, another thing he'd pay for when he returned.

With a last nod, the manager left.

People had shifted. His sister and her HeartMate were back on the sofa, along with his mother, the kitten snoozing in his sister's lap.

T'Cherry stood facing Winterberry. "Any update?"

The guard glanced at Raz, then took the stool before the mirrors, swiveled on it to face them.

"Our investigation is progressing. A known ex-Downwind petty thief has recently left Druida. After he came into some gilt." A smile flickered across the guard's face. "He bought a seat on a luxury airship to Gael City."

"You told that to the Gael City guards?" Raz's father asked.

Winterberry nodded. "They have his description. He's not as well known there, and we don't think he's conversant with the town. He may stand out. Make a mistake." Winterberry met Raz's father's eyes. "Though I believe he was hired for the job and is not the principal in this matter. He might not know anything even if we do catch him."

Raz's father nodded. "Understood."

"And we still don't know what the thieves might be after. Have you had any additional ideas?"

Lips thin, T'Cherry shook his head. "No."

Winterberry studied Raz. "You're an observant man. Examine your home carefully, see if you can deduce what the thieves want."

"He's not a guardsman," Raz's father barked. His jaw flexed, a mannerism Raz had gotten and used off stage, instinctively, and deliberately while performing. "Not a trained investigator. What have *you* found out?"

Winterberry raised his brows. "Since I was assigned this case yesterday?"

T'Cherry flushed but his chin went pugnacious. "It's been twenty days since the burglary and vandalism of Raz's apartment."

Raz's mother leaned her head on her HeartMate's upper arm. T'Cherry sucked in a breath and sifted it out, his voice became lower, steadier. "The more you can tell us, the more we might be able to help. The more Raz can use his observational skills at our southern house to give you information."

Winterberry inclined his head, stood with a fluid grace that matched Raz's own. "We know that other than the valuables, the main items that have been taken or destroyed are papyrus and holos. The worst destruction was to the model of *Nuada's Sword* and Raz's tapestry map."

"You're sure?" Raz and his parents asked together. T'Cherry continued, "You believe that's significant?"

"Yes," Winterberry said, staring at the new tapestry hanging over Raz's couch.

"A gift from Del Elecampane," Raz said. He wanted to scry her, now, invite her on the trip with him. Would she refuse?

"GrandLady Helena D'Elecampane was in Mombeij when the first theft occurred, in Steep Springs at the end of that week, then Gael City, and here in Druida the day of the theater thefts."

"You checked up on *Del*!" Raz clenched his fists.

"Of course," Winterberry said. "But given she was talking to a Guildhall clerk when we believe the destruction and thefts occurred here, she is not a suspect."

Raz just stared. With his mouth open.

Winterberry lifted and dropped a shoulder. "She came into your life nearly at the same time this string of events began."

"Del is the most honest woman I know." Raz bit off his words.

"Not to mention incredibly wealthy," Raz's mother said.

Winterberry bowed to her, said softly, "We don't think this is about gilt. Whoever is behind this situation wants something else. Something gilt can't buy." The guard shifted his gaze to Raz's father. "What would you have sold those old maps in your yard office for?"

T'Cherry straightened to his full height. His shoulders seemed to broaden. "I wouldn't have sold them at all."

"For any price, because they are Family heirlooms and you don't need the gilt," Winterberry said.

"That's right."

Raz's sister cleared her throat and rose from the couch. Her husband, holding her hand, stood with her. They walked to join Raz's parents, matching gazes with the guard. "You think all this"— she gestured at the room—"is because someone wanted—wants—a Family heirloom?"

"We—" started Winterberry.

"Not 'we,' guardsman. *You, Winterberry.* The guard assigned to the FirstFamilies."

It seemed to Raz as if a sigh was trapped in the man's chest, but Winterberry answered, not dropping his gaze. "Yes, I do." He glanced around at the room, the empty shelves. "The item least damaged was the model of the starship, *Lugh's Spear.*"

Raz and his father winced, exchanged a glance. "Still looks pretty bad to me," T'Cherry said.

A notion struck Raz like a bolt, made his mind fizz with static, settle into a new pattern. "The Tabacin Diary."

"What?" Winterberry asked sharply, his sensorball glowing as it recorded.

"I was at *Nuada's Sword* today. The Ship mentioned the Tabacin Diary."

"Which is?" Winterberry asked.

"Lost." Raz's mother wrapped her arms around his father. "Lost for generations."

"A journal of our first ancestress," his sister said, "before she chose the name 'Cherry,' her name was Tabacin." His sister's brow wrinkled. "She was a member of the crew of *Lugh's Spear*, born on the Ship, but made the trek from where *Lugh's Spear* landed to here, Druida City. They say she kept a journal of the trip, and before—of Discovery Day and the landing."

"They say she recorded where *Lugh's Spear* might be," T'Cherry said in a strong voice.

"The lost starship," Winterberry murmured. "The location unknown, but Flair and technology has developed sufficiently that we might be able to uncover the starship now."

"Others have searched for it. No one has found it," Raz said.

"What a treasure," Raz's brother-in-law breathed. His eyes had glazed.

"The diary is *gone!*" His mother's voice was shrill. T'Cherry hugged her. His sister handed his mother the limply sleeping kitten.

"That's right," Raz's father said. "It's gone. Misplaced or lost or even stolen a long time ago. We don't have it and don't know where it is." His face hardened. "Am I gonna have to shout that to the newssheets?"

"I doubt if they would believe you," Winterberry said. "Whoever might be searching for the journal probably doesn't believe that your Family could have lost such an important item." Winterberry glanced at Raz. "And you've become involved with a noted explorer and the best cartographer on the planet."

Raz's father winced. "Does look bad. But we don't have the book. Winterberry, you tell the FirstFamilies of this, all your colleagues. I'll set the rumors going around my set." His father looked at Raz. "My son can get the word out to the theater people and everyone who associates with them." T'Cherry sighed. "That's all we can do."

"I'm afraid so," Winterberry said.

"Raz, you check the southern estate for any missing documents, holos, papyrus." His father shrugged heavily.

"I'll do that." Raz kept his own voice soft, but he was heating again from inner fury. All this destruction for an object they didn't even have! He wondered if he could get his hands on the villain.

"I'll authorize gilt for damage repairs," his father said. He glanced at his timer. "The next express airship to Gael City is a ten-seater luxury one and takes six septhours. It leaves in a septhour and a half. Can you be on it?"

"Yes," Raz said.

T'Cherry squeezed his wife. "Long day already. Let's go."

"Yes." Raz's mother sighed and handed the kitten to his brother-in-law.

His father nodded to Raz. "Scry after you examine the place."

"I will."

Cocking his head at the suppressed anger in Raz's tone, his father said, "Let the guardsmen do their jobs. That's why the Councils pay them." With forced casualness, T'Cherry continued, "You might want to come back by glider. Pretty two-day trip to share with someone." After a last glance to the guard, his parents exited the room.

With his easy stride, Winterberry went to the door. "Please keep me informed."

"Please keep *us* informed," Raz's sister shot back. She jutted her chin. "My parents and me and my husband and Raz."

"I'll do that. Like GrandLord Cherry says, let us run this case. We *are* the experts." Then the guard was gone, too.

His sister shivered then took a step from her husband and offered both hands to Raz. Her face had crumpled into sadness.

He took her palms; they were damp from perspiration or wiping tears from her face.

She sniffed then said, "Thank you for going down and taking care of this mess for us, Raz. You're the best brother."

"I'm your only brother."

She buried her head in his chest and he patted her on the back.

"I really couldn't face going there. Maybe never again if it's too awful." Her words hitched. "Could you . . . could you . . ." Tears were back in her voice. "Look for my dolls," she whispered. "See if they were . . . hurt." She swallowed hard. "Bring back those you can . . ."

Both he and her husband flinched, shared an angry look. They didn't like her unhappy.

"I will," he promised as he patted her again, knew her Heart-Mate would soothe her later.

She shivered, released her hold, and took a pace back. Her husband's arm came around her. They were all a very demonstrative Family. Raz liked that.

Setting her chin, she caught Raz's gaze, managed a faint smile. "Are you whisking Del Elecampane away with you for a romantic retreat?"

He nearly flinched. *Del* had wanted time away and he'd retreated from her. But he pasted a lopsided smile on his face and answered, "I hope so."

"Good." She hesitated, shook her head, then swooped in for a wet kiss on his cheek. "See you later."

"Yes, later."

As soon as the door closed behind them, he pulled out his perscry.

*A*t the garden party, Del thanked her hostess and drifted from the room no more than a quarter septhour after she had obtained the information she'd wanted. She'd had a "casual" conversation in a secluded corner of the garden with Amberose's agent.

Amberose wanted full creative control of the production of her play. She wanted to name the actors and the director and choose the theater.

Del had a throbbing headache from the very thought of all the things she would have to do to give Amberose what she wanted so she would give Del what she wanted. Right now she'd made noises

to the agent that she was considering "getting into the theater business." She might even have to buy a theater. She couldn't believe it.
What would she do with a theater in Druida?

She was still determined not to stay in the city. She'd picked up
a cold three times, gone to a Healer to zap it three times. She'd had
no health problems traveling outside the City. There were too many
people here.

Del hadn't caved in to the agent. She was the one with the gilt,
after all, and she'd sensed that he wanted to make his commission.
She also got the vague feeling that the usual major players had turned
Amberose down. Del could play a waiting game. She *had* named
Raz, Johns, Galangal, and Trillia as actors she respected. She'd muttered something about Lily Fescue's negativity and watched the
agent blink as he absorbed that.

Before she'd left the party, she'd glanced to see who else might be
talking to the man. Nobody. That was a plus. Maybe.

Del had enough irritation energy to teleport home but believed
she wasn't getting her gilt's worth from the monthly hire of the
glider and asked the chauffeur to pick her up. She was standing on
the cool portico looking at the rain, her skin prickling at the chill
breeze that whisked through, when her perscry barked.

Bringing the small stone from her moderate sleeve pocket, she
said, "Here."

The holo expanded until she saw a shabby office, with a full-
length GreatLady Danith D'Ash standing wearing a wide grin. The
woman held up a small kitten. The Fam was pudgy with baby fat,
but Del could tell that it would be a solid, stocky cat. She liked its
colors: primarily a bluish gray with mottled black and lighter gray
mixed in. The young cat had a white mask around its yellow eyes.

Del smiled and felt her muscles easing.

Danith D'Ash said, "What do you think? Zanth, T'Ash's Fam,
just brought her in and dropped her on my feet. I'm sure she is his
get, but he just grunted when I asked. So only half a pedigree." The
woman nuzzled the kitten. "She's so soft."

"Looks perfect to me," Del said.

"She's healthy," D'Ash said.

A black glider pulled up to the portico and the chauffeur came out and opened Del's door. "I'll be right there," she said and signed off, hurrying through the rain to the vehicle. Sliding over the seat, she picked up a clump of fox hair before it attached itself to her clothes. Shunuk sat in the corner, tongue lolling.

"To T'Ash Residence, Danith D'Ash's office," Del told the driver.

He nodded and they pulled away smoothly.

Shunuk yipped and huddled against the opposite door.

"Not for you," Del said. Shunuk had gotten a cold, too, and been taken to D'Ash to get zapped. He hadn't liked it, something about his nose being scoured and compromising his sense of smell.

"D'Ash has a kitten for Raz." Del continued to smile and leaned back against the furrabeast leather seats. Her third gift for the man. Not that she'd give it to him now. He'd pulled back from her, so she had withdrawn. From hurt and pride, but it was good strategy. He retreats, she puts even more distance between them. She might even have to walk away.

She just realized that she could do that. She'd *hate* it, but the connection between them was strong, and she trusted that bond. They were HeartMates; he wouldn't forget her.

Shunuk sidled over, sniffed at her new silkeen gown. *Nice smell.*

Yes. She smoothed the fabric. *Silk from Chinju.*

Farther smell than we've ever been.

That's true, too. Del sighed. At one time she'd thought she'd sail to Chinju, work on that continent where the decedents of *Arianrhod's Wheel* had settled. Now her future was different.

Previous visualizations had been of herself traveling and surveying and mapping, then her and Shunuk. An image couldn't form when she tried to include Raz . . . or Doolee.

Del jerked a shrug. As she changed, so would her goals and her trail . . . her life's journey.

Twenty-three

The moment they arrived at D'Ash's office Shunuk hurried to investigate the Fam adoption rooms, apparently sensing another fox. From what he'd said, *Maybe Raz would like a pretty fox more than a stupid kitten*, Del figured the fox was female, a vixen.

Del's lingering hurt at Raz's rejection had decreased. She'd taken steps to win her man by setting wheels in motion with Amberose. If Del hadn't been on her way to pick up Raz's pet, she'd head out again, just her and Shunuk, into the country for some relief. Find a nice rustic place to stay with trails into the hills or a long beach to walk . . . somewhere she could hunker down and regain her balance.

But when she held the grayish-blue and white and black mottled kitten in her hands, she wondered about taking such a young life away from the city. It was so soft, hardly overflowed the palms of her hands placed together.

It blinked up with big yellow eyes, perfect for Raz in all its variety.

Yawning and showing a very pink tongue, it said mentally, *I am a SHE and not an it.*

Del sent a startled look at D'Ash.

That woman nodded and chuckled. "Yes, I heard her, too. Fams are becoming stronger in Flair all the time. More people than just HeartMates can easily hear Fam companions. They broadcast better."

I want FOOD! the little one shouted and both women laughed. Del stroked the round belly with her thumbs. "How often does she need to be fed?" Del knew little about young of any kind.

"Every two septhours." D'Ash beamed.

Del flinched.

D'Ash took the kitten from Del and placed the young cat on a counter with a small saucer of milk. The tiny cat lapped at it enthusiastically, splashing her whiskers white. The scene tugged at Del's heart.

"As long as you leave some fresh-spelled milk out for her, she can feed herself," D'Ash said.

Didn't sound as if Del should take her into the wilds, though. "How curious is she?"

"She's been all over the Residence," D'Ash said proudly.

Del stared at the kitten. Her tail twitched in a fearless manner, but the baby would be an easy snack for any animal out there.

Yet, the more Del thought, the more she wanted to get away from town. Smell non-city smells, walk through tangled hedges . . . an idea came. There was a small inn near the Great Labyrinth. Lately the place was becoming more popular. Nobles who showcased their Families with offerings were taking care of the great meditation crater more, especially the younger generation of FirstFamilies who were beginning to make themselves felt in powerful circles.

Talk was that if you wanted to look at the powerful and important, a trip to the Great Labyrinth might snag you a sight or two. Or if you wanted to catch a GreatLord or GreatLady to ask a favor, that might happen, too.

Del studied GreatLady D'Ash. "You said that Fams are increasing in Flair . . ."

D'Ash laughed. "Not only Fams. We're seeing increased Flair in Earthan descended animals and hybrids, like housefluffs of rabbits and mocyns—"

"People, too," Del said.

D'Ash nodded. "People, too. No one can argue that the prophet Vinni T'Vine has incredible Flair, or young Avellana Hazel." D'Ash shuddered.

Del eyed her. She'd heard strange, hushed rumors about seven-year-old Avellana Hazel, but at the look on D'Ash's face, decided it wouldn't be wise to pursue them. Del sure didn't want to become addicted to noble gossip like her parents. She was curious, and it was hard not to press, but she continued with her point. "It's easier for people to teleport in one jump to and from Druida City to the Great Labyrinth, isn't it?"

Appearing surprised, D'Ash nodded again. "Yes. Some nobles usually teleport into the center of the Great Labyrinth if they don't want to walk in. *No one* can teleport from the center of the crater to the rim, it's bespelled forever that way. Walking fast—not meditating—with no stops, the path takes at least a septhour around and up the crater. But from the city to the site in one teleportation jump . . ." Her brows knit. "Yes, I think I could do it."

"You are a noble GreatLady."

"I was born a commoner, but do have GrandLady status by my own Flair. I could probably 'port there. My HeartMate, T'Ash, could, of course."

"All of the FirstFamily nobles."

"Probably."

"And GrandHouse-level Flaired nobles."

D'Ash said, "Maybe. I'm sure you could, D'Elecampane."

Del grunted. "Prefer to ride. Never know when you might need the energy to teleport out of danger, and take your mount and Fam with you."

"Good point." D'Ash's expression showed her high approval. "*Have* you teleported yourself and your mount and Shunuk out of danger?"

"A time or two. Left me nearly unconscious and flat on my back." That was literally true; she winced as she recalled landing on sharp stones poking at her back and her butt. Good thing she'd been wearing her best and newly bespelled leathers.

Finishing her quick meal, the kitten circled herself in a ball and fell asleep. Del couldn't help herself, she picked up the little cat. The kitten gave a sleepy burp and purred. Del crooked her arm and set her in the corner of her elbow.

"So, I bet the up-and-coming middle class who are gaining more Flair will be able to teleport to the Great Labyrinth soon," Del said.

"Maybe. I don't think I'll be telling my friend Trif Winterberry about that, though."

Del smiled. "She'd try?"

"Oh, yes, and she's pregnant. It isn't wise to teleport when you're pregnant, not even newly pregnant, you know."

Del didn't, didn't care to. She shrugged, stroked the kitten's ear, smiled at D'Ash. "I think that the Great Labyrinth will become more crowded. You might tell your HeartMate that the FirstFamilies Council should consider limiting access."

"Oh, no!"

Del gave D'Ash a hard look. "Not to nobles, but to the amount of people allowed in during a day."

"It's a meditation center for *all.*"

"We don't want it to be a dusty labyrinth path for all."

"The bowl is filling up with more and more shrine offerings. You have one, don't you?" D'Ash said.

The Elecampanes had made a shrine after they'd channeled their Flair to scrying. "We have an arbor and a trio of birdbaths that can be used as scrybowls within the labyrinth. Outside scrys don't work in there."

The medium-sized pet door flapped in and out as Shunuk trotted

in. His head was high and he radiated displeasure. Uh-oh. Felt like
he'd been rejected, too. Del examined him. His fur was sleeker,
he'd put on a little weight so he didn't look scrawny. His color was
uneven, but she thought he looked fine.

Shunuk sniffed. *Is that our new kit?*

Obviously the vixen had not thought he looked fine.

"Yes, the kitten for Del's HeartMate, Cerasus Cherry," D'Ash
said smugly.

Del hadn't told D'Ash that.

D'Ash slanted her a glance and said, "My best friend is Mitchella
Clover D'Blackthorn, Straif's wife, Doolee's mother." D'Ash gave a
relieved sigh. "Thank you for letting them keep Doolee; they love
her very much."

What had Del gotten herself into? She'd known, of course, that
there were circles and allies and cliques and what all among the
nobles, the FirstFamilies. But her parents had been interested in that,
not she.

Shunuk had jumped on a table close to Del so he could snuffle at
the sleeping kitten. She awoke and hissed, swiped at his nose. Then
sat straight up on Del's arm, eyes narrowed. *Fox breath BAD.*

Shunuk growled but turned his head aside. He squinted at the kitten, gave insult for insult. *Cat has little muzzle, hardly pointed at all.*

That was true, though the kitten didn't have as squashed a face
as some cats Del had seen.

My nose is nice, Shunuk said.

Del wondered if the vixen had said something about Shunuk's
muzzle. Looked good to her, but who knew fox standards?

"I guess you didn't get on with Alapex," D'Ash said.

Grunting, Shunuk said, *Born and bred in Druida City. Not
for me.*

Del had had the idea that he wanted a city vixen as a mate.
The hard feelings of rejection would wear down, especially if they
crammed their lives with new events and other emotions. "Yes, this
is the new kit. We'll be keeping her with us for a few days." Until
Del got over *her* hurt. "I thought tomorrow morning we could ride

north to the Great Labyrinth and spend a couple of days there."
Through the weekend and the first day of the week when the theater
was dark, leave Raz on his own, though she would sure miss the
loving—physical and emotional.

OUT of Druida! The kitten gasped. It wriggled with excitement
and curiosity.

"The Great Labyrinth is safe enough. Bespelled not to allow
dangerous animals. But countryside, not city, and fun to explore . . .
for all of us." Del glanced at D'Ash, the expert.

The GreatLady tilted her head, examining Del. "You really aren't
a city woman, are you? You won't be staying in Druida."

"No." Del tried not to snap the word.

D'Ash opened her mouth, closed it, nodded. Del thought she'd
stopped herself from commenting on Raz. Then D'Ash raised her
hands, palms out. "Go with my blessing. Exploring the Great Labyrinth sounds wonderful; usually people just walk the meditation
path." Her mouth quirked. "I don't think there's any schematic plan,
any, ah, map of the Great Labyrinth. Where each Family's shrine is.
That might be good to have."

Work. Del slanted her a look, but the woman appeared innocent.

D'Ash rubbed her chin. "Hmmm. I think T'Ash would pay for a
good three-dimensional rendering. Maybe Mitchella could market it
as a decorating item or a meditation tool, a small table-sized three-
dimensional model of the Great Labyrinth. *I* would buy one. T'Ash
might do so, too. Maybe a huge landscape globe of it."

Del's mind boggled at the thought of forcing a landscape globe
into a certain shape with her own Flair. The very thought made her
head hurt—and the word *model* made her insides ache since she
associated it with Raz and starship models.

Maybe she could do a three-dimensional colorful holo of the
place, but for a real, solid sculpture . . . that would be something she
and Raz could cooperate on . . . "Someday, maybe."

D'Ash walked with them as they left the small room and went
through her offices to her separate entrance. "Yes, I would pay good
gilt for something like that—a holo or a sculpture or a landscape

globe of the Great Labyrinth. At the very least, I'd bet the Guildhall would like a plan."

"Maybe," Del said.

"Probably lots of nooks and crannies most don't know about," D'Ash said, waving them out with a cheerful smile. "Sounds fun." Then she drew herself up to her full, small height and grinned wider. "Though everyone knows that the center of the Great Labyrinth is T'Ash's Family's World Tree."

Bye, Danith, the kitten warbled mentally to D'Ash. *We go, go, GO!* They all faced forward and walked to the waiting glider, slid onto the back bench.

Del's pocket hummed, then Elfwort's voice said, "Hey, Del, you have a call."

This time Raz was scrying.

"To D'Elecampane house," Del told the driver as she carefully slid into the seat while holding the kitten. Shunuk had leapt in before them.

Aren't you going to answer? Shunuk asked.

"Vixens or men, city folk are city folk," Del grumbled.

I am city folk, the kitten said. She peered at the perscry in Del's hand, nosed it, then batted it. *I am here!*

Del snatched the glass stone as it went tumbling. She grimaced when Raz appeared in holo, standing in the glider, at least most of him: she couldn't see his feet.

Did she catch an expression of relief on his face before he offered one of his charming smiles? Maybe so.

He lifted and dropped a shoulder. "Looks like I'll be going to Gael City after all."

There was a hint of trouble in his eyes, but Del didn't ask. Not her place to ask about his private business, if she wanted to be stubborn about her moods, and she did. Now he wanted her company. Huh. "Have a good trip."

He grimaced, then offered an appealing face. "Del, wouldn't you come with me? Reconsider?"

"I've planned a different outing," she said.

He huffed a breath. "I'm sorry. I apologize for this morning."

Del blinked. She'd heard a man apologize. But Raz was an actor and flexible enough to do something he didn't like to get what he wanted. Not flexible in his honor—his father had raised him strictly enough about that, she figured. But she couldn't see T'Cherry apologizing much.

Raz's smile turned rueful, an expression she particularly liked. He'd know that. "I said something I regret this morning."

She wondered how long it had taken for him to regret that he'd rejected her invitation, growing closer to her. She had no illusions. He might have regretted his action and tried later to smooth it over, but some new circumstance had him going to Gael City instead of taking time off from work to be with her. Earlier he'd chosen his career instead of their relationship. The safe and known passion.

"Haven't you said or done something you regretted, Del?"

There would be few things more important to him than his career. "What happened?"

He frowned and she groped for words. "Trouble shows in your eyes . . . and anger." She wouldn't mention that she was aware of it in their bond now she was thinking again instead of concentrating on her own emotions. "Another break-in? Does your Family have an estate near Gael City?"

"You're very quick." His smile faded as his gaze pierced her.

She hunched a shoulder. "Just logic." Now she was faced with a choice. She wanted to soothe him, but her pride got in the way. Fear, too. She loved the man and he didn't love her.

Yet.

But he wouldn't be learning to love her if she didn't spend time with him. "You hurt my feelings when you refused my invitation."

Wincing, he said, "That wasn't well done of me."

Meaning that he would have tried to have been more suave about turning her down.

"Del, come with me," he said softly and it seemed to echo words he'd said in bed and her insides melted.

She frowned. "Your third present was delivered early. I suppose I should give it to you. Might have kept it for myself."

Curiosity lit his eyes.

Shunuk turned to the kitten. *Del speaks an untruth. Humans do that. We would not have kept you. I am her Fam.*

The kitten snapped out and bit Shunuk's leg. He howled.

The driver flinched. "D'Elecampane?"

Del grabbed the kitten around her plump middle and put her on the other side of herself, glared at Shunuk.

"What was that?" Raz asked. His gaze had been flatteringly on her face.

Del gave up—yielded to her own yearning to be with him, to the prospect of wondrous loving, to giving the new little troublemaker away. Though if she had her choice, they'd all be part of a Family.

A new Family. It was coalescing around her without her realizing until this minute. Her smile at Raz was shaken when she answered him. "Yes, I'll go with you to Gael City."

I will go with him to Gael City, too, Shunuk said.

An adventure to a new place, FUN! said the kitten.

"We leave in a septhour and a quarter. I'll pick you up there after I pack. Shortly." His eyes turned tender. "Thank you, Del."

Del's face froze. "No. I can't."

Anger flashed across his face. "Are you playing games with me, Del? Getting your own back?"

"Stup," she said. "I don't play games, city bo—man. I have another appointment I must keep this evening." She made a face. "Straif is coming over with Doolee and T'Apple for our first holo sitting."

Raz huffed a breath. "I keep underestimating your honesty."

"Yeah, and that's not a compliment from a lover."

Now his expression was a mixture of sincere emotions, heat at the "lover" as if he'd recalled times in bed, annoyance at her irritation. He inclined his head. "I apologize again. My father made the arrangements, let me contact him and see what else Cherry Transport has on its schedule for Gael City." Brief surprise showed in Raz's eyes. "I don't know the schedule by heart anymore," he murmured, then said louder and with a little bow, "I'll make arrangements for the trip, and we will be staying at Cherry House in Gael City."

Shunuk stuck his head in the viewing area.

"He's going, too," Del said.

"Thank you, Shunuk," Raz said. "I'll get back to you. May I come over as soon as I've packed?"

Del hesitated. Straif, a FirstFamily lord who knew Raz was her HeartMate, would study him. Doolee, the child she wanted to spend more time with—both the little girl and Raz would distract Del from interacting well with each of them. All under the very observant eyes of an older, master artist who was also a FirstFamily lord. This was getting far too messy for her.

So don't consider every angle, go with the simple, what her gut wanted. "Yes, you can come on over."

"I'll see you soon," Raz said.

Twenty-four

Raz spoke with his father and got seats on a commoner-class airship flight to Gael City that would take seven and a half septhours. He was disappointed; he'd wanted to give Del the best. He'd make sure the glider drive back would be special.

He'd had to work harder than he'd anticipated to get Del to accompany him to Gael City. He supposed that was good for him—women had always tended to fall into his bed—but it ruffled his pride. But Del wasn't a city woman, a sophisticated woman who prized the arts and preferred to take lovers from that milieu.

Lover. She'd used the word, he liked the word, and it stirred him up to hear her say it. Despite their retreat today, they were still lovers. Intensely lovers.

He studied a jacket and put it aside, too trendy for the smaller burg. Packing was taking too long, he was too conscious of his clothes and the image he wanted to project to Del.

She probably threw in a few leather suits and a dress for the theater, gave nothing else any more thought.

But as honest as he wanted their relationship to be, he wanted to show himself in a good light, too. Clothes that fit, that were appropriate for Gael City and the theater . . . that was important. Trillia was excited he was coming. The other actors would be judging him, as would everyone connected with *Heart and Sword*—the producers, the manager. It never paid to be discourteous or sloppy in his business.

When he drove up the gliderway, Shunuk met him. An air of impatience surrounded the fox. *They are all in the playhouse.*

"Playhouse," Raz said, thinking of an amateur theater or an amphitheater.

Shunuk snorted, sent Raz a detailed mental image of a miniature pink house with fussy castle facade, and a little girl. Ah. Playhouse. His sister had had one.

He followed Shunuk down a neglected path. The playhouse was a small cottage and old enough to have seen many generations of young Elecampanes. "Is there a tree house?" Raz asked, thinking of his own past . . . and how his sister had preferred the tree house, too.

Shunuk gave him a disbelieving look. *I don't know. Lots of people here. All watching each other. Boring.*

"Ah, you're ready to go on the trip."

The fox glanced aside. *Get out of the city for a while.* He stopped a moment and groomed his whiskers with his paw. *Vixens will appreciate me more when I come back.*

"Female problems," Raz said sympathetically.

Shunuk slid him a sly look. *Mating is important.*

Mating. That idea sent a jolt through Raz, but then a high, piercing shriek of glee hit his eardrums. He heard music and grinned as he walked to the open door of the playhouse.

Jazz beat at the walls, and Del and Doolee were dancing. Del was shuffling to the beat, Doolee was hopping up and down. Both laughed. The afternoon sun highlighted their golden curls, shadowed the dimples in their cheeks.

"It's going to be one of those kinds of 'sittings,'" murmured an older man as his hand moved rapidly over papyrus, sketching with a drawstick. With just a few strokes he captured the vitality of the two. The great T'Apple whose hololight paintings cost the same as an elegant mansion.

Raz swallowed; he'd met the man a couple of times, but not enough to claim an acquaintanceship. "What kind of sittings?"

T'Apple looked up at him with a quick and beautiful smile. "Exactly. I think they might sit still for maybe five minutes. If I'm lucky."

Clearing his throat, Raz said, "That was my assessment."

"Straif T'Blackthorn," T'Apple muttered. "*He* didn't tell me it would be this sort of commission. Drawing on the run, both them and me. I'm getting too old for this."

He was Raz's MotherSire's age, tall and elegant, with a head of white hair and turquoise eyes. "I doubt it," Raz said. He chuckled, said something he always hated hearing from others. "Think of it as a challenge."

"Ha."

The music ended and both females fell onto the thick and faded carpet the color of dirt. Del hooted with laughter, then her squeals matched the child's as Doolee climbed over her.

A wide smile on his face, Straif T'Blackthorn drifted over, thumbs tucked into his belt. "Absolutely must have a holo painting of them."

"Get a viz camera," muttered T'Apple.

"Think of it as a challenge," Straif T'Blackthorn said.

Raz and T'Apple shared a glance. Those who didn't practice the arts didn't understand the work that made something perfect look simple or effortless.

With an innocent expression, T'Apple answered, "Perhaps you should carve them—likenesses of all your children for your HeartMate."

Raz's brows rose. "You sculpt?" he asked Straif.

Straif frowned. "I whittle."

T'Apple stuck the drawstick behind his ear, clapped Straif on the shoulder. "Your creative talent is strong." He glanced at Raz. "And you are one of the best in your profession."

"Thank you."

The older man went on, "Yes, Straif, I should drop a word in Mitchella's ear about your whittling miniatures of your child—"

Straif raised his hands. "No. Please."

"Then you should have considered how easy these two would be to capture in a holo painting."

Both Del and Doolee were up and consulting about the next music selection. Del was jiggling the little girl in her arms and Doolee was wiggling.

Raz's throat tightened. The child looked enough like Del to be her own, and he'd never seen her face so soft with tenderness.

Still grumbling, T'Apple flipped pages on his pad, grabbed his drawstick, and began again. "How do you expect—"

"This is only a preliminary meeting," Straif said. He winked at Raz. "You don't need to work today, T'Apple."

"Ha." He continued making rapid sketches. Del's face stared out at Raz from the sheet, then a rounded one beside hers, Doolee's. For some reason he saw differences on the papyrus where he'd only noted likeness before.

Straif peered at the pad. "She's going to be a beauty."

"She already is," Raz said.

Both men stared at him.

Raz met their gazes with an impassive one of his own.

"Da, da, da!" Doolee broke the moment by toddling over to Straif, who picked her up.

With a wicked smile, T'Apple sketched the two of them. Straif frowned. "I'm not paying you for one of me."

"No, but your wife will. You should have a Family portrait."

Raz became aware that the music was a low and throbbing ballad. Instinctively he crossed to Del, took her in his arms, led her into the slow dance.

She looked up at him and her eyes had deepened into a darker green and all that mattered was that they moved together.

They danced for a few minutes until Doolee yelled, "Del, Del. Me. Me!"

Raz realized Straif had been "dancing" with Doolee and she wanted to switch partners. Del's laugh roared and she stepped away from Raz, turning to the little girl. Who held out her arms to Raz.

Plucking her from Straif's arms, Del smiled down at the child a moment. "He's a handsome one, isn't he? Raz Cherry."

"Wwwwzzzz. Ch. Ch. Ch!" Doolee said, fluttering her lashes at him.

He took her, not recalling the last time he'd held a child in his arms. His sister when they were both young, maybe. None of his friends had children. Most of his friends were unmarried actors.

Doolee gave his cheek a wet kiss. "Mmmm," he said, and though he was amused, he'd wanted to finish his dance with Del.

He spun in a quick dance step, around and around, good training, knowing that Straif T'Blackthorn couldn't match him in those steps.

Doolee shouted with delight.

When he returned the girl to Straif, T'Apple was checking his wrist timer. "I have to go." He nodded to Raz and Straif, rubbed Doolee's plump cheek, bowed to Del. "It was a fascinating experience." His eyes glinted. "I accept the commission. I consider it a challenge."

Del flushed, shifted, lifted her chin. "We're active."

"I can see that." He glanced around the playhouse.

Del offered her hand. "Thank you. Great meeting you."

T'Apple shook her hand. "I can fit in another 'sitting' next week." He raised his brows at Doolee hopping up and down. "And perhaps you and Doolee can actually sit."

Del's dimples creased as she smiled. "We can try."

"Good. Merry meet."

"And merry part," Del and Straif and Raz replied. Doolee said, "Mmmmp."

"And merry meet again," T'Apple said. He tucked his supplies away in a satchel and stepped outside. The man's presence was such that Raz felt it when he teleported away.

At that moment the tinkle of a child's tune sounded. "Scy!" Doolee yelled and shot toward a scrybowl on a chest in a dim corner.

Del frowned and strode behind her. "I didn't know there was a scrybowl here."

"H-h-hr," Doolee said as she touched the bowl.

"Ah, GrandLady D'Elecampane, at last!" Then the man sputtered, his ruddy jowls quivered as he bridled. Del sighed and picked up Doolee. She stared down at the bowl. Raz joined her.

"Greetyou, T'Anise," Del said expressionlessly.

He beamed at her, then at Raz. "Greetyou, GrandLady D'Elecampane, GrandSir Cherry." The man's face vanished as he bowed. "I would like to invite you to a social event tomorrow night at the Antiquarian Club so we can discuss the agenda for the next New Twinmoons ritual."

"I'm going out of town," Del said. "I don't know when I'll be back. I'll let you know when I'm available—"

"The Bloom Noble Circle needs you. As a noble you have a responsibility to this city and planet—"

"I've always fulfilled the terms for my NobleGilt, so I'm a responsible noble. I'll be in touch when I'm available." Del flicked a finger on the scrybowl water. Her body was tense.

"I've heard they do good work," Straif said neutrally. He came over to take Doolee, who was sputtering at the scrybowl.

"I'll be out of town for a few days," Del repeated.

Raz tucked her fingers around his arm. "We're going to Gael City."

Straif looked serious. "I'm sorry for your troubles."

"We'll get through them," Raz said.

"Yes," Straif said. He kissed Del on her cheek and Raz didn't like the casual gesture, even from a man with a HeartMate. Doolee gave Del several smacks. "Bye!"

"Fare well." Del brushed a hand through the child's locks, kissed her back.

"Bye!" Doolee grinned at Raz and he kissed her, too. She smelled like child and city and . . . Blackthorn. He didn't say so.

"Good-bye," Raz said.

"Take care," Straif said, looking at Raz, who knew he'd be held accountable if anything happened to Del.

R_az was back. Here on her estate, for her. Del's whole being had shivered in delight when she'd seen him. No break of their relationship. This time. The misstep she'd made in her wooing had only cost her a few septhours of misery. Enough to tell her that if this affair didn't transform into a HeartBond soon, she would be aching for a long time.

Before she tried again.

Take the trail for years, maybe.

But that hadn't happened, and perhaps it wouldn't, if she was careful. Though she was damn tired of being careful. She was glad when everyone else left . . . even Shunuk, taking a last tally of his food caches before they left Druida.

There should have been awkwardness, but there wasn't. They'd managed to get over a disagreement with one brief scry, and she wasn't even good at this. Amazing.

Raz scanned the place. "Interesting."

Del chuckled. The playhouse had one large room, a little no-time area, and tiny toilet closet. Old furniture, much of it child-sized, was pushed up against the walls. The walls themselves were covered with drawings in various tints against a creamy background, none that would give T'Apple any competition. There were maps. Her maps, both imaginary and real, one was a rough drawing of the estate, with the dark block of the house. "I think Doolee likes it here."

"It's a good playhouse for a girl," he said.

She turned and stared. He shrugged. "I always liked tree houses better."

"Tree houses," she said, watching him. "You know, all sorts of things can drop down on you from tree branches."

"So? You _do_ sleep under trees in the wild, don't you?"

"I have a good tent," she said.

He chuckled and rubbed his cheek against her head.

They sat on a twoseat and had about two minutes of peace before Shunuk barked and a mew came as did a small mental kitten-voice. *Me, Me, ME! Time for Me to be a surprise. I am in the box, now.*

"What was that?" Raz asked, tilting his ear, probably also sensing something through their link.

Del stood. "Time for your third present, before we leave."

His eyes lit. "Something good for the trip?"

She smiled, hoping it was mysterious. "I've always found one good on the trail."

Shunuk hummed appreciation in her mind.

Not much quiet time for her and Raz today. Maybe there never would be. He was outgoing, his energy high when he was around people. Now they both had Fams, and if they became a Family . . . four individuals. Much noise.

Shunuk ran through the open door and hopped onto the large rounded arm of the twoseat, his tongue out and happy anticipation in his eyes.

Del went into the small room that held the no-time cabinet. Atop it was a white box about four times the size needed for the kitten, wrapped with a big red bow, the kitten's choice. There were large air holes in the bottom.

I am ready! the kitten prompted.

With one last big breath, Del picked up the box. She was sure Raz would love the kitten, but Familiars and humans should be matched and . . . Danith D'Ash had known the kitten would be for Raz. Mind simmering with a trace of anxiety, Del took the box in. Shunuk nudged Raz with his muzzle. *You will like this.*

Well, one of them knew this was a good move. She put the kitten box on Raz's lap.

He opened the lid, looked sincerely surprised. "A kitten!"

The kitten hopped out with glee, landing on Raz's chest, squeaking, *I am here and you are MY FamMan!* She curled all of her claws into his shirt. Del hadn't thought of that, but it wasn't one of his expensive silkeen shirts. Anyway, he'd learn that having a Fam could be expensive—emotionally as well as financially.

"A kitten Fam. I saw you with your sister's," Del said.

He tilted his head back to look at the little being—who was purring and kneading his chest—in the eyes. "She's beautiful."

Leave it to Raz to know at a glance, or in one sentence of a mental voice, that his Fam was female.

He picked her up in both hands and Del got a mental flash of comparison of this Fam with his sister's. His was chunkier, would not have the delicate, sinuous lines of his sister's Fam. But this kitten was much more colorful with its mixture of furs, her loud mental voice . . . though her purr wasn't as loud.

"She's beautiful," he repeated. "What's her name?"

The kitten glanced at Del and she was touched the Fam would let her pick her name. "Rosemary," Del said. She smiled. "For remembrance."

Raz stilled and looked at her. "You're not going anywhere soon?"

"Only with you and Rosemary to Gael City."

Shunuk yipped. *I am ready to go!*

Rosemary lifted her nose, as parti-colored as the rest of her, a third pink, a third brown, and a third black. *I was ready before YOU!* She grinned up at Raz, showing little pointy teeth. *You are a beautiful person; you will fit with ME.*

Raz turned her around, looked at her straight, short black tail, her white mask, her mostly blue gray self. "My theater friends will love you, Rosemary."

She butted her head against his hand. *I am a Cat of many colors,* Rosemary purred. *I am SPECIAL.*

All cats think they are special. Shunuk lifted his head. *Are we going soon or not?*

ADVENTURE!

The fox looked down his nose. *May be adventure for you, but regular traveling for me.*

I am hungry. I need more FOOD, Rosemary said.

Del went into the playhouse and pulled two bowls of milk from the no-time, set them down.

"You certainly are special." Raz set her carefully on her feet in front of the smaller bowl. Shunuk lapped at the other. Raz cocked an eyebrow at Del. "How much does she eat?"

"Don't know." Del indicated a papyrus pamphlet and a viz record sphere in the box. "Instructions from D'Ash on how to care for your new FamKitten in two formats."

"Looks like quite a lot of information."

D'Ash knows EVERYTHING, Rosemary said.

"Sure," Raz said. "I won't be memorizing this, however."

As soon as the kitten had finished and Del had stowed the dishes in the cleanser, Raz picked up Rosemary and met her gaze. "You and I will make up our own rules, too. Like never going outside my dressing room at the theater."

The kitten glanced aside.

With another yip, Shunuk bounded off toward the house, where Del's duffle was. "Did you come by glider?" Del asked.

Raz nodded. "I'll drive it to Southern Airpark and someone will take care of it." His smile showed white teeth. "Probably my father." Then he frowned, cuddled his kitten closer on his chest. "We'll be taking a large airship down to Gael City, thirty twoseat couches, seven and a half septhours. Is it all right for Rosemary to be with so many other people?"

"Good for the kitten, D'Ash said. To be socialized."

Raz snorted. "As if she wasn't socialized by being in D'Ash's menagerie or will be in the theater."

When they reached his glider, Raz put Del's duffle in the trunk, lifted the passenger door, sat, closed the door, and said, "You can drive if you want."

"I don't know how to drive a glider," Del said.

"And I don't have time to teach you now. Cherry is fully automatic, so just tell her where to go."

Hoping she didn't show her sudden nerves, Del took the driver's seat.

"Just push the steering bar out of the way." But Raz did that for her, clicking it into the console. He said the Word to envelop them in the web safety shields she'd rarely noticed. "Go ahead," he said.

"Southern Airpark," Del muttered. She wasn't sure she wanted to learn how to drive a glider. Gliders were useful only in cities. Though they could go off gliderways and roads, they didn't handle rough terrain well, and this sports model . . . definitely a status symbol.

Shunuk hopped in on Raz's lap, laughing at his expression and the kitten who sat on his shoulder. Rosemary hissed at the fox, but he only waved his tail at her.

When the vehicle raised its landing stands and moved smoothly along the gliderway, Del acknowledged that the ride was a lot easier than on a stridebeast, or even a horse. No jolting at all. From what Raz had said, he'd become attached to his glider as much as she was to her animals. She didn't know how that could be.

You are crowding ME! Rosemary snapped at Shunuk. He ignored her.

The driver's area, even with the steering bar lifted, was a little too cramped to hold Shunuk on her lap.

Rosemary hopped through the webbing to the little ledge at the bottom of the window and sat in the middle, back turned on them all, staring out. The tip of her tail twitched.

Del turned her head to see Raz's lips pressed together, laughing silently, but telepathically she heard, *Thank you very much, dearling. She will be constantly amusing.*

You're welcome.

My third gift.

Deciding to let Rosemary enjoy her sulk, Del continued to talk mentally with Raz. Shunuk could overhear if he wanted, but he was watching Druida City speed by. *How did you like the tapestry?*

Twenty-five

I like it very much, it's very vivid. He winked. I bought mine when I *passed my apprenticeship tests to become a journeyman. I didn't replace my tapestry after I became a Master Actor. I think your weaving is a higher quality.*

Del shrugged. *Like I said, I have several. I love maps.*

As usual, Raz reached out and took her hand. She intertwined her fingers with his, both glad of the contact and wary. His touches were becoming necessary to her. She was beginning to love him too much. She'd seen other people set aside their needs to focus on their mate and it had never ended well. She'd always thought that she was too strong for that. But how she wanted him!

The glider slowed and stopped. Shunuk hopped out. Raz picked up Rosemary, who'd curled on the ledge and fallen into a snooze. When they followed the fox to the end of the line of the people boarding the airship, Raz murmured, "Rosemary is a wonderful gift, Del. A lifetime gift."

That wasn't the only lifetime gift she'd given him. She could only hope he'd keep her HeartGift with as much joy as the kitten.

They landed in *Gael City in the wee hours of the morning.* Del stepped into cool night air and a galaxy-studded sky that seemed a thousand times brighter than in Druida. All those shields in the capital city—security shields, weathershields—slightly distorted the atmosphere.

She shook out her limbs and inhaled deeply of the slight mechanical scent, letting the middle-class passengers file by her to the free Cherry Transport shuttle that would take them to the center of town. She began to trail after the people at the end of the line, and Raz tugged at her hand.

He'd kept a touch on her since they'd met again, his hand on her waist or fingers laced with hers. Close enough that Rosemary could hop from his shoulder to hers, though they'd both kept a small safety field around the cat in case she fell.

Del turned and saw a young woman dressed in a pilot onesuit striding toward them.

The pilot nodded. "GrandSir Cherry?"

"Yes." Raz flashed her a smile and the serious expression vanished from her face as she smiled back. She had to make an effort to switch her attention to Del. "GrandLady D'Elecampane?"

Del nodded.

The pilot blinked, sent a long breath out, and inhaled, grinned even wider at Del, holding out her hand. Del shook.

"Really pleased to meet you." The woman cocked a hip. "I'm one of the pilots on the new canyon run. Top-of-the-pyramid fun! Got a glider for you."

Remembering the zooming papyrus transports in her dining room, Del repressed a shudder. Give her a nice, steady stridebeast any day.

The pilot had already turned and was walking away. Raz's glance had fastened on her butt. Del squeezed his fingers and he laughed, raising his eyebrows. He was a man and appreciated women and would never hide that, HeartBonded or not.

Since she was equally amused watching him, she winked and said, "Straif Blackthorn has a nice butt, too."

"I didn't notice." His tone was actor-cold, but his eyes were dancing.

They were pleased with themselves, she realized. Just happy being together . . . and away from all the city pressures. She breathed deeply again.

Or it might just have been that he'd noticed the midnight blue sports glider sooner than she.

It looked sleeker than his red one. The pilot flung up the door with a flourish and gestured to the leather interior. The vehicle had a small carpeted bench in the back.

"Nice." Raz shared an appreciative look with the woman. "Very nice."

"Hot from T'Elder's shop," the pilot said, running a hand along the subtle metallic curve of the front.

Raz slid into the driver's side, flexed his hands.

"I'm sure it is fully automated," Del said.

Raz and the pilot stared at her. "You don't let your horse or stridebeast go where they want, do you?"

Actually, she did. They sometimes had better trail sense than she did, but she knew when to keep her mouth shut.

Shunuk barked a laugh and hopped onto the back bench, stretched his front paws to the back of Raz's seat, and delicately lifted the kitten with his teeth from Raz's shoulder to the bench beside him.

I want to sit on FAMMAN. I want to SEE, Rosemary objected.

"Let Raz drive without distractions, Rosemary," Del said firmly. She went around the glider to where the pilot had raised the passenger door and sank into cushioned leather. Better than the airship twoseat, and that had been nice.

Her door clunked shut and the pilot went back to Raz, leaned down. "Sorry for your Family's troubles."

Raz tensed. "You haven't had any problems here?"

The pilot shook her head. "No."

Smiling up at her, one of those actor's smiles that masked his face—and the young woman didn't seem to realize that—Raz said, "I don't think you will."

Her shoulders relaxed. "That's what T'Cherry and GrandMistrys Seratina Cherry said, but we have guards now."

"It will be over soon." Raz's fingers flexed again and this time Del thought he was imagining getting his hands on the culprits who'd upset his Family. "We think thieves are after an old diary. One the Family lost," Raz explained.

The pilot snorted. "Lost old diary? Huh." She shook her head in disgust, clearly firmly rooted in the present and looking toward the future.

"Spread the word about that," Raz said.

She gave him a little salute. "Will do."

Del only had an instant to brace before Raz said the Word and they zoomed into the night. To distract herself from the blurring of dark scenery, she said, "Your Family doesn't think there will be problems here?"

"No," Raz said grimly. She sensed that he barely concentrated on his driving, the road familiar. While she admired his skill, she wished he'd slow down. "My FatherDam built this yard. Our original Gael City yard was more northern but was torn down and housing constructed as the city grew."

"Gael City is growing," Del said. Unlike Druida, which had been built by colonists of an overpopulated planet and still had empty areas within the walls.

"Druida is growing in populace." Raz shot her a look. "It's just harder to notice. You said yourself that it's busier each time you return."

Del sighed. So much for steering his notions to work somewhere else. "True," she said. "The press of people and Flair, the *hurrying* is greater in Druida than when I first took the trail."

They fell into a silence that was only broken by an occasional *Whee!* from Rosemary and arrived at the Cherrys' Gael City house in a quarter septhour. Del was disappointed to see that it was a smallish estate among a lot of other small noble estates. The lights of the neighbors' houses could be easily seen. Only when she felt her spirit depress did she realize that she'd hoped that this would have been an option for them in the future, living in Gael City.

The glider stopped in a bricked courtyard area several meters from the house. As she stepped from the glider and watched Shunuk shoot into the brush to explore, the buzz of humanity slid up her skin like an irritant and the press of people living close together clogged her throat. This was not a place on the outskirts of town, but an old established community.

Rosemary hopped from Raz's hands and made a bolt for the bushes, too, but he scooped her up before she could escape, held her up at eye level to talk to her . . . that was already becoming a habit. "You must stay near to me so we can bond well," he projected in a serious voice. He'd watched the holo of D'Ash's instructions on the trip.

The kitten stopped wriggling, mewed in a small voice, *We are together, so we ARE bonded.*

Raz shook his head. "We have to be together for a while before we have a bond."

Rosemary's expression turned suspicious. *How LONG? I can talk to you. You can talk to Me.* She offered a cute kitten smile. *You can call when you want Me to come.*

"And you will always come when you're called?" Raz asked.

The kitten didn't answer.

"I didn't think so. I'm not as stupid as you think. I know something about cats. Please stay close to me."

Shunuk gets to explore, Rosemary said sulkily.

"Shunuk is a FamFox used to the trail," Raz said.

"He's been on the trail for years," Del said. "He wasn't born in the city."

A cough came from near the door. "GrandSir Cherry? Gael City Guardsman Patrick here. Been waiting for you." Another cough, this one deprecating. "We haven't cleaned anything up. Wanted your first impressions of what's missing. The insurance woman has already been here with a recording sphere. T'Cherry authorized that—authorized everything."

Raz had tensed beside her, then put on a casual, one-of-the-guys manner and loped toward the front of the house. It was dark, and as Del approached she saw the globes on either side of the door that should have flickered with spell light were the odd grayish color that showed their spell technology had been tampered with, all their power drained.

With Rosemary tucked securely under one arm, Raz held out his hand and gave the guard a lopsided smile. "Sorry to be late, and sorry to have a strange one-sided conversation—"

"It wasn't one-sided." The guard smiled back. He was a middle-aged, solid man, well-spoken. Raz had gauged him right. "I could hear the kitten. New Fam?"

Raz sighed. "Very new. We are trying to get our rules set."

"Always good to have boundaries with young ones," the guard said with the air of a man who had children. "Pretty Fam."

"Thank you."

I know, said Rosemary.

The guard laughed. "The door is fine; the burglars came in through one of the side windows."

"I can guess," Raz said. "The west side of the house that has the grove between us and our neighbors?"

"Yes, dense, brushy area, that. You might consider trimmer landscaping."

"I'll tell T'Cherry, or my sister, GrandMistrys Cherry. They're the ones who will be making the decisions on this. I'm just a pair of convenient eyes."

The guard looked as if he doubted that but said a Word that would unlock most doors and the door swung wide. The lights of the small entry hall lit.

"They didn't drain the interior lights," the guard said.

At first glance, nothing looked bad.

Then they all stepped inside and Del saw doors to each side of the entryway were open and the rooms beyond were a shambles.

Though she'd sensed Raz had tried to prepare himself for this, he flinched, braced further.

"Broken glass and china," the guard said. "Hard on bare paws."

Raz set Rosemary on his shoulder. "I need you to stay with me," he said to her. "Attach Fam to clothes," he ordered. Rosemary tried to lift a foot from his shirt, hissed when she couldn't.

"Please, Rosemary," Raz said, voice thick.

Rosemary subsided. Blinked big eyes, mewed in sympathy.

An intelligent Fam and fast learner. Or she was acting. Del wondered how much cats *acted* around their humans. Well, however much it was, Rosemary would do it, learn from Raz.

He'd stuck his hands in his trous pockets and let the guard go first into a room that appeared to be the den.

"This is the worst," the guard said.

It was plenty bad. The walls had been lined with built-in shelves. Now all the contents were jumbled on the floor—some broken, some not. Some deliberately smashed. At least one shelf of each section had been destroyed.

Raz said, "Druida Guardsman Winterberry said that he would tell you of a lead on who might have done this to my Family. Have you caught the man?" His voice was all suppressed anger.

Obviously Raz wanted to get violent hands on the guy. Carefully stepping over upturned chairs, righting them as he went, he moved toward one corner of the room . . . where a spotlight showed rawly splintered shelves. On the floor were bits of metal, some gleaming as they'd twisted to show where tint had never been.

He crouched down. Del joined him, standing helplessly as his hand hovered over the metal and grief at the destruction throbbed from him.

The guard made a commiserating noise in his throat, then said, "We've got recordings of everything, you can move it."

Raz inhaled audibly, picked up a battered model. "*Lugh's Spear*. Again it's less damaged than the others."

"It's a smaller model, right? About half the size of the ones in Druida?" the guard asked.

"That's right."

The man nodded; his face went grim. "Not much left of *Nuada's Sword*." He gestured to an object a couple of meters away tilted against a desk chair, as if the model had been flung. Sharp, flat strips and planes of metal showed broken lettering.

Raz winced but said nothing. He stood, holding the crumpled *Lugh's Spear*, tilting it this way and that. Rosemary leaned forward and sniffed at it, mewed pitifully again.

"Not as bad," Raz said.

"You can see that there wasn't any room to hide anything inside it, like a diary," the guard said.

Turning to look at him, Raz said, "You're well informed."

"Winterberry respects our department."

Raz nodded, looked down at the model once more, grimaced. "My father and I made these together."

"Always tough," the guard said.

Del wasn't sure what she should be doing. She wanted to summon spells to put everything back in order in an instant, but it wasn't her place. She linked her arm in Raz's and sent him love and comfort. Then she righted a table that had held a vase that was in broken shards around them, but the bouquet of flowers treated with a stayfresh spell was still pristine. She set the flowers on one end of the table. Raz put *Lugh's Spear* in the middle. "We can repair this," he said briskly and glanced down. "*Arianrhod's Wheel* and *Nuada's Sword* are hopeless."

Del didn't want anything in Raz's life to be hopeless but could only say, "Let me help."

He looked down at her and smiled, but that didn't reach his eyes. "You *are* helping. Just by being here."

ME, too! Rosemary said. *I am sad because FamMan hurts.* She licked his face.

"Thank you," Raz said. "I think the best way you could help would be if you sat, ah, here,"—he placed her on a high shelf—"and supervised. I've found cats are good at supervising."

Sighing, he gestured to one of the bookcases along the wall. "We had several bound editions of *The History of Celta* and *The Encyclopedia of Celta*. They're all gone."

The guard said, "No real books or holospheres or vizes left."

Raz's jaw flexed. "We had a library, not just objects on the shelves."

"Figured that," the guard said.

"At least we didn't keep any memoryspheres out. Losing those would be devastating." Letting out a sigh, Raz started picking up the remaining whole objects, stone figures of the Lady and Lord, a battered brass scrybowl with etching around the rim, all its power drained, too.

"GrandSir Cherry, I think you should tour the house," the guard said.

"Yes, of course." Raz had taken a chest that had had its top ripped off and put the fragments of the starship models in it, along with other models of what might have been transports, airships, and gliders. He found the curved top to the chest and carefully placed it on the box.

Del had been occupied with a brisk cleanup and hadn't realized that sadness and depression had flooded his thoughts. She put her basket away, dusted her hands, and linked arms with him.

His smile was crooked as he lifted Rosemary to his shoulder.

They walked across the entryway into a mainspace and he flinched, his eyes scanning the room. His mouth flattened. "We had three very good holo paintings—works of art—in this room."

The guard made a note. "Gone?"

"Yes. The safe was in the dining room." With quick strides he passed through the door at the end of the mainspace and moved into the dining room, stopped just over the threshold. Del kept pace.

"The safe was open and empty," the guard said.

"I can see that." Raz raked his fingers through his hair, set his shoulders. "I'm not sure of the contents." Now he gave a casual shrug that belied his distress, an actor again. "You'll have to speak to my father or sister."

"Some gilt and jewelry," the guard said. "Original property documents."

"Ah," Raz said, but it was more like a noise stuck in his throat. He turned back to the mainspace and Del pivoted with him. Good thing she could keep up with the man. Her arm was clamped against his side and he was gaining comfort from her but not thinking of her. Thinking of his past and his Family, as he should.

His observant gaze scanned the mainspace. "Lighting full," he said, and the room brightened to summer daylight. The silkeen wallpaper hung down in strips near the corners where apparently the thieves had been looking for secret compartments. Occasional gouges in the wall showed.

The guard cleared his throat. "They were diligent about looking for hidey-holes."

Raz flinched, said in an emotionless voice, "I guess that means that every wall of the house has been marred."

"I'm afraid so."

"Right." Raz slid his hand down to Del's fingers, moved quickly around the room, cataloguing the missing items for the guard.

"We think the break-in occurred a couple of days ago," the guard said. "None of your neighbors noticed anything."

Rosemary mewed. *I need food.*

Raz ran a hand down her. "Of course you do." He gave the room a last glance. "I've detailed the loss in here, let's head to the kitchen." His mouth twitched in a false smile, his eyes were dark and aching. "Not that I know much of what might be gone there." He took Del's hand, frowned as if he tried to visualize the place. "Were the no-times opened and food—"

But the smell of spoiled meat answered that. The kitchen was a wreck, with doors of the no-time food storage units opened. Again their power had been drained.

"Cave of the Dark Goddess," Raz muttered.

Del recognized regular no-times that would have held all meals and snacks at the exact temperature they'd been when placed inside. She saw one that must have contained special food for rituals, some elegant platters were bare of treats. There was a whiff of cider and cinnamon.

The huge meat no-time was empty, and most of the contents thrown on the floor, looking like a rotting massacre. The whole had a containment shield around it that prevented more spoilage and kept insects away, but the odor remained.

"We did what we could," the guard said gruffly.

"Of course you did."

Rosemary *eeped* and buried her head in Raz's neck.

Del plucked her up, cuddled her, and strode back into the dining room. She put the kitten down and removed a package of bite-sized soft furrabeast bits she carried for Shunuk and herself from her duffle, snagged a nearby saucer with only a slight chip on the bottom, and dumped the food into it for Rosemary.

"A good woman to have in a crisis," Raz said. His smile was strained.

Her mouth lifted on one side. "Not much of a crisis, feeding a kitten. But she needs milk."

His face hardened. "I'm sure we don't have any." With deliberate steps he moved close to her, took her hands, looked into her eyes. "I want a tracker on this case. Now."

The best tracker in the world was Straif T'Blackthorn.

Del hesitated—it was a big favor to ask Straif—but she nodded. "Fine." She moved into the kitchen. Raz frowned.

Taking her perscry out, she tapped it and said, "Straif."

Twenty-six

Raz waited tensely. *After a minute there was a buzz and a grumble.*
"Here!" Straif T'Blackthorn said. No image showed in Del's perscry;
the man had blocked it.

Then Straif swore, said, "Looks bad."

Raz recalled that Del's perscry was full-sized, not showing just a
head or torso. He looked at the meat and the destruction; again his
stomach turned and he had to glance away.

Del said, "We need your help tracking the vandals."

Straif cleared his throat and an image formed, showing him sitting up in bed, hair tousled, his wife opening sleepy eyes beside him.

"Straif, this is a life-sized perscry," Del said.

Straif stared. He grabbed a robe and moved from the bed. Raz
noticed the man's limbs were ropier than his own. He had scars and
looked tough as old leather. When he faced them again, his gaze was
that of a FirstFamily lord. "Cherrys', Gael City?"

"Yes," Del said. "T'Cherry can have transportation for you on the way in a coupla minutes." She glanced at Raz and he understood he should be contacting his father. He nodded and moved away but kept an ear on the conversation as he scried his father and let him know what was going on.

"Can't teleport to Gael City," Straif was saying in the background. "No place midway. Damn mountains, too. Tricky."

Raz's father's brows rose high when he heard that Raz had called on the FirstFamily lord to help. T'Cherry, too, had a rumpled and satisfied look. The creases in his face were heavier than a few days ago. "I'll have a glider sent to T'Blackthorn's or he can 'port to the Nobleclass lounge at Southern Airpark. An express private ship will bring him to you." His father's eyes gleamed. "We'll try the new pass. A good test."

"Yes," Raz said. "I doubt any of your pilots would think of zooming crazy at night with a FirstFamily lord as a passenger."

T'Cherry rubbed his graying whiskers. "Got that right." He nodded again. "A good test." His face set. "We'll find the gilt to pay the man his going rate."

Astronomical. Raz said, "I have savings."

"We'll work it out. Maybe the lord would work for a silver favor."

"I heard that," said Straif. "I will."

Del walked closer and the images of Straif and T'Cherry stared in astonishment at each other.

"How can this be?" asked T'Cherry.

Del coughed. "My perscry is an experimental one." She lifted her chin. "Given to me by my late cuz, Elfwort, who developed them."

"Got to get the technology and spells," Straif muttered.

Del rolled a shoulder, pointed her scry at Raz's perscry.

T'Cherry's head bobbed out of sight as he bowed. "T'Blackthorn. I'm grateful beyond words that you'll be helping us." He straightened his shoulders. "Ah, payment—"

"One silver favor for my Family, to be cashed in at any time in the future, with the standard conditions," Straif said.

Raz was foggy on the conditions, but his father would know.

"Done, and many thanks," Raz's father said. "I can have a glider—"

"I heard that part, too," Straif said. "I'll 'port to Southern Airpark." His eyes narrowed. "I'm more familiar with public teleportation pad twelve than anything else."

"I'll have a pilot meet you there." Raz's father rubbed his unshaven cheek again and the rasp came through. "You should be in Gael City about four and a quarter septhours from now."

Straif blinked. "That soon? More new technology?"

"Express run, new pass." T'Cherry puffed his chest out.

"I'm impressed."

"Good, then you can tell the FirstFamilies about it." He winked and ended his scry.

Straif met their eyes in turn. "Keep the containment shield on the kitchen and the trail fresh for me. Later." His full-length image vanished.

"Lady and Lord," the guard said. He was rubbing his temples with forefinger and thumb. "Straif T'Blackthorn." He eyed Del. "You have him on your perscry by given name."

Del shrugged, stuck her scry in her pocket. Her nose wrinkled in distaste as she scanned the kitchen. "He'll be here in a little over four septhours."

"I'm heading upstairs," Raz said.

"GrandSir Cherry, it's bad there," the guard said, shaking his head as he tromped from the kitchen. "All this waste. So much Flair and energy needed to restore." Anger laced his tones, enough to set off the lava flow inside Raz again. Once more he kept it from erupting, spewing. Kept his temper. He didn't think even Del understood how furious he was.

At his side, her arm entwined in his, she nudged him from the kitchen and he realized his skin had heated; his skin would be ruddier than ever. He started breathing and sending his anger away, through his feet. It would be best if he could find a grounding pad. There was one in the exercise and fighting salon.

Out of the kitchen, he scooped up little Rosemary, who'd curled into a ball next to the dish. His mother wouldn't be pleased that this set of dinnerware was broken.

He put the kitten on his shoulder and immediately felt nearly as good as when he'd taken Del's hand. The little cat stretched out, burped as her tummy came in contact with his muscle, purred before she fell back to sleep.

Again he went through breathing exercises to control his emotions. The thieves had been setting the pace, and the plot, and the action, his Family reacting or letting the guards take care of the business. Now *he'd* taken action, moved onto the stage, ready to do what had to be done, no matter the gilt or the personal cost.

He hadn't liked bringing Straif T'Blackthorn in, admitted to himself that he might not have done so if Del's ex-lover hadn't been HeartBound to another woman.

"Lights," Del murmured, and Raz comprehended that he'd been stalking through the dim house and Del didn't know the place. Now the spell lights in pretty round, efficient globes lit and he stopped at the stairs and swore again. The Family portraits marching up the wall above the stairs had been slashed.

Del put her arms around him and he leaned his head against hers.

One big breath, and another, and he could speak. "Mostly reproductions from those in the Residence." But "mostly" wasn't good enough. He forced himself to look at the originals, narrowed his eyes as he realized the oldest were the most defaced, though squares where a holo painting had projected were drained and gone forever.

"The oldest of the Family . . ." Del murmured.

"Yes."

"You don't have a pic or holo of your ancestress, the colonist? Tabacin?"

"No." He smiled grimly. "She didn't like images of herself. We're not sure who she looks like, if there's any Family resemblance at all."

Del nodded and they ascended the stairs. These walls, too, were marred.

"How much do you know about Tabacin?" Del asked, and Raz knew she was trying to divert him from the destruction.

Meanwhile his anger had grown enough that his ears felt hot, he thought the top of his head would sizzle. He kept his breathing steady, his steps even, but his voice was tight when he answered. "Not a lot." He managed a hitch of his mouth in a semblance of a smile. "She liked cherries and baking, I think. Made the trek from *Lugh's Spear* to Druida with the rest of those colonists. Was supposed to have kept a diary about all the journeying. Married late in life and had several children. Four? The colonists were more fertile than we." He hesitated, turned left down the corridor to the sparring salon. He *needed* that damned grounding mat, his feet burned as hot as his head and he wondered that he didn't leave smoking footprints in the carpet behind him.

Del cleared her throat. "Surely, if you had something as valuable as the diary, you'd keep it in the main estate's HouseHeart."

Raz's teeth clicked together as his jaw clenched. "You would think so. But it's not there, not in the HouseHeart safe, not in the Residence. Nothing of Tabacin's." He made an abortive gesture. "I'm supposed to have some divination cards that she created. If so, she was a good artist."

Del's eyes widened. "Cards."

"They do seem to be homemade, and of materials more Earthan than Celtan. Of the old Earth image system, not the Celtan Ogham."

"Fascinating."

The door to the exercise and fighting room hung off its hinges.

"Lights," he said. Sucking in air, he marched forward. A grounding strip ran along the base of one of the short walls. A few seconds later he was there and shoved the anger roiling within him through his soles to the mat. His feet no longer burned, red no longer edged his vision, though his muscles trembled as his rage renewed when he saw more long slashes in the walls.

"I'm sorry about this." Del wrapped an arm around his waist and the heat he felt from her told him that she was using the grounding mat for her anger, too.

He buried his face in her hair. "This wasn't even my favorite place. I've always loved the Residence and Druida more than this hick town."

"Oh."

"I didn't say that to Trillia when she was auditioning for a part down here, though."

Del stroked his head, sifting her fingers through his hair, and they sighed together. "I'd forgotten about seeing that show," she said.

He raised his head. "You don't want to see *Heart and Sword*?"

"Sure I do. I love plays."

On another steady inhalation he examined the room. The exercise mats were too thin to have held anything, but they'd been cut up. The ballet barre was broken in three pieces. He shook his head. "The thieves really tore this place up."

Del leaned against him and he felt the wave of comfort she was sending him. "Thank you," he said.

"Welcome."

"Mirrors," he ordered and the upper panels shimmered and turned reflective. There were some dark spots here and there, but they looked better than the wood, and whatever they were made of hadn't shattered. "Not too bad," he said.

Del grunted and he didn't think it was agreement. She said, "Comparatively better."

"Yes." He nerved himself, sent the awful anticipation away into the grounding mat, too. "The nursery next."

"Nursery?"

"Where my sister's dolls are." He swallowed hard. "She loved— loves—this place and didn't want to come. She wanted me to check on the dolls."

Del stepped behind him and put her hands on his shoulders, dug her fingers into him in an excellent massage. First she worked on his tense neck. He deliberately relaxed his back, groaned as she loosened a tight knot, let his head fall forward.

When his thoughts began to drift, she dropped her hands and stepped off the mat, offered her fingers. "Ready to do this?"

"Yes." He took her hand, dry and warm and strong, as usual.

At the door he turned left. "At the end of the hall." They walked and he saw drunken cabinets where a leg had been snapped, more walls damaged.

The nursery was nearly as wrecked as the den. The plank floor had been torn up, most of the toys broken. No books or holos or vizes remained here, either, not one single page. "Cave of the Dark Goddess, they took all our books!"

"Bad," Del said. "Full lighting."

"Terrible," Raz said. He trod gingerly around holes in the floor, the jutting or sunken wood. Stopped. His stomach clenched when he saw the pile of dolls in the corner, like bodies. He froze. Could not take one more step forward.

Del let go of his hand and walked to the corner; she bent down and her fine, taut derriere stretched against her summer trous, and Raz welcomed the distraction, the curl of lust inside him driving out dread, transmuting the anger. Another way to ground fury—turn it into lust. He didn't think Del would mind doing that with her own anger, coming together in wild sex tonight.

After this endless tour of the house was over. "How are they?" he rasped.

"Not too bad." She stood and turned, holding a doll no larger than her hand. "Mostly just tossed aside. Do you know which one was your sister's favorite?"

"Yeah." He was afraid to hope that the face hadn't been smashed in, cut up, the eyes . . . no, he wouldn't let his imagination rule. He took the room in bounds, jumping over messes. When he reached the corner, he found that Del had sat most of the dolls against the wall. They didn't look too bad . . . until he saw his sister's favorite soft-bodied one slit open from neck to legs.

"We can have her restuffed and mended," Del said.

"Good." He changed the topic. "We'll need to clean a room for Straif."

"He isn't fussy."

Raz didn't believe her.

They worked on a guest room, swept the crumbled bedsponge into a trash receptacle, pushed the broken furniture against the wall and used a housekeeping spell to cleanse it. Raz wasn't pleased with the poor result and his jaw hurt from where he'd clamped it shut.

"We can sleep here." Del studied his old room. "I have enough energy and Flair for a housekeeping spell to get rid of the sponge."

"Not a decent bedsponge in the house," Raz said.

Del patted her duffle. "I have two groundmats here." She smiled. "One will be crowded, but I don't think we'll mind."

"No."

"The other we can use for Straif."

I need My own cushion. A FAT one. Rosemary had awakened and eyed the flattened pillows. *A feather pillow might be good. I like feathers.* Her little teeth showed. *But it MUST be plumper.*

Raz knew answers to statements like this. "Why don't you pick your pillow or your cushion out from whatever is in the house?"

She wrinkled her nose.

"We can purchase a pillow for you later today," Raz said. "But now all the best establishments are closed."

The kitten made a small huffing sound. Her ears rotated and she turned her back.

Del rolled out the groundmat, waved a hand, and it inflated. Raz eyed it warily. Sure wasn't a bedsponge.

"Well, I'll be going," said the guard who'd arrived on stage with one line like a minor player. "Little Miz Rosemary, if I were you, I'd take the middle couch cushion from the mainspace. Dark red would complement your coloring."

Raz couldn't see that, a blue gray cat on deep red.

Rosemary's back rippled in a cat shrug. *YES.*

"And I can 'port it up for you," the guard said. With a frown and a Word he did so.

The kitten went over to it immediately, hopped atop it, began kneading.

"How does it smell, Rosemary?" asked the guard.

She lowered her nose, then looked at him. *Smells like FamMan and Family and knife metal and furrabeast glove.* She touched a slash.

This cushion was the least harmed of all. The guard had known that, had observed the location of the cushion well enough to be able to transport it, had enough Flair to do so. Perhaps Raz'd underestimated the man.

"Ah," the guard said. He nodded to Raz, bowed toward Del.

Raz stepped forward and offered his hand. "Thank you for your work." He added a sincere smile. "You've been a great help."

"It's nothing. My job," the guard said gruffly. He set a tiny disk down that would include all his contact information. "Scry if you want, or if you come across anything you think I should know. I'll use the upper-story teleportation pad."

Neither of the teleportation areas had been drained of energy. Probably so the crooks could escape.

The guard passed Shunuk as he trotted in, smelling of cool air with a hint of damp. He grinned when he saw Rosemary. *Kitten needs to sleep on a pillow?* His teeth were a lot sharper than Rosemary's. Then the fox snorted, angled his head so he was looking at Del. *Kitten would not be good on the trail.* He fluffed his tail, flicked it. *Not even when she is grown. She is a demanding cat.*

"No," Del said quietly with an odd note in her voice. "Rosemary is not meant for the trail." She left the room carrying the other rolled groundmat. Raz watched her, tried to figure out what she might be feeling through their link, but only sensed a weariness.

MY cushion needs to be moved so the morning sun will fall on Me.

Shunuk rolled on the floor, hooting with laughter. *This room does not have any eastern windows, cat. Take yourself down the hall, then.*

Rosemary turned her back on them and curled up in a pouting cat-circle, tail over nose.

Del walked in, all quiet competence and with the air of a task well done. There was not a less demanding woman on the planet. Had he truly understood that? Valued that? Now that he had a FamKitten that wanted things *her* way from the start, the contrast was staggering.

His lover walked up to him, wrapped her arms around him, and they leaned together. Almost like a unit like his parents were, like his sister was with her HeartMate.

No! He didn't want a HeartMate or a wife to distract him from his climb to stardom.

But Del felt so good in his arms. "Lights off," he said and peeled her shoulder tabs apart.

Twenty-seven

*D*el sighed, stepped away, and dropped her trous, loosened her breast-band a little until it only draped over her breasts, didn't lift and form them into delectable mounds. They looked fine to Raz anyway. "You don't need the breastband," he said. He didn't have the energy anymore to have lusty sex with her . . . anger had been worn down by grief and melancholy and the sheer *work* of trying to recall all their Family possessions and report on what was lost.

"Straif will be here soon."

"Oh, yes." He grimaced, pulled his clothes off until he was wear-ing only his loincloth. Del was dressed in breastband and pantlettes. She took a loose onesuit from her bag and put it near the left side of the bed.

They matched in that. He preferred the right side of the bed. He swung her up into his arms, kissed her, and when their lips met, it was with a gentle tenderness, a promise of other times. He'd needed her taste. He opened their bond wide, found it was wide on her side, too. Then he sank onto the bed, let his ragged emotions sink into her. He wrapped around her and in an instant was asleep.

He was awakened by a knock on the front door that echoed loudly by spell through the room. "Straif Blackthorn here."

Raz flung sleep away with a shake of his head, rose, and drew on trous, saw a shadowy Del slip into the onesuit from the corner of his eye. Coughing to clear roughness from his throat, he projected, "Raz Cherry on my way down. Thank you for coming." For the first couple of steps he was stiff from the groundmat, then he balanced his energy and moved across the floor with an easy glide.

Del was one step behind him as he went through the door and he reached back and caught her fingers. They moved through the dark in silence.

You forgot ME! Rosemary mentally shouted.

Shunuk stayed in his corner.

"Come along, then," Raz said. "We did a quick cleanup of the floors, nothing to hurt your paws."

There was a skittering and she ran to keep up. He paused at the head of the stairs following D'Ash's instructions. "Always keep the cat in sight when negotiating stairs. Let the cat proceed first." He wondered how many broken bones Healers had put together from cat/people tangles on stairs.

"I wonder how many cats D'Ash has Healed from stairway incidents," Del murmured.

Rosemary was prancing at the doorway. *Time for T'Blackthorn to see ME.*

"His FamCat is Drina," Del said, then Raz heard privately. *Do not let Rosemary talk to Drina under any circumstances. She is the original Queen of the Universe Fam. She will give Rosemary ideas.*

Raz smiled wryly as he picked his kitten up, mentally whispering back to Del, *I think Rosemary already has a lot of ideas.* He opened the front door, his brows rising as he took in FirstFamily GrandLord Straif T'Blackthorn. The man looked scruffier than Raz himself. His leathers had stains Raz didn't want to contemplate and Straif wore the oldest celtaroon boots Raz had ever seen.

"Greetyou." Straif adjusted his wide-brimmed hat.

Raz recalled his manners. "Thank you for coming so soon."

I am a beautiful Kitten and Drina is OLD, Rosemary announced.

Straif's gaze went to her as she sat on Raz's shoulder. His eyes crinkled. "Older than you, for sure."

Raz stepped back and Del did the same, moving like they were a unit. He didn't want to think about that, had plenty of other things to think about. "The kitchen is this way. It's bad."

"Not too bad," Del said. "No dead animals or people." She and Straif shared a look and Raz disliked the annoyance that bit at him.

They walked to the kitchen as Rosemary listed all her good qualities. At six weeks. Opening the kitchen door, Straif stared at the meat and scowled, turned to Raz. "Using my Flair, I saw traces of two men throughout the house, but their tracks are much stronger here." He narrowed his eyes. "They ate some of the food, would have left saliva, a better identifier. Good job on the containment spell." Straif rubbed his hands. "I'll get to work."

"You don't want to sleep?" Del asked.

Shaking his head, Straif said, "No, the fresher the trail the better. I slept on the luxury airship. I think I'll have to keep a Cherry airship on retainer."

"Excellent idea," Raz said.

"Excellent service," Straif said. He crossed the room to a point that didn't seem the least interesting to Raz. He looked at Del. She shrugged. She must not see anything, either.

The man was using his powerful Flair for tracking. Raz's interest was snagged. He always enjoyed watching people work. It came in handy later when he was shaping a character. Straif had straightened, walked with smaller steps, studied the floor, the counters, glanced at a gouged wall or two, stared at the no-times. Then he nodded and strode to the back door. He waved a hand. "Later."

He was gone before Raz could ask about the two thieves and he was left pondering how much Straif could tell about them. Not their names, surely, but something of their looks?

Del yawned. "Let's send this mess to the city salvage and get back to bed."

"On three," he said, staring at the spoiled meat. Flair ran up and down their hands as Raz tried to recall the location of the Gael City facility. Del augmented his memory with her own fragments of the place. Raz was unsure their recollection would be sufficient.

It is like this! Shunuk grumbled, as if roused from sleep by a stupid problem. The fox added perfect lighting for this time of year.

Del met Raz's eyes. "He must have been there lately."

"We'll transport the mess to the intake station on three," Raz said.

When it was done, Del said a housekeeping Word that Raz didn't know and strength was siphoned from him. In a few seconds the kitchen gleamed.

"Rosemary?" Raz called. She'd hopped down and had seemed to be sniffing at the trails Straif had followed. She'd disappeared when Raz wasn't looking. The kitten didn't answer and he sluggishly tried to think of what might bring her to him and keep her where he wanted her. He walked to the pantry, crossing the open end of the U that were the counters. No kitten in sight. He didn't want to call her again, preferred to use guile.

Reaching up for a small stray tube that had rolled back to the darkness of a pantry shelf, he tore it open. "A snack for Rosemary before we go back to bed." Again he projected his voice. "Come along, kitten dear." He infused his voice with love. Still no answer. He tsked. "You should stop acting like a tracking dog."

Dog! She hissed and shot out from one of the bottom shelves of the pantry, between his feet. *I am NOT a dog. Nothing about Me is doglike.*

Raz cocked a brow. "Many dogs track. They are very good at it." Damn, wrong thing to say. "Not as good as you could be, of course, but very good. Perhaps you could hire out for it."

Hopping with anger, black tail straight up, Rosemary hissed again. Raz hoped she wasn't going to pee on his bare feet.

She lifted her nose. *You may pick Me up and give Me a snack.* She stared at the tube of caviar. *What is that?*

"Caviar, a delicacy. Fish stuff."

Del glanced sharply at him, then shook her head. *Too late,* she said privately.

I think I have heard of this caviar, Rosemary said. *I think D'Ash gave it as a treat to a cat once.*

"A treat, yes. For good behavior." Raz corrected his mistake. Thank the Lady and Lord that the tube was small and the portion he would give the kitten would be equally small, just a little squirt.

Rosemary purred. Raz could hardly hear it. She licked her muzzle. *I CAME when I was called.*

Not quite, but he was tired. He scooped her up with a hand under her belly and took her to the feeding station in the dining room, hesitated. The chamber looked worse now that the kitchen was cleaned. He grunted, turned back toward the kitchen.

Rosemary wriggled in his hand, fell lightly to the floor. *I eat in the dining room.*

Del coughed. Raz glanced at her sparkling eyes. He didn't have to use his bond to know what she was thinking. He and Rosemary were establishing patterns. Caviar. Eating in the dining room. He began to squeeze the treat onto the plate Rosemary had used before and she said, *This is NOT a clean plate.*

It looked clean to him, not a crumb, not a smear of a previous meal. Del turned on her heel and went back to the kitchen, returned with a whole saucer of thick pottery.

The kitten scowled at it. Looked at the "dirty" plate of fine porcelain. *I will eat on the dirty plate.*

"Fine," Raz said. "Because I don't have the time or inclination to clean it right now. And I don't have plates like this at home or in the theater. I don't have a dining room or caviar."

Rosemary just ate her caviar.

* * *

𝒟*el awoke to the lovely feel of Raz's body all along her back and a* bare, unfamiliar pale blue wall ahead of her. She stared, blinked, and memory filtered back. She wasn't at the inn at the Great Labyrinth. She *was* on a trip with Raz, but not an intimate getaway. This would not be the relaxing time she'd wanted with him to focus on each other.

This time together would be an emotional mess.

Her gaze dropped to the ripped carpeted floor as she extended her senses. Rosemary was up and exploring, but an indulgent Shunuk was with her.

Do not leave her, Del admonished her Fam.

Shunuk didn't answer, but she got the vision of him carrying the kitten by the scruff of her neck back to the room, kicking the door shut, and him teleporting away . . . when he became bored with her.

Thank you, she said. Today they'd have to clean the house, start the replacement of furniture, find someone to mend Raz's sister's dolls. Del didn't know Gael City well enough to do that, doubted that Raz did, so they'd have to depend on someone else—guardsmen, she supposed. Raz wanted to viz the play Trillia was in, *Heart and Sword,* and Del didn't know how to arrange that, either. She'd be stuck with cleaning the house.

Beyond the house there was a hum of busy Flair. In some ways Gael City was harder for Del to tolerate than Druida. A more fluid class structure made for a very bustling town. The energy was high, the personal space between people closer. Del considered a couple of kilometers a good personal space between herself and everyone but Raz and Doolee and Shunuk.

Soon it would be a month since she'd been on the trail, riding her stridebeast up to Steep Springs and the letter that had changed her life. So long in Druida City, and now Gael City. What was she doing here?

Raz's hand covered her breast and played with her. Passion speared straight to her core. She arched against him, found him hard and throbbing. Her breath went ragged and thoughts fell apart. "Mornin'," he said in a naturally raspy voice he hadn't bothered to clear, from a throat he hadn't bothered to limber up. That touched her, too. He wasn't thinking like an actor, just a man.

Her man, her HeartMate.

His fingers slipped lower, under her pantlettes, down where she was rapidly dampening, her body loosening for his. She let out a whimpering pant and he arched as if the sound had roused him further.

She liked the feel of his sex, long and hard. Her skin flushed with hot need and anticipation.

He grabbed the side of her pantlettes, yanked, and they were gone. He rolled over and slid into her in a quick smooth move and only sensation mattered.

And emotion. When she closed her eyes she saw sparks, fireworks, heard their unsteady breathing, felt the slickness of their bodies as they plunged in rhythm. Need. She craved him—his touch on her breasts, him inside her. She was addicted to his raging emotions pouring through her, cracking and shattering whatever brittle shield she'd begun to build around her own feelings.

Rounds of golden rope shone in her mind. The HeartBond, for her to send to him and they would be linked together for life, in all aspects of their lives. But her body demanded release and . . . just . . . *there*.

She flew, she fell, she exploded, and when her mind came together again, she heard him whispering. "Lover, lover, lover Del."

She found wetness on her cheeks. He knew they were Heart-Mates, otherwise the bond wouldn't have appeared. But he wasn't admitting it to himself, let alone to anyone else, and definitely not to her.

Because a life with her would mean work and compromise, now and in the future, and the only work he wanted to do was on his career.

That hurt.

They'd been so close, physically. His desire had rushed through her and he'd felt her own. So fast, so hard, so passionate. Now he rolled back and held her, snuggled with her, one of his hands low on her stomach, one on her breasts, their legs tangled together. Love enveloped them. Love he thought of as affection or caring or tenderness.

Del swallowed her stupid, untimely tears. She was tough, she could handle this.

She'd get through this step-by-step. Win or lose.

He wanted to give Del something.

She had given him so much, and though he'd given, too—taken her around to all the theaters, involved her in his life, that wasn't enough. The safes in the house had been opened and robbed and drained of any locking and shielding Flair, but perhaps a young boy's hidey-hole might have been missed.

Come to me outside when you are done in the waterfall, Raz said. He'd already cleansed in a different room.

Fine, Del said.

He left the house through the sunroom door and walked to the trees where his father and he had made a platform. The tree house was one of his favorite places in his youth. The platform was suspended midway in a close circle of trees. As far as he could tell, the permarope was still good.

He didn't think that the thieves would have bothered it.

With a quiet inhalation and a lift of his hands he levitated straight up, grinning. He hadn't forgotten *that* skill. He separated thin, whippy branches with their multitudes of leaves and stepped into the green light of his hideaway. The trees arched over him; the space was still taller than he. As he stepped a pace, the floor swayed a little. Ah. He'd reached his full growth, had the muscle mass of an adult man. Half closing his eyes, he tested the thick wood planks of the platform and the permaropes for soundness. Fine. Good for another fifty years, another few generations of young Cherry boys.

"Raz?" Del called.

She stood near him but couldn't see him and the secret delight of hiding from an adult washed over him as if he were ten.

But nicer to share this with her.

He held a couple of branches away with his arm. "Up here, Del. Trust me to 'port you?" That took a lot of energy, and he could only do if she was nearby.

"Of course," she said.

As she landed, the platform rocked and she hung on to him. He liked her clutching his arms. He bent down and kissed her. Carefully, she wrapped her arms around his neck, opened her mouth. His brain buzzed with passion, need, as if they hadn't made love a few minutes ago. Then she ended the kiss, slid her hand down to link fingers, looked around. "Wonderful place."

"My playhouse."

Her mouth twitched. "I would have liked this better."

"It isn't pink."

She laughed. "No." She lifted her face as if studying the sunlight filtering through the leaves, the arch of the branches around them, drew in a slow, deep breath as if tasting the place. "Wonderful," she repeated, squeezing his hand. She took a step away, squeaked a little as the floor swayed beneath her. "Oh. Even better."

"I'm glad you like it. The thieves didn't find it, or they didn't care."

"Is there something here?"

"Yes, a boy's treasure box."

With one smooth move she sat. "May I see?"

"I have a gift for you."

Her dimples showed. "Thank you."

He reached for the box. It was no longer above his head. He'd made it of the hardest wood on Celta and it had weathered the years well. About the size of both his hands, it was black with age and the lid had warped so that there was no opening it with the pry of fingers. He sank to the wooden platform with a sigh.

Del's eyes were large and round. She had an anticipatory smile on her face and hope that looked nearly painful shone from her eyes. As he gathered Flair for a delicate spell, he asked, "When was the last time someone gave you a gift?"

Her smile froze, her eyes shuttered. "You've given me flowers."

"Not enough," he said, "and not often enough." He set the box aside, took her hands. They sat cross-legged, knee to knee. "When was the last time, dearling?"

She glanced at the box, back into his eyes, let out a quiet breath. "I don't recall."

A yip came in the distance, floating from one of the open windows of the house.

"Shunuk gives me occasional 'gifts.'" She wrinkled her nose. "I'm appreciative but have never liked mouse feet or heads."

Raz choked. He'd decided right then that everything in the box was hers, and he needed to give her something more. He knew just what.

Dropping one of her hands, he slid the box over to her. "Yours," he said.

She stared.

He finessed the box open with a short spell; it creaked but didn't break. The lid lifted slowly, then fell aside showing a cheap red faux silkeen lining.

He glanced in, then away, shrugged. "A boy's treasures."

"Raz, these mean a lot to you . . ."

Not so much that he'd thought often of them over the years. But he'd known they were safe and he'd retrieve them someday. More focused on the future than the past.

"Please," he said gruffly. He caught the gleam of amber and reached in and pulled out the bracelet. The jewelry wasn't as beautiful as he recalled and he winced. Surely she could pick up amber stones like these on her travels, the workmanship was amateurish . . . but then his boyhood friend had been an amateur.

The golden drops were roughly tumbled to polish, hung on a gold-toned chain.

"Oh." Del blinked and Raz knew to the bottom of his soul that she was awed and grateful for the small gifts. *Saw* through their link that her last present had been from Straif T'Blackthorn, years before. One small carving. Her last expensive gift had been from her parents before she'd become an adult.

He took her wrist and draped the bracelet around it, latched it shut. "A friend of mine gave me this when I gave him a model I made—our creative Flair. Not exactly T'Ash's work."

"And you two were how old?"

"Ten."

In a feminine gesture Raz had never seen before, Del moved her wrist to a patch of sunlight and twisted it to see the stones shimmer. The lady had a weakness for jewelry. He'd remember that. He hadn't seen her wear much.

"Where is your friend now?" she asked.

An old ache stabbed, but Raz replied calmly. "He died in the last epidemic that came through. That winter. I wasn't here."

Del nodded. "Celta can be harsh."

"But it's better than living in generational starships," Raz said. "I remember that from the old stories."

"Better than Earth, too, I'm sure," Del said as she began lifting things from the box. Pretty pebbles he'd picked up in the stream running through the estate, a couple of gaudy feathers . . . three rolled and beribboned papyrus that Raz had totally forgotten.

He flushed as she began to open one papyrus and read it.

She chuckled. "I should have known. Are all of them awards for recitation at the local fair?"

"Yes," he muttered.

"First place."

He straightened. "I won three years in a row. Then the rules were changed so only folk who lived here all year 'round could enter."

"Ah." But she caught his slow smile and said, "Since you couldn't compete here, you did so in Druida?"

"That's right."

She carefully rerolled the papyrus and put all the other small treasures of his childhood away in the box, ran her finger around the rim. "I think your mother would like the papyrus, and you should keep the pebbles and feathers and box, but thank you for the bracelet."

He wanted her to have it all, knew she valued the moment, knew she was being generous and not rejecting him, but he wanted her to have it all.

She leaned forward and kissed him, her soft lips lingering on his, and the sweet warmth of tenderness moved through him. He touched her nape, curved his hand around it, and opened his mouth to slide his tongue against hers. One perfect moment.

INCOMING scry! Rosemary and Shunuk sent mentally.

Twenty-eight

*W*ater in the scrybowl is red, Shunuk said. Don't know the woman.

Then Raz heard the tinkle of the house scry. He drew back, looked into Del's soft gaze. Her eyes were shiny. He brushed her cheek with his thumb. "My mother, probably."

SCRY! Rosemary shouted.

We are coming, Raz said. He tucked the box under his arm and rose, pulled Del up, and stepped into her, wrapping her close. "On three I will 'port us."

"Yes," she said.

"One, my sweet Del, two, Lucky Raz, three!" She gave him power—or rather, he used his Flair and some of hers to teleport them to the pad near the bedroom where they'd slept, the only room that had a working scrybowl. The small bowl had rolled under a cabinet and not been drained of Flair, though he'd had to reset the spell. "Mom must be trying the house scry."

"Lucky that the bowl was spared."

"Yes." He kept his arm around her waist as they walked back into the room.

*R*az's *mother briskly planned the house restoration and buying new* furniture. She'd commandeered Del and sent her off to deal with various people the rest of the day. From the gleam in the older woman's eyes when she'd given her orders to Del, Raz's Family was completely aware of who his HeartMate was. She hadn't taken this many orders since she'd been training with the old cartographer. Though she grumbled, and interacting with so many folk was tedious, she still felt pleasure at all she'd accomplished when she'd reported to D'Cherry, and flushed with pride when she was complimented for her good work.

Since Del had been taught all the cleansing spells a person would need for a house or a Residence, and learned the same for a campsite, she took the lead in the housekeeping department. They were an odd and small circle—Shunuk sitting on her feet, Rosemary on Raz's shoulder, and Raz and she holding each other's hands. But Flair and love connected them and their power was large enough to clean the whole house to sparkling without depleting their energy. That had garnered more compliments from D'Cherry.

Late that afternoon, with a half-smile on his face, Raz led Del out to the glider and handed her in, then drove to a large space of packed earth out of town, exited his side of the glider, and came around to open her door and haul her out. "Now I will teach you how to *drive*, not just put a glider on autonav. Anyone who has a glider should know how to drive it," he said with a mock frown.

"I only have the Family glider and it's antique, may not even work anymore." She got out of the small vehicle and looked at it—a glider fun to drive.

She still preferred animals. Stridebeasts, the rare horses. Anything live, though as she scrutinized the glider and remembered Raz's, which he'd actually named, she wondered if the things could ever come alive. Be malevolent.

She hoped not.

With a flourish, he seated her in the driver's side. He tapped the molding, which she understood to be a bespelled soft metal covered with thin furrabeast leather. Sometimes cloth was used, she thought. Hadn't her parents put white silkeen in the Family glider as well as the house?

"This is the console."

She looked at the studs and dials as he named them, repeated them back when he asked. Accompanied by Rosemary's loud mental recital. *SPEED DIAL, FLAIR METER, NAV INDICATOR TURN LEFT, NAV INDICATOR TURN RIGHT, WEB SAFETY SHIELD, WEATHERSHIELD, GLIDER HEIGHT FROM GROUND INDICATOR "HFG," LANDING STANDS.*

Rosemary was lying perpendicularly on the console, her head hanging over to look at the controls.

Raz rubbed his temples. "You know the commands: Go, Stop, Pull Over. You can also initiate all the spellshields verbally as well as manually." With a grin he plucked Rosemary from her spot and placed her behind the front seats on her pillow. "Like 'Privacy Screen.'"

A transparent field shimmered between the back and front seats. From Rosemary's open mouth, Del thought she was yowling, but Del couldn't hear anything.

I want to be up THERE! Rosemary whined telepathically.

Del could hear *that* easily enough.

Del doesn't need your distraction right now, Rosemary. You can see fine from there, and I think you will be too delicate to drive a glider. You should let me drive you or, maybe later in my career, a driver.

Del winced. "Maybe you shouldn't have offered that." She studied Raz. Like his father, she didn't think he'd ever give up driving.

Raz shrugged and tapped a blank space on the console and a rounded rectangle appeared. "Navmap," he said.

Of course Del knew that screen; it'd been in gliders forever, but she hadn't ever studied it. Now she leaned over.

"There are magnifications. Zoom in and out," Raz said.

Del frowned. "I don't think this map is accurate." She didn't like the color indicators, either, dirt brown for the packed earth glider-ways. "It should have more land contours. Everything's flat."

Raz raised his brows. "I'm not sure most people would appreci-ate contours, and that might need more Flair in the spell than most want to spend."

"Huh." Del frowned, then shook her head. "If Elfwort were alive, it would be a challenge for him. We could have worked on it together." She swallowed.

"The nav will recognize various features: cities, intersections, parks, addresses. The more often you go to a particular place, the more it will recognize that as important to you, it will do the same with routes. You can decide to use different routes to the same place. Not that we have a great deal of glider traffic; most of the vehicles on the streets are of transport services, noble Family gliders, and PublicCarriers."

"And people and beasts."

"Those, too, but more and more people are becoming Flaired enough to translocate even large objects and teleport themselves."

Del figured that was good.

"This is the steering bar." Raz pulled it gently from its rest in the console. "It's very sensitive and works by a combination of Flair and finger pressure in this type of model. Some Family gliders are fully automatic." His tone held disapproval, but Del could appreciate that quality. He set her fingers on it and she could feel oval spots of warmth beneath them. He showed her how to turn left and right, go faster, slower, stop, back up, all without opening her mouth.

She had left the packed area—the fairgrounds—and was driving down a shady lane with overarching leaves when she found a little spot at the end of the rounded steering rod. "What's this?" She tapped it and Rosemary bulleted from the back through the now-gone privacy screen.

Raz shouted; his hand caught the kitten before she hit the inside of the window, but she escaped his fingers to tumble downward. "It's the manual engage-release of the privacy screen, which Rosemary had con-tinued to fling herself against." He grabbed at the kitten and missed.

"Stop!" Del yelled.

The glider slowed, moving toward the side of the road.

Rosemary fell under the console.

The glider screeched. Halted. Stands came down and they rocked violently back and forth, then the stands gave way and the glider sank with a bump onto the ground.

Del drew gasping breaths through her mouth. Adrenaline pumped through her, but she was caught in the web safety shield and could only tremble. Her hands tightened on the steering bar, but the warm spots were gone.

"Webshield open!" Raz snapped, and ducked under the console to look at Rosemary.

Scared, SCARED! BAD GLIDER, Rosemary whimpered as he lifted her to his lap, stroking her.

Del's webshield had vanished, too. She stared at the shivering kitten. "Oh, Rosemary."

"She's not hurt," Raz said, his fingertips poking and prodding the kitten. "She's just frightened."

Del let out a whooshing breath, flung up the door, and adjusted her seat so she could stretch. She looked at the glider on the ground, its air pressure gone. "I don't think I've ever been on the ground in a glider before."

"Emergency power-off," Raz said. "Rosemary must have hit the switch when she was flying around the cabin."

He took Del's hand and slid her fingers along the underside of the console. She could feel a small round peg sticking out.

"Feel that?" Raz asked.

"Yes."

"All right, pull down and toward us slowly. The Flair spell will reset and activate and the glider will rise to its usual meter above the ground."

She drew the switch as instructed and the vehicle vibrated around them.

"A glider has forcefields around it determined by the nav screen. Usually a glider will not run into anything. If it happens to bump something unexpectedly, it's mostly at very low speed and the landing

stands will lower. This switch is for emergencies but is rarely used."
Raz scowled at Rosemary.

She was sitting up on his lap, staring at the switch. *I can't SEE it.*

"It's the same color as the console. You don't need to see it. You
don't need to know it is there; most people forget that it is there."
He held her up to stare in her eyes. "If you'd had your webshield on,
you would have been fine, even with a hard stop." Then he cradled
her next to his chest. "Hear my heartbeat? You scared me, Rosemary. Please don't do that again."

Del leaned against Raz, gazed down at the kitten's wide yellow
eyes. "You scared me, too. Are you all right? Will we need to take
you to D'Ash for an exam when we return to Druida?"

NO!

Del figured that would be the answer.

I am a CLEVER Cat. I am fine.

A snorting, hiccupping sound came and Del felt paws on her leg.
Outside the vehicle, Shunuk chortled. *Glider going smooth, then
bump, then down! Very funny.*

"I'm glad you think so."

Glider is not like a stridebeast.

Del sighed. "No, it isn't." She was a much better rider than a
driver and decided that would always be true.

*R*az had spent the rest of the afternoon arranging the viz and interacting with the theater manager, crew, and actors. When he returned to
the house they rearranged the new furniture and ate a simple meal.
Raz had stocked the no-times as soon as they were repowered.
Rosemary grumbled about furrabeast bites instead of caviar and
then vomited from the excitement of attending the theater.

The play was wonderful, capturing Del's attention from the
moment the curtain raised and Captain Bountry walked out on stage.
The holos behind him that showed infinite space made her shiver.

Backstage was equally fascinating. Del liked Raz's friend, Trillia,
very much and praised her acting, though Del also sensed that the

two had been lovers. When Trillia plucked Rosemary from Raz's shoulder and beamed a smile at Del and said, "You don't mind giving Raz and me and this wonderful kitten a septhour to catch up, do you?" Del could only smile back. "No, I don't mind." She kissed Raz's cheek and strolled away.

Shunuk? she called mentally.

I am here in front of the theater. Only six theaters around this oval, not like Druida. He sniffed. Del's insides tightened. She hoped her Fam wasn't turning into a snobbish city fox. If worse came to worse, she couldn't bear to lose both Raz and Shunuk.

She went through the outer doors into the warm night with other stragglers and found the fox sitting under a spotlight, appearing a whole lot sleeker than when they'd ridden into Steep Springs. He *looked* like a city fox, well fed, groomed, bushy tail. He'd had the aspect of a trail fox and dangerous predator before.

People were smiling approval at him and he waved his tail at them.

His eyes narrowed. *You are a little sad.*

All this time in cities is wearing on me. She rubbed her arms.

I will not leave you. He hopped to his paws and licked her hand as she bent and stroked his head.

His eyes slid slyly toward her as she straightened. *But we may not be taking jobs a long way from the cities?*

She didn't know. Rolling her shoulders, she said, "I haven't been downtown in Gael City for a while." She grimaced. "It's changed. Getting more 'fashionable.' Let's walk." An idea occurred to her. "No, let's go check on my stridebeast."

*R*az *thanked the viz techs and took the spheres they'd recorded,* then followed Trillia to her dressing room. She stopped at the door and preened a little. "My first star."

It was brass inset on an old oak door. He kissed her temple. "You deserve it."

"I do." Opening the door, she went to the dressing table and set Rosemary down, then Trillia stared at herself in the mirror, running her hands over her face to dispel the enhancement spells for her last scene. She fluffed out her hair and it turned from deep black to her natural midbrown.

"You didn't tint your hair?"

"I didn't want to. Thank you for arranging for the viz and smooth-talking the stage manager into it." She gave a little sigh, put Rosemary on her lap, and swiveled on the stool to face Raz instead of meeting his gaze in the mirror. "I'm excellent in the part and I'd like those in Druida to see it. My Family, too."

"It's mainly for *Nuada's Sword*."

"The Ship." Her teeth were very white when she smiled; she began to pet Rosemary. "Good for it. But my Family has connections, one of them will see it." A small line etched between her brows.

"You're frowning," Raz said.

She smoothed her face out, but her eyes were serious now. "I know that Druida is where the action is, the best parts, where I should focus my career, but I really like Gael City. Well, not the city so much, but the . . . I guess you'd say the pace." She shrugged. "Or maybe it's the freedom. Things, circles, are not as stratified here." She made a wavy motion. "It's more fluid." Inhaled deeply. "It would be easier to play different parts here, less typecasting. It's just a question of how to handle my career. Staying here and being a big fish in a small pond or rising through the levels until I'm a star in Druida. Maybe a balancing act until I feel my reputation is such that I can jump back as a star. But I like being on my own, too, not always having to satisfy Family expectations."

You need to pet Me more, Rosemary said since Trillia had stopped during her unburdening.

Trillia laughed and rubbed the tiny head with her forefinger. "You are precious, Rosemary." She winked at Raz. "She is perfect for you and will be an excellent theater cat. I do like you, Rosemary, and Raz is lucky."

Yes, Rosemary agreed.

"And I like Raz very much, too." Trillia jumped to her feet and flung an arm around his neck and gave him a smacking kiss. "And I think your HeartMate is perfect for you, too."

Twenty-nine

Raz froze. "HeartMate."

"Del Elecampane. She's a very nice lady and an excellent contrast in character to you."

"She's not my HeartMate."

"Of course she is." Trillia pulled back and looked at his frozen face. "Uh-oh."

Of course Del is, Rosemary said, hooking her claws into Raz's tunic and climbing up to his shoulder.

Dread washed through him. He'd known for a long time but hadn't wanted to admit it, had willfully been blind to it. Now the words and confirmation were out from another's lips—mind—and he could only deny it.

Trillia stepped back from him. "What's wrong? She's a great lady."

"She's eight years older than me." It shouldn't have continued to bother him, it didn't . . . but it was the rationalization that sprang to his mind to keep himself from believing she was his HeartMate, the block he'd used.

"Really? She doesn't look it. She's in very good shape. And that's still plenty young." Trillia wiggled her brows. "And I've heard that older women only get better in bed. Certainly true of older men."

Raz couldn't prevent a flush.

"Interesting." Trillia shook her head. "Del Elecampane."

"She's a GrandHouse lady."

Shrugging, Trillia went to the screen in the corner and began undressing from her last costume of a ship's uniform. Rosemary hopped down from his shoulder to explore the room.

Trillia said, "You're the only son of a GrandHouse"—she peeked around the screen—"and from what I understand of the strata of nobles in Druida, in Celta, your Family is higher up the social scale than hers. Than my GraceHouse, too." She ducked back, then came out in a comfortable onesuit a few seconds later.

Blackness edged his vision. Now that he admitted that Del was his HeartMate, bad choices loomed. His knees were locked, his hands fisted, and there was a distant panic that he was going to lose and the loss would be hard.

"What's wrong?" Trillia crossed the small dressing room to a twoseat and perched on the arm.

Raz licked dry lips, stared in her general direction but didn't meet her gaze. "Del Elecampane is a *cartographer.*"

Another shrug. "Even I know that."

"A cartographer who is often on the trail. Always on the trail. Far away from Druida or any other city." His chest was tight. He wasn't breathing right. He settled into his balance and began a good cycle of counted breaths.

Trillia gave him a three cornered smile. "You could be a traveling player."

"*I haven't trained for more than a decade to be a traveling player!*"

Wincing, Trillia said, "Sorry, bad joke."

"I will not leave Druida. I have my career to think of. I don't *want* to leave Druida."

"Plans change. Mine did," Trillia said.

Raz opened his mouth, shut it.

"Good," Trillia said. "I think you were about to insult me." She came close and stared up at him. "Del could move to Druida."

He meant to shake his head, but his whole body jerked, he was so stiff. He'd risen from his grounded balance and hadn't even noticed. His body had betrayed him, after all the long training. Is this what he had to look forward to with a HeartMate? Being completely off balance? Again he softened his knees. "Del has problems in the city. She's become pale, lost some weight." Other things he hadn't wanted to notice or admit. "She's sleeping less, more restless."

Trillia pursed her lips. "Just not a city person."

"No."

Her chest rising and falling with her own deep breaths, Trillia nodded. "All right," she said with a calm that he never associated with her. She tilted her head. "What did you plan to do next with your career?"

Raz felt like he was standing on a narrow bridge spanning a chasm; either way he fell would be terrible. He pulled his thoughts together and spoke from cold lips. "Johns and I have discussed this new play of Amberose's; we're hoping—"

"A new play by Amberose." Trillia clasped her hands and held them to her breasts. "Really?"

One more deep breath and he was on solid ground, wouldn't think about it right now. Later. As he'd been putting off "later" for so long.

"Yes." He eyed Trillia. "Two male parts, two female, I think." He frowned. "But Johns knows better. We heard Amberose's agent contacted Lily Fescue, too."

"Lily," Trillia said darkly. She flopped back down on the twoseat, captured one of the cushions to squeeze.

"Scry Johns," Raz said. "Maybe, if we're approached, we can drop your name."

"Thanks."

A knock came at the door.

"Who's there?" asked Trillia, but Raz already knew. Del. He wasn't ready to see her. He could call on all his acting ability to be "natural," but both of the women—and his Fam, and Shunuk—would know he acted. So he had to be himself and right now he didn't want to be with her.

"Del Elecampane," Del said.

Trillia glanced at him, then said, "Come in."

Del strode in with the hint of a smile on her face. "Have a good talk—" Her face closed down as she caught the mood.

"We were just discussing Amberose's new play," Raz said as Shunuk came in.

"A lot of that going around." She glanced at him.

Rosemary took that moment to leap onto Shunuk from the counter, he shook her off, and Del jumped and caught the flying kitten before she hit the dressing room mirror. She cradled the cat.

I got you, Rosemary said to Shunuk.

Shunuk rolled his back and ignored her.

"What's that smell?" Trillia wrinkled her nose.

Del said, "Stridebeast. I have one stabled here."

"Oh," Trillia said.

*T*he short glider trip from the theater to his Family's place was taut with tense silence between Raz and Del.

Instinctively, he'd narrowed the bond between them. Shock and grief and anger had rolled through the thread from her. She was stiff beside him and had a mask on. Trying to hide her feelings from him, as he was trying to hide his own shock and fear and anger . . . and grief. They sat, nearly vibrating with emotions that they weren't talking about. It might have been amusing if he hadn't felt so wretched, for himself and her.

When they returned to T'Cherry estate, they got another shock. Straif was sprawled out in a large chair drinking good alcohol and three guardsmen awaited them—none of whom Raz had met before.

"What's wrong?" Raz asked.

Straif looked at him, impassive. "I found your man."

Raz tensed, then deliberately relaxed his muscles. "Oh?"

"Not good," Del said quietly.

"Not really. He's dead." Tossing back his drink, Straif sucked in a breath, then stood. The guards did, too. "I've told these gentlemen as much as I know. I'm sure that the petty criminal was murdered by the other man. All the signs point that way. The other guy was the one in charge. Don't know if he's the person behind all this." Straif's nose twitched. "I'm inclined to think he isn't. His clothes and his personal smell don't quite match, like he lives in someone else's House."

Straif swept his gaze to each of them. "A noble house or even a Residence, but not one I know. Don't think the victim lives here. He had the scent of Druida on him." Straif stretched, a physical man limbering every joint in his body after a long day; Raz noted the movement for use in the future.

Then Straif's deep blue gaze bore into him. "My trail lies in Druida City. I took the liberty of contacting T'Cherry and requesting a seat in the last express airship there." He gestured to the guards. "These gentlemen want to talk to you, show you a holo of the dead guy." Straif rolled his shoulders and there were a couple of pops, then he bowed to Raz. "Good seeing you again." He glanced around and his mouth twisted. "Nice place."

It was emptier than Raz—and his Family—liked, but the destruction was gone. "Thank you," he said.

Raz saw from the flicker in the lord's eyes that Straif had noticed he didn't hold Del's hand or have an arm around her waist. Raz thought the tracker knew to a millimeter the amount of space between them, sensed their tension with each other.

Straif prowled toward them, took Del's hand, and lifted it to his lips in a polished gesture, a FirstFamily GrandLord gesture. "See you later, Del. You and Doolee have another appointment for your holo portrait in three days." He sniffed. "Don't come by stridebeast, that takes two weeks."

"We leave tomorrow," she replied coolly. "Raz is driving a glider back for T'Cherry by the new route through Fairplay Pass. Glider's shorter than stridebeast, longer than airship."

"Right." Straif reached over and rubbed Rosemary between her blue gray ears. "Cute kitten."

I AM! Rosemary replied and started her thin purr.

Straif glanced back at the Gael City guards. "My thanks for your help."

The local guardsmen looked dubious.

"I'll teleport to the Airpark." Straif strolled from the chamber into the entryway, picked up a duffle, and 'ported away.

One of the guards cleared his throat awkwardly, holding a sphere. "Will you two look at the crime scene and body?"

Raz lifted Rosemary to meet her eyes. *I think I heard a mouse in the main bedroom this morning. It should be out and running around by now.*

His FamKitten narrowed her eyes suspiciously. *You THINK?*

"Yes." He kept his face guileless.

She sniffed, commenting on his wish to get her out of the way. He stroked her from head to tail. She was just a baby and didn't need to look at dead bodies . . . unless they were mice she'd dispatched herself. Without a sound she vanished from his hands and he heard a tiny thump from the MasterSuite.

Del had walked over to the guard, glanced down at the image in the sphere. "I don't know him." She frowned. "That looks like one of the fairground groves."

"Yes."

"We were near there earlier today, about WorkEndBell."

"So T'Blackthorn informed us. You didn't go into the grove?"

"No. We were on the fairground itself and the three western gliderways. That grove is to the east."

Raz strode to the guard, held his palm up for the holo, braced himself. When he glanced down, he saw a strange scene in an eerie gray and white that revealed every detail of the night. He caught his breath at the sight of the body, a person whose life had fled, violently. The man was small with even features and a weak chin. He lay on his side and black liquid—blood—had pooled under him. His mouth was open slightly, his eyes, thankfully, were closed.

"How'd he die?" Raz asked.

"Knife. At about the same time the lights went on after *Heart and Sword* ended," the older guard said.

Raz nodded, saw Del do the same. "I think I've seen him before." Raz closed his eyes, forced away the afterimage of the body. Thought of the man alive and standing, moving. "It would be better if I'd seen him moving."

"Dead don't move much," said another guard.

Raz shrugged. "I think he was one of the thieves at T'Spindle's party who vandalized my glider. He had enough Flair to teleport himself and the other man away."

The guard grunted. "Or enough practice."

Raz opened his eyes and gave the man an edged smile. "That's all I remember. You can contact T'Spindle about it."

"We'll talk to Winterberry, who is the Druida liaison. Leave it to us." They all stood. "Thank you for your help," the older man said. None of them offered their hands but turned and left the house with brisk solidity.

Raz poured himself a brandy. This little surprise had diverted him from the thorny problem of his HeartMate.

*R*az had slammed a door between them.

Something had happened in the theater. Del didn't know what it was, but now that the guardsmen were gone, they could deal with it. Trillia must have made some comment about her. "What's wrong?"

"Nothing."

A lie and she didn't think he'd ever lied to her before.

"You don't want to talk about what's bothering you, say so. Don't lie."

He lifted eyes that swirled with hot emotions that she couldn't define, stood. "All right." He bowed. "My apologies." His jaw flexed. "Everything's wrong and I don't want to talk about it." He went past her through the dining room and the kitchen; she heard him put the snifter in the cleanser. His voice floated back. "I'll be sleeping in the blue guest room tonight; take any room you want."

That stabbed. Her blood drained from her head and clamminess wrapped around her. Her gut churned with nausea.

He didn't want loving, sex, closeness. Easier to tell her when he wasn't looking at her? Not even in her presence?

She took a deep breath and stood in his way when he returned. He didn't meet her eyes.

"You don't want to be in my company? Fine. I'm not the one due at work in two days." She lifted her chin, met his surprised gaze. "You and Rosemary go ahead in the glider. I'll pick up my stridebeast and Shunuk and I will ride back to Druida City. Doolee and T'Apple can wait. I want my mount in town, anyway. For the moment." Until they headed out again on an empty winding road away from him.

Lady and Lord, she hurt. She didn't know she could hurt so bad. She talked around the lump in her throat. She would not show him how devastated she was. She didn't want to understand how devastated she was herself.

"You're walking away?" No actor's voice here; pure man, reacting.

She trembled inside. After a mental spell to keep herself from shuddering, she said, "Yes."

The atmosphere sizzled between them, with anger and hurt, not passion. Raz's jaw clenched and unclenched. He said nothing.

Del gave a sharp nod. "Right." She turned on her heel and strode toward the door.

He caught up with her in three steps, caught her hand, lifted it to his mouth. "I'm sorry. Please. Don't go."

Even with the spell, she flinched, dammit!

He took both her hands, held them tight, spoke fast and husky.

"I don't want you out of my life. Not yet. Please don't go . . . yet. I'm not ready for this to end now. I've hurt you and I'm sorry. I . . . I . . . care for you, Del. You must know that."

She did, but she wanted more. She wanted *everything*. So much, too much. "Now"—he wanted to live only in the moment. She was once good at doing that.

"My lovely Del." He opened the link between them and she was flooded with emotions overwhelming her. Sparkling yearning urgent need . . . his and hers.

She hung on to him as she strove to master the emotions clashing inside her, rocking her, only managed a whisper. "I won't go . . . yet."

He dropped her hands to grab her close and wrap his arms around her. His breath was ragged in her ears. "Stay with me, for now."

She wanted forever. She shut out the future, croaked, "For now."

They made love on the floor and later he carried her upstairs and they bathed and loved again. But after he'd fallen asleep, she was left empty and staring at the ceiling, contemplating a lonely, winding road.

*T*he next morning she awoke before dawn as usual and thought of Raz's behavior the night before. He'd had a few shocks. Hell, so had she, viewing that murder scene. Murder brought this mess of thefts and vandalism to a whole other level. Not much she could do but be careful and protect her own.

Her own Fam, her own man.

Just how long he'd be her man, she didn't know, but she knew enough that she was going to have a very hard time walking away from him.

But she had tentative plans for a compromise . . . maybe. Where could they live that would please them both?

She hadn't seen the HeartGift she'd given him. What did it show as Raz's perfect home?

What if it revealed something in Druida?

She didn't know. Maybe she could get something from Healers to help her live in the city, or the starship *Nuada's Sword* might have a remedy, but she flinched at the thought.

Wouldn't a HeartMate's home be a place where she could live, too?

She didn't know. Maybe HeartMate love didn't mean living together, but would stretch to living in different places, or one being on the road and the other in a city. The thought made her feel hollow.

She didn't know what would happen when they went back to Druida City, either. The more time she spent there, the more she felt like a spring was winding tight inside her, ready to snap. This trip had loosened it a bit, and a two-day glider ride through countryside would help, but a heavy dread waited.

Raz woke then and opened his eyes, they went from blurry to sharp as he smiled with a sweetness that made her clench. Surely he would come to love her like she loved him? Maybe not; she loved him so intensely it felt as if it had sunk into her very bones, never to be removed.

Never wholly her own self again.

Thirty

They had nearly recovered their previous easiness by the time they took a waterfall together—and made love again—and dressed, preparing to leave Gael City.

Del packed her duffle, swept the room with a practiced glance to see she hadn't left anything. Knew she had left a lot of herself here: her quiet satisfaction at being alone with Raz; her innocence before she got involved in a murder; much of her hope that she and Raz would live together as HeartMates. "Ready?"

"Wait," he said, adjusting his cuffs, then taking something from his trous pocket. She wore her good leathers, he wore a fashionable linen trous and shirt suit with minimal blousing of the sleeves and legs. He'd always be the better dressed of them.

He set a circle of papyrus about five centimeters wide above her left breast, tapped it. Del felt a warmth as whatever design on the sheet was transferred to her leathers. With a grin, Raz took her fingers and led her to the mirror. "Look."

The ancient symbol of the theater—a happy white mask and a sad black one—was now inscribed on her leathers. Raz circled his finger around it. "You're now a lifetime member of the Theater Guild."

Turning over the hand he held, he pressed more circles of papyrus into her palm. "For all your leathers." He cleared his throat. "I like the looks of it."

"I do, too. A wonderful gift, thank you." Her own voice was husky.

Rosemary and Shunuk trotted into the room; they'd been wandering, "out looking for a last wild nibble." Both appeared satisfied.

Time to go? A new ADVENTURE, glider ride home! Rosemary said.

"Time to go," Raz agreed. Once more he scanned the room. "I've done the best I can for this place." He shrugged. "I'll let my sister and parents take care of the rest, make it what they want."

Del got the feeling that he'd crossed some inner threshold, that whatever place this house and estate had had in his life had changed forever. She recalled the holo murder scene and figured that would affect anyone.

He glanced at her. "I don't think others of my Family will have to view that holo. I'm glad."

Because this was their place more than his. "I'm glad, too."

They did a tour of the house and estate, left before WorkBell dawn.

To Del's surprise, Raz had already arranged transport for her stridebeast to Druida and stabling in the city.

As soon as they reached the outskirts of Gael City, tension dropped from Del like a heavy load off her back. She sighed and thinned her window to open air. Raz thinned the roof.

Rosemary hopped up and down in her web sling with glee. *Go, go, GO!*

Raz did. He drove faster than any glider on the road, not that there were many. They headed out on the standard route of hard-packed earth toward Druida. Del shut her mind to the destination and lived in the now.

They would travel over plains and foothills and camp in one of the mountain valleys tonight, then take the new airship and glider route through Fairplay Canyon the next morning. At the speed they were going, they'd cut several septhours off the usual glider trip. More than she'd anticipated.

Soon Raz put the glider on auto and they tilted their chairs back and snacked. The small food storage no-time held exotic cocoa and caff drinks and Del admitted that this particular glider travel was superior to stridebeast.

Raz was an easy traveler. He took enough breaks that kept Del and the Fams happy with stretching and play, and lunch was cheerful with food and a game. As the day progressed, they rebuilt the foundation of their relationship that had crumbled the night before, but Del was all too aware that the peace between them was fragile. Life could so easily break them.

There was a looming dread that she wouldn't be able to make it come out right. If Raz wasn't willing to make it come out right, too, it was hopeless.

They entered the Hard Rock Mountains late in the afternoon and turned off the main glider road. A few miles later they came to a verdant valley and the glider began to slow.

Raz turned to her with a smile. "I've always liked this place—Verde Valley. You can see that abandoned resort from the road and air."

Del squinted as the estate came into view and memory clicked in. There was a medium-sized house that had been there since she'd started her career. A few years after that someone had built a larger hotel and billed it as a spa resort, so it must have hot springs. There were other outbuildings, barns, and stables for stridebeasts and horses.

Both a river and small lake graced the property. "Not a wise investment. Too far away from Gael City and Druida."

"About halfway." Raz's forehead wrinkled. "But I don't think that's too far."

Del shrugged.

He did, too, at the same time. They laughed together. He said, "But we made the trip by glider at least once a season, by airship, too."

"Beautiful valley." Lush and green with hills in the foreground and towering mountains in the back. She narrowed her eyes. "This will be the main gliderway to the new Fairplay Canyon route."

"Yes."

"Hmmm." The house was a sprawling one-story building with a large half-round sunroom of many-paned glass facing the lake. "Charming," she said. She was never one for a totally straight-walled building.

"Yes," Raz said. "Slow to minimum PublicGlider speed through Verde Valley." The place came into greater focus. "You know"—he scanned the estate—"the Family that owns this might be able to make it work again if they sank some gilt into it, what with our new route. Good place to spend the night. Luxuries, you imagine?"

"Well, spa—hot springs, probably. Large inn building, excellent quality . . . but plenty of noble Families have estates in the south near Gael City, nothing special to bring them here."

"But on their way there and back . . ." Raz shook his head. "It was a thought. Lovely house and inn."

Shunuk gave a lusty sniff. He'd stuck his head out his window, but the rest of him was in a webshield. *Lots of good smells, good game, good hunting.*

PRETTY! Rosemary said.

Raz rolled his shoulders and pulled the driving bar from the console. "The opening to Fairplay Canyon isn't that much farther, three kilometers or so. I thought we'd camp there tonight."

"Sounds good."

"Dad said there was one of the new four-rod pavilions stowed in this vehicle."

"Huh," Del said. She glanced back, saw four hand-length tubes under Rosemary's portion of the ledge.

The kitten grinned at her, bounced in her sling. *OUT soon.*

"For sure." Del nodded. It had been a good day, spent with Raz and the Fams. Lively with talk, but with some nice quiet periods of like-minded silence or throbbing jazz that filled the vehicle. She cherished the time together.

They stopped in the shadow of the mountains just before the entrance to the narrow canyon.

The pavilion went up with a chanted four-line rhyming spell, the hand-sized rods lengthening until they were over Raz's head, and the protective shields curving around it in a sphere. They'd made the area spacious, about as large as Raz's bedroom.

All the bugs and small animals were driven from the sweet, high grass under the watchful eyes of Shunuk and Rosemary. Del thought Raz had given the prey a helpful, Flaired "push to escape" since both Fams pounced several times and missed.

Raz set out mats, a large one for Del and him, a smaller one for Shunuk, and Rosemary's new feather pillow . . . properly bespelled to keep clean.

Del made the fire and brought raw kebabs from the no-time in the glider, set them cooking.

The night was incredible, eating and laughing with Raz, watching the sun set and the sky deepen into black studded with stars that were all the brighter for not being in the city. Sitting cuddled with Raz in the silence of the wild . . . crickets and birdsong and the rush of wind in the whispering aspen.

Perfect.

Until they realized Rosemary was gone.

Raz's fingers clamped on Del's fingers as fear spurted through him. He'd been drawing her away from the fire and to the pavilion for sex under the stars. He'd glanced at Rosemary's pillow and she was gone. Not anywhere in the safe area.

Calm! Del said mentally, but her body had tensed and her pulse was racing. *You have a bond with her, you would have known if anything happened.*

Nausea and panic had him fumbling for his small connection

with Rosemary. He hadn't known her for that long, but he loved her. A thin thread. Tiny, really, as small as a blue gray kitten that would blend in with the shadows in the night.

Yes! There it was. She was all right. Curious, but not exploring. He couldn't tell how far away she was.

His grip eased on Del's hand; she bumped his shoulder in friendly support. After a couple of regulated deep breaths, he called, *Rosemary! You are not on your pillow.*

No answer. Anger surged to replace the panic; he slapped it down.

Rosemary?

The kitten didn't respond and his link with her wasn't strong enough for him to understand what she was feeling.

His link with Del was another matter. Her panic had fled, too, and now she was amused.

"I can't locate Rosemary from my link."

"Shunuk isn't with her but knows she's fine. He wants to hunt, won't be any help."

Another big breath. Raz rolled his shoulders to loosen them, brought Del's fingers to his mouth for a kiss. Then he said, "You must have a small bond with the kitten, too, and you're used to Fam links. With your help, I'm sure we can find her."

"Of course."

Suddenly it was open, that bond between them, the HeartMate bond that scared him so, but he was willing to use it to find his wayward Fam. Del was willing to give, as always, and Raz hesitated. She'd been so generous, he'd taken so much from her, though he was certain that she'd searched for him. But his kitten journeying alone in the wild took precedent now.

He joined both hands with Del and the Flair rolling between them doubled. Closing his eyes, he traced his link with Rosemary until he could tell what direction she'd gone . . . about three kilometers to the southwest, longer by glider.

She was at the abandoned estate!

Del sighed beside him. *Not surprising for a curious kitten.*

Shunuk and I have been this way before, so he has explored the place. Naturally, I did not.

Naturally not.

Best if we walk; how're your shoes?

He thought of his elegant half-boots and knew brush would ruin them.

There can be marsh here, too.

"Oh, joy," he said aloud.

A wisp of smile curved her lips then disappeared, along with her dimples.

"You think we can get onto the estate?" he asked.

"We'll find a way or lure Rosemary into the open where we can see that nothing is around her and—"

"Teleport her." Raz's free hand fisted. "This isn't good."

"She's just a baby," Del said matter-of-factly.

"We'll have to set behavior parameters."

"Good luck," Del said and started walking.

It wasn't too long before they reached the boundary of the estate, though Raz's appreciation of the landscape had deteriorated as he walked through brush, a patch of marsh, and stumbled over a few rocks.

A thin spellshield rose before them. Raz frowned.

Del said, "Won't keep much out, probably the larger animals haven't tested the space lately, but when they do, there will be trouble. You know who owns this?"

"No."

"Neither do I. I'll ask at the Guildhall when we get back and notify them." Del's blond curls, silver in the waning twinmoonslight, lifted in the breeze when she shook her head. "We may trigger an alarm."

There is a hole in the spellshield. Shunuk appeared before them, grinning, his plumy tail waving. *Even storyman can get through.*

Raz knew then that his whole travel suit was ruined, as well as his boots. He sighed. "Lead us to it."

After another half septhour of walking, they reached the

gliderway to the estate where it branched from the main road. Raz shivered at the thought of his kitten wandering this far.

The "hole" was a thin place in the shield as it collided with the spellshield of the public gliderway that had been put up by the local council. Shunuk hunkered down and wiggled through, so did Del, and the view of her butt was the nicest thing that had happened so far. Her leathers didn't have a mark on them.

He lowered to the ground and inched through on his belly, feeling the threads of his shirt and trous catch and pull.

Then they were inside the estate and his breath caught.

"There's something about this place," Del whispered. "Special."

He was better with words than she, but he was speechless, too. A breeze carrying the heady scent of flowers prickled across his skin.

Del had marched down a crushed white gravel path that glinted as bits of mica caught the moonslight. She stood staring at the house, hands on hips. "There's a lot of Flair in this land. Why, I'm not sure. Might have been an old settlement or something, though I didn't know about it." She shrugged. "Another bit of research. Definitely a spring infused with Flair nearby. No wonder someone thought a spa would be a good investment."

She sniffed, turned to where her nose pointed.

Nice pond in that direction. No fish, though. Much Flair, Shunuk said.

"Now that you're here, would you mind leading us to Rosemary, please?" Raz asked.

Shunuk trotted toward the house. Raz followed, then realized that Del still stood, staring in the direction of the hot springs. She must be accustomed to soaking in hot springs on the trail, and for a moment the notion tempted . . . Del and him naked in hot springs together, playing, exploring . . .

Shunuk yipped and Raz was grounded from his fantasies. But, damn, he was going to talk to Rosemary when he got his hands on her.

Raz proceeded slowly, glancing over his shoulder until Del reluctantly came after.

They found the kitten curled up and sleeping in a small enclosed garden at one end of the house. She was tucked under a wooden bench that circled a tree. Raz would have never seen her, but Shunuk poked his nose at her.

"Rosemary," Raz said in tones of doom.

The kitten froze. Then she pranced out, head tilted up at an ingratiating angle, eyes big. *Greetyou, FamMan.*

His hands itched to pick her up and pet her, so he crossed his arms and glared down at her. "You are not on your expensive pillow. You are not in the pavilion. You are not in the camp. All of which you promised to be."

She shifted from paw to paw, looked aside, licked a patch of shoulder fur but still watched him.

"No caviar for a year."

The kitten hopped to her feet then into the air. *A YEAR! I will be OLD!*

"And since you don't like to stay with your pillow, I am going to take it away until I can trust your word."

She hunched in on herself, looking pitiful.

Del walked up.

THEY cried and they called and I had to come, Rosemary said.

"What?" he and Del asked in unison.

Rosemary sat up straighter but kept her eyes wide and round, not hard to do in the low light. *I thought they were KITTENS.*

"Kittens?" Raz looked around.

Shunuk barked with a note of scorn. *No kittens here.*

Raz had the uncomfortable feeling that at one time Shunuk considered kittens as food.

Del was frowning and prowling, lifting her feet as if feeling something through the ground. Raz snatched Rosemary up; she wiggled, then caught his stern look and went limp. He set her on his shoulder with a "stay" spell. Closing his eyes, he sent his awareness around him. Now his anxiety about Rosemary had eased, he felt the full effect of this place. It felt . . . old. . . .

"Kittens," muttered Del, then shook her head. "Nope, I don't sense anything like 'calling and crying kittens.' Do you, Raz?"

He opened his eyes. Saw the world in shades of black and gray and silver. "No."

They are right under THERE! Rosemary insisted, kneading his shoulder with paws and snagging her claws on his shirt. Despite its name, this suit did not travel well. *They are SAD, they have been ABANDONED. They CRY.* Rosemary thrashed around on his shoulder.

Thirty-one

*W*e *believe you," Del soothed, glanced around again.*

Shunuk sniffed. *No young of any kind around here.*

Rosemary plunked her bottom onto Raz's shoulder stubbornly. *YES THERE ARE.* She sniffed right back at Shunuk. *They feel like the LITTLE WARMTHS in Del's house.* Another, final, sniff.

"I don't have any young things in my house," Del said. "Only when Doolee and Antenn come over to . . ." She sat down on the tree bench, held out a hand to Raz, and he took it. When she tugged, he sat. But he'd felt Del's burst of understanding.

Del leveled her gaze at Rosemary. "Little warmths, not quite intelligent?"

You KNOW! Rosemary trilled. She hopped up and down on his shoulder, a small weight.

Del was shaking her head and again he noticed the twinmoons-light on her hair. Extraordinary hair. She looked more vulnerable by moonslight, shadows tinting her face. Raz stroked her hair. "What?" he asked.

"HeartStones?" Del asked. "A House becoming a Residence?"

"HeartStones?" Raz let surprise tinge his voice. He looked at the low house, its many windowpanes. "That means the house has been here longer than I thought."

"Me, too." Del cleared her throat, glanced at Rosemary. "Can you, uh, communicate with the little warmths?"

Rosemary lifted her nose. *They were HAPPY to see Me. I LISTENED to them and kept them company.*

"Ah," Del said. "Why don't you try telling them that you must go but that we'll see they aren't abandoned." She rubbed her face and grumbled, "Hard enough to get folk to watch D'Elecampane House, here . . ."

Purring and humming, Rosemary grew warmer on his shoulder. She was using Flair, Raz realized. The link between him and his Fam was open, but it still wasn't strong and wide, not like his link with Del.

Yet, he could vaguely sense that she was sending emotions to something else. A shiver went through his bones. He'd never felt emanations from HeartStones, not even when he'd been T'Cherry Heir as a child.

Flair was increasing with every generation.

I have told them, Rosemary said in a little voice. *They are not happy, but they will wait.* She curled her claws into Raz's shoulder until he yelped. *They must NOT be abandoned again.*

Del stood. "I said I'd take care of it, didn't I?"

Rosemary didn't answer.

Del grunted and turned to walk away. Raz caught her hand, recalled that strangely familiar feeling he'd had, and said, "As long as we're here . . ."

"You want to look around?" Del sounded surprised.

He grinned. "Guilty pleasure, exploring a secret and forbidden area."

She slanted him a look. "We don't go in the house or the hotel." Her mouth turned down. "Or the springs if they are enclosed."

"Fine," he said and took her hand again.

So they walked around the house, long and rectangular except for the large semicircular room that extended in the back. They strolled through overgrown gardens filled with wild roses that fragranced the air. They stood and looked at the hotel, agreeing that it was still in good shape.

Inside one of the large outbuildings, Raz said, "Wonder what this was," then stopped. The acoustics of the building were extraordinary. He dropped Del's hand, began moving around, reciting bits and pieces of plays, throwing his voice, listening to the sound.

"What?" Del asked.

Instead of answering, he took her hand and pulled her to one end of the building, turned her in his arms and launched into the role he was playing now, curving his arm around her waist. "Darling, I was so worried." He raised his brows. She'd seen the show often enough to know the lines. "And you say . . ." he prompted.

She went sticklike in his arms. "What?"

He shook his head. "No, that's not right, you say—"

"You fool!"

"That's not right, either."

Shunuk snickered from where he sat watching, an audience of one.

Raz said, "The line is: 'I didn't mean to worry you, but I found the locket!'"

From Raz's shoulder, Rosemary put in, *FamMan was worried about ME!*

"This is a play," Raz said, then he turned to look into close yellow eyes. "Yes, I was. Don't wander off again."

Del gasped. "I can't do this!" She pushed against him.

He tightened his grip and grinned at her. "Sure you can. There's only Shunuk and Rosemary to see. They won't be critical."

"Ha." Del snorted. "Much you know about Fams."

He eased back from the pretend-kiss. "I don't think my lady in the play ever makes that sound."

"Not a strong character. Can't see clues in front of her face, gets into trouble," Del said.

"Maybe you're right." She was right, of course. "A mystery might not suit you."

We know Summer Flowers *best,* Shunuk put in.

"Ah." A show that had been vized two years ago. His first lead. It had been a very young man's role. Everything swam back into his memory, and his posture altered, his attitude, as he became the youngster sweeping his equally young lover up into his arms. He gazed down at Del with burning intensity. "I have loved you for years." His voice trembled with the remembered note.

"I have loved you for years," Del whispered huskily, her voice low and vibrating with truth and not sweet and high and gushing with youthful enthusiasm. But this was right, the mood and the words and the way her eyes caught his, the way her feelings opened to his, the way the bond between them pulsed.

All was true. Hurt throbbed, his and hers. A touch of despair. He didn't know how he could bear it when she rode out of his life. But he didn't know how he could give up the fulfillment of his career, either. Didn't want to consider the choices.

OUCH! Rosemary screeched. *I DON'T like that FEELING. And I am hungry!*

The moment was broken.

Stup kitten, Shunuk said, yawning. *To leave safe camp with good food. Lucky she didn't become dinner herself.*

"The fox has a point," Raz said. "Which is why I was worried about you." Reluctantly he placed Del on her feet. He glanced around the building, shook his head. "Excellent acoustics." His smile was lopsided. "Like everything else here, this place has possibilities. Let's go back to camp."

"I know the coordinates and the light well enough in these mountains to 'port us there," Del said, her hand warm in his.

He wanted to bend down and brush her lips with his, but he was still disturbed. Instinctively he'd retreated—and so had she, their bond had narrowed, both of them trying to protect themselves from pain. He wondered if that would work, for either of them.

* * *

The next day a little after noon they were out of the mountain pass and on a newly improved gliderway through the rest of the range into Druida City. His father would be pleased that they'd shaved a good six septhours off the trip. He could almost see the man grinning and rubbing his hands at the gilt he could charge the Councils for widening and hardening the ground of a public road. All those who had gliders—and that would be upper-class nobles—would prefer this way for sure.

The Family who owned the hotel could make gilt, too.

He'd let Del drive the glider cautiously along the mostly straight road through the mountains. She even reached top speed once and occasionally appeared as if she was enjoying herself, though she didn't care as much for guiding a glider as she did for riding—stridebeast or horse. But she valued a new skill.

That pleased him. Once again he had given her something she prized, and when she returned to her estate, she'd find that her ancient Family glider had been refurbished by the Cherrys. Next to that vehicle was a two-year-old previously owned glider in Cherry red that Raz had purchased for her through his father. It was a sturdy vehicle easy to drive and navigate. Thinking of her surprise and satisfaction at the gift—he *had* heard her mumble that she'd have to buy a new glider—made him smile.

"Why don't you take the glider all the way into Druida?"

A horrified expression crossed her face. She glanced at the control panel with all the dials and buttons and pressed the "auto slow" one, ordered, "To the side of the gliderway, please." The vehicle lost speed and pulled over, though they'd only seen one other glider and a few heavy-duty transports. Del dismissed the safety webshield, flung up her door, and stretched. Raz got out and appreciated the flexibility of her body as he stretched himself. He walked around the glider, grabbed her waist, swung her around in the sheer joy of being with her.

She flung back her head and laughed and he nibbled at the taut line of her throat, enjoying her fingers tightening on his shoulders, her mind hazing with desire. He slid her down his body, humming at the feel of her against him, his sex hardening.

Rosemary is running away! Shunuk said.

Growling, Raz set Del on her feet, saw a tiny bobbing black tail heading toward a gulch. Holding out his hands, he said, "Return to me!" and grasped a hissing, struggling kitten.

Rosemary glared at him. *I need to pee.*

Raz raised his brows. "Really? Didn't we stop the glider ten minutes ago so you could dig in the dirt and pee and dig again, and investigate the brush? That *was* you, wasn't it?"

With a glare past him, Rosemary didn't answer.

Raz turned to Del and stilled. She was looking toward Druida. Following her gaze, he saw the ripple of air in the distance—all the many shields of the city. A glint of metal as the sun gleamed on *Nuada's Sword,* maybe even the hint of a gray line that was the city walls.

Del's expression held a weary resignation. Checking on the open bond between them, he felt an underlying dread at returning to Druida. An image came to her mind of the landscape around them, the tree-covered hills, the mountains behind them jutting into the sky, the plains beyond that. All seemed to narrow down into a tube—like the tubelike corridor Raz had felt around him in the starship. That's what Druida City meant to Del—constriction.

She was taking deep breaths as if filling her lungs with country air, inhaling the essence of nature around them, ready to hold it against all the irritants of civilization.

It hurt to see her, to feel her dislike of all that he loved . . . the lights, people, entertainment, the knowledge that he could go somewhere any minute of every day and night and find something to do.

How could they be HeartMates? Surely two people should be better suited by lifestyle. He couldn't grasp how they could blend their lives.

Del lifted her hands and fluffed her hair, as if wanting the scent of sage and sunlight on her scalp for a few more minutes. She glanced at the glider and for the first time since he'd been a child unable to drive, Raz saw it as confinement.

He didn't know what to say, felt as if any words he'd speak would be wrong, would emphasize the differences between them.

She scanned the area, her eyes focused on a trail up a hill, a massive protrusion of rock hiding a path that was too narrow for a glider. She *knew* where that path went. Her mind showed him, flowers and brooks, patches of snow and more trails beyond with crystals embedded in hillsides. She *yearned* for that trail.

Just as he yearned for the applause of a full theater.

How could they be HeartMates?

With one last breath, she shook out her legs again and walked from the driver's side of the glider to the passenger door he'd left open. She let out a loud whistle. Better than he'd ever learned. *Shunuk, leaving in two. 'Port your tail to me.*

There was a distant yip.

Raz thought that he might even have been forgotten in this small pattern of theirs. He shoved Rosemary back onto her pillow behind his seat. Restlessness filled him and he couldn't figure out whether it was because he wanted to head back to the city or wanted to head off with Del and make love with her for days. And after that, what would he do? He was at home in a theater, not on the trail, especially any trail that wasn't made for a glider.

A small *pop* sounded and Shunuk sat at Del's feet. His coat looked as if he'd rolled in dust, and he had a satisfied smile that meant he'd caught and eaten something.

Mouse. Shunuk swiped his muzzle with a quick tongue. *Very tasty mouse, fat off the land.*

Del's eyes lingered on the path. "Plenty of good game this summer. It's been a bountiful year."

Raz had never hunted in his life. He slid into the car, thunked the door down, murmured the webshield on.

Del walked up to stand next to the glider and stretched again. "I don't miss hunting for food . . . rabbit or Celtan rabbit—mocyn— or wild clucker. Occasional wild furrabeast. But a person can only carry with her so many rations." She slanted him a smile. "Especially if she packs a lot of vizes or holos of plays."

Raz ordered the glider to auto into Druida, turned to Del. "Our lives aren't very alike, are they?"

She met his eyes. "No."

Honest, as always. He didn't think of Del as being a woman who would compromise. He took her hand, raised it to his lips. "You are a very special woman, Del."

"Thank you. I think the same about you."

He flashed a smile. "My thanks, too. I have to return this glider to T'Cherry Residence and report to my father about the trip . . . and the break-in and thefts."

"Of course."

"I want you to stay with me at T'Cherry Residence tonight."

She raised her brows. "With your Family?"

"Yes." He didn't want to speak the *HeartMate* word. Didn't want to get into any discussion of that. His gut squeezed as tight as a miser's pouch at the thought. Not now.

But there was a shadow of a notion in the back of his brain about the thefts and diary that needed to solidify. He knew if he gave it a couple of hours, it would coalesce, and he sensed he needed to be in T'Cherry Residence for the revelation.

Tilting her head, she met his eyes. He felt the feathery brush of her mind through their link. She frowned, then nodded.

"Good," he said. "You showed Dad and me around D'Elecampane House, let's show you around T'Cherry Residence." Again he kissed her hand, tasted her unique flavor . . . wild herbs. "I can promise you a fine meal and fine wine and entertainment."

She smiled back. "How can I resist?" Her brows dipped. "I have a change of good clothes, though they need to be freshened."

I have not roamed the T'Cherry estate, Shunuk said. *It will be fun.* The fox slid a glance to Rosemary. *You will love the other kitten.*

OTHER kitten! Rosemary screeched.

She is very elegant, Shunuk went on. He scratched his ear with his hind leg. *But you are bigger, though she is older.*

Rosemary hissed.

"We won't be staying," Raz said. "I don't live there anymore, won't be living there in the future." He thought of his apartment that he loved, thought of his career and the general idea he had of buying his own small house in the area where most actors and artists lived. That almost seemed a lost dream.

Too much brooding on old plans. An actor needed to be flexible in his mind, his body, his parts to make a good career.

"I also have a . . . feeling . . . about the diary."

Del's eyes widened and he smiled inwardly; it was hard to impress the woman, get any strong reaction from her—out of bed.

"I'll let you know when we get home."

She stilled and so did he. He'd meant T'Cherry Residence, but it wasn't truly home. Nor was his apartment. He thought of the landscape globe he'd chosen from her workshop that was sitting on a shelf in his dressing room, wondered if anything was showing in it yet. Something had been building in it the last time he looked.

No, he wasn't sure what was home, but was sure that it would be in Druida.

Home, a hard and sticky subject between them.

"Let's ride," Del said and slid into the glider, and Raz knew she was wishing she was on the back of a stridebeast.

They made excellent time and were at T'Cherry Residence in a couple of septhours. Raz and his mother showed Del around the Residence and she appreciated his childhood home.

The concept of home again. He itched to get his hands on his landscape globe but didn't want to leave Del. He was afraid she'd ride out—more afraid that he wouldn't stop her.

After dinner the Family went into the mainspace and Raz sat with Del on a twoseat, his arm across the back, nearly embracing her. He wanted her close . . . until she left.

Playing with her fingers, he waited until his parents and his sister and her HeartMate settled. Then he projected his Flair through the room until everyone looked at him.

He kept his voice low, a standard murmur that might not alert a certain entity—and might not arouse the kittens who had hissed and fought and then curled up on pillows in opposite corners to nap, ignoring each other. "I have done some thinking about the diary."

Everyone's attention keenly focused on him. He liked that just as much as in the theater, and if this show progressed the way he thought it would, he'd be a hero. Anticipation was sweet on his tongue.

He glanced at Del. "Del gave me an idea when she asked whether the diary should have been in the HouseHeart."

Del snorted. "Obvious question."

"It's not in the HouseHeart." Raz's father's brows knit.

"But when the diary went missing, this house wasn't a Residence," Raz pointed out.

"We still had a HouseHeart," Del's sister said.

"Also true," Raz said, then sank his voice lower. "But when the diary went missing, we couldn't *ask* the Residence if it might be here."

He snapped, "Residence, review all your spaces, check for an object that is not part of your structure but resonates of a human Family member, a box, perhaps, that has been hidden."

"Yes, Raz," the Residence said. "There is the box in the MistrysSuite placed there by D'Cherry."

His mother flushed, threw up her hands. "Gifts. I hide holiday gifts!"

"And Seratina's satchel in the HeirSuite bedroom." His sister blushed, too. "Never mind that one." The image of sex toys flashed into Raz's mind . . . everyone's minds, he guessed since they all stared at her. Her HeartMate's ears turned red and he sat stoically looking straight ahead.

"The gilt wallet in this mainspace hidey-hole," the Residence continued.

"Dammit," his father said.

"And an item that I have been forbidden to reveal by T'Cherry . . ."

"Cave of the Dark Goddess," his father exploded.

"Stop!" Raz said, carefully not looking at any of his Family. "Let me rephrase that."

Bunch of secretive pack rats, Del teased. *I suppose you have another treasure box here, too?*

Raz didn't dignify that comment with an affirmative answer. Del was just too used to having minimal possessions when she traveled. "We are interested in an object that resonates of a long-past human Cherry, that has been there since you have become aware of yourself. A box, perhaps, and if you can sense so far, inside the box might be old books."

"I am aware that there were journals," the Residence said with dignity. "They have been spoken of often, all the hidey-holes and secret caches have been searched."

"All of them that we know. But what of something that is not you, but has always been with you, never moved, yet has lingering human traces." He studied his Family, all of whom wore dubious expressions. No, not a hero this time.

Del squeezed his hand. *It was an excellent idea.*

"There is a small warmth..." the Residence said in nearly a whisper.

Everyone leaned forward. "Rather like my HeartStones. Always there. Always mine."

"But not a HeartStone," Raz's mother said in her most comforting, soothing voice.

"No. It is not in the HouseHeart."

"Maybe it should be," his father said gruffly.

"I like it where it is."

"May we please look at it?" Raz's sister asked. "Please? We want it, too. We won't ever take it away from you." Her glance swept around the room and they all nodded in agreement with her words, even Del.

"It is mine," the Residence said.

"It is ours, yours and ours, as all is."

"Someone is hunting it, hurting your Family looking for it." Del's voice was practical, and sharp.

"Where is this thing that is all of ours?" Raz's mother asked.

Thirty-two

A change in air pressure had the windows sighing. "It is behind the pantry."

"The original Cherry *was* a baker," Raz's mother said.

Everyone had instinctively risen to their feet—except Del. Her face was impassive. "I'll stay here."

She was his HeartMate, but neither of them had admitted it.

"Oh, but—" his mother started, then stopped and nodded.

So they trooped through the house to the large kitchen, through it. The pantry was large enough to hold them all.

His father cleared his throat. "Thank you very much for helping us, your Family. Where is it, Residence?"

"To your left, third shelf up." The Residence's voice had become smaller, younger, but there was trust in it.

The shelf might have been too high to see for older generations, but Raz's father could reach it. He pulled down a multitude of jars, grimacing as he did, handing them to his HeartMate. She frowned, too. "Your great-great-FatherDam's gooseberry jam."

Raz's sister stuck her tongue out. None of them liked gooseberry jam. His mother sighed. "These should have been thrown out years ago, but I forgot about them." The jars were over her head. She chuckled. "Of course the Residence didn't remind me of them."

Soon the entire shelf was bare, but there was no evidence of a safe or even a seam in the paneled wall. Raz's father stuck his hands in his pockets.

Raz said, "Residence, can you open the space for us?"

With a slow creak and a fall of dust, a panel square swung out. Inside was a polished box of gleaming cherry.

Raz's father hissed a breath, lifted it out, stared at it.

"Please shut the alcove," Raz said.

The panel swung shut, clicked in place. Raz put all the jars back up as his father continued to stare at the box.

"The breakfast room," T'Cherry said.

It was one of the oldest in the Residence, the most intimate for a Family of four—or six. *We are meeting in the small breakfast room,* Raz told Del. "Residence, can you give Del directions?"

They took their usual places around the circular table . . . and Del sat next to Raz. His parents were near the door, Raz next to his father, his sister between her husband and his mother. Del was the last one in, every footstep echoing with a creaking board . . . the Residence being nervous.

"We'll put the box and contents back, Residence," his mother said. "We will want to read the journal, and perhaps viz it for copies, but we *will* put it back."

Thank you, the Residence whispered in their minds. The curtains around the windows fluttered, though the room was usually without drafts.

Raz's father continued to stare at the box without touching it until Del sat. Raz took her hand, saw his sister was grasping her HeartMate's and mother's hands. Raz put his other hand on his father's near shoulder; his mother did the same.

Del reached across the table to take his brother-in-law's hand and the connection between them all snapped into place. Raz felt a vibration through his body, not only from the Family energy but from the floor beneath his soles to the crown of his head. "Residence, we feel you," he panted. "A little less energy, please? We know you will survive beyond us, and you are one of the threads that keep us Family."

A soughing came from the hallway.

"Residence, that's enough. Stop acting like a distrustful child," Raz's mother scolded.

The lights flickered at the reprimand but then brightened and remained steady.

Raz's father cleared his throat. "All right." He lifted the lid; it came easily and emitted a slight *whoosh* as a long-ago spell gave way and left the scent of rosemary . . . bread made with rosemary and sea salt, an old Family tradition.

The Cherrys sighed.

Raz's brother-in-law licked his lips. "Smells good."

"I haven't made that in too long," Raz's mother and sister said in unison, then smiled at each other. His sister gave a watery sniff.

T'Cherry lifted a book out. "There's two," he said. He passed the first one to his wife, took out the second.

"We don't have time to read all the entries tonight." Raz's mother stroked the cover of one and the connection among the Family diminished. Raz's sister put her free hand on her mother's shoulder and once more all let out a sigh as they became connected—everyone.

The books didn't look like books made on Celta. Four centuries old. Raz's heart pumped hard at the thought.

"Could you just read near the front and the back to see if she mentions any map? Flip through it for a drawing?" his sister asked.

But his father already was skimming the pages. "Plenty of little drawings, faces, the ship . . . *Lugh's Spear.*" He stopped and stared. "Broken." He whistled. "Lucky there weren't more casualties."

Del's grip nearly crushed Raz's hand. He squeezed back.

The pages fluttered faster, sped by Flair instead of fingers.

"It appears that mine is the first." Raz's mother turned to one of the opening pages, frowned. "The entries are hard to read, old script." She lifted her chin. "But I can do it."

It wasn't often that Raz was reminded that his mother had been a scholar; she'd always been such a charming hostess and caring mother.

She cleared her throat and began hesitantly, pausing between sentences, then continued smoothly.

All of my life I've lived on the Ship. I was born here and thought I'd die here like the generations before. I would look out the portholes at the black and white of the darkness and stars, the other colors I sensed but could not really see, and knew that the Ship was my home.

Like the two other Ships I could sometimes see out the portholes . . . the shining things not shaped like *Lugh's Spear*.

I didn't believe in the "mission" to get to another planet, a home world that was like those pieces of rock that we would occasionally pass.

I didn't believe that there were actually "golden ones," people who had boarded on Earth and not been born on the Ship, those who were whispered to sleep until we reached a planet. Which no one believed we would. Even kids knew that we were off course and there would be no planet.

Then word spread that there was a mutiny on *Nuada's Sword* and one of the most golden of the golden ones was awakened to handle this.

Everything must have changed there, because it affected us here. One of the few golden ones that traveled with us, instead of the newer *Nuada's Sword*, was awakened, too. He did have a golden glow around him. They said it was the remnants of the liquid in the tube that he slept in for so many years.

But they were wrong. I saw him once, the new Captain, walking in the hallway. There was a glow to his skin, but his aura also glowed. Golden.

And today for the first time in my memory, the Ship didn't just automatically alter course to avoid something, but *turned*. And we faced a green-tinged brown and blue and white sphere. I was in one of the viewing lounges when we turned and saw it for a moment.

They said it would be our new home. Celta. Named centuries ago back on Earth.

I am terrified.

Raz's mother paused.

"Imagine seeing a whole new world from a spaceship." Del's hushed voice sounded dazed.

Raz's sister shivered. "I'm quite happy here on the ground."

Raz's mother set the book facedown on the table and went to the kitchen, came back with a tray with carafes of caff and cocoa and six mugs, poured and doctored each cup. When Raz took his he found caff hot and strong and sweet, perfect. Del's dimples showed as she sipped her cocoa.

His mother drank deeply of her own caff, then picked up the book again and began to read.

The Ship broke!

"Landing" was horrible! I was gathered with my bunkies midship, like everyone else, in those rooms built to sustain stress. We were tossed around like dice in a cup. I have bruises everywhere and terror still lives in my heart.

Screaming and yelling started, but Captain Hoku controlled it. Said in that deep, calm voice of his that only the lower hull had been breached, that only people in Section Four who hadn't gone to their safe places were hurt and dead. I don't know that I believe him.

Doors all around the Ship opened and we were told to exit in an orderly fashion, taking only what we could carry.

I ran with the big satchel I'd made, taking these diaries.

Out into the light—a different light than I'd always known. Someone said it was too blue or white or something. But there were no walls! Even in the great greensward in the Ship, there was the hint of distant, curved metal walls.

Nothing surrounds me now. Anything could come from the sky, or from around me.

People fell down on the ground and screamed and shouted and cried.

I did, too.

Raz's mother paused, turned a page, and continued.

I am calmer, not so scared that I can't take writestick to paper and record my thoughts, and my fears, and my doubts. I'd always thought that I was a strong woman, but I shake nearly every minute of every day. I know nothing will ever be the same and I fear—everything, even people.

People I've known all my life have changed. Some broke and can't deal with the sky and the dirt and the trees and the horizon in the distance. I feel like that, too, but I will not beg to go back into the Ship.

They say we will have a gathering tonight, and everyone who wishes will speak and we will all decide on options. That is very strange. Me, a baker, having a voice in how the Ship—how the settlement is run? It makes me shake more.

I yearn to go back and live in the Ship. Many of us do. But the golden ones speak of making a town. So far no one has been allowed to reenter the Ship, our home.

I don't know what to do. Everything is too strange. The shakes have come again and I can't write.

Raz's mother's voice ended on a wobble. She leaned against his father, as his sister and husband angled together.

Del sat straight in the chair beside him. He put his arm around her shoulders and she relaxed a little.

"How awful, I never thought . . ." Raz's sister said.

Her HeartMate murmured love words, stroked her hair, said, "It all worked out. After all, we are all here."

"How courageous she must have been, they all must have been," Raz's mother said.

"Especially the generational crew," Del said. "The cryonic folk had it easier, the FirstFamilies."

"Yes," Raz's father said heavily, "those who survived the sleep." He leaned over and kissed his wife and HeartMate tenderly on her lips. "Can you go on? I'm fascinated."

"We all are," Raz said, his hands itching to hold the diary, to read, to act out this most personal Family memory.

Raz's mother nodded, glanced down at the page. Raz's father pulled his chair closer, followed her gaze as if he would read along with her.

His mother jolted in her seat, and they all stared at her.

After a long breath in and a short one out, his mother continued.

The Ship is gone!

We all woke to this terrible noise, this rumbling, breaking shaking noise! I staggered from the tent with the others and saw the ground give way and the Ship tilt down and more ground cover it up. Some people ran to it and were lost, too.

My home is gone.

"She saw it go down," Raz's father said. Everyone else exclaimed, too. Raz wasn't sure what came out of his mouth. Del's voice cut through the babble.

"Did she leave a map, give any directions?"

"No," his mother said. "Still no map. More about her feelings and less about her surroundings."

Del frowned, said slowly, "A woman like her, who'd lived on a starship all her life, might not be good at distinguishing flora and landmarks. You shouldn't hope for a map."

"Certainly we haven't seen anything at first glance," Raz's father admitted. "Skip to the end of your book, darling."

Raz's mother nodded.

I have thought long and hard. This is a pretty place, but I want more people. Hoku, he says not to call him Captain anymore, told us that the crew and most of the colonists—those who paid for the Ships and the trip and slept in the cryonics—have begun to build a big city where *Nuada's Sword* landed. Their machines work.

I don't know what a city is.

But I know what walls are and I think walls are a good thing. The walls of *Lugh's Spear* are gone forever.

The walls of the shelters—houses—being built here are not big enough for me. They only surround one group of families.

I will go with the two-thirds of us to this new city of Druida.

I only shake a couple of times a week now. But they are not our Ship "weeks" anymore. They are longer.

I had no say in that.

Raz said, "So she ends that diary when she ended her time at the settlement near where *Lugh's Spear* landed."

"Seems so," his father said, opened his own book, cleared his throat, looked down. With a shake of his head, he said, "I can't read this. I thought I could at first, but the letters are all squiggly." He smiled at his wife, then at Raz. "You two were the ones who studied the old language." Puffing out a breath. "Just for this moment, eh? In case we found the diary?"

His wife elbowed him with a mock frown. "I thought that was why you married me?"

"Yeah, I was trying to work out the script on those old cards. The divination cards! Raz, you still got those?"

"Yes. They weren't harmed in the break-in in my apartment. The pouch was opened and they were scattered, but the deck's complete."

"Lucky." His father's breath whooshed out. His thick brows

lowered. "But there isn't much info on the cards, is there, just draw-ings and the ancient script titling each card?"

"That's right. Though I found a couple with *Lugh's Spear* in the background."

"Really?" asked his sister. "Which ones?"

"Eight of Cups and"—he lifted Del's hand to his lips—"The Lovers."

His sister frowned. "Change."

"Ah, right," Raz said.

"Cards," his father murmured. "She might have mentioned them in here." He tapped the volume, then reluctantly slid it over to his wife. "You might see if a 'search volume' will find it."

"I'll read the opening page first," his mother said.

I did a sketch of the one now calling herself Dame Sea—after that old belief system they talk about all the time—and she liked it and gave me more paper. Now I can earn my way on this trek. People, those beginning to call themselves the FirstFamilies, and the upper echelons of the crew, are paying me for my sketches. It is a relief.

There is no baking to be done while we travel.

Divination cards have always worked for me, and I need something to keep my mind and hands busy on this journey, so I have decided to make some. I would prefer flexiplastic, but I don't have the resources of the Ship.

I think I will always miss *Lugh's Spear*.

"See if she mentions a map." T'Cherry shifted restlessly in his chair. When Raz's mother continued to scan the pages, he tapped it, said, "Find the word *map*."

"This volume is four hundred years old. Surely you don't think . . ." Raz's mother started, but the pages flipped.

"Some of her descendants read it, bespelled it. There were Flair security shields on the box and books." He craned to see, shook his head, and muttered, "Still can't understand it."

"I can," his wife said smugly. She ran a finger down the page, then read.

Every night when we gather around after dinner, he-who-was-Captain shows us a map of where we have been and where we are going and the progress that has been made. It is not like the only other map I have ever seen which was the inside of our lost *Lugh's Spear*. Like most everything else about this strange journey, the few who were in the cryonic tubes of *Lugh's Spear* have an easier time reading the map, though I study it. It is a top-o-graph-ic map.

I want to learn. I don't want to be stupid.

Stupidity has taken a toll on this trip, people have died or wandered away and never been seen again.

Those who were in the tubes and Hoku-who-was-Captain say we are lucky that it is summer. Again, it is something the rest of us do not understand, though our leader has patiently explained it more than once, a season is when the temperature and plants around us vary.

I try hard to learn, because not to learn will be to die.

"Cheerful," his sister said with a shiver.

"We can't possibly understand what they went through." D'Cherry patted her daughter's shoulder.

"The captain had a map." T'Cherry scowled. He rubbed his cheek. "What happened to it?"

Del shrugged. "Who knows? Do we even know what Family name he took?"

They all stared at each other. "ResidenceLibrary, are there any notations in any of your archives as to what Family name the *Lugh's Spear* Captain chose? He would have been a FirstFamily, wouldn't he?"

"No record," said the ResidenceLibrary's light female voice that sounded a lot like D'Cherry. "The Captain of *Lugh's Spear* was offered membership in the FirstFamilies, of course, but he declined."

"He *declined*!" Raz's sister sounded astonished.

"Hard to believe," T'Cherry said.

"The entry regarding him states he was very tired of leadership after *Lugh's Spear* and the responsibility of bringing the colonists from the landing site to Druida City."

"He was a great man," Raz's sister's HeartMate said.

"Yes." More lines dug into T'Cherry's forehead. "The original settlement, those who stayed near *Lugh's Spear*, died out, right?"

"History has it that the settlement was moved several times from the original location, then, yes, after a couple of generations the people were gone . . . dead or migrated to Gael City or Druida City."

"Sad," Raz's sister said.

"Yes," Raz said. "Celta is *still* a hard planet on her human inhabitants, and for new colonists . . ."

"Fatal to many," Del said.

"But not Mona Tabacin," D'Cherry said. "Not her. Let me read the final page . . ."

So I am finally settled in Druida. It isn't what I expected, but I have a fine stone house and a man and am happily pregnant. I have a Family.

Life is better for me than it was on *Lugh's Spear*. There I would never have been more than a minor crew member working in the kitchens. Here, I bake better than anyone else in the city.

I don't shake much anymore, the journey got so tiring that I had no energy to do so, and I am happier, have accepted this new life and new ways.

I am no longer Mona Tabacin. I am Cerasa, Dame Cherry.

"Yes, she lived and prospered," T'Cherry said. He poured more caff and cocoa all around, lifted his mug. "To Cerasa D'Cherry."

They toasted.

"To us!" Raz proposed, his fingers twining with Del's.

"To us!"

Hope spun through the room, strongly enough that Raz just felt the emotion and didn't question that things would turn out all right with his HeartMate.

Thirty-three

That night, Del slept in his arms in his own room in the Family Residence. Raz's mind swirled with odd thoughts—everything from knowing that two other HeartMate couples—both HeartBound— slept in the Residence; concern about the Residence itself and knowledge that his father and sister would be visiting the HouseHeart, reassuring it; and at the outreaches of his brain the tiny notion that if the play *Heart and Sword* was a hit, maybe he could interest another playwright, maybe even Amberose, in a story based on the diaries.

Most of all, though, he twined around Del and tried not to wonder about his future with her.

The next morning, Del woke to kittens jumping on her and the scent of baking bread. The sun was bright in the room.

Raz wasn't in the bed, and she sensed he was back down in the breakfast room with his Family. Last night, a page-by-page perusal of the books showed absolutely no maps, and more quick peeks didn't show any exact directions—except for baking. Recipes. Some of them made her mouth water to think about, ancient treats that no one had revived in years. From the gleam in Raz's mother's eyes and a new spring in her step, Del saw another Cherry business about to be born.

Real cherry pies, even. Now that the great greensward of *Nuada's Sword* was available for use, there might be true Earthan cherry trees there . . . certainly would be DNA.

Rosemary bit her ear. *Time for breakfast.*

"Haven't you already had yours?"

Yes, but the people have locked Us out of the breakfast room. If We go with you, We get back in, the FamKitten belonging to Raz's sister said.

Del grunted. "Guess I'll eat in the kitchen then. Probably food there."

YES! Rosemary kitten said. *But WE want in the breakfast room!*

"What you *don't* want is a Residence mad at you. Can you both promise not to put a pad or paw or tongue or claw in the journals?"

They both plopped their butts down in front of her and gave her big-eyed stares.

YES!

Yes.

Del still didn't think so. There was such a thing as overwhelming temptation. Del had *never* thought she'd spend a night in Raz's bed in the Cherry Residence. But the whole Family had appeared shocked after the discovery of the journals, needing comfort from wherever they could draw it, including from her.

With a Word, Del opened the door. *Run along now. I'll be down after a waterfall.*

The kittens eyed her, then the more trusting one, the one who lived here, trotted out. Rosemary appeared torn as to whether to stay or go, but when the other kitten squeaked *Fooood,* Raz's cat left.

In the waterfall, Del shifted from foot to foot with concern. Finally she spoke. "Residence, are you all right?"

"I am very well, D'Elecampane." The Residence's deep voice had returned. "You are the first to ask this morning."

"I've been spending a lot of time in houses with stones barely aware, ready to become Residences or sink back into dull rock. You have been blessed, Residence, with a long and caring and lively Family."

She hadn't put scent in the holder over the fall, but sweet herbs wafted around her. "Thank you," she said to the Residence.

Thank you, D'Elecampane. None of my folk will ever harm me.

"No. They love you." She ordered the waterfall off, dried herself with a whisking breeze, and went back in to look at the clothes she'd reluctantly hung in the closet. The wrinkles were gone, of course, but she was tired of wearing each and every tunic and trous, even her leathers. She put on her best and hesitated with her hand on the door latch, finally understanding that one of the reasons she didn't want to join the others was because two other couples were HeartBonded and she and Raz weren't.

A hum came from her duffle and her calendarsphere appeared. *Septhour before your holo portrait sitting with Doolee for T'Apple.*

She could grab some food here, poke her head in to the Family—the one who belonged in this Residence—gathered in the breakfast room reading their ancestress's journals—and wave good-bye to them, kiss Raz, then take off for her own house. Her house that she knew would never be her home, but that she'd come to have a fondness for.

Yes, she'd take the quick and cowardly way out for once.

*E*veryone was pleased with the portrait session. Straif was gone from the city, actually trusting Del to get the thing done. Both she and Doolee held landscape globes. Doolee played with hers, which didn't show a place, but her Family . . . Straif and Mitchella and the other two Blackthorn children. Doolee would shake it and beam as the figures would take up different positions . . . sometimes Doolee was being held by a parent, Straif sometimes wrestling with his boys. Del thought once she'd seen the children jumping on the couch in the playroom. So Doolee's "home" was her relationship with these people. Something Del hadn't considered before, but it sounded fine to her.

She stared out the playhouse windows at the gardens around her. She was fine with leaving the estate to Doolee.

Del had returned to ten messages from T'Anise about charity work and social gatherings and Bloom Noble Group rituals that Del should do. Invitations to this afternoon meeting, that dinner, some other working breakfast.

"Expression, Del," T'Apple reminded her. He smiled. "Squeeze Doolee."

That usually worked to cheer her up, and it did now. The toddler had fallen asleep for a few minutes and was limp in her lap. Del smiled back at the artist and thought of Doolee, which apparently gave her the expression he wanted to capture. This time.

The man had threatened to do one of her in her leathers, with that "distant, cartographer's expression," the "frontier woman." As *one* of his studies of her. She suppressed a snort.

"Can you shake your landscape globe again?" T'Apple asked.

Del tilted the oval-domed globe T'Apple had chosen from her workroom. Del thought it was because it had a great many bits of found city items, but maybe it was the shape. She glanced down at it and her eyes widened as she saw a fleeting image of what might come—the property in Verde Valley, the pretty white house with the large, multipaned round sunroom, the larger square of the hotel, the building that could be a theater.

"Expression, Del," T'Apple said again, this time absently, his fingers weaving light in glimmers and flashes and splashes, adding color that nearly had her mouth dropping. Again. It was wonderful to watch him.

"Expression!"

So Del composed her face and shifted the child, thought of Doolee. The girl would have changed her life even if Del hadn't gone looking for Raz.

"Yes! That hint of a strong woman in love. Perfect! One of the other studies I want to do is with more of that expression . . . but not . . . just . . . now."

He bent light, tinted it, and it flowed. Del strove to think of Doolee and how the child played in the HouseHeart, this playhouse, ran as fast as her toddler's legs could go along a corridor glorying in the freedom of being home. With her Family, in her very own house. Would the landscape globe later show this place? Del hoped so.

"You are a very challenging woman," T'Apple said.

"No," Del said.

"Don't try to deceive an old man," T'Apple said. He was old, but he radiated health and vitality, sheer pleasure in his work. An artist—would Raz be like that in the far future? "You're a challenge. Good thing I've lived long enough to know what to do with a woman like you."

"Do? What?"

He met her eyes, fingers still working. "Appreciate you. From a distance."

Several days passed for Del with an increasing tension between her and Raz, and when she was clearheaded enough once during loving she understood why. He knew he was her HeartMate.

But he was fighting the knowledge.

That hurt.

He was sometimes "too busy" for her, and that hurt even more. But as the week went on and possibilities grew in her mind, she came to understand what to do. Discreetly she inquired about the estate in the valley near the new glider route.

Despite the fact that she told the Family who owned it that the stones in the house were becoming intelligent and of the new glider-way through the valley, the owners were uncaring. Their Family had taken a huge loss on the property two generations ago when they'd built a resort. Since then they'd decided nothing of any interest existed outside of Druida City.

Since her parents had felt that way, Del was familiar with the attitude. She offered an insultingly low figure for the estate and the bid was accepted so quickly doubts assailed her. But she'd seen the place herself. The buildings were sound.

Raz had liked the house, as she had. He'd thought the valley pretty, she was sure he'd said something like that. He'd acted in that one building. It could become a theater, couldn't it?

Wouldn't Raz enjoy owning a theater, choosing the plays to put on, acting in them?

She could only hope so, but her gut pitched acid. Every day here in the city began to itch more under her skin.

Concentrating on rehabilitating the property, she called people in Gael City who had worked on the Cherry's house. On one of Raz's matinee and evening performance days, she squeezed in a quick express airship trip down to Gael City, hired Trillia to look around the "theater." The actress grinned with approval, nearly bounced with every step as she considered the space, went to a spot and belted out a song, surprising Del.

Trillia approved and dropped the information that she'd told Raz that Del was his HeartMate. Trillia approved of Del, too. They could become friends. If all went well.

Del had an awful feeling that all would not go well. She was putting plans in place for them to live together, love together, but really didn't know if he would accept them. Soon she would have to confront him.

*R*az carried anxiety around with him like a cold fog that had sunk deeply into his bones. Del was restless. She'd left the city and hadn't told him. He'd learned from newssheets that her job mapping the old Downwind area was finished. He'd heard from his parents that T'Anise, the antiquarian and head of Bloom Noble Circle, continued to remind Del that she had "responsibilities" for molding the city and the culture by attending rituals. Something Raz couldn't imagine her doing.

He couldn't visualize much of a long-term nature with Del . . .

except her moving out of his life down a road with a stridebeast and Shunuk. Walking away from him.

She *wouldn't* live in Druida, he knew that in that cold marrow of his.

He *couldn't* pursue his career the way he wanted to outside Druida. He needed top-notch productions and shows to fulfill himself, his destiny.

He yearned for Del, for a life with her, but still the taste of ambition lay on his tongue and he couldn't give that up.

He tried not to think that they were HeartMates, denied it as he had denied it for so long.

As he denied that he loved her.

She wasn't a woman who would compromise. Every time he withdrew, she stepped back even more.

He used the busyness of the week to dull his anxiety. Lily had been wretched to work with from the moment he got back, had demanded more rehearsals since he "was no longer fresh." It was easier to go along with her than fight and imbue the theater with more negativity.

His Family had wanted to read the diaries aloud and study them and wanted him near, and he couldn't object to that, either, though Del didn't always come with him. He and his father had visited *Nuada's Sword* and gone to D'Ash after a FoxFam kit had been left at T'Cherry Residence.

Straif T'Blackthorn had left Druida, too, following a lead back south to Gael City.

So Raz decided to think about the HeartMate thing much later.

An eightday after they'd left Gael City, Del nervously prepared for the New Twinmoons ritual. Mitchella D'Blackthorn had invited her and Raz to attend the FirstFamily ceremony. A big deal. Good for Raz to attract attention for his career, but also underscoring that *she* should be participating more in noble stuff, maybe even FirstFamilies stuff, that she'd never wanted.

She'd decided that she would claim Raz as her HeartMate after the ritual. He'd had her HeartGift for an eightday and a half. Since before they'd traveled to Gael City.

Legally, she figured she could claim him as her husband and HeartMate. But she wasn't fool enough to do so in public, not when she didn't know how he would react—not when she feared how he would react.

She curled her lip at the thought of publicly announcing he was legally her HeartMate. Force. She wouldn't do that to him or her own pride.

But she couldn't go on this way, with all this tension between them. Better to get everything out in the open, work through their problems, their options.

Del picked Raz up after his evening performance, driving her new glider carefully, taking them to the midnight ritual at GreatCircle Temple.

T'Ivy and D'Ivy, the officiants, were pompous and arrogant, looked down on her until Raz charmed them. It didn't take him long to beguile everyone in the room, certainly by the time Vinni T'Vine, the young prophet, helped the Ivys arrange the circle. Del was hand in hand between Raz and Signet D'Marigold. As the woman's catalyst energy zoomed through her, Del smiled coolly at young Vinni. Did he think she needed changing? She had changed so much.

The ritual itself emphasized self-knowledge and modification as the Ivys spoke of circling into the spiral of the self. Del strove not to shift from foot to foot. She knew herself, knew she'd changed, accepted it.

Then the work of the FirstFamilies began, with raising and sending energy to the round temples of Druida City, particularly the less well attended, to keep them clean and strong and sacred. After that, they checked on the state of the city, and when Del provided a clear and detailed visualization of the new streets of old Downwind there was a murmur of approval.

Then, to her pleased surprise, the circle focused on the Great Labyrinth north of the city. Other than the path in the crater and up the bowl to the rim itself, it was a tangle. As the energy cycled around, spots on the map in Del's head brightened, as if each Family sought out their own sacred space with their own offering and sent Flair there.

By the time the ritual ended, she was dizzy and leaning into Raz. He was thrilled and energized at being a part of the FirstFamilies' ceremony. She fought a headache and the edge of nausea. No, she wouldn't do this again.

She stayed silent by Raz's side as he complimented everyone and said good-bye, glad for the breath of fresh, cool air when they finally left the temple for her glider. Raz seated her in the passenger side, then took the driving bar.

"I'd like to go to your place tonight," Del rasped. She felt his glance but didn't elaborate.

"Sure."

The drive was quiet. Now they were alone, Del sensed Raz was letting himself feel the wonder of the great ceremony they'd taken part of, the surge of immense Flair and psi that the FirstFamilies lords and ladies could command. The awe in shaping their own world, actually making a difference.

Del knew Raz considered his career as one of art and entertainment, of exploring personalities and conflicts. He thought of his profession as a calling, satisfying to himself and his coworkers and his audiences. But to actually *affect* and change the world . . . that awed him.

It would awe her, too, once she got past the sickness and headache. The circle was too strong for her, the links too intimate for her comfort, and she wasn't ashamed to admit it. But she sensed Raz had sipped a euphoric and addicting drink, another difference between them. She shivered. The early morning air was cool, not to be warm again as the year wound down. Soon the autumnal equinox would be upon them, and in two months, the new year.

Would she spend it with Raz?

The last time she was this nervous was when she took her master's examination. She trembled, never wanting anything as much as she wanted Raz.

Raz parked the glider on the street in front of his apartment building. The street was wide enough for PublicCarriers to pass, and there were no other vehicles. The glider glowed with a new alarm.

The intensity of the moment condensed around her, the faint scent of herbal cleanser wafting from the building's interior, the rush of chill air as Raz opened the door for her, his smile—that smile she thought he saved only for her; a loving smile?—the slide of his smooth hand across her calloused fingers.

Her heart thumped hard. She tried to keep all emotions through their bond steady and easy. It was an effort. She couldn't smile back at him.

"Del?" he asked.

"When we get inside," she said, squeezing his hand.

But his body went tense and emotions surged within him and through their link, distress.

Damn.

They entered the building silently, though when she stepped in, a humming energy caressed her skin. Others in the place had done New Twinmoons rituals. How could he live with so many people around him?

But he liked it.

She found she was shaking her head when he opened the door to his apartment and bowed her in.

Inhaling deeply, she glanced around. Over the weeks, he'd added objects to the wall shelves, and they all looked good, but she sensed the room yet seemed bare to him.

She sensed too much from him.

One thing she didn't see was the HeartGift she'd made. Wasn't it here the last time she'd looked?

No, it was in his dressing room at the theater, on a high shelf, layered with shields.

Damn. She could have used it to make her point.

"Lights on," Raz said and closed the door behind him. He sniffed and she realized that scents from others' rituals had drifted into his space and he liked that. The herbs seemed to coat her skin, another irritant.

"Del?"

She wasn't sure when he'd dropped her hand, or had she dropped his? Didn't matter. She turned to him and held out her hands. He took them, lifted each to his lips, and kissed them, and her throat closed so she had to pant a couple of times before she could force words out.

"I claim you as my HeartMate," she said.

"No!" He stepped back. She lost the warmth of his touch. His face drained of blood.

She fumbled for the connection to the HeartGift in his dressing room, grunted with the effort of translocating it here, had to jump to catch it as the slick glass slipped through her sweaty palms. *Damn!*

"You accepted this HeartGift from me," she croaked, flooded with panic, his and her own. She wet her lips and struggled on. "You are legally my HeartMate. HeartBond with me."

"No." He shook his head.

Everything inside her broke. Her knees weakened. Thankfully her vision narrowed until she could only see the top of his shirt, rising and falling rapidly with his breaths. A great rushing filled her ears, blocking further denials from him.

She looked down at the landscape globe, thought she saw the estate in Verde Valley, shook her head and had to hunker into her balance. She would *not* peel the shields off the HeartGift and accept sexual madness. That's not what he wanted, and she wanted all of him. She was bleeding from a thousand cuts, all inside. She hurt, hurt, hurt. But she would not give up. "You're my HeartMate. I know it and you know it."

Thirty-four

Raz stared at Del.

"You have accepted my HeartGift." She held up the landscape globe and heat flashed through him. Knowledge he'd hidden from himself, like everything else, sexual heat as he looked at it, knew that if he removed the shield he'd sensed, they would have sex where they stood.

"You chose it before we left for Gael City. Legally I can claim you as my HeartMate." The skin on her face was taut, her bones showing all angles. Determination.

Her lips compressed. He sensed she didn't want this confrontation any more than he did, but that issues had been raised that must be dealt with. No running away for either one of them. Her eyes blazed power and Flair, as if she, too, had had a small shield over her, one he hadn't noticed. She was magnificent, and if he let her, she could overwhelm him. He couldn't allow that.

"Legally I can claim you as my HeartMate and no one could deny me." She smiled thinly. "But morally that isn't right." She sucked in a breath. "I am an honorable woman, and you are an honorable man. Do you want me as your HeartMate?"

He wasn't ready for this.

He felt trapped. Completely. If he didn't do something about it, he'd be trapped forever.

Traveling with Del as a wandering player. He couldn't do that. He couldn't give up the full houses of applause. He couldn't throw away his career to walk lonely trails with her.

"No," he said for a third time. Wasn't there a rule about a three-time refusal? He didn't know. He *did* know the rules about Heart-Gifts. He'd taken the one she'd made for her HeartMate—*chosen* hers of his own free will. Kept it close.

All the weight was with her, as usual. The law, riches, power. All the things he'd told himself didn't bother him rushed forward into his mind and fear spewed words out of his mouth. "I don't want a HeartMate or a wife or a family," he said.

She dropped the landscape globe. He lunged and caught it.

HeartGift. Given to him. Desperation swelled through him. He didn't want this, didn't want the words between them, though he wanted the sex and the woman and the loving.

He couldn't have his own identity and his career and her, everything. Though he wanted to keep the HeartGift closed in his fingers, he pried them open, threw it back at her.

She didn't reach out to catch it and it fell.

Rosemary shot from the shadows, pounced, and rolled with the globe onto the carpet before the glass hit the wooden floor. The kitten squealed as the globe escaped to spin behind the couch.

Del nodded once—as she had in that argument they'd had in Gael City. Her face was completely impassive, a hard mask. Something was tearing inside him and he didn't have the wits to stop it. Couldn't fight the sensation of being trapped and pry his mouth open and say the right words. He didn't even know what kind of words he could say.

She was going to walk away. All his insides chilled, clench-
ing into a small frozen knot, but heat burned on his skin from
anger that she would wreck what was between them, force him to
acknowledge what they were to each other before he was ready. He
was embarrassed that he couldn't speak, couldn't smooth this over
with words.

The contrast of fire and ice hurt. He didn't know what else to do
or say that would make his life right, that would blend their lives
together.

Emotions roiled wildly between them, the pain so intense he
slammed the link between them shut, only to feel emptiness in his
body and mind and heart.

He shuddered, saw that she trembled, too.

"Take care." Her voice was low. She pivoted, her back straight,
head high, shoulders tense and set, and left.

He didn't call her back.

She didn't know how she got out of the building, but stood in the night.
Why had she believed even for an instant that he was happy to be
her HeartMate?

She couldn't teleport, her brain was too scrambled. When the
glider caught her eye, she turned her back, began to shamble away.
But she couldn't walk the streets of Druida.

Couldn't.

Too many people around since it might be the last New Twinmoons ritual that could be done outside in parks.

Her eyes burned, too dry, though she thought somewhere inside
there was a tender soul racked with sobs. Stupid idea.

She could barely shuffle her feet.

Shunuk joined her. His tail slapped into her sweaty palm. *Follow
me to the public teleportation pad.*

Right.

It was at a dead end in a narrow crack between buildings. A
service teleportation pad for middle-class workers.

Del reached down and lifted Shunuk to her, buried her face in his thick pelt, he visualized the house, and they teleported there.

She couldn't stay here, either. The rooms would be haunted by her HeartMate.

Three more scrys had piled up in her cache from the persistent GrandLord T'Anise. The man was determined to get Del in his clutches, reform her into a pattern of a responsible Druidan Noblewoman.

Never.

Del packed quickly, headed out of the horrible town and north within a septhour by stridebeast. Her eyes had cleared but her gut still churned. She wouldn't be forcing down food anytime soon. All of her ached or occasionally went numb from sheer devastating overload, and she welcomed that.

Where are we going? Shunuk asked after a silent septhour on the dark road, far from dawn. *North to the fishing villages? All the way to the Great Washington Boghole?*

The last sarcastic bite to his tone brought her dull mind back to the present. Good thing she was riding and had a Fam, though the gliderway was well tended. No more damn gliders for her. Good.

"To the Great Labyrinth," she croaked. Maybe she should stick with telepathy, her throat hurt, and her voice was bad.

Why? Shunuk asked.

Why not? We'll stay at an inn there.

It was a few septhours ride for a summer's night. With each step of her stridebeast, Del seemed to sink into herself, find herself. Her new self.

She'd have to return to Druida, if only to settle her house and accounts so she could be gone a long time away, finish the holo painting with Doolee.

Straif had been right. Good to have a painting of them at this time in their lives, when they'd found each other, before Doolee became more Blackthorn than Elecampane and Del became ... whatever. Not fossilized and a caricature of a frontier woman. She'd escaped that fate.

Occasionally a glider passed her. Every time she flinched. Not good.

Shunuk coursed along the trail or rode on his pad. He had reverted more to the wild, feral fox on the trail than the sleek, city-dwelling Fam. He didn't intrude on her thoughts.

At dawn, Del rode to the rim of the huge crater of the Great Labyrinth before going on to the inn. Good thing about stridebeasts, they could take small trails between uneven brush and ground instead of needing wide packed earth. And they could whiffle with concern for their rider, turn their heads back and stare at her with big, loving eyes.

Del slid down from the stridebeast's back, set her face in her mount's side. He wasn't as intelligent as a horse, but not as delicate, either. Stridebeasts might never become Fams as she'd heard horses might become, but Del was glad to have the simple warmth and limited caring of the beast in her life.

Shunuk yipped. *What are we doing here? The inn is around the rim another kilometer or so.*

Swallowing and clearing her throat, Del took a softleaf from her pocket and rubbed her face. No tears. She thought tears would be a relief, but all the wild hurt was dammed up inside her, couldn't get out. Not safe to let it out on the trail.

Shunuk tilted his head. *You hurt, should let water come from your eyes.*

"Sometime soon." She inhaled the warm and city-odor-free air, let it settle in her lungs like a blessing and release, set her mind in the now.

Another good, deep breath and she focused only on the huge bowl beneath her. It was three kilometers in diameter, with a wide floor and walls angling up six hundred and fifty meters. A quarter of the rim had collapsed. Inside the bowl was lush and mostly trained vegetation. The path of the labyrinth was clear and well defined, as many feet had made it over the centuries.

Between the labyrinth loops were shrines that more and more noble Families were establishing. The FirstFamilies had started the tradition centuries ago. T'Ash had the huge World Tree in the center, T'Vine an arbor and bottles of wine, T'Hawthorn hedgerows around a small glade, sweet smelling in the spring. Mapping this place would be easy, the wending path was already ingrained in her mind. Noting the Family spaces would be interesting—the benches and altars, the mosaics and fountains . . .

Making a model would be challenging.

When her throat tightened she put that thought aside, too. Let someone else make a model. She'd map the place, leave papyrus and three-dimensional holo at the inn, take one to the Guildhall in Druida City, maybe give one to Mitchella D'Blackthorn for the FirstFamilies, then leave Druida for a long time.

Even before all the talk of the lost starship of *Lugh's Spear*, Del had been interested in crossing the Bluegrass Plains, checking out Fish Story Lake again, refining those maps. Now she had the Flair for it, she could make topographical holos.

Shunuk sniffed. *Walking back and forth on that path is boring.*

No doubt the meditation of the Great Labyrinth would work on her and she'd be ready for the next stage of her life. "For you, maybe. But you don't have to walk the path. I'd like you to do something different. You know that Families are making spaces to show off their characteristics and their work, shrines for whoever comes or if no one comes, for the Lady and Lord." She slanted a look at her Fam. "There's food sometimes. I don't think anyone knows exactly how many shrines there are or which Families are represented. The Great Labyrinth just came back in fashion a few years ago. So you should help me double-check."

He hummed in his throat, slid a glance toward her. "Have the Cherrys made a spot?"

Yeah, there came the stabbing pain. "Maybe."

Shunuk turned his pointy nose toward a dark green shadow halfway up the crater. *I will find it.* He looked back at her with glittering eyes. *We should not have left Druida City.*

The very thought of staying there, living there, made her gorge rise. She widened her stance, gritted her teeth, stared down at her

Fam and said more words that might rip another loved one from her life. "I can't live in Druida City, any city. There are too many people, too many shields, too many expectations. I can do many things, but that's not one of them. I have spent too much time in the wild. I would be like a caged bird, dull and unhappy. I would fade away, not be the person I am." She lifted her chin. "At least I know this weakness. If you want to live in the city, go. I'm sure our Fam bonds will thin and then vanish." Pain engulfed her; she hung on to her stridebeast's mane.

Shunuk fell to his belly, put his paws over his muzzle. *I am sorry I made you hurt more. I would have liked the city, but that is not for us. I will stay with you.*

She couldn't speak aloud. *Thank you.* She stroked her stridebeast's soft lips; for a moment she'd thought she'd be ripped into more pieces. Too many pieces lost and she wouldn't ever get herself back.

Lifting his paws from over his nose Shunuk stood and shook himself, glanced at her, and said, *HeartMates are forever.* Then he stared at the Great Labyrinth and trotted along the trail around the rim.

HeartMates were forever, but she would never ask Raz to bond with her again.

The couple who ran the inn made her welcome. It wasn't a big place, only five or six rooms and two suites. Del took the most expensive suite. It was fussy and feminine and that was so different than the places she'd been staying that it was good.

She'd become accustomed to spending a lot of money lately, refurbishing the resort spa and house and planning a theater in Verde Valley. Before that, attending expensive city amusements, buying city clothes. At least that part was over. Her leathers had never felt so comfortable.

She wasn't the only guest, but she took a tray in her suite instead of joining the rest for meals that day. The owners of the inn were cheerful and comforting, nearly pampering, and she thought they understood she'd had a bad shock.

She didn't sleep much the first night, just lay in the bed and existed, drifting in and out of sleep, still empty, still dry, still burning inside.

Shunuk spent the night exploring.

The next day she dressed and rode to the labyrinth, left her stridebeast in a nearby meadow to graze while she walked to the rim of the huge crater. The crater had been made by the impact of a satellite sent by *Nuada's Sword* to examine Celta to see if it was a good planet to colonize. Even that bit of history hurt, since it was something she'd been reminded of by the play *Heart and Sword*. She thought of Rosemary's delight, of holding hands with Raz, of the wonder of the production that had taken her from her theater seat into space and centuries past. Her throat closed, but tears didn't come.

She didn't go to the center and the great ash tree, but stepped off the path to visit various noble offerings. Several yards off one of the wider rings, she wound through trellises to see a deep pond. The plaque showed one of the FirstFamily's names, the Seas, mind healers. Del studied the water and knew it would be full of soothing herbs. Good.

Del was gone from Druida. He only needed to step outside to sense her absence. There was only one D'Elecampane that smelled of wild herbs brought on the summer breeze, that left a trace of unique mapmaking Flair in the atmosphere.

He wondered if that's how Straif T'Blackthorn tracked, and misplaced jealousy bit him hard. No, not jealousy, the damn panic-fear that she was gone and Raz was a fool. Fear and foolishness that he couldn't prevent.

It shamed him to think that he had chosen his life and career over his HeartMate, but when he was on stage and that applause came at him, when he *acted*, he was giving the best of himself.

Good riddance. With a smug smile, Rosemary curled up on his dressing room sofa. The wall above it was empty, he hadn't been able to bear looking at the tapestry, had translocated it to storage in T'Cherry Residence.

No more fox. No more woman. Now I have you all to Myself.

Raz had Family and theater people and friends and Fam, and was deeply and disturbingly lonely like he'd never been in all his life. If he kept still he thought the edge of a dark doom would overtake him. So he wasn't ever alone, slept at one of the rooms at the Thespian Club. He concentrated only on his work and the diaries and his Fam.

Lonely. He had never known the true feeling of the word before, though he had acted it.

Loneliness was awful.

For a couple of days Del wandered the labyrinth, noting the Family shrines, recording them on a sphere.

Shouldn't some artist instead of a mapmaker be doing this? Like T'Apple? Then she thought of the man, knew he'd change the composition of the shrines to what he believed would be more visually pleasing. He probably wouldn't get the measurements right, either. Wouldn't care about that.

She did. It was the main focus of her days. She still waited for her emotions to break loose, for the relief of tears that didn't come. Knew she couldn't go on with her life until that happened. Stupid female thing. But she was a woman, one who had *grown.* Better to have too many emotions than none.

She didn't feel good enough to walk the meditation path. Once she did that, she'd be facing her deepest aches—the loss of her HeartMate—and she'd have to give up the past and set her feet on the trail of her future. She figured the tears would come then, and if she was walking the labyrinth, everyone she met would know her pain, see her vulnerability. Maybe pity her.

Her pride wasn't ready for that, either.

She was civil to the people she met in the inn, most of whom had only come in for a day and stayed overnight. Now and then, from excited comments they'd made during meals, she understood that in her rambles she'd missed a FirstFamily lord or lady.

Then she realized that rumor of her project had reached Druida and some of the Families were sprucing up their shrines for her. Which meant another circuit around to make sure she had new holos, the correct dimensions—and some of them had extended their space, dammit.

One day she saw a teenaged boy uncrating bottles of wine with great care and putting them in a rack and a no-time in the T'Vine arbor. Restocking his offering.

She stopped. Vinni T'Vine, the great prophet of Celta. One who was known to lay out your future to you . . . or reveal a glimpse or two . . . or make cryptic comments.

But it was the middle of the morning and she recognized the wrapper around some cheese and the label on the bottle of blackberry wine and got the first hunger pangs in days. Ignoring her rumbling stomach, she walked up to his shrine and bowed to him. "Merry meet, T'Vine."

Thirty-five

*M*errily *met, D'Elecampane." Approval beamed from the teen's eyes.*
He set the cheese on a sturdy marble-topped no-time and sliced the
cheddar, put it on crackers and those on plates, poured a glass of
wine for himself and a quarter of one for her.

He glanced at the spheres in her hand, the roll of papyrus under
her arm. "May I see your work?"

"Since you're feeding me, sure." As soon as he cleaned off a
glass-topped table she unrolled the papyrus, tapped it with a finger
to lay flat, and with a sweep of her hand, let the thing form into
three dimensions.

The young man stood looking into the large bowl of the crater
and the Great Labyrinth and Del took one of the floral-patterned
white wicker chairs. Didn't seem at all like T'Vine.

"The women of my Family insisted," the youth said absently and

Del's mouth went dry as she recognized he'd heard her thoughts. A very powerful GreatLord indeed.

T'Vine laughed and turned to her. "You think I'm mind reading." He gestured to a mirrorlike sculpture of the sun hanging from one of the arbor lattices, twisting gently in the breeze. "Your expression at the furniture gave you away."

Del sipped her wine. "Thanks."

A resigned look came to his eyes. "People are wary of me because of my prophetic gift; I don't need to be considered a receiving telepath, too."

"Guess not," Del said, munching another cracker.

He glanced at the wine racks and no-time. "Though being cautious of me doesn't seem to prevent folks from drinking my wine and eating my offerings. I have to restock every couple of weeks now."

"Really good cheese. Thank you."

His smile lightened his face, making it more boylike, though she didn't think he'd been a boy for a while. "You're welcome. You do excellent work. I think this map needs to be several places in the labyrinth, at the center with T'Ash's World Tree, and at the rim where the path ends, near the Elder's new pavilion."

Del shrugged. "I'll send the original and holos to the Guildhall—they can distribute as needed—leave one here with the inn people."

Vinni sat next to her, swallowed cheese and a cracker or two, sipped his wine. They ate in silence as the shade deepened in the arbor and the scent of ripening grapes gently infused the air. She sighed, relaxed, even let her eyes close. "Wonderful cheese." Cheese didn't travel well, and she loved it.

"You can always get the best in Druida City."

Pain. She opened her eyes. "I have Family there, I'll be back more often."

"Good."

"Or did you know that? Something you want to say to me, GreatLord T'Vine?"

He smiled. "Call me Vinni."

Which made her wonder how close they would become, but she shrugged. "You gonna tell me something, Vinni?"

His eyes had changed color, a slight tinge of red came to his cheeks. "Walk the labyrinth, GrandLady D'Elecampane."

"Del," she corrected. "That's all?"

His gaze was direct. "You don't want to know your future, do you? And hearing me wouldn't affect your decisions, would it?"

"Maybe."

He shook his head. "No. You will do what is right for you and yours. That means a place outside of Druida, but visiting Druida more than you have. Just as you've already decided." He hesitated. "Knowing the future would only distract you. Be careful."

Del stared at him, but he said nothing more. So she nodded, glanced at her work, thought about finishing touches, double-checking with Shunuk.

As if she'd conjured him with her thoughts, the fox slid into the arbor, sat before Vinni, and smiled ingratiatingly. *Greetyou, Vinni.*

"Hello, Shunuk. Thank you again for taking care of that celta-roon nest on my estate."

Del raised her brows. Shunuk had been ranging farther outside of Druida City proper than she'd known.

Shunuk panted. *You are welcome.* He sniffed. *I love cheese.*

Vinni laughed, went to the no-time, and broke off a hunk of cheese, threw it, and laughed again when Shunuk leapt to catch it in his mouth. The fox rumbled happily around the treat. Vinni dipped his hands in a basin Del hadn't noticed, said a Word to wash and dry them, then looked at the labyrinth path with a pained expression.

People could teleport into the labyrinth, but never out of it.

The boy set his shoulders, looked at Del. "This will be good for me."

She nodded.

He stepped onto the path and when he looked back at her, his eyes weren't the usual hazel. "Be careful," he said again, then began the walk out.

* * *

The rest of the day she and Shunuk consulted on the shrines, verified the spaces and each of the objects with the most recently recorded holos and vizes. They used small animal tracks to ascend the crater. Del was careful to keep those dirt paths as tiny and hidden as possible. The Great Labyrinth was a very special place, both historically and for Celtan culture, the meditation path helpful for all.

In the morning she'd walk the path, from the rim down to the center and back. At a slow meditative pace, without stopping, that would take her about three septhours. She decided to allocate a full day, with as many stops as she wanted. She'd use the time on the labyrinth to make her decisions about her life. Then she'd head back to Druida and take care of business.

She was haunted by dreams that night, yearning for Raz, his touch, the loving she'd gotten used to. But she wasn't going to participate in erotic dream sex if he couldn't give his whole self. As she would have given her whole self.

She woke up sweaty and unsatisfied, with the edging light of dawn filtering over the horizon. The first hint of autumn to come had kissed the morning with cool breath. Time was passing and it was past time she made decisions for a new life.

After a waterfall she dressed in her favorite, shabbiest leathers, saddled her stridebeast. Shunuk joined her without comment and kept pace.

The Sallow Family, who specialized in animal training, kept a small meadow next to a stream for horses and stridebeasts along with a salt lick and squares of feed. Her mount blew his lips in pleasure when he realized where they were going.

Soon they were at the rim of the crater where the path to and from the Great Labyrinth began and ended, due east.

The sun had risen and Bel's rays slanted obliquely over the land, touching the green and verdant earth with the gold of summer, barely outlining the lip of the crater opposite her. Del was surprised and a little disappointed to see that she wasn't the only one here at dawn. An older couple, surely in their eighteenth decade or so, were already treading the path down, the woman in the lead. Small and white-headed, they were still making good time. As Del watched, the woman passed her mate something to eat, a fruit or a bar, and Del understood they'd come well prepared.

Del had decided to leave her sustenance up to the Lady and Lord, which actually meant taking advantage of all the Family offerings. She'd have milk and honeycakes in half a septhour.

A faint crackle came and Del glanced toward the pilgrims who had stopped at a shrine that offered specialty caff no-times. The woman had a piece of papyrus and Del noted it was an old plan of the labyrinth. Del's smile widened, and a bit of serenity eased her. Soon everyone would be using *Del's* three-dimensional holo papyrus map. That was something she could be proud of: her work.

So she stepped onto the path of the Great Labyrinth, most of it still in shadow, the branches of the huge ash tree barely visible in the darkness at the center of the crater.

As she walked and regulated her breathing, she thought of her work. Slowly comprehension seeped into her that her great work of traveling Celta and mapping it was over . . . she didn't want to be away from Doolee that long. There would be no more yearlong trips with no stop in Druida. Even the trip to the Bluegrass Plains that had seemed appealing in the first rush of grief over losing Raz didn't feel right anymore.

She had finished the detailed survey of the area that had once been the Downwind slums, had recommended changing a few streets and parks to make the neighborhood more like the rest of Druida City.

There had been an interesting energy there, obviously the result of FirstFamily rituals in rehabilitating the land where despair and loneliness and other negative emotions had seeped into the ground for centuries.

That was done, as was the labyrinth chart.

She'd left a legacy of maps that would help later generations and was very proud of that. She had nothing and no one to prove herself to anymore, was considered the premiere cartographer of Celta. That was enough of a contribution.

So what did *she* want to do?

Find a home base.

She stopped at the Hickorys' shrine that was blessedly equipped to disperse negative energy with chimes that corresponded to different bodily fields. She breathed and sounded the chimes to lower her grief and frustration, then, as the sounds echoed back to her, she took care in placing the notes for the best echo, and that exercise increased her serenity.

As she walked again, Vinni T'Vine's words came back: *a place out of Druida*. More layers to that phrase than she'd first heard, as if a place outside of Druida would be good for everyone, almost a warning.

When she'd first started on this quest to find her HeartMate, she hadn't considered his feelings; he'd been a dream lover, not a real man with wants and needs.

She wouldn't move to Verde Valley until she could share it with him, have *him* put his mark on it as much as she. She'd stop the renovation of the theater until he was with her.

Sometime within the next few decades he would be with her. Her laugh was choked and garbled. That should have been a balm, that HeartMates were forever, long-range planning was good. But she wanted him *now*, had no patience to wait. Too greedy for that part of her life to begin, for loving.

She hadn't comprehended how lonely she'd been, wasn't as self-sufficient as she'd thought.

A good thing.

The meditation path worked on her. Occasionally she'd stop for snacks, watch others move ahead of her, kept an eye out for the older couple who progressed to the center. They'd be the first to T'Ash's tree, not that the labyrinth was a race.

Del let her mind rest, having faith that when she finished the walk to the center and back to the rim, she'd have answers.

When she crossed from the darkness where the morning sun

hadn't touched, into the area that had been warmed by it, her chest finally loosened and the tears of grief rose and washed her cheeks.

She wept silently until her body began to shake and groans came. As she wiped the tears away she saw the path to D'Sea's hidden arbor and the spring. Not coincidence. The labyrinth working on her, her knowledge of every shrine.

Stumbling along the blue flagstones to the pool, she stripped and fell into warm, scented water. There was a slight rushing of an intake spout and she moved to it, used the noise to hide the sobs that ripped out of her.

This was good, this weeping. It meant she cared. She *loved*. She'd lost her HeartMate.

She didn't let herself howl or wail, but gave in to the tears, under the downspout, letting herself go, then taking wrenching breaths and dipping her face, her head, her whole self into the water.

Better.

She was not a careless, emotionless stick of a woman. Not the woman she would have become if she'd had no HeartMate and no Doolee and no Shunuk and continued mapping Celta.

She was a woman who had a glory of emotions. A better woman, a wholer woman, a woman who could experience great grief . . . and someday when Raz came to her, great joy.

She wept until she was empty and the horrible tearing pain inside her was gone and she was filled with soft sadness. Other sensations sifted back into her. The gentle lap of the water, the footsteps and cheerful voices of people passing the hidden spring. People she actually felt connected to.

They, too, walked the labyrinth today and that was enough commonality for her to appreciate them.

She was not alone and a loner. She was a woman who was valued by Doolee, and Straif and Mitchella, and others. Her skill was appreciated. It was enough. She'd never be completely without emotional ties again. She *liked* the emotional connections she had.

Birds chirped and rustled, a woman with a trained voice sang as she walked the labyrinth.

Enough indeed. She washed her face one more time in the water, then rose, her toes and fingers wrinkled from long submersion.

But Del was calm and had a future to plan. She dressed and the fine linen of her underwear felt good and her soft leathers slid across her body. She was alive and life was an interesting trail before her.

Shunuk moved into the bright sunlight of late morning and sat. *You are better.*

Yes. Again her throat hurt and she didn't want to speak. *The past is done. We must craft a future. Are there any towns you'd like to live in? Not Druida, not Gael City.*

I like the valley best.

Raz . . . It hurt to even think of his name in her head, to see him in her mind's eye. She started over. *Raz must help restore that place for it to be a true home.* She hesitated. *What of Steep Springs?*

Shunuk's gaze slid away, he shifted on his bottom. *I don't like Steep Springs.*

Amusement welled in her and she appreciated it. Shunuk probably wouldn't be welcome in Steep Springs. More cluckers or rabbits missing, she supposed.

Toono Town, he said.

Del blinked. Another town, more in the hills than the mountains. A very arty community of brightly painted houses.

Once she would have rejected the notion, shuddered at the thought of living among such folk. She nodded. "Deal."

She wended her way down the rest of the crater to the World Tree, passing folk and being passed, everyone at different places on their lives' journeys. The older couple nodded as she stood aside in a shrine and watched them walk upward to the rim. She understood that the woman recognized the recent puffiness of tearful eyes, yet she said nothing, raised her hand in blessing.

As Del took the path again, she explored the rhythm of herself, steps and heart and breath. Delving deeply as she hadn't been able to during the last New Twinmoons ceremony or in the numbness and pain of grief.

When she reached the World Tree and stepped into the center a mind-blinding epiphany shook her so she had to lean against the great trunk.

She was pregnant.

Thirty-six

What had he done? He'd been a stup, a fool. An immature child.

Raz paced his dressing room before the last act of the matinee performance, glad he had only this one bit to get through before he could go after Del.

Who'd have thought that of the two of them, Helena D'Elecampane, tough frontier woman, and Cerasus Cherry, acclaimed actor, he'd be the more rigid, the less flexible?

He wouldn't have. He'd always considered Del the uncompromising one, the one who couldn't, wouldn't change. The one whom life had carved and scoured so she couldn't stay in Druida.

But he'd never had life smack him in the face like Del had.

His parents hadn't approved of his choice of work and that had been a bitter thorn in his side. The acting profession wasn't an easy one and he'd had his share of rejections and foul-ups. But he hadn't had any true tests of his character—life-and-death tests, life-changing tests.

He'd failed abysmally and he didn't like that, and as soon as this afternoon show was over, he'd figure out how to get her back, how he could *be* the man he'd thought he was.

*P*regnant.

Del spread her hands over her flat belly, lowered herself to the ground.

Pregnant after two eightdays of sex with her HeartMate.

That didn't happen on Celta. On Celta it took time for women to conceive.

At least it had with everyone she'd ever known, everyone she'd ever heard of. Naturally there would be exceptions to that rule. Naturally. She gave a gasping laugh. Being pregnant was one of the most completely natural things that had ever happened to her. If the quality and heat of the loving between her and Raz had anything to do with conception, she wouldn't be surprised if she was carrying triplets.

She sank deep into that inner awareness, softly, softly, unable to do anything to jar this miracle, hinder her child, stop the wondrous event. Yes, there was just one baby.

Del wasn't Flaired enough or in the right way to sense her child's sex. She thought she'd heard that some people knew instantly . . . instantly when they or their mate was pregnant and the sex.

She couldn't tell Raz. Her jaw clenched. He'd said he didn't want her, or a family. The words had echoed in her ears, descended to taint her heart like a painful disease. He wanted a career. He wanted to be the individual star of his life right now.

She wouldn't be able to bear it if he changed his mind about marrying her, HeartBonding with her, because they were having a child together.

Voices came toward her. Without thought she moved around the large trunk of the ash tree, away from the opening of the labyrinth.

T'Ash had placed a no-time next to a small stone altar, and there was milk inside since he and his HeartMate had children, expected some children to walk—or run, or skip, or play—in the labyrinth.

After drinking a tube of rich milk and setting it in the reconstructor, she nodded to the group who had unpacked a picnic under the tree, then she set off up the path. The baby made all her choices easier.

For a moment she considered if she could stay in Druida, thought hard. No. The city affected her negatively physically, mentally, emotionally. That couldn't be good for her child. She had too many contacts with the theater and noble circles. She wouldn't hide his child from Raz, but she wouldn't flaunt the babe, either. She didn't want even a hint of a chance that this child would be unloved by his or her father.

Raz had too many ties to Gael City, too.

Not to mention the fact that Del figured everyone she knew would want them back together, would expect Raz to submit to his fate. There'd be no lack of meddling on the part of the Cherrys . . . or the Blackthorns.

Right now, this child was *hers*, and only hers. She wanted a little time to become used to the idea. Time alone with her new life.

Shunuk loped up, panting, grinning up at her, suspiciously happy. He knew how to open several no-times. "Greetyou, clucker-breath," she said.

He snapped his mouth shut and tried to look innocent. He didn't do that nearly as good as the Cherry kittens. Del accepted the pang of memory, knew it would happen often, moved past it.

Drawing in a deep breath, she said, "I'm going to have a kit."

He sniffed as he trotted beside her. *I know.*

That had her slowing her step a little as dizziness rippled in her brain. "You do? How?"

You smell different.

She wanted to ask when but decided it didn't matter. "All right. What do you think of living in Thomastown?"

Shunuk angled his head so he could look at her. *Not Toono?*

"No." Not the quaint mountain artistic enclave, but a town near a research HealingHall that was on the far edge of Gael City. Del could live within easy glider distance, slightly longer stridebeast distance if worse came to worse.

She was determined that worse would *not* come to worse. She wanted this child, this bond between herself and Raz. Stepping off of the path to sit on a bench, she examined her link with Raz. She couldn't cut it off or shut it down, but she made it as narrow as possible. He would not learn of this child from that bond. "We'll leave Druida City for Thomastown the day after tomorrow." As soon as she had a full prenatal exam by Lark Holly. She'd set up the appointment when she got out of the crater, speak to Lark herself, and make her promise to tell *no one* but her HeartMate, who must promise not to speak to anyone.

A while later they rounded a curve and stepped from sunlight into shadow, the path still cool from night. Shunuk yipped, looked at her from the corner of his eyes, at the trail circling up. *Long path. We can take one of the animal ways.* He waved his tail. Del hadn't put the animal tracks on any of her maps but knew them all.

"It is best for the kit and me to walk the meditation path. We won't be back here for a while if we're living south in Thomastown." Not during her entire pregnancy. She'd be stuck in one place. The timing was good, at least. Warm autumn days to find a house and settle in, get everything ready for the winter. Then the winter and the spring for her pregnancy.

New celtaroon nest in the middle southwest quadrant, want to see before I kill?

"No." She gestured. "You go on, be careful. They are deadly and poisonous. I'm going to slow down, I'll reach the rim in a little over two septhours."

With a flick of his tail, Shunuk ran through bushes and up the crater. Del settled into a slower pace. Time passed as easily as if she were walking beside her stridebeast toward the next section of topography to chart. She didn't know how long she'd stay in Thomastown, but she'd make sure that the place would be good for her and her child for several years. For an instant she wondered how long Raz would ignore his little family, how long it would be before he would hear. This month? The next? Healers were supposed to be the souls of confidentiality, and Del already knew carrying this baby to term would be tough. If she phrased it that way . . . a woman rejected by her HeartMate, her feelings tender. She grimaced. Not her style.

Not her former style.

But she acknowledged and accepted that there would be new and wondrous changes in her life in the future and that she was looking forward to them.

Raz reached mentally for Del. The bond between them was tinier than ever. It had been larger when they'd only been having dream sex.

He winced, rubbed his hand over his chest. He hadn't stopped hurting since she'd walked out of his life . . . since he'd sent her away . . . and the idea of dream sex, how that had become loving, hurt.

Setting his jaw in concentration, closing his eyes, he tried tugging on the minuscule bond between them, caused his own heart to squeeze with pain. North.

He didn't have good navs in the glider for the north. Pulling his perscry from his pocket, he rubbed a thumb over it and said, "Guildhall Map Division."

"Guildhall Maps," said a young woman in an irritated voice. She blew a bit of blond hair away from her eyes. It was not a good look for her, but Raz put extra appreciation into his smile.

"I am sorry to bother you, but I would like to stop by and get glider nav flexistrips for the north."

The woman huffed a breath. "You and everyone else. The Great Labyrinth is very popular all of a sudden. I'll be glad when D'Elecampane gets her maps of the place back to me."

"Ah. She is there?"

"Yes." The woman narrowed her eyes at Raz. "Maybe I shouldn't have told you, shouldn't have told anyone else, either."

"Who else was interested?"

She shrugged plump shoulders. "T'Anise, the antiquarian."

"I've heard the name but don't know the man." Hadn't Del

complained of him? More than once? A tingle whisked down his spine . . . something . . . something.

The clerk's mouth drew down. "No loss." Again she stared, this time pushing her hair away from her face. "Come on by, GrandSir Cherry. I'll have the flexistrips." Her image vanished from his stone.

Raz sighed. It seemed as if everyone in Druida knew what a stup he'd been. He scooped up Rosemary and she grumbled sleepily as he attached her with a spell to his shoulder. "We're going to find Del and Shunuk."

The kitten sat up and hissed. *No. She will take Us away from Our stardom.*

He hadn't seen Rosemary doing anything except being loved by the cast and crew, with the exception of Lily.

She will take Us away from Our theater.

"There are things more important than the theater." Nearly heresy, but what he'd finally come to understand.

What?

He plucked her from his shoulder, looked into her topaz eyes. "Love. HeartMates. I love you."

But I love the theater.

The kitten could stir up all his anxieties if he let her. She was a clever cat who was learning him well.

"Del is a very generous woman. We will overcome our problems together." That phrase sounded like a new, good mantra for when his doubts bit him. "Very generous," he repeated. "She gave me you, didn't she?"

Rosemary sniffed and subsided.

Even as Raz was closing the door to his dressing room, his scrybowl flashed white. He stared, went back, and answered, "Here."

"Captain Ruis Elder," the man said, the water in the bowl burbling his words. His image was too wavery to see more than a vague gray profile of the man. Raz was still impressed. He'd thought the technology *Nuada's Sword* was incompatible with scrybowls.

"How can I help you?" Raz projected his voice in case Captain Elder was having a problem hearing him.

"I'm a little concerned," Captain Elder boomed. "Ship has notified me of a series of requests he's had over the last year for maps from *Lugh's Spear*, plans of the Ship itself, and any information on the Tabacin Diary. This all came up when a lord purchased one of the new sets of ship diagrams and models of *Lugh's Spear*."

A name was slithering through Raz's mind, but he needed to hear it.

"GrandLord Pym T'Anise," Elder said.

Everything fell into place. T'Anise, a man who owned an antique shop. A man who was interested in the past. Perhaps obsessed with the past? Raz scraped his memory to recall when Del first told him of the GrandLord. *After Del had started seeing him.* Del, a great cartographer. Raz, a Cherry who might have evidence—a diary—showing where *Lugh's Spear* had landed.

"Thank you. I must go."

"The man asked about Del's maps of the east, too."

Raz could only nod. "I'll take care of it."

"I can call Straif T'Blackthorn."

"Blackthorn's out of town. Del's *my HeartMate*." Raz didn't wait, he raced for Cherry, calculating how fast he could get to the Great Labyrinth. About two septhours.

He fumbled for his perscry, called Winterberry. The guard was in Gael City with Straif T'Blackthorn.

No one Raz knew could teleport to the center of the labyrinth, even knew enough about it to try.

He flung the bond between himself and Del wide, but it was still narrow on her side. He tried her perscry but there was no answer, not even to cache a message. Probably in the great bowl of the labyrinth.

He heard nothing but the thunder of blood-ridden fear in his head.

*A*s she reached the top of the bright, sunny rim of the crater, and was a pace or two from the end, Del's own words from the past, from her former life echoed in her head. Words she'd said to the shop owner in Steep Springs. *If I want to get pregnant, I will.* She laughed as she stepped from the labyrinth.

She turned and looked back at the bowl, bowed formally in thanks, kept the image as a memory. Halfway down one side she saw a thrashing of dust and figured Shunuk was enjoying himself cleaning out the celtaroon nest. Maybe she should try once more to get him a vixen from Druida who would like living in a tiny settlement with Shunuk. Good and symmetrical.

Del pivoted to walk from the path and saw a thick-bodied, middle-aged man heavily descend the few steps of the Elder's new pavilion. He progressed carefully over to her, a smile plumping his cheeks into round pouches. She blinked as she recognized T'Anise.

When he reached her, he bowed. "Finally we meet merrily, Grand-Lady D'Elecampane."

She suppressed a sigh, raised a hand. "I'm not staying in Druida. I've left the city and won't be returning."

He bent a commiserating look on her, clicked his tongue, shook his head. "I've heard."

Del gritted her teeth. She supposed all the damn noble circles had gossiped about her and Raz.

"But there was another, more sensitive matter about which I wish to speak personally with you." T'Anise gave her a toothy smile. "I would like you to consult with me, GrandLady. It has been centuries since the boundaries of my estate have been surveyed." A tiny cough came from his throat and he reddened and looked aside. "There might be a dispute . . ."

Wasn't that always the way? People. "I'm sorry," Del said, "I'm not avail—"

He named an extortionate fee. "The estate is a little south of Gael City, not too far off the glider paths or airship route. It's not a big estate, but it's a jewel and I love it."

Del paused to consider. Work, close to her home, something to do other than preparing for the baby. She'd be practicing her craft. Taking a job like this might lead to others in the area. "I'm listening."

Thirty-seven

Over the next septhour and a half, Raz pushed the glider to its limits. After a glance at the navmap he cut some time by going over ground instead of following wide curves. It was rocky and they bounced but kept up good speed. He'd turned on the emergency flashers and sound pulse and zoomed from the city. The few gliders on the road had pulled aside for him.

The image of the dead thief kept flashing in stark black, bright white into his mind.

The blows from the big man when they'd fought ached.

Del was tough and strong.

She'd fight.

To the death.

*   *   *

*A*s she and T'Anise discussed the location of his estate and the details of the job, he offered his arm and Del put her fingers on it, then disliked the proper action as strange energy pulsed under her fingertips. When a large boulder rose ahead of them, she went around it to the left as T'Anise went right, continued down the path to the meadow where her stridebeast was.

"My lady, where do you go?" T'Anise asked.

"To my stridebeast."

"My man can take care of that. Come join me in my glider." With a wave, he gestured to a large man dressed in gray on gray livery.

Del hesitated, but as T'Anise's man came closer, there was something about him that she didn't like. The guard spoke with T'Anise and turned in her direction.

"We can talk at the inn," Del said. "I'll meet you there."

"I have maps in my glider," T'Anise said. He moved toward where it sat, large and luxurious and gleaming gray, the only glider in the small bulb of cleared ground.

Shrugging, Del said, "I'll be with you in a bit."

The large man strode to her in a few paces, took her elbow in a tight grip.

She broke it, stepped away, turned to run.

Was grabbed around the waist. She hesitated. She was pregnant, couldn't 'port, couldn't fight. That might harm the baby. Rage mixed with despair filled her.

"Get her!" The high shriek came from T'Anise but didn't sound like a sane man at all.

"*Shunuk!*" she cried mentally and with all the breath in her lungs.

*S*hunuk! *Raz yelled telepathically. Raz had just thought of the fox.* Whose mind was clouded by the bloodlust of killing.

His words were echoed by Del.

She was afraid yet didn't call on him. Terror flooded him.

Shunuk, go to Del! Raz was too far from the labyrinth. He cursed steadily. He didn't know the area well enough to pull over and 'port.

He sent all the Flair he had into powering the glider, overrode the top speed limitations. He could burn it out, drain his Flair, but Del needed him *now*.

*T*he big guy stuck her in the back of the glider, with T'Anise. Del swiped her nails down T'Anise's cheek, and he squealed. "Get her out of here. Put her up with you, fool."

Del raked at T'Anise again, missed, got blood on a papyrus and tore it as the guard grabbed her around the waist again. He stuck her up front in the passenger seat.

Shunuk! she called again. He didn't answer.

Raz did. *Del! T'Anise—*

Del wanted to slam her mind against Raz, against the shuddering pain of hearing his mind voice. *He has me, at the Great Labyrinth—*

An open-handed slap rocked her head back and destroyed the mental connection.

"Go!" screeched T'Anise, hurting her head. "Keep slapping her if you think she is mindspeaking."

The guard turned his head and grinned at her, his gaze lingering on the bruise rising on her cheekbone.

Del tamped down her fury, her fear. She *couldn't* fight back. She grabbed the webbing and said the shielding Word. Neither of the men donned the shields.

Silver glider. Del risked a short spurt to Raz and Shunuk.

"Go to T'Anise southern estate," the large guard ordered. The console navmap flickered but didn't show the whole route.

T'Anise's man leaned back and looked at Del, letting the glider run automatically. He stank of sweat and she recalled the odor from the Cherry's kitchen in Gael City. That was what had alerted her.

He was one of the thieves and had killed the other man.

The privacy shield was down and T'Anise said from the back, "Now, D'Elecampane, you will tell me everything you know about the Tabacin Diary, of the maps you have made for the Cherrys to find *Lugh's Spear*." T'Anise's breath whistled in and out. "I will be famous beyond belief when I discover *Lugh's Spear*. I will never be forgotten, *Anise* will never be forgotten, even when I die and the Family is no more. I will be the most important member of my Family, ever. Everyone will remember and honor me."

"Not so much when history shows that you stole and murdered for such an honor," she said.

The guard slapped her again. Smiled.

He'd like killing her, too. She kept her hands from covering her belly in a betraying gesture. "All right, I'll tell you," she said. "The newssheets were right about the journal. The Cherrys told the truth," she said through puffy lips; a cut dribbled warm blood down her chin. "There were no maps in the diary."

The glider turned south, accelerated from a crawl to slow.

This time the slap had her ear ringing as she turned her head.

Shunuk hopped high, so she could see him in the window as he ran along the side of the vehicle. It wasn't moving too fast. Yet.

She opened her link with Raz a little more. A rush of staggering love and fear inundated her, pulsing with the word, *HeartMate, HeartMate, HeartMate.*

Another blow to her head.

"Can't. Think." She gasped.

"Be a little easier on her," T'Anise said in an annoyed tone. "She's not as tough as we thought. We'll get the information."

A red-furred beast appeared on the hood of the glider, scrabbled, wide eyes and sharp teeth.

T'Anise screamed.

The guard flinched.

Del lunged forward, found the emergency lever and pulled.

The glider stopped, the men went flying, the guard hitting the console, the front window. Thumps came from the back.

Webbing cradled Del, moved with her. Kept her safe.

Landing gear failed and the glider fell to the ground.

Del was out of the glider in an instant, running toward the labyrinth crater lip, ready to slide down. She'd lose the men.

"Del!" It was Raz, leaping from Cherry, running toward her.

She waved to him, turned back and ran to the silver glider, slamming and sealing the back door on T'Anise. His face purpled with rage. She hurried to the other side of the glider and sealed that back door, too. T'Anise shouted Flaired Words, but Del's spells held.

He pounded on the windows. "You don't understand. I *must* be the one to discover *Lugh's Spear*, the lost starship, so I can increase my Flair. The ancients knew *all* about Flair, and it's all locked up there, in that starship. *Nuada's Sword* has been no help. When I find *Lugh's Spear*, riches and knowledge and Flair and fame will be mine. I will never be forgotten!"

The man was mad.

There was the sound of flesh on flesh and Del swung to see Raz smiling fiercely, jabbing his fists into the face and stomach of the guard, ignoring his own blackened eye and bleeding cheek.

The man hit his head on the upper edge of the door opening and Raz pummeled him back into the vehicle. Raz slammed the door and said a Word and the glider was sealed shut. He pulled his perscry from his pocket and snapped a report to a guard station.

Then he came to her, his eyes narrowing as he saw her swollen face. His stride lengthened and he feathered his fingers over her cheeks. "Lover," he whispered. "HeartMate." He brushed a kiss on her mouth and the yearning inside her flashed like fire. "Mine."

She let herself lean on him.

Shunuk hopped around them, barking. *You are here, stup man.*

"Yes, I am here." Raz drew a little away, his eyes an intense blue. "Be mine, Del. Don't ever leave me again."

"Things have changed," Del managed.

Raz frowned. "We need to get you to a Healer. 'Porting on three. One, my HeartMate—"

"No. No 'porting." Del stepped from his arms, kept her gaze locked on his. "I'm pregnant."

He stared at her.

We will have a human kit, Shunuk affirmed.

Raz folded to the ground. He opened his mouth, closed it, opened it again, thumped himself on the chest as if loosening his voice. "Pregnant?"

Del opened the link between them wide. He was stunned, as she had been, but there was no revulsion, no horror, just plain shock.

She put her hands on her hips. "I'm starting a Family early." She lifted her chin.

A wash of love came from him to her. He cleared his throat. "*We* are starting a Family."

Rosemary kitten pranced over. *I am Family.*

Shunuk yipped, *I am Family, too. Del and me and Raz and you . . . and the other Cherrys.*

"My parents," Raz said, dazed.

Del turned and began walking back down the gliderway to the Great Labyrinth and her stridebeast, ignoring the pounding and swearing from T'Anise and his man. They couldn't even rock the glider, evidently didn't know of the emergency lever.

Raz caught up with her and slipped an arm around her waist, looked down at her. "I love you, Del. Don't walk away from me."

She eyed him sideways. "Or else?"

"Or else I'll have the next person we meet be priest or priestess and recognize my HeartMate vows to you."

She felt a smile curving her lips, closed her eyes for a few steps. All she could feel from him was love. "What of your career?"

"You, *we*, are more important than my career."

"Same here," she said, then touched her stomach. "So is the baby." Then she turned and looked at him fully, saw his mobile face radiating love. He lifted her hand to his lips.

"My lover, my love, my HeartMate. Bond with me."

She had to cough to clear her own throat. "Yes. About our home—"

"My home is with you."

"I have some ideas on that."

* * *

*D*el had three sets of pillows propped behind her as she lay on the bedsponge in Raz's suite in T'Cherry Residence. She felt stupid. Selfishly, she wanted to be back at her own house. But Raz and the other Cherrys had hovered over the new HeartMate and the prospective first child of the next generation.

His mother and sister had actually *cooed* over her. His father, T'Cherry himself, often took breaks from his work at home to come up and check on her.

They'd convinced her that she would be easier served in T'Cherry Residence. She wasn't used to being served, but everyone was worried about the baby, including her, and she should have the best care.

She still felt stupid.

She shifted and muttered. From what she could tell with her own body, all was well, but she *wouldn't* jeopardize this child.

Her and Raz's child.

At least there wouldn't be continual bed rest. This was only precautionary after the frightening and active events at the labyrinth. T'Anise's mind had cracked beyond all mending and he had been placed in D'Sea's, the mind Healer's, most private facility. His estates had been confiscated.

His guard and distant relative had been more interested in the treasure *Lugh's Spear* might hold than his lord's wish for glory. The big man had been tried for murder, found guilty, fixed with a DepressFlair bracelet and exiled to an island. Like others with the same fate, he wasn't expected to live long. When the FirstFamilies acted, they moved fast and deadly.

Del was still concerned about being tied to the Blackthorns through Doolee—they tended to hover, too—but was becoming resigned to a lot of Family around her. At least she liked the Cherrys and the Blackthorns . . . and the Clovers that she'd met, Mitchella Blackthorn's birth Family.

She had a large Family again, who would have thought it? She wasn't quite ready for them all, but she was stuck.

For a while. Until the property in Verde Valley was ready. Sin
she'd done much of the original arrangements and Raz insisted c
it being a mutual HeartMate partnership project, he took an enth
siastic lead now.

Del glanced at the timer, he'd be back from negotiations wi
Amberose and her agent soon. The final negotiations. If they couldr
agree on the casting of the play and having it open at the new Cher
Theater of Verde Valley, that particular project would be scrapped

Since Raz was muttering about hiring a playwright for a sto
about the Tabacin Diaries, that wasn't too bad, except Del felt t
press of time.

She shifted in the bed. She felt fine. The baby was fine. There h
been myriad tests, resulting in this one eightday of bed rest. Whic
was becoming more tiresome with every second.

She sighed and picked up the ancient divination cards Raz ha
given her to amuse herself.

At first she just looked at the people in the foreground. Sh
smiled when she saw hints of features in those she knew. T'Ash. Ru
Elder. Vinni T'Vine. Then a river and hills caught her eye and sh
began to pay more attention to the backgrounds and landscapes
the cards.

Here, as Raz had said, was *Lugh's Spear*, looking not at all lil
Nuada's Sword. An older type of ship or something. She tried
figure out *where* it might be, but there wasn't enough detail. So sh
set that card aside and began sifting out those that showed mo
geographic features.

Her heart began beating hard as she started to recognize t
areas, the journey Tabacin had described . . . surely that was an ed
of Fish Story Lake, those were the Bluegrass Plains. Del put them
order, though she was still frustrated. Just not enough detail. She h
a copy of the diaries, too, and flipped through them to the few scen
sketches . . . Tabacin had been afraid of the outside world, had pr
ferred to draw people, especially if they paid her for likenesses.

Frowning, Del lined up the cards in the order of the journe
east to west, then south to north. Her hand hesitated over the t

of wands. Surely that was *their* valley. Verde Valley. Her head went a little dizzy. Verde Valley. An old, old name. As old as the *Lugh's Spear* colonists?

The door creaking open had her jolting. "Sssh." Raz came over, leaned down and hugged her. "Just me."

From the wild sense of triumph that pulsed from him, Del knew they'd gotten everything they'd asked for. She grabbed his face for a hard kiss and he returned it enthusiastically.

He raised an eyebrow at the large cards spread over the bed, shrugged and straightened, paced to the window and back, too restless to sit with her.

Del grinned and when he turned, he matched that.

Rosemary was hopping up and down on his shoulder, as far as her "stay" spell allowed.

Raz said, "Not only did we get the cast and the director we wanted, but . . ."

"But?"

"Amberose herself will come to the theater opening and mix and mingle."

"Wonderful. That will be a big draw."

"Yes. She is interested in a 'country' theater. I got the impression that she might have an estate near there." Raz winked. "Good for types that don't care for the city much."

Del nodded. "Good for nobles driving a glider from Druida to Gael City and their southern estates. With the landing pad we will put in, it will serve airships, too."

"And as people become more adept with teleportation, it can be a stopping place," Raz said casually. They'd discussed all this. He paused and his eyes gleamed. "And . . ."

"And?"

"I happened to take a copy of the Tabacin Diaries with me, talked to her about the story. She's hooked. I think she'll write it."

"Wonderful!"

Raz was pacing again, rubbing his hands. "After the Evening Primrose Theater does *Heart and Sword* next year, audiences will be ready for more colonist tales. We can premiere the play when *Heart and Sword* closes up here."

"If it closes; the Gael City production is still going strong." She hesitated. "Are you sure you want to premiere *Tabacin* at our theater? We agreed that you would take some runs here in the city."

"We did." He came over and played with her fingers. "But if our inn and theater go well, I will rethink that. I'd like being a big fish in a big pond. We own much of the valley, but not all, and I can foresee an artistic community growing here."

"Huh." Del wasn't sure about that.

Raz glanced at the cards, his brows drew together. "What's this?"

He'd observed it, too, the distinctive crooked mountain against the sky, a view they could see from their home in Verde Valley. He picked up the card. "I never noticed this before."

Del gestured to the cards. "I think this is the journey Tabacin made. I even think *Lugh's Spear* colonists stayed in our valley for a while, named it maybe."

Raz's mobile face had gone still. The link between them was wide and his emotions of awe and love for her rushed through it. Del flushed.

"*You* are wonderful."

I want to SEE! Rosemary shouted. *Unstick.*

Flicking fingers and murmuring a Word, Raz dissipated the "stay" spell.

Rosemary hopped onto the bed, staggered around the cards, disarranging and flipping them.

"Rosemary!" Raz chided, grabbing her.

But knowledge exploded in Del's brain as she noted the backs, the minuscule symbol that looked like *Lugh's Spear* on one card. "Wait, wait!" She panted. She gathered the cards and began laying them out, back side up. Shuffled them around.

"What?"

"It's a map!"

"A map! It doesn't look like a map to me, just bands of different colors, pale yellow to deep purple."

"But it is! Tabacin mentioned that the leader of the colonists, the Captain of *Lugh's Spear*, showed them a map and progress they made on it on their trip. The map he would have used would have come from the ship, been taken by *Lugh's Spear*."

Raz stared, shook his head. "I don't see it."

"It's a little fuzzy," Del admitted. "And the woman *did* like her color palette. But I recognize the scale, and we also have the map that was transmitted from *Lugh's Spear* to *Nuada's Sword*." She pointed to a big purple blob. "Look, this is the edge of the Deep Blue Sea." Touched another purple area. "And Fish Story Lake."

Her finger quivered as she touched the card with the symbol of *Lugh's Spear*. "And there is exactly where they landed," she whispered.

"We have a map," Raz said blankly.

"*The* map. The map to *Lugh's Spear*."

"Just as we'd always been told," Raz said. He put a hand on her shoulder. "If you want to go . . ." His voice was expressionless.

Yearning twisted inside Del. If this had been only two months ago . . . but two months ago she hadn't known Raz and none of this would have happened.

"I love you." Her voice was thick with conflicting emotions. "And I love our child and the thought of more children with you. They can't be jeopardized." She squared the cards, lifted her chin, and returned the love she saw in her HeartMate's eyes. "The discovery of *Lugh's Spear* has waited this long, it can wait until our children can make such a trip. The logistics of finding it, maybe excavating or raising it, will take massive planning."

Raz bent down and kissed her tenderly on her lips. "My Heart-Mate, my woman, my wife, the mother of my children. I can only love you more each minute."

Sounded like mushy actor stuff to Del, but it touched her all the same, and dammit, that was just what she felt, too.

*   *   *

𝒜 month later Raz stopped the huge and heavily shielded glider just before the pillared gateway of their Verde Valley estate. Del opened the door and got out. She heard the voices of workers putting the last touches on the hotel for the grand opening at Full Twinmoons just after the new year in a few weeks.

The male HeartMated couple who were to run the inn had already arrived, as well as Del's Healer.

Their house had been finished yesterday. The white tinting around the many-paned windows gleamed. At last everything was ready for them to move in. Within her satchel was the HeartGift Raz had given her, an exquisite model of *Lugh's Spear*. Well shielded until she placed it on a shelf in their bedroom next to his landscape globe that night.

Rosemary and Shunuk tumbled from the glider, shot through the pillars into the estate.

Raz wrapped an arm around her, his hand resting lightly on her stomach. They looked at the estate, the hotel in the foreground, their house near the lake. The red and gold tinted theater gleamed like a jewel.

Del let out a long breath. Finally free of Druida City! "My journey has ended," she murmured.

Raz rubbed his chin against her hair. "Our journey together begins."

"Yes." She wrapped her arms around her HeartMate, kissed him, and leaned into his embrace. "Our journey together begins."